FROM OUT OF NOWHERE . . .

The helicopter came at them down low, skimming the hills, the sound of its blades muffled, absorbed by the open space. Then, seconds before it reached them, Marquette heard it, the distant popping slap of the blades. His horse's ears pricked forward as he caught it too. The adrenaline hit Matt's heart like a sledgehammer.

Marquette twisted around and screamed, "Get down! Take cover!" In a single motion, he came off his horse, his eyes searching the earth. Behind him, the cowboy drew rein, his mouth open, the carbine coming up.

The chopper hurled into sight, so close that Matt saw the bottom carriage clearly, the pontoons streaked with take-off oil.

He dove for a small castle of rock, hit, rolled, pressing as tightly as he could against the stone.

Then the first volley of rounds came, blowing silently out of the aircraft's overriding noise . . .

CODE
BLACK

CHARLES RYAN

AVON BOOKS · NEW YORK

AVON BOOKS
A division of
The Hearst Corporation
1350 Avenue of the Americas
New York, New York 10019

Copyright © 1997 by Charles Ryan
Published by arrangement with the author
Visit our website at **http://AvonBooks.com**
Library of Congress Catalog Card Number: 97-93018
ISBN: 0-380-79131-5

First Avon Books Printing: October 1997

AVON TRADEMARK REG. U.S. PAT. OFF. AND IN OTHER COUNTRIES, MARCA REGISTRADA, HECHO EN U.S.A.

Printed in the U.S.A.

WCD 10 9 8 7 6 5 4 3 2 1

To Don Hedges, with whom I shared youth, about a million cold Budweisers, and that endless search for the perfect wave.

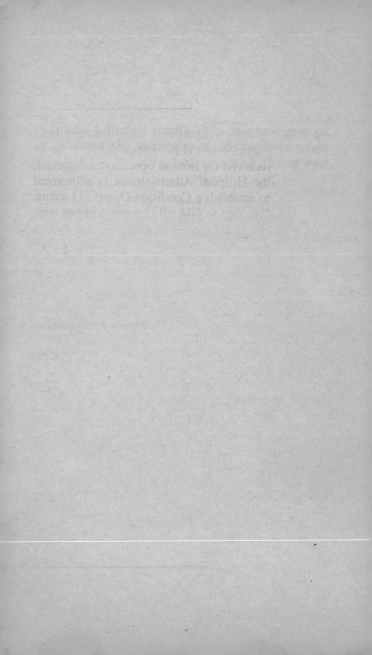

received for normal operational disposal, the Hospital Administrator is authorized to establish a Condition One (C-1) status

Item XXI: When all Emergency facilities have been maximized and no further patients can be received for normal operational dispersal, the Hospital Administrator is authorized to establish a Condition-One (C-1) status. Persuant to this, all communications with Hospital Emergency personnel, police and other emergency agencies will be logged under the standard reference of Code Black.

Manual of Operational Procedures
Harborview Hospital
Trauma Center
C/P-1995

prologue

March 2

It had rained heavily for three days across the jungled mountains of the Daying Confluence. Situated in the north-western corner of Laos, the area formed the country's borders with Myanmar and China. Through it ran the Mekong River. Now near crest, the river was swift, mud-thick and filled with whirling flood debris.

In a delapidated hotel in the town of Muang Sing, ten miles south of the confluence, Jack Stone waited out the rain with mounting anxiety. The continual downpour had prevented his scheduled meeting with the intermediary. Instead, he sat through the soggy, heat-saturated days getting drunk on Burmese jackburr beer.

Finally, the rains eased off. At noon, the intermediary—a tall Cambodian named Ban Phu Keun—appeared in a beat-up Land Rover. Ban Phu was a Pakxeng shopkeeper who, for a price, arranged for things to be smuggled across borders. He did so with the approbation of the ex-Kuomingtang army commander named General Ho, who controlled a vast drug empire on the frontier.

The two men immediately left for the border. As dark approached, they reached the river crossing of Muang Nan. A cable was strung across the river, and on it hung a rusty metal box for ferrying people. On the near bank stood an abandoned customs blockhouse.

The Cambodian parked in the jungle on a slight grade so they could watch the blockhouse. They waited. It began to rain again, sudden roaring cascades that quickly turned the dirt road into a rushing stream.

The gray storm light slowly faded into hissing darkness, and a tiny light appeared down the road. A moment later, an old man on a bicycle came by, pumping hard through the water. The light was a tiny lamp clipped to his handlebars. He wore a cone-shaped paddy hat and dark serape. He passed without looking at the vehicle.

Ban Phu touched Stone's shoulder. "Now you get out," he said.

"What?"

"Get out and walk down the road to the customshouse."

"Are you coming?"

"No. Do you carry weapons?"

"Yes, a pistol."

"Leave it here. Knives?"

"In my boot."

"Leave that, too."

Stone left the weapons and climbed out of the Land Rover. The rain pounded at him, straight down, in huge, chilling drops. He dipped his head and started down the road. The water made pressure wavelets against his boots.

Around him, the jungle droned with rain and the roar of rushing water. Ahead, near the blockhouse, he saw several lights suddenly appear among the trees: the feeble glow of kerosene lanterns.

He reached the blockhouse. It was a square chunk of cement with rotted cross beams above the twin doorways. All the window glass was gone.

A man stepped from the underbrush beside it. Stone heard him before he saw his shadow. The man wore a pith helmet on which the rain drummed hollowly.

"You the American?" the man asked in Cantonese.

"Yes."

Stone waited. Neither he nor the man moved. Then a soft glow appeared inside the customshouse. A moment later, another man came to the entrance holding a kerosene lantern and waved Stone in.

The building was a single room. The floor was cluttered with broken bottles, and the walls bore Laotian graffiti. It smelled of urine and mossy cement. Inexplicably, an old Jeep tire rim stamped with "U.S. Army" lay in a corner. Someone had defecated beside it. The turds were now stonelike agates.

Three men were there. All were Chinese, armed with Russian AK-47s and dressed in Western-type bell-bottom jeans and military camo serapes. Two wore straw peon hats, the other a red bandanna.

"You have the money?" Bandanna asked, also speaking Cantonese.

"Yes."

"Give it to me."

Stone took out a small canvas pouch with a drawstring. He opened it. Bandanna held up the lantern and took out four packets of American bills. Two hundred thousand dollars. He riffled through the bills, then put them back into the pouch.

He snapped an order. One of the other men brought out a small leather valise and set it on the floor before Stone. The American immediately knelt and opened the bag.

It was filled with loose straw. From the straw, he withdrew a small, brightly-polished sphere about the size of a grapefruit. There were two shallow depressions on opposite sides of the ball, finely milled. Stone turned it over in his hand, the surface gleaming in the lantern light.

Bandanna watched him, narrow-eyed. "What is your name?" he growled.

"Stone."

The Chinese snorted mirthlessly and said to his men in Mandarin, *"Sey-ching ya."*

Oh, shit! Stone thought. A sliver of ice stabbed his spine. Bandanna had just used an ominous expression: "This man has an evil tooth."

"Why do you say that of me?" he asked brusquely, trying

to conceal his fear. He knew his position had just turned very dangerous. Now that they had the money, these men might easily kill him.

Bandanna's eyebrows lifted with surprise. ''Ah, you understand Mandarin.''

''Yes. Why do you say that?''

Bandanna nodded at the sphere. ''Because that is a very evil thing in your hand.''

''No more evil than those.'' He pointed at the men's assault rifles.

''No, it is not the same.''

Stone quickly replaced the sphere in the straw and re-zipped the valise. He stood up.

Bandanna and his men stared coldly at him. Finally, the leader snapped his head toward the entrance. ''Get out, *gokyan*,'' he growled.

Stone nodded, turned and went back to the road. The rain had lessened but he could sense the close passage of clouds just above the trees.

He hurried along, grinning broadly, testing the slight weight of the thing in the valise. Bandanna had called him evil. Well, screw him, Stone thought triumphantly. It had taken months of clandestine negotiations with General Ho to get this little ball. Now, with it, his plan was complete.

March 15

At precisely 6:31 P.M., the bulk carrier *Mars Luden* crossed the primary boundary of the Puget Sound Vessel Traffic service area southeast of the entrance to the Strait of Juan de Fuca. Holding to a steady nineteen knots, she was inbound for Victoria, British Columbia. Her deep bunkers were filled with Malaysian bauxite, and there were crates of machine parts from Singapore stacked on the main decks.

The sea was choppy, whipped by the March wind that still held the sharp bite of Canadian winter. To the northwest,

barely visible rain squalls moved in gray sketch lines against
a layer of deep purple.

The ship slowed to seventeen knots and turned directly
into the wind. Once into the strait, she would encounter swift
eddies in the ebbing tide that could shear her into outbound
separation lanes if she carried too much momemtum.

As the ship settled out of the turn, a figure darted across
the shadowed boat deck. It was the third officer, an Austra-
lian named Tommy Hook. He paused between the stem of
the number four lifeboat and its Steward davit, reached up
under the boat's canvas tarp and took out a small leather
satchel. He'd hidden it there after it was passed to him in a
whorehouse in Singapore.

He quickly moved forward, dodging between the strapped
machine crates until he reached the fo'c'sle deck ladder. Behind and high above him, the steaming lights on the bridge
wings and radar trunk looked like bright crystals tethered to
the night.

At the top of the ladder, he scurried to the hawsepipe
where the starboard anchor chain reeved through the hull.
Unstirred by the wind, the cramped space smelled of oil and
old iron from the huge chain links.

Hook unzipped the satchel and extracted a hand-held Electronic Satellite Navigation unit. Extending its little antenna,
he switched it on. Instantly a tiny screen glowed with the
digital readout of the ship's present coordinates.

Next he took out the sphere. A tiny locator unit was now
strapped to it with twin metal bands. Once more, he checked
the ESN, then hunkered down to wait.

It began to rain. Ten minutes later, the coordinates 124.01
long., 43.23 lat. blinked onto the screen.

Hook flipped the sphere over in his hand and tapped its
locator unit lightly against a riding chock to activate it. He
held it to his ear. Very softly, he felt the unit's spaced pulses.

He leaned over the chain and hurled the sphere through
the hawsepipe. Then he tossed out the ESN unit. Without
looking to see them fall, he headed for the fo'c'sle ladder,

chuckling pleasantly. He'd just earned himself twenty-five thousand dollars.

For the last three days, the female mako had cruised near the coast of the Olympic Peninsula. She was a big shark, fourteen feet and at least seven hundred pounds. She was also newly pregnant. Her cloaca, or genital opening, was still slightly swollen from a recent mating.

In these fish-depleted waters, she hadn't fed well since encountering a small shoal of mackerel coming in from open ocean nearly two days before. Now her high-powered metabolism was creating ever more desperate hunger spasms.

For a while she dallied about a pair of fishing boats slowly moving north. They gave off no blood scent, so she turned and moved into deeper water.

Soon after, she felt the distant engine throb and hull hiss of the approaching *Mars Luden*. Experience told her that often these gigantic, mobile objects left edible things in their wakes. Turning sharply, she threw on a burst of speed and headed for the increasing sound vibrations.

She caught up to the ship and paralleled it, then dropped back, twice crossing its stern, searching. But the vessel was moving too rapidly for her to keep up.

Suddenly, the pitch of its engines changed and it slowed. Once more she came abreast of it, into the turbulence of its wave vibrations. Despite that agitation, her auditory nerves picked up a series of faint pulses near the ship. The pulses were high frequency, like the distress cries of a wounded fish.

Instantly, she whirled. Rising toward the surface, she zigzagged, homing in on the sound. Even in the blackness, she went right to it. The thing was bobbing wildly in the churn of the ship, a small round object like an inflated balloonfish.

She swung past it cautiously. Again. Then, pectoral and caudal fins lashing, she struck, swallowing the thing whole. Her momentum hurled her through the surface for a few seconds.

Afterward, she continued to range the area, looking for

something more to eat. But there was nothing save the oily scent of diesel fuel and the receding rumble of engines.

At last, she rolled and sounded, aware of a peculiar, spaced pulsing in her stomach.

1

The mako hit the trotline like a Texas tornado.

The line was a small set, twin fifty-five-gallon oil drums floating sixty feet apart with a hundred-pound pig-iron anchor. Spaced along the connecting rope were three six-fathom drop lines sporting foot-long hooks and chunks of smelly mackerel. The shark had struck the middle line, coming straight up from the depths.

A half mile away, Matt Marquette snapped his head up at the sudden erratic pendulum swing of the line's pole light. The rain made it seem deceptively far off, isolated in the ocean fifteen miles off Washington State's Olympic Peninsula.

The light disappeared for a moment then reappeared, snapping back and forth crazily.

Marquette had just emerged from the number-two ice hold in the stern of his forty-foot Benson troller, *Big Blue*. He and his crewman, a part-time University of Washington student named Rick Hammil, had set the trotline just before sunset. For the last two hours, they'd been crisscrossing the area with their outriggers extended, trolling for cod.

Matt slammed the ice shovel against the gunwale to get Rick's attention and pointed out at the pole light. Hammil nodded and swung the helm. The boat hesitated for a moment, then came around, tilting sharply and catching the full face of the north wind. He put full power to the twin GM-

6-71 diesels, and they surged toward the light, breasting the wind-rough, rocking.

Head and big shoulders tilted against the icy shrapnel of the rain, Marquette dismantled the two trolling booms, gurdying in the stainless steel lines until their lures trailed on the deck. He quickly unhooked the trolling line from the starboard winch, cranked the booms back into their slots on the crosstree and reeved a hooked lifter-cable from a block on the masthead through the winch buckle.

The trotline was approaching fast, the light still flailing wildly. Sixty yards from it, Rick cut the throttle, angling slightly to the south. Then he swung into a tight left turn, and they came up into the wind with the starboard side parallel to the line.

Gripping a boathook, Marquette stationed himself forward of the winch, his six-foot-three frame jackknifed over the starboard gunwale. Under the wind, he heard the barrel cables squealing against their swivels, the sounds like birds being slaughtered.

As the boat lost headway, he leaned far out and snagged the trotline. It instantly exploded at the end of the hook. Something very powerful was down there. He felt the jolt of it come up the shaft, strain through his shoulders. Counterbalancing with his weight, he held on as Hammil, armed with a gaff, scrambled aft to help.

Two minutes later, the shark appeared, first the hump forward of its dorsal coming up gray-brown, and then the huge snout, the eyes catching light from the cockpit for a second, black and round and dead as obsidian coins. The rain furred off the head into a soft cloud of shattered droplets like smoke.

"God *damn*," Rick yelled happily. "That's one big motherfucker."

The animal had twisted itself into the drop line, the stainless steel leads looking like silver cobwebs wrapped around its body. It thrashed furiously, whipping the water as Matt hauled the line closer.

"Put the gaff to it," he hollered. "Now."

Rick swung once, missed, swung again. The gaff head went into the shark just back of its left jaw. The animal slammed down sideways, hurling water.

When it came up again, it was still for a moment, then began to thrash once more. Both men were panting, gasping with the effort to control the animal's fury. Their shoulders and back muscles started to burn.

Again the shark went suddenly motionless. Matt, holding the end of the boathook's shaft under his arm, scooped up the lifter cable hook and jerked out a few feet of cable.

The bow of the boat had fallen off the wind slightly. The lee drum was now behind them, banging and skidding off the transom. The shark exploded again, coming up, twisting. Marquette sank the lifter cable hook into the back of the jaw near the gaff.

For a second, the winch cable went loopy on the deck, and then the automatic drag came on and it snapped taut, hurling splinters where it crossed the gunwale. As it started to reel in, *Big Blue* heeled so sharply that both men were thrown against the gunwale. The cable twanged beside their knees.

Hammil shot a glance up at the mast. It was bowing. "Watch out!" he yelled. "That son of a bitch's gonna snap."

"No, she'll hold," Matt shouted back. "Stand by the winch. You hear her crack, cut the drag."

Marquette turned and dove through the cockpit door. A moment later, he was back with a twelve-gauge Winchester shotgun.

The shark was still fighting the cable. But slowly, inexorably, it was being drawn above the gunwale, which was now taking water in the sharpness of the heel. The mako's tail lashed back and forth, gouging out reams of surface water.

Matt jacked a round into the chamber and lifted the weapon. Braced against the gunwale, he sighted along the shark's underbelly. In the faint cabin light, it looked as white and sheeny as the albumen of a boiled egg.

The first round, carrying 00 buckshot, blew a hole just aft

of the dorsal fin, flinging bloody flesh and cartilage. The second, almost missing, tore across the animal's head, paring off a thick layer of skin. The wound was like a plate suddenly filled with blood.

The mako went limp. It hung, twirling slowly in the wind as the winch brought it up the rest of the way, the little motor whining with strain. Matt pulled the boathook free and got another purchase along the lower flank.

Within a minute, they had the shark aboard, down between the winch and sideboard. The troller rolled hard back to port as the weight came off the cable. A foot of water sloshed back and forth on the afterdeck. Blood and bits of white back flesh turned it dark as wine.

Matt unsheathed his belt knife, a Marine Ka-Bar. He leaned over the shark and ran the point across the huge head wound until he found the partially exposed brain. It was tiny, shaped like a tuning fork. He jammed the blade in and severed the twin sides.

They cut the drop line, saving the wrapped lead wire. The boat, now abeam of the wind, cleared away from the drums. Using a fantail bitt as fulcrum for the winch cable, they began to haul the carcass back toward the ice hold.

A half mile away, the oculate strobe light of an aircraft suddenly appeared through the rain. It approached from the northwest, skimming just above the surface.

Quickly the light grew larger, and then there was the whomping crack of blades. A few seconds later, a small helicopter flashed directly over the boat, the bottoms of its pontoons showing oily black in the masthead lights.

It made a wide turn and once more skimmed just over the top of *Big Blue*'s mast. On the third pass, the aircraft came in slowly and hovered just off the stern.

Marquette made out two men in the bubble cockpit. The chopper's body was white with a logo of three intertwined red *S*s on its right side. The blades' downwash lashed at him, agitating the lee surface into a ring of peaks and wavelets that resembled the breast feathers of a hawk.

A spotlight snapped on, flooding the boat with brilliance.

Matt squinted against the white-hot center of the spot and made a questioning gesture with his left arm: *"What do you want?"*

The helo remained for a few seconds. Then it snapped into a steep bank and whirled away, the spotlight going off as it gained altitude. It headed northeast toward the strait.

Hammil watched it go. "Who the hell was *that* asshole?"

Matt shrugged. "Just a couple guys curious about the shark."

He knelt beside the mako again. There were tiny sparkles still on his retina from the spotlight. He blinked them away. As he did, his gaze rested on the animal's savaged head, its upside eye.

It was glassy, as menacingly expressionless as in life. It suddenly seemed to him to contain all of death. The empty deepness, void of bottom. His mind rove up the image of the buckshot tearing the mako to pieces. He winced as he had when he'd first pulled the trigger.

Unlike in other days, Matt Marquette now hated to kill anything. Ever since that hot, wine-heady moment in Barcelona, Spain, death had become a complex and meloncholy affair to him.

On Kelli Pickett's computer screen, the simulation model of the Golden Gate Bridge was done in wireframe, a complicated network of white lines on a blue background. It was part of a test being run to track torsion vectors and molecular wave propagation within the Gate's strut system as it was exposed to increasing wind forces.

Kelli was in the electronics lab in Guggenheim Hall on the University of Washington campus. At different consoles scattered around the large, icy-aired room were other team members of the university's AI-F/B-3 Project, designated CRYSTALBALL.

Using her mouse, Kelli occasionally shifted the image on the screen, making it revolve slowly as if the simulation camera were changing perspective. Lined along the right side of her monitor were two columns of numbers indicating wave and vector progressions.

The project director, Troy Gilhammer, paused at her shoulder to squint at the readout. He was forty, blond and bushy-haired, a mountain climber who always smelled of the cherry gumdrops he constantly sucked on.

"Well, the random moment span's still looking stable," he said. "Let's give her another click."

Kelli's fingers quickly tapped in a command sequence. Instantly, her number columns began to change.

Gilhammer glanced over at a nearby console that displayed a graph bearing two horizontal line sets. One was black and showed the predicted change in the bridge structure under various force vectors. The prediction parameter was based on Bayesian Probability, or BP, norms. The second set was red and as yet incomplete. It indicated the real-time feedback coming off the model as the vectors increased in strength.

So far, both sets were almost perfectly aligned.

"What's gust speed?" Gilhammer called.

"One-two-four knots," someone answered.

He began to pace, head down, thoughtful. "Okay, that's high enough. Let's start with the P and S waves. Two-second period, intensity four."

So far they had been exposing their simulated bridge only to wind gust forces. Gilhammer had now initiated a second vector force: wave impacts from an earthquake. Instantly, operators began to call out monitor changes.

With part of a grant from the National Science Foundation to explore artificial intelligence, CRYSTALBALL's mission was to design general concepts for computer software programs and toolkits. These would analyze, predict and unify smooth countertransitions from states of chaotic divergence in malfunctioning systems.

The test runs covered a wide range of systems, from steel structuring to bioengineering of pathological cells, from chemical and enzymatic reaction transistors to human insulin pumps. The Golden Gate run was the sixty-third in a projected series of two hundred.

The research team used the latest in computer technology: MIRROR-t programs, high-speed Tera-FLOPS, and processor-in-memory integrated circuits. Their theory base was keyed to Bayesian Probability and Fuzzy Logic concepts that allowed degree parameters far beyond the simple on-off switching of binary systems.

"What's L and R horizontal wave divergence?" Gilhammer asked.

"Eight percent, point-zero-nine meters."

"Let's have intensity six."

Reaction changes were called out. On the graph monitor, the red line still shadowed the BP set.

"Okay, this time let's give her a real boot in the ass. Punch up to intensity nine."

For eleven seconds, everything remained in stable progression. Then Kelli said, "Oh, shit, I'm starting to get particle shimmer."

Gilhammer darted to her console, swore, dashed away.

Another operator shouted, "Troy, I'm showing pre-chaotic frequency onset."

"The trip-P's fading," Kelli called. The computer network's parallel processing power, the ability to "consider" all possible solutions at the same time in order to offset escalating chaotic divergence, was falling behind the rapidly changing wave sequences.

Gilhammer came around again. "Goddammit," he moaned. "There she goes." On the graph monitor, the red line began a wild up-and-down divergence from the BP set. Within seconds, it looked like the printout on a violently shaking seismometer.

Kelli's wireframe bridge came apart.

Everybody slumped, cursing.

For the next thirty minutes, they held a post-run bull session, throwing ideas and what-ifs at each other, trying to decipher the glitch in their program that had allowed runaway.

But the team was visibly tired; they'd been at it since eight that morning. Finally, Troy called a halt. There was a hectic bustle as everybody shut down equipment, gathered up notes and took off.

Within three minutes, Pickett was alone in the lab. She poured herself another smidgen of coffee, leaned back in her console chair and gazed wistfully at the ceiling.

She was a beautiful woman of thirty, long in the leg, high-breasted, hair the glossy color of a raven's feather. But it was her eyes that caught instant attention: emerald green, full of light, capable of pouting impishness or quick passion or hot corundum anger. With a master's in structural engineering from Stanford, she was deputy director of CRYSTAL-BALL and an assistant professor in computer logic.

At last, she put the tip of her running shoe on the edge of the desk and scooted the chair across the console platform to a phone. She punched in the number of the Seine Cafe in Dungeness, a small fishing village on Puget Sound, twenty miles from Seattle.

A woman picked up after the first ring. "Seine."

"Bev, Kelli."

"Oh, hi, hon. How's the brain trust?"

"Frustrated."

"Ain't we all."

She heard the background clatter of dishes, the sudden guffaw of a male voice. "Has Matt been in this evening?"

"Not yet, hon. Somebody said they saw him south of Flattery this afternoon."

"If he gets in before midnight, tell him I'll be at home."

"Will do."

"Thanks."

She replaced the phone. For a moment, she pictured Matt Marquette as she had seen him a week before. He'd come into the city to pick up a new fathometer for his boat, and she'd gone with him to the chandler's shop. Knowing how strapped he was for funds, she'd offered to buy the fathometer for him. Just a gift, she said. He didn't comment on her suggestion, just looked at her and then paid for it himself.

She did, however, manage to get him to accept lunch. It was rainy and cold as they drove up from the waterfront. She chose the Space Needle's Emerald Suite with its 360-degree view of the chilly, gray city far below them.

Afterward, they went to her houseboat, moored on Lake Union, and lay naked in her bed, getting slightly drunk on home-brewed beer that someone from the university had given her and watching a lone rowing shell from the Naval Training Center stiffing it out on the wind-whipped water.

She'd been going exclusively with Marquette for nearly a year. They'd met when Gilhammer rented his boat for an afternoon of deep-sea fishing with some of the other college teachers. It hadn't taken Kelli very long to realize how easy it would be to fall in love with this particular man.

Remembering that gray afternoon, she felt a sudden sexual warmth ripple through her groin—achingly sweet, yet there was something sad there, too.

Sighing, she finished her coffee, turned out the lights and headed for home.

The road between Port Angeles and Dungeness ran along the edge of the sound. Ahead of the rented Toyota, it was slick with soft rain. Near the town of Agnew, it turned inland, then back again and into a small ocean forest of cedar and needle pine. The rain was like fog in the trees.

Jack Stone had a blistering headache. He was hyped, on a high wire of energy and frustration. His back muscles felt like taut cables. In the passenger seat, his company's chopper pilot, Jay Basset, whistled tunelessly, his close-cropped head bobbing.

They had left the helicopter in a transit slot at the William Fairchild airport in Port Angeles. Before leaving, they'd drained some high octane from the aircraft into a stolen five-gallon can. Now it sat between Basset's legs, the fuel sloshing inside on the turns.

Stone gave his companion a studied glance. Basset was jived, looking forward to what was coming. He sat there whistling those same two bars of a country song. In profile, his face looked as if it had been pushed flat before hardening.

A fucking stone-killer, Jack thought.

Basset had once been a cop, small-town-deputy type in Idaho and Montana. But he'd been too brutal, even for that country. He'd also spent time in the Marines. They had taught him to fly a helicopter, and he was good at it.

Stone had first met him during the early days of his company, Stone Security Systems, in Boise, Idaho. Back then, he and his partner, Gus Fettis, both ex–Army Intelligence and Drug Enforcement Agency men, had been cash-strapped. To make ends meet, they'd run drugs. No big-time; just a few wholesale drops in places like Boise and Missoula and Idaho Falls. Basset became their enforcer with recalcitrant cowboys. To this day, he still carried a Marine combat blade in an upside down scabbard along his spine.

Stone snorted, venting his impatience. He readjusted his lanky, rawboned frame against the seat and agitatedly clawed a hand through his curly, graying hair. At forty-eight, his horsey face had leaned itself out into long, somber lines, like a man in perpetual mourning.

"Don't you know another goddamned tune?" he finally said.

"How's 'at?" Basset asked, sliding his ice-blue eyes around. He had a slow slur to his voice.

"Fuck it."

"Man, you all keyed up, Jack. I tole you we shoulda took them boys out on that boat. Then we wouldn't have to go a-sneakin'."

"Yeah, right. With half the fucking fishing fleet in the area."

"Hell, we coulda smacked 'em, *wham!* and been gone." He slapped his palm against his knee for emphasis.

"Bullshit."

In contrast to Basset, Stone hated what lay ahead—not out of any moral injunction, but simply because it had been forced onto him by a glitch. He hated glitches, those small accidents particularly endemic to clandestine operations.

The freighter drop of the sphere should have gone off

without a ripple. In Nam with the CID, he'd run hundreds of such drops off hostile coasts. Later, with DEA in Malaysia, he and Fettis had garnered comfortable pocket change smuggling China White and black-market gems off the coast of Thailand with similiar drops.

Yet here, off a goddamned *American* coast, it had blown up—not because of Coast Guard or cop patrols, just two jerkoff fishermen. What were the odds that they, without homing gear, would stumble onto a tiny silicon ball in all that ocean? Astro-fucking-nomical!

Yet here it was, and their intrusion had now forced him to deal with them. It was bad shit. Stuff like this could create bigger problems down the line. . . .

They reached the outskirts of Dungeness. It lay in a shallow bowl that funneled out into wide wheat and corn fields to the south. Protected from sea storms by the huge hump of the Olympic range, the area was called the Banana Belt because it always remained unusually warm and dry.

They crossed a bridge and slid down into the downtown area: darkened storefronts, a bank, a couple of saloons, a small drive-in with leather-jacketed punks on gleaming Harleys giving them the slow once-over.

They crossed two one-way streets and eventually reached the Dungeness estuary. Fed by a long entry channel, it curved around to form a small harbor. Inside were mooring jetties strung out like the tines of a comb. A few fishing boats, mostly trollers and gillnetters, were berthed among houseboats.

Jack eased along the waterfront. They passed a boatyard, and he stopped. A few seagulls and shearwaters squatted on posts. They turned their dark, shiny eyes into the headlights. A moment later, a pickup went by. It followed the water's edge to a small cafe up near a huge, abandoned-looking packing shed.

Stone switched off the lights and engine. He rolled down the window, and the pungent aroma of oily water and cedar and mud flats wafted through. The air was chilly and wet, like that coming off the walls of an ancient icehouse.

Basset gazed around, sucking noisily through his teeth. He looked over. "You sure we gon' be able to spot him comin' up that channel?"

"He's got to turn here to get to the piers. That'll put him close enough for us to pick up signal."

Stone had a small, handheld frequency scanner. Although not as sensitive as the aircraft's unit, it would easily ID the fishing boat. And once on board, the scanner could indicate the general location of the sphere from its pulse strength.

"What if he don't come in a-tall? Maybe we misread the port name off his stern. Besides, some of them boats stays out for days, don't they?"

"We didn't misread nothin'. And that was a small day-troller. He'll be in tonight."

Basset sighed. His shoe hit the gas can, made it ring. "Man, I gotta piss," he said.

"Then piss."

Basset opened the door and climbed out. The clear line of his knife and scabbard showed against the back of his faded leather aviator's jacket when he bent forward. With his dark glasses dangling cop-style off the neck of his T-shirt, he walked away into the darkness.

Jack stared out into the estuary. On the far side, the land climbed up into pine-covered bluffs. Here and there, house lights shone through the trees. Far beyond, along the dark ridges of the Olympic range, little bursts of friction lightning snapped like the quick glow from flashbulbs.

He lit a cigarette and studied his hands. Perfectly still.

Jay climbed back into the car. He sat silently for a moment, then started his two-bar whistling again.

"Goddammit," Jack barked. "Will you can that fucking song?"

A little grin crept into Basset's face. It had a cold, lethal merriness in it. "Okay, Jack," he said lazily. "But, hey, you ought to chill out."

They sat in silence for several minutes.

At last, Basset said, "I could use a cuppa coffee. How's about me walking down to that cafe and gettin' some?"

"Don't be stupid."

Basset said nothing. After a while, his fingers began to tap on his knee, then on the top of the gas can.

Jack closed his eyes. He listened to the soft thumps and felt himself coming up to it. The adrenaline beginning down below his skin, then coming up into the nerves of his fingers, into his scalp. Just like during the waiting before combat or a dangerous drug strike—that hollow feel of isolated suspension with the rising throb of his body the only motion in the air.

It was always like that just before the killing.

2

Holding her engines to a throaty idle, Marquette took the troller up the leeside of the Dungeness Spit, a four-mile-long stretch of sand that hooked into the sound. They were headed for their mooring slip in Dungeness.

Beyond the running lights, the shoreline of the spit looked softly luminous, as if it had absorbed the day's feeble sunlight and was now letting it seep gently back into the air.

At the Del Maro cannery loading dock, Matt eased *Big Blue* up against the tall, barnacle-encrusted pilings. He gave a blast on his horn to notify Tobacco Willie. Willie, a fat Tulalip Indian, was the cannery's night receiving clerk.

They unloaded their catch into one of the company's soggy, coffinlike fish boxes. It was meager, barely two hundred pounds of lingcod and snapper. They left the mako in the after hold. Matt knew a Japanese restaurant owner in Port Angeles who would take it right off the boat for a decent per-pound price.

After weighing the catch and getting their voucher, they walked back down to the boat. Matt slapped Hammil's shoulder. "Come on, kid, let's go eat."

"No, you go ahead," Rick said. He seemed distracted, kept glancing down toward the mooring jetties. "I'll tie her up and then head back to Seattle. I got early classes tomorrow."

Matt chuckled. The kid was in heat. Rick had a Dungeness girlfriend named Julie. Whenever he got the chance to be aboard alone, Hammil would signal the girl on the horn, and she'd sneak out to meet him. They'd make love in one of the troller's forward bunks.

"You sure?" Marquette teased. "Hey, I'm buying."

"No, really, I ain't hungry."

"Okay." He grinned at him. "Keep it safe."

"Yeah, right."

As Rick took the troller farther into the estuary, Matt crossed the factory tracks and walked down to the Seine Cafe. The wind and the rain were gone now. Save for the distant rumble of *Big Blue*'s engines, the night was silent, as if a great bell jar had descended over the town.

The Seine was squeezed between a shabby Korean hardware store and a tiny doctor's office. Several pickups were parked out front. Inside, it was steamy warm, the air laced with the greasy odor of fried meat and stale beer.

Several men were seated at the counter, hunched over coffee or long-necked bottles of beer. Fishermen in yellow sou'wester rubbers or high-neck Canadian sweaters, their faces and hands leathery and wind-reddened.

In recent years, the ocean hadn't been good to these men. Most of the sound's fish stocks were now badly depleted from decades of overfishing, pollution and hydroelectric dams inland. Much of what had survived was then decimated by Japanese long-liners fishing just outside the national territorial boundaries.

As a result, the fleets had rapidly declined throughout the entire area. Thousands of boat captains had either sold out or lost their boats to creditors. Those few who remained hung on by a thread, always looking for that miraculous summer run that would put them back to square one.

Until that time, they were forced to take part-time jobs in Seattle and Tacoma. Or go sharking. Or even charter out to tourists—landlubbers who usually ended up getting drunk and puking all over their boats.

"Hey, Marquette," a bearded man in a peacoat called. He was half drunk. "How you do today?"

"Landed an eight-hundred-pound mako female."

"No shit?"

"Yeah. But the damn bitch nearly took off my mast."

The men laughed.

Matt pulled off his jacket and cap, brushed a hand through short, chestnut-brown hair. At forty-four, Marquette was quite a handsome man, chocolate-eyed and full-faced with a well-shaped, warm mouth that always seemed just about to lift into a smile of sardonic mischievousness.

The cafe owner's wife, Bev Boudeen, poked her head out the kitchen door. "Hey there, Matthew," she drawled. She drew a cup of coffee and slid it up the counter with her thumb. "I hear you say you scored a big jack?"

Matt nodded. "A *damned* big one."

"Well, that oughta by God put some jingle in your jeans." Bev was sixty, thin and dry as a stalk of desert corn. "What'll it be, hon?"

He ordered two hamburgers and a bottle of Bud. Bev shouted the order and then leaned against the counter.

"Kelli called about a hour ago," she said. "She was fixin' to head home. Said for you to call if you got in before midnight."

"Okay."

Bev gave him a lifted eyebrow. "I like that little ole gal, you know? Make somebody a damned fine wife someday."

He feigned surprise. "Oh, you think so?"

She snorted. "You know it, cousin, an' I know it. You better damned well think about it before somebody *else* knows it." She headed for the kitchen.

Matt checked his watch. Ten after twelve. Not wanting to talk to Kelli on the cafe's phone, he crossed to the door and checked the public phone a block away at Albin's Car Repair. Someone was using it. He went back to his seat.

Bev brought his order. The beer was achingly cold with tiny slivers of ice in it. For a few minutes, Bev chatted with him. Then two men came in, and she went back up the counter.

He quietly finished his hamburgers and ordered a second beer. Through the cafe's steam-frosted window, the neon sign outside formed a scarlet sunburst on the glass. It suddenly seemed an oddly isolated image, as if the color were really a sound muffled into hushed poignancy.

From it evolved Kelli Pickett's face. Idly, he wondered what she might be doing at that precise moment. Drinking a last glass of wine before sleep, or perhaps sitting in the tub with her hair up, humming as she soaped the smooth, linear lift of her arms, the full rise of breasts.

The picture slipped into the memory of the day she'd spent with him in Dungeness several weeks before. Gilhammer had given her and the entire CRYSTALBALL team the day off. She'd driven over and surprised him.

Bev had packed a lunch and a twin-pack of beer for them in an old picnic basket. They hiked out to the end of the spit, racing the last hundred yards with him lugging the basket and Kelli cutting ahead, her long legs in sweats pumping hard, hair fluffed and aerated by the chilly wind. Far across the sound, a fog bank was slipping in, shadowing a tanker as it worked its slow, majestic way toward Vancouver.

They ended the afternoon at his place, an old Victorian on a hill overlooking a valley carpeted with winter wheat. He rented it from an old California couple who rarely came north.

In the master bedroom, they made exhilarating love while the house creaked in the sea wind, whispering as if there were ghosts in the walls. Afterward, they lay in each other's arms, feeling a glow like warm sunshine in the air.

Suddenly Kelli had sat up and looked at him, right into his eyes, for a long time, she herself having fallen into a wistful silence. Then she had risen, still wordless, and gone barefoot to the white-tiled kitchen and made coffee.

Remembering that, he felt an aching tug at the heart. He knew what she had been asking with her eyes, her suspended stillness. Something deeper between them, something far beyond the sex. He also suspected she was in love with him, or at least well on the way. And, in his own fashion, he knew he loved her, too.

Yet—

For a long time, something had been missing in Marquette's life, something he'd once had in grand proportion. It was a thing that a man must have to feel himself whole. It was that sureness of self, of ability to control what he was or could be.

At times, it was hard to recall those earlier times when he *had* possessed it. In college, for instance, when as a powerhouse tight end he'd nearly won an All-American berth. Then in Nam with Navy SEAL Team One, all gung ho and macho disregard, facing death and dispensing it without particular terror or remorse.

And, finally, as the hard-charging rebel on the International Formula One circuit. Matt-the-Cat Marquette, the hotshot who took no prisoners and creamed anybody who got in his way.

But in a brilliant collision during the 1992 Spanish Gran Prix in Barcelona, it had all disappeared, evaporated. In its place was a sudden, overwhelming sense of guilt and fear, as if all the deaths he had seen, all those he had conspired in, had been lying in ambush for this precise moment of critical mass to regenerate themselves, forming now in that crazy, time-slowed flight of Andre de Neauve's car cartwheeling off toward the stands and the people wildly fleeing and the blue-white explosion and Andre still strapped in his seat hurling through space, a black, broken mummy.

All because he, Marquette, had pushed the envelope once too often.

The Bureau of Alcohol, Tobacco and Firearms chief agent, Albert Kizzier, snapped on his flashlight to check his watch. Two minutes after one.

He touched his radio button. "You set, Jo-Jo?"

"Yeah," Jo-Jo came right back. "Somebody's inside, all right. A radio's on in one of the rooms."

Kizzier was parked in a brown van in front of a small, white clapboard house on Deeder Avenue in the unincorporated section of Boise, Idaho. Called Garden City, it was a shoddy area of cheap motels, country-western honky-tonks and blocks of dilapidated houses built in the thirties.

A half block away, partially hidden by a smashed fence, a pair of Ada County Sheriff patrol cars was parked. Four deputies in yellow windbreakers stood around, waiting. One carried a thick-barreled battering ram, resting it on his boot.

Kizzier got out of the vehicle, reached back through the window to flash his headlights. Twice. Immediately, the deputies scooted around the end of the fence and broke into a run across the weed-grown yard between the house and street.

Kizzier went after them. Unlike the deputies, he wore a navy-blue windbreaker with the letters *BATF* stenciled in white over the right breast.

He and his partner, Jo-Jo Azevedo, were members of the bureau's Rapid Response Team based in Boise. Earlier that evening, an anonymous phone tip to the Federal Building had claimed that a man named E. J. Goodell was holed up at this particular house and that he was carrying illegal guns.

The team had been watching for Goodell. He was a known member of both the Aryan Nations (AN) and an Idaho militia group called the Grassrooters. Many such volatile antigovernment, white-supremacist groups were scattered throughout the Sawtooth and Salmon River Mountains in central Idaho.

In 1994, inflamed by the bloody incidents at Waco and Ruby Ridge, these isolated "camps" had begun to merge. Insurgency plans were rumored. Rabble-rousing leaders began to call for open guerrilla warfare against the U.S. government. And massive stockpiles of heavy weaponry and ammunition were secretly being cached.

Goodell had already been arrested for violations of federal gun laws and the illegal manufacture and sale of machine gun conversion kits. But so far the ATF and FBI had been unable to put him away.

The deputies reached the house and bounded up onto its small porch. An emaciated yellow cat, spooked by the sudden thud of boots, hurled itself over the edge of the porch and disappeared into the darkness.

The lead deputy slapped his palm loudly against the door.

"You inside, open up! Sheriff's Department!"

He stepped out of the way, and the man with the battering ram smashed it into the door. The wooden face blew apart, both hinges flying to the side. Weapons drawn, the men rushed in, jostling one behind the other.

The interior of the house stank of sewer gas mixed with the wet-hay, smoky odor of marijuana. A lighted living room was to the right. It was strewn with filthy clothing and empty beer cans. The furniture was sparse and shabby except for an expensive-looking television set in one corner. There were several videocassettes piled on the set. The screen was blank.

Kizzier, directly behind one of the deputies, headed down a narrow hall. A crash sounded from the back of the house. A moment later, Azevedo and two deputies burst out of the kitchen.

Kizzier reached a door off the hall. He paused for a moment, then kicked it open and dove through. A man and woman were on a brass bed, both naked. The man, heavily bearded, had already started to leap off the bed and head for a closet.

Kizzier caught him before he reached it. He shoved the muzzle of his Beretta 92 sharply against the man's backbone. "Ease up, E. J.," he said casually, "or I'll blow your goddamned spine into next week."

Goodell relaxed, glaring over his shoulder at Kizzier with tiny, dark eyes. He was a young man, but his head hair and beard were flecked with gray. There were twin tattoos on his shoulders, crossed swords inside a circle formed by the phrase "Posse Comitatus."

"What is this shit, man?" he growled.

Kizzier cuffed him and shoved him back to the bed. He leaned over and turned off a small plastic radio on the windowsill. Goodell lowered himself slowly, still glowering. He had a barrel chest covered with curly hair.

The woman disgustedly crossed her legs and watched the policemen. Her makeup was heavy and her body skin very white. Her dark patch of pubic hair seemed an indelicate obscenity. "Goddammit, Koster," she said to the deputy, "not again."

The deputy chuckled good-naturedly. "I keep telling you, Angel. You gotta leave these goddamned shit-kickers alone."

Kizzier glanced over at him. "You know her?"

"Yeah, name's Angel Eberhard. A stable lady for a local pimp, name of T-Bucks Scoot."

Resignedly, Angel got out of bed and began to dress. She had bony hips and, up close, looked to be in her late thirties. "Man, this has been one puke-shitty day," she grumbled.

Jo-Jo came in. He was stocky and olive-skinned. Locks of hair, black as a Gypsy dancer's, curled out from under his turned-around BATF baseball cap. He and Kizzier began to search the room, starting with the closet. They found a worn-looking brown suitcase hidden under some clothing. Jo-Jo dragged it out and took the straps off.

Goodell said, "Where's your gawddammed warrant, man? I don't see no warrant."

The agents ignored him. Inside the suitcase were parts of four MP-5 submachine guns with several boxes of ammunition. Under that were two chromed Colt single-action Peacemaker .45s, along with a small plastic pouch containing several dime bags of marijuana and four packets of what looked like crack.

Kizzier grinned coldly over at Goodell. "Congratulations, fuckface. If them P-5s are stolen like I figure they are, you just earned yourself a triple nickle in the Dump."

"That ain't my shit," Goodell said. "I never seen none of them weapons before. This ain't even my house."

Angel stared at the suitcase, suddenly alarmed. "Hey, wait a minute," she cried, "I don't know nothing from machine guns. I just come here for a straight lay. Check with T-Bucks, he'll tell you."

"Who owns the house?" Azevedo asked Goodell.

"How the hell do I know? I jes' borrowed it for a little quick pussy."

"Who from?"

"A guy I met in a bar."

Bumps and thuds sounded from different parts of the house as the other deputies continued to search through it. Azevedo went out to help.

"I want to put my pants on," Goodell said to the deputy. "I don't like settin' here with my gawddammed dick hanging out."

Kizzier turned to Angel. "You ever trick here before, sweetheart?"

"No. This dude brung me here."

A few moments later, Jo-Jo poked his head around the edge of the door. "Al, you want to come out here a minute?"

He led Kizzier into the living room. The television screen had a picture now. Azevedo nodded toward the videocassettes on top of the box. "Typical survivalist BS. Guerrilla tactics, sniping, crap like that. Some porno flicks, too. But there's something on the one running now you gotta see."

He leaned down, punched the VCR stop button, rewound and started the tape through again. There was a moment of scattered static lines across the screen. Then the picture came back on.

The scene was a typical American small-town street. A Rexall drugstore was on one corner, and there was a small restaurant called Fran's across the street. At the end of the second block, in front of an Exxon service station, a single stoplight was suspended over the intersection. Up and down the street, pickups were parked, hunting rifles racked in the rear windows and big logging toolboxes in their beds.

The camcorder suddenly jumped to a higher magnification, focusing sharply on two men talking beside a green pickup in the Exxon parking lot. One man wore a plaid logger's jacket and hobnailed boots. The other was dressed in a U.S. Air Force flight jacket and dark jeans tight enough to show the outlines of his muscular thighs. His head was completely shaved.

Kizzier frowned, then leaned in. "Jesus H. Christ," he snapped. "Is that who I think it is?"

"Sure as hell looks like him, don't it?" said Jo-Jo.

He froze the picture, and both men got down close to study the man in the flight jacket. Finally, Kizzier straightened and shook his head, amazed. "Well, if that ain't Hans Halberstadt, it's his fucking twin."

Hans Heinrich Halberstadt was a twenty-nine-year-old neo-Nazi terrorist from Germany. A speed freak and senior officer in a skinhead organization called *Die letzten Stunden*, "The Final Hours." Implicated in gun-smuggling operations and bombings of Turkish and Muslim enclaves throughout Europe, he was wanted by the German State Police and Interpol. He was strongly suspected of having assassinated a Swiss diplomat in Prague in 1994.

"Get Goodell in here," Kizzier snapped.

The Grassrooter stood around sullenly. He was still naked save for his boots, which the deputy had allowed him to put on. "What video?" he said. "Them things is just fuck movies. They belong to the guy who owns the house."

"What about this one?"

"I don't know nothin' about it."

After Goodell and Angel were taken away, the two ATF agents scoured the house looking for anything else on Halberstadt. They found more dope and a beat-up old single-shot .22 rifle, but nothing on the German.

They went over the tape again. "You recognize the town?" Kizzier asked.

"Yeah, it's Salmon." Jo-Jo snorted. "Man, D.C.'ll shit rings over this. Hitler-Hans schmoozing with the 'Rooters and AN?"

"Fuck D.C.," Kizzier snapped. "This item stays off the six report. We let the goddamned suits and Feebies get wind of it, we'll have fucking reporters coming outta the woodwork."

Among the ATF's Response Teams, Kizzier and his people were known as rebels, Fast flyers who sometimes used unorthodox methods and unnecessary force. They were tagged "the Z-unit" after their roster code ID of Z-131. In the preceding two years, they'd been under internal investigation twice. But their arrest records were so outstanding, the incidents had neatly been backlogged.

"What about Goodell?" Azevedo asked. "He might leak something through his lawyer."

Kizzier thought a moment. "Then we'll let the prick go. No charges on the guns, just misdemeanor possession of drugs. When he bails, we surveil him."

"How we gonna explain no charges on the P-5s? County's already in."

"We'll just conveniently lose the goddamned things on the way to the station."

"Whoa," Jo-Jo said. "We fast-shuffle like that and Williams's gonna get nervous." George Williams was Assistant U.S. District Attorney for the Federal Criminal Division of Central Idaho.

"Don't worry about that," Kizzier countered. "He'll go along with the program. There's big coup to make here if we nail a cretin like Halberstadt—and maybe some of his AN scuzbags into the bargain."

He popped the videocassette out of the VCR and flicked off the television set. For a moment, he surveyed the room's squalor, his dark eyes narrow with revulsion. "Let's get the hell out of this shithole."

Thrashing her head back and forth on the pillow, Julie cried out, "Oh, God, don't stop. I'll goddamned die if you stop." Her words filtered off into a strangled, panting jumble.

Above her, Rick Hammil's back humped and straightened rhythmically as he plunged in and out of her. He felt her nails rake his nakedness. Groaning, he buried his face in the confluence of her neck and shoulder, tasted her skin.

The small forward berth space of *Big Blue* was cramped and cold, tinged with the tang of pudendum and the heavier odor of netting and dive gear and sour blankets. With elephantine counterpoint, like a giant metronome winding down, the boat periodically rocked in the estuary ripple.

Rick felt a furtive thud come down through the bulkhead

from the upper deck. Another. For a second, he lifted his head and gazed upward, studying the half-lit underside of the deck. Had someone come aboard? Matt? Julie's writhing body quickly drew him back.

His orgasm hovered on the edges of his groin. It was like a rising of sunshine, the heat intensifying. Caught up in ecstasy, he tried to hold it back.

Suddenly, he felt Julie freeze, the movement a tangent to their sexual flow. For one tiny moment, there was a pause. Then she let out a surging, frightened gasp and tried frantically to get out from under him.

His eyes shot open. In the half-light from the galley, Julie's face was contorted with shock. She let out a muffled scream just as he felt something slip over his head. A second later, he was powerfully jerked backward.

Confused and strangling, he tried to free himself. A rope was around his neck. It dragged him back until he was off the bunk, down onto his buttocks on the deck. Vaguely he saw moving shadows.

Julie started another scream that was cut off sharply as he heard something strike her face. It sounded thick, hollow, like a bamboo stick hitting a melon. She went silent.

A knee rammed viciously into his stomach, and a man's face came down close to his. "Where's the ball with the locator, kid?" a guttural voice demanded.

Rick continued to struggle. Someone else grabbed his arms, pinning him back and down. "Who . . . are you?" he managed to croak.

"Where is it, goddammit?" the man asked again. He viciously slapped Rick across the face. "Don't be stupid, asshole. You want to die?"

"I don't . . . know . . . nothing about a ball."

The man said something to the other one. Then he stood up. The rope around Rick's neck went slack. He started to push himself up, but something struck him at the base of the neck. It blew a white explosion behind his eyelids, and he lost consciousness.

He drifted for what seemed a long time, through vast, dark

hallways where he felt surreptitious movements around him, footsteps that seemed to form solid prints in the fabric of the darkness as if a man had walked through it with phosphorescence on his toes and heels.

He tried to move but couldn't. Gradually, a powerful smell seeped into his consciousness, filtered searingly into his nostrils. It was caustic, like ether. High-octane gasoline! Oh, dear God, he thought in terror. They're going to burn us.

Willing his body to function, he moved, first his eyes, then a hand. Another. He looked at his chest. It stung. It was soaked with gasoline. Dizzily, he got to his feet.

The entire berth space, bulkheads, the blankets of the bunk, were dripping with gasoline. Julie was lying half off the bunk, her face on the floor. The round curve of her buttocks looked white in the pale light, vaguely bikini-marked.

With his heart hammering crazily in his head and throat, Rick reached out, lightly touched her shoulder. "Julie?" he whispered. "Oh, God, baby?" Her body felt thick, heavy, as if the deck were sucking her to itself.

He recoiled, stood there, his chest heaving.

There were several heavy thumps on the afterdeck. Someone had opened the hatches to the ice holds. Desperately, he searched for a weapon and finally found a three-foot metal bar. Gripping it like a bat, he peered into the galley.

Things were strewn all over: cooking utensils, charts, navigation books. All the cupboards had been flung open and emptied. A five-gallon gasoline can lay on its side near the stove, a little stream of blue-tinged fuel still flowing out onto the deck.

Suddenly a man came down the steps from the control cabin, sliding down the rails on his palms. It was not the man who had talked to him. This one was dressed in a leather jacket, pug-faced, blue eyes like pale turquoise.

He stopped short when he saw Rick. Then his eyes narrowed. His right hand snapped behind his back. When it came out again, it held a knife.

He charged.

Rick swung the bar at him. The swing was too short. The

end of the bar slammed into the stove, hurling a grill cover against the bulkhead. The man ducked to the left and continued in low, his right arm shooting out.

Rick saw it all happen in slow motion, everything as pronounced and defined and crystalline as if he were seeing it through the purest of lenses. The fear in him was like a block of dry ice searing the insides of his ribs.

He swung back, the bar suddenly terribly heavy. It went sailing over the man again; his head was tilted as if he were looking up under something. He growled, the sound like an animal's. The bar crashed into the small butane heater unit beside the chart table, gouging open the screen. A small blue flash flicked from the pilot flame.

Rick felt the knife go into him. Under the high ribs, the blade a sudden scorching like a compressed sliver of lightning. The heat of it seemed to flash through the entire network of neurons in his body and then coalesce back again into the single glowing shaft of the blade as the man twisted, then withdrew it. As it departed his flesh, a fanning splurge of bright arterial blood burst out.

He fell backward. He wasn't aware when he struck the deck. He opened his mouth and tried vainly to suck in the gasoline-fumed air in front of his face. It seemed to have gelled into solidity that wouldn't pass through his lips.

Then he was gone.

The phone rang four times before Kelli answered.

Matt said, "Hi."

"Oh, hi." Her voice was hoarse, sensual from sleep. She cleared her throat. "How are you?"

"Okay. Got you up, didn't I?"

"No, that's all right. What time is it?"

"Around one."

"You just get in?"

"Yes." He leaned against the wall of Albin's garage. It smelled of old oil and grease. Beside the garage was a small grassy plot filled with car parts. Beyond was a lumber warehouse.

"How'd you do?" Kelli asked.

"We snagged a good-sized shark. Should bring about four hundred."

"That's great."

He pictured her, dressed in the old flannel nightshirt she always wore to bed. Her hair would be ruffled from the pillow, her face slightly pale without makeup, and the room would smell of her, a warm scent like freshly pressed cotton.

"I've missed you," she said.

"Me, too." He looked up at the sky. The cloud cover had thinned toward the east. A few stars showed through like luminous crystals of salt behind a thin gauze.

Earlier, Matt had decided not to call her. Instead, he had remained in the cafe for a while and then walked down along the factory tracks to the jetties, going slowly.

Hammil's bicycle was still locked to the main pierhead post. Matt stood beside it and looked out at the boat, imagining Rick and his girl there in the darkness. The moment telegraphed a sudden surge of utter loneliness in him. Silently, he had turned and gone back to the garage phone.

He inhaled, shifted against the wall. "How's the project going?"

She snorted with disgust. "Full of problems, as usual." She recounted that evening's blown wireframe run. He listened, grunting interest now and then, trying to follow. But like the other times when she talked of her work, he understood little of what she said.

Finishing, she paused, then asked, "When do I see you?"

"Are you free tomorrow night? I thought I'd come over and treat you to a pizza. Seeing as how I'll be loaded with shark money."

"I'd like that." Her voice had lowered again. The philter of its whispered headiness coiled through the mouthpiece, made his own throat thicken for a moment with longing.

A dog began to bark somewhere among the houses on Cooper Street, which ran off the entrance to the factory parking lot. The sound seemed remote, as if the animal were in a distant valley.

He started to say something, and there was a sudden, bright, blue-white flash from the direction of the estuary causeway. A fraction of a second later, he heard a whomping explosion. Flickering patterns of yellow light began to play across the asphalt parking lot.

"What the hell—?" he said.

"What's the matter?"

"I think something just exploded. Hold it a minute." He stepped a few feet to the right, holding the short length of telephone cord at arm's length so he could see past the corner of the factory building.

As he cleared it, his eyes shot wide open.

A boat was burning down on the last mooring jetty. Flames seethed off it, up into the air, churning smoke laced with bursts of gas that flared and disappeared. The masts and cabins of nearby boats made flat black silhouettes aginst the fire. The estuary itself, as far out as the breakwater, danced and flaked with orange highlights.

Adrenaline hit his veins like liquid oxygen. It was *Big Blue*! Then he was moving, the phone banging back against the garage wall and Matt going full-out across the parking lot and down the incline toward the causeway.

Behind him, lights began to flick on in the houses and people started to come out, looking north, their sleep-dulled faces going flat in that stunned look of catastrophe.

3

Clallam County Detective Lieutenant John Two Elks, a full-blooded Nez Perce Indian, stood six-foot-five and weighed nearly three hundred pounds. Wearing a curly-brimmed brown Stetson and a bulky winter coat, he lowered himself tiredly onto one of the pier pilings beside Marquette.

"This kid Hammil have relatives in the area?" he asked. He had to raise his voice over the steady drone of a mobile generator that had been wheeled out onto the dock to run two floodlights.

Matt shook his head. "No. He was originally from Iowa. His parents still live there. Marshalltown, I think. I've got their number."

He glanced toward the pierhead. A small volunteer fire truck was parked beside a pair of green-and-white county patrol cars. The crackle of their radios occasionally shattered the night.

It was now after three in the morning. The county medical examiner, Dr. Roy Byner, had already left with the bodies of Rick and Julie. They'd been burned extensively, body skin waxy and swollen. In places, there were oozy black patches like shavings of leathery coal rubbed in the thin oil of deep-tissue edema.

Beyond the vehicles and yellow crime ribbons, a cluster of Dungeness citizens huddled, murmuring and watchful. Fog had begun to slip in off the ocean. It created fuzzy halos around the streetlights of the town.

"I'd like to be the one to tell his folks," Marquette said, turning back. "I've talked to his dad a couple of times. It might be easier if the news came from me."

Two Elks shook his head. "This kind of news isn't easy coming from anybody. We'll have a Marshalltown officer do it. What about the girl?"

"Her name was Julie Polk. She was from Tacoma but was staying with an older sister here. The sister works nights someplace in Seattle, a packing company. I don't remember the name."

Matt had been the first to reach the boat, pounding out onto the pier and then up onto the stern. The fire was so hot it was like hitting a wall. The forward portion was fully engulfed. The cabin's top beams had already caved in, with individual frames burning fiercely. It made a deep roaring.

He immediately shut off the deck butane reservoir tank to prevent further explosions, then tried to go down into the galley. The heat drove him back. People had begun to arrive with handheld extinguishers, everybody yelling. The feeble extinguisher streams were useless.

The forward part of the boat had started to sink as the bunk area began to flood. Steam poured up through the galley stairs and out from under the eaves of the cabin.

Someone suggested hooking the cable from a small cherry-picker loader near the pierhead to the stern of the troller to keep it from going to the bottom. They reeved it out, and Matt quickly ran it through one of the after eye-ballards and back around the winch plate. With the winch drum grinding, they managed to anchor the stern tightly against the pier pilings.

The volunteer fire department arrived with foam cannisters and twin fire hoses that fed off the pump on the town's old fire wagon. They ran hoses out onto the pier and cut loose at the blaze. The thick jets of water hissed through the nozzles, looking yellow in the firelight, like streams of liquid gold.

The lieutenant took out a cigar, lit it with a tiny silver

lighter and puffed languidly for a moment. He leaned out to spit into the water.

"How come they were alone on board?" he asked. "Was that usual?"

"Sometimes. The kid didn't get to be with his girl much out here, so they'd use the boat if I wasn't around."

Two Elks nodded, thoughtfully twirling the cigar in his mouth. Although large, he had a certain grace of movement. In the eighties, he'd played seven seasons with the Seattle Seahawks as a defensive tackle. Four times he was chosen for the Pro Bowl.

He tilted his head and studied Matt narrowly. "Where were you?"

"Having dinner at the cafe."

"Which cafe?"

"The Seine."

"And you were the first one to reach the boat?"

"Yes."

"How was that?"

"I was on the phone with my girl—that phone up there, near the factory. I heard the explosion."

"What's your girl's name?"

He gave it and her phone number.

"You heard nothing else?"

"Just a dog barking."

A deputy came up. "Hey, Lieutenant, we're gonna have to take off. You want a man to remain?"

"Yeah, leave Jensen."

The deputy walked off toward the patrol cars.

Matt's gaze followed him. It paused at Rick's bicycle, still chained to the pierhead. He stared at it for a long moment, then swung around and looked at the boat. Wisps of smoke continued to drift off its fore end. With the stern up on the cable, the barnacle-encrusted copper bottom was showing. It looked sadly forbidden, as if an old woman were helplessly exposing her naked thighs.

Jesus Christ, he thought. Jesus Christ.

"You own this boat clear?" the detective asked suddenly.

"What?"

"The boat—is it yours free and clear?"

"No."

"Who carries the paper?"

He told him.

"What kind of engines she carry?"

"Diesels."

Two Elks stood up, groaning slightly. He spat into the water again, then looked off toward the town. "You got anything aboard you need?"

"No."

"I want everybody to stay off it. Including you. An' I'd appreciate it if you stuck around for a few days."

"Sure."

"You got a phone?"

"Yes." He gave the number, which the detective didn't write down. He merely nodded, turned and walked away without another word.

Dawn came in softly, grayly, through the fog. It was very cold, and there were knifeblades of ice on the boards of the pier. Matt still sat where Two Elks had left him.

A few fishermen had walked out to offer condolences in short, guttural, awkward sentences. Then they'd gone away again. At the first solid light, two trollers from adjacent piers headed out for open water. Their foghorns drifted back into the estuary like the moaning of a wounded man.

The deputy, Jensen, remained in his patrol car the whole time, his fur collar turned up. After awhile, an old woman named Norma Jean, from a nearby houseboat, came out and gave Matt a mug of steaming coffee. She didn't say anything, just handed the mug over, patted him on the shoulder and returned to her boat.

The deputy, seeing the coffee, must have decided to get his own. He got out of the car and, carrying his thermos, walked up past the rail tracks toward the Seine.

Matt put the mug down on the pier, stood up and walked over to his ravaged boat. When he stepped aboard, his weight made the cherry picker's cable squeak against the gunwale. He stepped over it and, ducking, went into the cabin.

The windshield had been totally blown out, and there were tiny pearls of melted glass scattered across the deck. The right side of the cabin was completely gone, as were the wheel and control pedestals and throttle mounts. The stairs down to the galley were merely scorched framing. An oil gauge lay under the Radar Direction Finder unit, its glass face turned amber by the heat.

He squatted at the head of the stairwell and peered down into what had been the galley. It was half flooded, the water black against the scorched keelson and frame struts. A thin film of fuel floated on the surface, making it appear smooth and shiny.

Everything held the odor of wet, burnt wood and spent fuel, and the dark, sweetish fetidness of incinerated flesh. The smell instantly drew up a picture in his mind, like a burst of light in a dark room.

Nam. Night incursions. Passing like dark ghosts through villages where there was nothing left but burnt huts, smoky from blasted wood and straw and death, the bodies of old men and women and children sundered and strewn like piles of forgotten laundry with the rats already feeding. . . .

He shook off the memory and stood. For a moment, he wandered distractedly around the cabin, touching this, checking that. Absently, he flicked on the depth indicator, a battery-operated Sonar RC-D120. Water depth was indicated by a digital readout on a tiny screen. It read 41.3 feet.

The screen flashed a series of white lines.

Again.

Matt looked at it, puzzled. Once more the lines appeared. He grunted. Apparently, an interference source, occuring in evenly spaced pulses, was being picked up by the unit. But where was it coming from?

He went around the cabin again. Everything was shut down. Intrigued, he stepped back to the afterdeck and surveyed the pier area. Could it be the police car's radio? No, he decided. Whatever it was must be below the waterline.

For the next ten minutes, he thoroughly searched the after portion of the boat. Finally, he pulled open the ice holds. Most of the ice had disappeared. In the number-two hold, the big mako lay on the carlings, partly submerged in bloody ice melt.

He dropped down beside it. The animal's body had hardened slightly from rigor, and its one visible eye was now as milky-white as an ivory cue ball. The gaping shotgun wounds still seeped blood.

He ran a finger along the side. The dermal denticles were rough and sharp as a rat-tail file. He stopped suddenly. A tiny pulse, faint as a butterfly's wing, had touched his finger. He pressed his palm against the shark. There was the pulse again.

It was coming from inside the animal.

A shadow loomed over him.

"Hey, Marquette, what the hell you doin' down there?" a man said sharply.

Matt looked up into the shaded glasses of deputy Jensen. "Checking my catch," he answered.

"The lieutenant say it was okay you do that?"

"Yeah," he lied.

Jensen grunted. For a moment, he gazed down at the shark. "Big prick, ain't he?" he said.

"Yeah."

The deputy disappeared. Matt heard him step back onto the pier. Quickly he unsheathed his Ka-Bar. He jammed the blade in just above the anal fin and drew it forward, slicing open the entire belly. Entrails, slimy with blue mucus and dark blood, gushed out onto the boards.

He slit open the actual stomach. A powerful stench of rot hit him as he reached up into the cavity for the contents. There was partially digested garbage, a tooth-punctured Pepsi can and half a rubber raincoat. He reached in again, felt something hard, gripped it.

It was a round metal-shiny ball. A tiny unit of some kind was banded to it, and there were milling dents in both sides.

In its mucal coating, it glistened like a large Christmas tree ornament as he held it in his palm.

It pulsed.

At that precise moment, in the Silicon Valley near San Francisco, a senior executive of InTronic Corporation arrived early for work. His name was Phil Holbrooke. He was the company's chief research engineer, a nationally known specialist in designing computer programs for robotic-oriented production systems.

Alone in his office, he stripped off his coat, tossed it over a chair and sat at his desk. First he sketched out his day's schedule, then turned to the mail and faxes that had come in overnight.

Among the letters and FedEx parcels was a plainly wrapped package roughly the size of a paperback novel. He examined the postmark. Twin Falls, Idaho. Puzzled, he thumbed the brown paper open. It contained a small, roughly hewn wooden box. Using the point of his letter opener, he pried the top off.

There was a small, sharp explosion. It blew off Holbrooke's right hand at the wrist.

Thirty minutes later, the sports editor of the *San Francisco Chronicle* received a phone call. What appeared to be a taped message followed—a male voice, digitally distorted. The man called himself the Horseman and claimed responsibility for the incident at InTronic.

The message was filled with rambling obscenities and threats directed at Jews and blacks, New Age religionists and homosexuals. But the strongest venom was aimed at scientists, like Holbrooke. They were all in league with the government, the caller claimed. Their goal was the total annihilation of the white American male, via advanced technology and a secret computer spy system operating through the country's phones and television sets.

The tape ended with the ominous promise that more strikes would be mounted until all the Holbrooke-type scum of America were wiped out.

In reality, this was the second Horseman attack. Four months earlier, a professor of electronics at the University of Colorado had been severely wounded by a similiar letter bomb. But save for transcribed copies of his messages and the nearly useless remnants of the wooden bomb, the FBI had no solid clues as to who the Horseman was.

"My God, Matt, I've been frantic," Kelli cried on the phone. "Are you all right?"

"I'm sorry I left you hanging. Something terrible's happened."

"I know; I called Bev. Oh, Matt, I'm so terribly sorry about Rick and his girl. God, it's horrible. What started the fire, do you know?"

He pressed the sphere tighter against his body under his jacket. With his other hand, he sipped at Norma Jean's coffee. It was cold.

"I think they were murdered," he said quietly.

"What?"

He repeated it.

"Good Lord!" There was stunned silence, then: "Who would do that? Why? Are you sure?"

"I don't know who, but I might know why."

He hesitated. Since finding the sphere, he'd been frantically trying to reason it out, to form explanations and linkages of cause and effect. He'd managed a few things.

First, the fact that the ball held a locator meant someone had intended to recover it from the sea. But who? Then he recalled the helicopter they'd seen the previous night. The two mysterious men gazing down at them. The intwined *S*s on the fuselage.

Were *they* the ones, homing in to the locator signal even from the shark's belly? Or had their momentary interest really been nothing more than curiosity? Still, if it *had* been them, they would have certainly seen *Big Blue*'s home port off her transom and known to strike in Dungeness.

There was something else: the powerful stink of gasoline fumes he'd caught when he first jumped onto the boat. It still faintly smelled of it—not ordinary gas; rather, the acrylic pungency of aviation fuel. That meant somebody had deliberately set the fire. To cover the murders? Obviously.

It occurred to him that Lieutenant Two Elks was quite possibly thinking along those same lines . . . with one ominous difference he was certain of. The detective's focus was on *him*.

"Matt? God, say something."

He slipped the ball from under his jacket and looked at it, felt the pulsing. It was growing fainter. Apparently, its battery was losing power.

What in hell *is* this thing? he thought. He was suddenly, profoundly aware of a dark, grotesque sense of vileness locked into the tiny pulsing. The demonic breathing of an incubus.

"Matt, please."

Should he tell her? Bring her into this? Perhaps endanger her life, too? No, she shouldn't know. Still, she might help without knowing.

"Kelli, have you got access to X-ray equipment at the university?" he asked.

"X-ray equipment? I don't understand."

"Do you?"

"Well, they have units at the Magnuson Medical Center on campus. But I wouldn't have ready access. Why would you want that?"

"I need to find out what's inside something."

"What?"

"It's a small metal or composite ball, about the size of a grapefruit." He heard the crunch of car tires and quickly put the sphere back under his jacket. Deputy Jensen's patrol car went slowly by the factory parking lot and disappeared beyond the lumber warehouse.

"Where'd you get it?"

"I'd better not tell you that."

"Matt, what's going on here? Are you . . . involved in something?"

"No. Look, think a minute. Isn't there any place with X-ray gear you can use?"

Kelli was silent for a moment. Finally, she said, "Well, there's an InVision CTX-5000 unit at the engineering building. They're running tests on it for the FAA. It's like a CAT scan for running baggage at airports."

"Can you use it?"

"I know some of the people over there. Yeah, I think I might swing it."

Jensen was back. He stopped outside the parking lot, waited a moment, then turned in and came slowly toward the garage.

"I've got to go," Marquette said. He checked his watch. It was forty minutes past six. "I'll meet you at the university around noon. Where is this engineering building?"

"It's directly east of our lab, across Steven's Way. Loew Hall."

"All right."

"Matt?"

"Yes?"

"I love you." It was the first time she'd said it in the cold light of day. Before, it had always been uttered in the throes of sexual heat when he himself had spoken it, growled it, a part of the spending.

Now the reciprocal words stalled on his lips. He watched the deputy's patrol car ease to a stop a few feet away. "I've gotta go," he said and hung up.

Leaving Norma Jean's mug on the top of the phone, he walked over to the vehicle. Jensen smiled at him, his dark glasses holding a miniature reflection of Matt.

"How you doin'?" the policeman asked.

"All right."

"I'm going off shift. You want a ride home?"

He thought about that, then nodded. "Sure, thanks."

He climbed into the patrol car, holding the sphere snugly, secretly against his body with his right elbow. The interior of the vehicle smelled of leather and radio gear. To it was now added the reek of the dead shark from his hands.

* * *

Two hours later, carrying a small, blue University of Washington gym bag, Marquette crossed the apron of the Port Townsend ferry dock and went up the car-deck ramp of the Olympic-class ferry *Kitsap.*

The fog had cleared off quickly over the sound. Now a stiff, cold wind blew down off the Haro Strait, soughing hollowly as it cut through the open-ended, car-filled deck.

Upstairs in the main lounge, he bought a cup of coffee and a croissant and found an empty booth on the starboard side. Motes of dust drifted in the cool sunlight coming through the big windows.

The ferry gave a long blast on its horn as they slowly moved away from the dock. Matt ate quietly, gazing out at nothing in particular. His sense of loss coupled with an increasing awareness of dangerous waters ahead had drawn him down into himself.

The withdrawal shamed him. In the past, he'd always been proficient at handling difficulty and bereavement, from his father's passing when he was twelve to the deaths of friends in Nam, all coming with brutal, stunning speed. Yet he had always exhibited surprisingly rapid assimilation.

But the murder of Rick and Julie haunted him darkly. And they *had* been murdered; he was now certain of that. The sheer randomness of it created a shock that penetrated right to his soul.

His father's death as an oil rig worker had been the result of intrinsically dangerous work. And in the military, a soldier's life always forced acceptance of death as the natural core of his work.

But here, *this* dying was too needless and unexpected.

Could he have interceded? If he'd refused Rick the use of the boat? If he'd been quicker in returning to it? Wrapped into that possibility, with its familiar sense of desolation, was the awareness that the old guilt was resurrected, newly honed to a sharper cutting edge.

He turned his mind away and momentarily considered the behavior of Deputy Jensen. It was obvious that the officer had been ordered to keep track of him. After driving Matt home, he'd lingered in front of the house for several minutes. When he finally did leave, he merely drove down the road a ways and parked beside a grove of maple trees.

Matt watched him a moment, then went in to shave. Afterward, he showered and dressed quickly: Levi's, running shoes, a Washington letterman's jacket. He looked young, athletic, like the first-string tight end on the Huskies football squad.

He phoned for a cab. While waiting for it, he wrapped the sphere in toweling and tucked it into his gym bag. For a moment, he paused, staring undecidedly at his dresser. Finally, he pulled open the top drawer and withdrew a Browning Hi-Power 9 mm pistol. It had been his personal sidearm while in the SEALs.

He checked the clip, put it into the bag with the sphere and covered them both with another towel to break the outline of the gun against the canvas.

The cabbie was a young Cambodian everybody called Won Ton. He arrived out front and honked twice. Matt went out and climbed into the car. As they passed the deputy, Matt waved at him. Jensen barely nodded.

They turned toward Port Townsend. Won Ton kept up a steady, aimless patter while Marquette watched out the back window. For a few minutes, Jensen followed them, hanging far back. Then he swung a U at the junction of State 101 and headed back toward Port Angeles.

"He finally go away?" the Cambodian asked.

"Yeah."

"Dat Jensen one sneaky bugga." Won Ton picked up speed.

Matt felt the vibrations of the battered Chevy tremble up into his body, and the old fear came, swiftly, as it always did. The strike of a snake. Tiny beads of sweat oozed onto his forehead, into his palms.

Since Spain, he couldn't tolerate speed.

"Goddammit," he snapped at the driver. "Slow the fuck down."

Won Ton had given him a puzzled, sidelong glance and eased off the pedal.

Matt inhaled and leaned his head back against his seat on the ferry. His heart began to slow. He closed his eyes, idly ran his hand over the sphere through the canvas of the gym bag.

A thought struck him. What if this thing were actually a bomb? Jesus, he was about to take it into the middle of crowds. To Kelli!

He ran his finger over the bulge again, exploring its contours. He recalled its precise weight in his hand. No, it couldn't be a bomb, he decided, relieved. Too light. Besides, whatever it was, it wasn't complete. The bevelings clearly showed that other components were necessary for it to be whole and functional. . . .

He caught the look right off.

Two men were sitting in a booth slightly behind him on the port side. One was tall, all angles and somber gray eyes, dressed in a Montana blanket coat. The other was younger, prizefighter-faced. He wore a faded leather aviator's jacket and silver-coated dark glasses.

Matt had caught the older one looking straight at him. The man quickly turned away. Too quickly. A moment later, his head came swiveling back around, the gray eyes scanning in seeming boredom. Again they touched Matt's and again ricocheted off and away.

Marquette's heart went *tick-tick*.

He didn't look at the two men again for the rest of the crossing. Ten minutes from Seattle, he got up and went outside. A young girl in a woolen serape was sitting cross-legged by the door, out of the wind. She listlessly played a violin, looking stoned.

He went past and leaned against the starboard railing. Wind whipped his hair, the gusts salt-scented and frigid. From the corner of his eye, he saw the man in the blanket coat standing inside the lounge door, watching him.

A mile away, the panorama of Seattle spread out. Tall, glass-faced skyscrapers were set off in sharp contrast by the spindly appearing six-hundred-foot-high Space Needle. To the right was the chunky, upside down bowl of the King Dome. Beyond it all stretched the cloud-shrouded cordillera of the Cascades and the snow cone of Mount Rainier.

The *Kitsap* slowed and sounded its approach warning: one long and two short blasts. Casually, Matt pushed away from the rail. He walked around the side of the main lounge, headed toward the bow. Instantly, the man inside, joined by the other, followed, keeping pace with him.

At the outside stairs to the car deck, he stopped. In that position, he was hidden from the lounge windows by the starboard curve of the pilothouse. He checked the lounge door, then pushed off the railing and darted down to the lower level, taking the steps three at a time.

Over the rumble of the ship's engines, he heard the lounge door slam open above him. The thud of boot heels sounded on the metal stairs. Running crouched over, he scurried between the parked automobiles.

People were sitting in their vehicles, reading, drinking coffee. He paused long enough to take the pistol from his bag. He jacked a round into the chamber and shoved the weapon under his belt.

Choosing a red Chevrolet Blazer in the second line, he ran to it and jerked open the passenger's door. The driver was dozing, his head back on the seat. He was a young black man in a light-blue pullover and dreadlocks.

He snapped forward and stared at Marquette, shocked and angry. "Yo, man!" he cried. "What the fuck you think you doin'?"

Matt slipped a twenty-dollar bill from his pocket and held it out. "This is yours if you get me off this rig, pal."

"What? Where you at, fool?"

"I'm trying to ditch my ex-wife, man." He waved the bill.

The young man squinted at him for a long moment, then snorted and whipped the twenty from his fingers. "Sheet," he said disgustedly.

The ferry, rocking slightly, eased up into its slot. The engines roared for a few seconds, then died. The barrier at one end of the car deck shot up, wobbling.

Matt caught sight of the two men. They were searching between the cars, dodging and ducking to peer underneath. One spotted him. He hollered to the other, and both converged on the Blazer.

The forward line of cars began to move up onto the exit ramp, funneling into two lines as the deck guard waved them out. The Blazer driver switched on his engine, geared and started forward.

The two pursuers planted themselves directly in front of the car with their right hands under their jackets. The older man slapped his other hand onto the hood and pointed at Marquette.

The driver braked sharply. He shoved his head out the window. "Get out the way, motha-fuckas. Or I be runnin' yo' asses into the planks."

At that moment, the deck guard came up, pumping his arm. "Come on, people. Let's keep it moving."

The two men glanced at each other, then broke and ran back on either side of the Blazer. The one in the blanket coat passed on Matt's side. He snarled something at him.

The Blazer pulled onto the ramp and swung left, past a docked fireboat and Ivers restaurant, to the overpass. The driver studied him narrowly. "You know what I'm thinking, man? That stony-ass bitch you trying to dump is wearin' two sets of balls."

Within a minute, they were lost in the thick flow of morning traffic on First Avenue.

4

In the Z-unit squad room, Kizzier had just logged in. He was slightly hungover. After the Goodell arrest, he and Azevedo had spent an hour drinking beer in a sleazy Garden City cafe.

Jo-Jo met him in the hall. "Williams just called," Azevedo said, giving Kizzier a sly grin.

"What?"

"Ole E. J. got whacked this morning."

Al's face opened with shock. "You're shitting me."

Jo-Jo nodded. "Somebody at the Madder Avenue holding barracks put a shiv made from window glass in his liver. In the toilet. Neat and quick, Beret-style."

"Well, I'll be go to hell." Kizzier frowned down at the worn floor. He had a pale face and short-clipped brown hair, and wore rimless glasses. They made him look studious, like the young athletic director for a small junior college. But his stare could go flat and cold in times of stress or rage. Behind his back, people sometimes called him Cobra Eyes.

He glanced up. "Any leads on the hitter?"

"No more than usual. But Williams wants to talk to you right away."

The Assistant DA was angry. "What the hell's this Goodell killing?" he barked over the telephone. "Goddammit, Al, the shit's gonna hit the fan over this. I need some answers."

"There's a lot more to it than what's on the surface, George."

"Yeah, Azevedo mentioned something about a German skinhead. What's that all about?"

Kizzier explained.

"Jesus Christ," Williams said, momentarily stunned. "Hitler-Hans Halberstadt is involved? You sure about this?"

"It's him, all right."

"And this video showed him in Salmon?"

"Yeah."

"What the hell's he doing in Idaho?"

"That's obvious. He's been imported by the AN. I figure something hot is in the works."

"Oh, Jesus," Williams groaned. "Like what?"

"Who knows? Some heavy drug deal, maybe weapons. It could even be a hired hit."

Williams expelled air.

"With E. J. gone," Kizzier went on, "we got no solid link now. If we increase AN surveillence and roust a few informers, that'll take time. I got the feeling we ain't got time."

"Wait a minute," the ADA said. "Maybe I've got something. I talked briefly with Goodell's public defender this morning. She didn't know much, had only talked with him a few minutes before they transferred him to Madder. But there was something."

"Yeah?"

"She said he was scared shitless of serving hard time. Was sure the blacks'd take him out. He told her that if he had to, he'd negotiate with some prime information."

Kizzier sat up. "What kind of information?"

"She didn't give me all of it, just something having to do with a *heine* and either Seattle or Vancouver, B.C. She didn't know what the hell a *heine* was. Actually, neither do I."

"It's a World-War-Two slang word for a German. Like kraut-head."

Williams grunted. "Well, the German meaning ties in, doesn't it?"

"Let me call you back."

"I'm scheduled for court in a half hour."

"Five minutes."

He huddled with Jo-Jo. "How long's it been since you bounty-hunted with that drug strike force in Washington State?"

Azevedo shrugged. "Three years ago."

"What hits you on this?"

"I ain't surprised Seattle's involved. The place has always been a hotbed for survivalist and antigovernment groups. And if they're bringing in guns or drugs, it'd be a better bet than B.C. The Canadians've really tightened up customs procedures ever since the chink mafia took over Vancouver."

Kizzier considered a moment. "How's the chance you still got some decent contacts out there? People you could sly-probe who'd know if a Nazi piece of shit like Halberstadt blew into town?"

Jo-Jo squinted at the ceiling a moment before answering. "Hard to say. I'd have to work the ground to see for sure."

"Okay, hold that thought." He got Williams back on the phone. "I want to send Jo-Jo to Seattle. Right now."

"That's shooting in the dark, isn't it?"

"Look, Puget Sound's a key stop in the skinhead underground. You know that. Besides, this is the only lead we got on Hitler-Hans."

Williams grunted. "All right."

"Also, I want you to stonewall this thing for awhile. Downplay it with the media. Tell them the Goodell killing was a cellblock love triangle, some shit like that. And keep the suits out of it."

"Wait a minute, not liaison with Washington?"

"Think about it, George. You get the newsies sniffing and those DC assholes in the loop, we're gonna blow seams everywhere. Am I right?"

"Well, yeah, that's true enough, but—"

"You're damned right. Look, this is our thunder. Just thrown into our laps with no Feebies or Customs. Jesus, let's not blow the goddamned thing."

The ADA was silent again. Finally, he said, "What about your cross-state clearance?"

"Cundiff'll sign, won't he?" James Cundiff was overall ATF administrator for the Idaho/Nevada/Wyoming Federal District.

"Sure, but then word would be all over Washington." Williams sighed again. "Still, we could maybe go through one of his deputies. Lawrence or Copeland."

"Can I count on that?"

"I think so."

"Good. Now who do we get for the international arrest warrant?" An IAW had to be issued by the State Department on the request of a federal district judge whenever a foreign national was involved.

"Faulk, easy," Williams said right off. "Once he gets a whiff of Halberstadt, he'll foam at the mouth. And State never questions his requests."

"How much will we have to specify?"

"I'm sure he'll give you an open warrant."

"How quickly can we clear? I want Azevedo under official status as soon as possible."

"Sorry, Al, there's a mandatory thirty-six-hour minimum on an IAW issuance."

"Okay, that'll have to work."

"All right. But you listen up, Kizzier. I want to know everything you're doing on this. You got that? You keep your man in check, no hotdog shit." He paused a moment. "Incidentally, where the hell are those P-fives you impounded from Goodell? County says they never showed up in inventory."

"I've got 'em." Al chuckled. "Hell, George, you know I always play by the rules."

"That'll be the day," Williams snapped and hung up.

After vainly searching the waterfront area for Marquette, Stone sent Basset back to Dungeness and caught a taxi to his hotel, the Downtown Hilton.

His partner, Fettis, had come in from Boise sometime during the night. He was asleep on the couch with the television on, the sound turned down very low.

Gus had stripped off his coat and left it lying on the floor. Although a short man, he had massive muscle definition from daily workouts with weights. His rounded shoulders and pectorals stretched tightly through his sweater. Beneath his short, brown hair, his brow was beetled from steroids.

Stone didn't wake him. Instead, he found a glass and a half-empty bottle of Jack Daniel's and took a drink. Another. The liquor hit his stomach with gentle fire but did nothing. He was still running on an adrenaline high, spiky and full of pulses.

Without the sphere, everything was coming apart, all the sweet complexity of his plans slipping away with inexorable velocity. He drew another shot and began to pace, staring unseeingly at the autumn-yellow walls, out the vast window.

He finally noticed Fettis's opened suitcase and walked over to it. Under a pair of folded shirts, he found two small, velvet-wrapped bundles. Gently, he took them out and placed them on the dining table.

He opened the first. Under the velvet was plastic tissue, and inside the plastic was a black cannister about the size of a twelve-ounce can of beer. It was made of an epoxy, and Jack knew it contained a timer and trigger assembly, plus a capsule of fulminate of mercury. Nevertheless, it felt nearly weightless in his hand.

The second bundle was heavier. It, too, was a cylinder, gray with a buffed surface. One end had a countersunk activation button with tiny white and green lights, the other a narrower cylinder concealing a graphite needle.

This unit had been secretly manufactured to his specs by the Sol de Rojo electronics company, a German-owned outfit based in Huatambampo, Mexico. After being built, it was smuggled into Boise aboard an eighteen-wheeler hauling computer panels for Stone Security.

He carefully examined both components, then replaced them in their velvet wrappings. He put them back into the suitcase and began to pace again.

He paused at the window. Pale sunlight flooded through, suffusing the gilded edgework of the room with a gentle glow. To his right, the sound stretched away, dotted with forested islands misty in the distance.

Directly across from his suite rose the Century Plaza Building. Layers of windows reflected the morning sun like squares of sheet ice. Beyond the northeast corner of the skyscraper, he saw the Space Needle. Its revolving top looked like a gigantic UFO momentarily tethered to the earth.

He stared at it. People moved slowly about the observation platform, colorful stick figures. There was a sudden, tiny flash: a tourist's watch or bracelet reflecting sunlight like the bursting into flame of an ember.

His mind's eye lingered on the afterglow. It seemed suddenly to symbolize something . . . a resurgence to life from apparent flameout. Yeah, he thought, goddammit, yeah. And he felt a new anger begin to sing in him, a rebirth of resolve. . . .

Jack Stone was not a man to easily abide defeat. Once his mind settled on an object desired, he always homed relentlessly to it like a smart missile. Attainment *would* be achieved. At all costs, through whatever means, regardless of the consequences.

Once when he was nine years old, out in the putty-colored gumbo plains of Red Elm, South Dakota, he had lusted after a horse, a big, buckskin stallion, sixteen hands tall and laced with lean-muscled firepower. It belonged to a Swedish farmer named Eckman. Often Jack walked the three miles to Eckman's farm to feed the animal brown sugar cubes and stroke its wild beauty.

His hunger ate at him, distorted precepts. One morning, no longer able to hold back his longing, he stole the stallion, rode him all day out yon-way among the gravel and creosote draws of the plain. Not once did he consider the consequences.

As evening came on, he returned home and hid the buckskin in a small cottonwood stand near a muddy wash. Two hours later, Eckman drove up to the house in his old flatbed Ford. A shotgun was braced on the dashboard.

"Stone," he bellowed out in the darkness. "I come for

my horse. I know you got hit. My wife seed your gottam son take hit.''

His father questioned him. He readily admitted the theft. His father swore and went out to talk to the Swede. He offered to give him the pick of his own horses for his inconvenience. Eckman said to hell with it, retrieved his stallion and drove off.

His father whipped him with a lariat until blood came. Jack didn't cry although it hurt like fire, and went on hurting for a whole week. But afterward, his eyes held a deep spark of triumph. That old buckskin had been his for a whole day and half a night. . . .

Fettis coughed and sat up, flexing his shoulders. "So, did you get it?"

Jack shook his head slowly. "No."

"Oh, shit, you gotta be kiddin' me."

Stone explained about the ocean search and how the fishing boat had picked up the sphere before they could reach it and then how they'd waited for it to come into Dungeness.

He swore. "We'd have had the damned thing, too. It was somewhere in the stern. But the kid started the fire before we could pinpoint it."

"What kid?"

He told him. The young punk and his girl, fucking below, and then the fight with Basset and the kid slamming an iron bar into a butane heater, which triggered the inferno, forcing them to get the hell off the boat fast. He finished with their failed attempt at the other fisherman on the ferry.

Fettis listened, watching from under thick eyebrows. When Jack finished, he shook his head, chuckling mirthlessly. "Jesus, you guys sound like Laurel and Hardy. Well, I guess that's all she wrote."

"Not yet. What we gotta do is find that fisherman again. He took something off the boat, under his jacket."

"How, for Chris' sake? You don't even know his name."

"The newspapers'll probably have it. Besides, sooner or later the bastard's gotta return to Dungeness."

"But we only got two days, remember?"

"I'm telling you, we'll find him." He walked back to the bottle, poured another shot.

Gus fumbled through his coat for his cigarettes. He lit up and gazed thoughtfully at the floor. He snorted disgustedly. "Wouldn't you know that dumb fuck Basset'd stick a knife in the guy? There goes what could have looked like an accidental explosion."

"Maybe not. That high octane went fast and hot. Body burn might hide the wound."

"Don't bet on it."

Stone nodded toward Gus's suitcase. "Both units check out all right?"

"Near perfect. The timer was off by a tenth of a second, but that's no problem." Suddenly his eyebrows lowered. He'd been idly watching the silent television. He picked up the channel selector and turned up the sound.

"Hey, check this out," he said.

The program was *Seattle Today*. A perky blonde was giving a news update: "... name is not available. He was known to be a senior research executive with InTronic. No details on the bomb have been released, but reliable sources say a caller contacted the *San Francisco Chronicle* and claimed responsibility for it. He referred to himself as the Horseman, the same name used in an earlier—"

Gus glanced over, grinning broadly. "There you go."

Stone smiled, too. "Score one for our side."

"No, score two," Fettis corrected. "I didn't tell you. The Goodell bust went off right on schedule."

"Did ATF get the video?"

"T-Bucks said yeah."

"What about the hit?"

"No word yet."

The phone sounded, a soft purr. Jack leaned over the counter and snapped up the receiver. "Yeah?"

"Stone?" A man's voice, deep and rich. "Grady."

"You're late."

"Sorry about that, pardner. Had to bail an old boy out of jail this morning. So, are we all set?"

"Yeah, everybody's ready on this side."

John Wayne Grady was a well-known Seattle lawyer. Smooth and prone to a folksy style and turn of phrase, yet he could become savage in cross-examinations when warranted. Born in Lincoln County, New Mexico, forty-nine years previously, he always sported denim horse-cut jeans, a jacket and a black Stetson with a silver-and-turquoise hatband. It was his signature, sometimes even in court.

Grady's clients were mostly drawn from the fringes of society—hard-core scum cases that seemed hopeless, Chinese mafia thugs from Vancouver's Saltwater City, drug hit men out of California, and especially the militia and anti-government types who infested the Northwest. For them he had secret sympathies.

Now he was to be a key player in Jack Stone's plans, although he had no idea of their true purpose.

"Mighty good," Grady said.

"Have you spoken with Keck yet?" Dieder Keck was a sixty-year-old German from Frankfurt. Merely a low-echelon administrator in the German government, he was very powerful within the European neo-Nazi movement. Grady was acting as liaison between him and the militia for the purchase of weapons.

But unknown to the lawyer, his involvement as a go-between was merely a cover, part of a much more complex plan worked out by Stone and Fettis. Like the Horseman's bombs, which had been designed to draw a false trail. Like Goodell's arrest and the planted video to lead ATF agents to the German and his militia connections.

It had taken the two men months to neatly set all the disparate pieces of the puzzle into play, keyed to a precise timetable. It even included the exact locations where Halberstadt would be taken once he reached Seattle, in order to establish a scapegoat whose tracks would obilterate their own once they struck.

"Yes, this morning," Grady answered. "The ole boy arrives in Victoria in two days."

"What about Halberstadt's itinerary? You damned sure they'll stick to exactly as I set it up?"

"To the click, pardner."

"Who's gonna be your liaison?"

"A lady friend of mine. Sweet ole gal, sharp as a ten-dollar razor."

"What if she starts asking questions about who she's squiring around?"

"She won't. As far as she knows, them two boys'll just be friends of a friend who're lookin' for a good time."

Gus asked, "That Two-Gun Grady?"

"Yeah."

"Tell him his Grasser buddies are getting antsy as hell having the Nazi shit-for-brains as a houseguest."

To the lawyer, Jack said, "They're getting jumpy about the kraut in Idaho."

Grady chuckled. It had a crafty throatiness, like a man who'd just pulled three aces. "Yeah, I can see how they would."

"Okay, I'll call you with their exact arrival time."

"Looking forward to it." Grady hung up.

"Whoa, here we go," Fettis cried suddenly. He leaned forward and tapped his fingernail against the TV screen.

On the set, the anchorman of *Seattle Today* was just beginning an interview. His guest was a youthful, attractive man in a dark-brown leather sports jacket. He wore large, dark glasses like those of an aviator, and his hair was swept back into a small ponytail. His name was Jerry Cornell, chief executive officer of PrimeData Corporation, the software giant based in Seattle.

Founded by a computer genius named William Ballard while he was still a student at Oregon State University in Corvallis, PDC now supplied nearly three-fourths of all software in the world. It had made Ballard and all his partners billionaires several times over.

The two men indulged in a moment of cutesy joshing, and finally the anchor got down to business. "Tell me, Mr. Cornell. What exactly is this STAMINA-2000 you'll soon be introducing to the American consumer?''

Cornell crossed his legs, eased comfortably back into his chair. ''Simply put, it's a trusted security system that's literally tamperproof. It creates an impenetrable protection environment for any computer, particularly those logged into network operations like the Internet and the World Wide Web.''

''What you're saying is that with this system, I could surf on my PC all I wanted and never worry about a virus injection or a data theft?''

''Precisely. Besides that, the system's extremely user-friendly. No code injunction sequences to remember.''

The anchor tilted his head in feigned skepticism. ''Come on now, is it *really* possible to gain total security? Isn't every system eventually vulnerable?''

Cornell gave him an unruffled smile. ''We believe *our* technology can and will prevent all system transgressions for at least the next decade.''

''What makes STAMINA-2000 different from earlier security systems?''

''Its basic architecture. Are you familiar with the Orange Book?''

''That's the bible of security-systems testing, isn't it?''

Cornell nodded. ''Right. Well, our S-2000 is a quantum leap beyond the highest Orange Book standards.''

''Very impressive.''

With the sudden explosion of worldwide computer networking, protection of data against hostile invasion had become ultraimportant. As a result, numerous companies had instantly come out with their own systems.

But these were all B2-and B3-level domains, almost immediately breachable even by amateur hackers. PrimeData, with its massive research power, had so far been the only seemingly viable developer for a newer, more shielded system.

But Stone and Fettis's company, Stone Security Systems, had also developed a highly advanced design. In fact, they were actually only a month or so behind PrimeData in making their public release announcement.

During their years in U.S. intelligence organizations, both men had learned the workings of most of the super-secret, A-1 platforms used by the government: TEMPEST, ROGUE, even NASA's SPYGLASS systems.

Their program was based on these advanced platforms and had taken over two years of intensive research and testing to develop. It was called BODYGUARD-t. Unfortunately, it had eaten up all their cash reserves, and SSS was now deeply in hock.

Back at the company headquarters in Boise, their line engineers were still trying desperately to speed up completion of final tests, disposing of last-minute bugs. Everybody was aware of the fact that the first company to bring out its product would control the entire market.

"Will the program be expensive?" the anchor asked.

"Not at all. Any PC user will be able to afford the entire system."

"I understand PrimeData owner and originator Bill Ballard will be making the formal announcement of public release himself, right here in Seattle."

"Yes. Day after tomorrow."

"From all reports, STAMINA looks like it'll break market records—sales, leases, government contracts, all that. And it'll also create a bonanza for PDC stock. So, how realistic are these projections?"

Cornell gave a shrug. "Well, as they say, the firstest with the mostest takes the day."

Snarling an obscenity, Stone hurled his glass at the wall. It shattered, leaving a dent and a tiny fan of liquor. "Don't count your money yet, asshole," he hissed.

In Port Angeles, Lieutenant Two Elks swung off Caroline Avenue into the parking lot of Olympic Memorial Hospital. Continuing past the Emergency Room entrance, he parked beside Dr. Byner's Jeep Cherokee in front of the small cinder-block annex that housed the Clallam County morgue.

The ME was sitting with his feet on his desk in a tiny, cluttered back office. He wore bloodstained green scrubs with plastic booties over his running shoes. He was eating a jelly roll.

He grinned as the lieutenant came in. "Hey, Big John," he called. He leaned forward to push a pink pastry box between the stacks of folders spread across his desk. "Set yourself on down and have a roll."

"Mornin', Doc," Two Elks said solemnly. He settled his bulk into a chair, unzipped his jacket and reached for a bear claw.

Byner studied him, a merry glint in his eyes. He was in his early thirties and sported a blond grenadier's mustache. "Looks like your hunch was right about those two kids in Dungeness," he said. "I haven't done the full post yet, but my prelim shows solid evidence of homicide."

The lieutenant grunted without comment, chewing slowly.

Byner licked jelly off his thumb and rummaged for a moment through the folder stacks. "Well, shit," he said. "The protocol's still back in the suite."

"Just fill in the high spots."

The doctor swallowed, sucked through his teeth. "Well, first off, both had deep-tissue burns over at least eighty percent of their bodies, along with general blast lacerations, mostly on the female's buttocks and the male's face, thorax and upper legs."

"You got any idea of what type blast?"

Byner nodded. "Rapid gas ignition rather than compressed blowout. This wasn't a bomb."

"What kind of gas?"

"Possibly butane or propane, but judging from the stink on that boat last night, I'd say it was aviation gasoline. It's also more consistent with the degree and profile of the burns."

"Yeah, we found fragments of a gasoline can . . . were they doused?"

"I'd say so."

Two Elks nodded, his thick face expressionless.

"There's more," the doctor went on. "Both of them were already dead before the explosion. The female had a blunt injury fracture to the left temporal and malar area." He indicated the positions on his own skull. "Right about here and here."

The doctor paused for another bite of pastry. "The male was stabbed—a left, upper-angled entry just under the third rib. Judging from initial workup on blood scrapings from the deck, he exsanguinated explosively. That indicates penetration of the left ventricle."

"You certain they were dead?"

"Positive. Body blood shows sudden aplastic anemia and catastrosphically low levels of hemoglobin."

The lieutenant scratched the back of his hand with his chin. "The wound was on the left side. So the killer was right-handed."

"Yep."

"What was the weapon used on the girl?"

Byner shrugged. "Hard to say—tire iron, crowbar, something with solid weight. I'll know better when I get in."

"I wonder why the same weapon wasn't used on both victims."

"This is just a guess, but I think the boy was killed first. And the knife might have momentarily become stuck in him. It was a powerful thrust. There's evidence of subcutaneous hilt bruise."

"What's the story on the knife?"

"Entry wound shows sharp and dull markings. And it was fairly wide. That means a single-edged blade, thick, nonserrated, with a deep blood channel. Cross section would probably be an elongated pentagon.

"Again, I won't know for sure until I see the blade chattering marks on the rib bone. As to length, I'd say probably six, seven inches."

Two Elks's eyes were dark and still. "A fillet knife?"

"No, too thin."

"How about a hunting knife?"

Byner shook his head. "Not a standard commercial one.

No, I'd put money on a military-type blade, heavy-duty. Something like a Marine Ka-Bar, maybe a K-nine.''

Two Elks nodded, took another bear claw.

The ME shook his head sadly. "Actually, they were in the middle of coitus when the attack came. Vaginal swabbings and fluorescent scan show the presence of preseminal fluid. The boy hadn't come yet.''

The lieutenant squinted his eyes. "Ain't that a helluva way to go? Were they high?''

"I don't know. I'm waiting on the tox report.''

"Could this have been some sort of kinky sex that got out of hand? I mean, like the kid freaking, killing the girl, then himself?''

"Not consistent. Vaginal tissue shows strenuous intercourse, but not the violent tearing usually associated with S and M activity. No anal entry and no marks at all to indicate sadistic fantasy or torture.

"Besides, he couldn't have put that knife into himself. The angle's all wrong. No, this was a blitz attack, pure and simple.''

Two Elks sighed and stood up, wiping his hands on his handkerchief. "When can you get me a full ME-one?''

"Later this afternoon.''

"Okay. Thanks for the chow. See you.''

"See you, John.''

The lieutenant returned to his car, opened the door and slid in. The maple trees near the Emergency Room entrance rustled in a freshening breeze off the sound. He watched two women joggers go past with blond hair in ponytails, spandex shorts hugging their buttocks like molded blue metal.

He keyed his radio. "KT-one, D-six.''

The dispatcher came right back. "Go ahead, Lieutenant.''

"Who's on DE sector?''

"Collins and Lomelli.''

"Vector them to Dungeness. I want a pick-up-for-questioning on one Matthew Marquette.'' He gave the address. "If they don't score, put out an APB on him—Seattle and Tacoma PDs and the Highway Patrol."

"Right, Lieutenant."

Two Elks started the car, adjusted his Stetson and drove off.

5

The Blazer driver dropped Matt at the southeast corner of Seattle Center. From there he walked the block to Denny Park and caught a taxi to the University of Washington campus.

The day was bright and cool. Sitting in the warm cab, he thought about the ferry attack. It had been close. He wondered whether or not those men would actually have killed him, right out in front of everybody.

Or, more importantly, would he have fought back? *Could* he have killed again? Even in his own defense? The very fact that that had occurred to him at all left him dejected and oddly restless.

It was a few minutes before noon when he arrived at Loew Hall. It was an old, two-story building made of red brick with a domed, Quonset-style roof. There were tall Victorian lamps and winter-shorn chestnut trees in the courtyard.

Kelli was waiting beside one of the spindly lampposts. She looked fetching in denim jeans and a gold-and-blue ski sweater. She waited as he paid the cabbie, then walked across the courtyard and silently hugged him.

She eased back, her eyes searching his face. "Are you all right?"

"Yeah, I'm okay."

"I still can't believe what's happened."

"Neither can I."

"What's going on here, Matt? You hinted at something on the phone."

"I honestly don't know yet."

"*Are* you involved in something?"

"I am now."

"Tell me, I want to know."

He held up his gym bag. "First let's see what's inside this thing I have. It might explain some of it."

They entered the building. Just inside the main door, two students were seated at a desk, playing chess on a computer. Kelli asked where Peter Dvikas's office was.

"Second floor," one of the young men answered. He had a Three Stooges beach cut and pimples. "Third cubicle."

The upper floor looked as if it had once been a chandler's loft into which floor-to-ceiling partitions had been built. The walls were old, with dark-brown wainscoting, and the area had the odor of old newspapers overlaid with the acrylic scent of electrical gear.

Dvikas, Kelli explained, was a young doctoral assistant in the electrical engineering department. They found him working on a small laser in a tiny office cluttered with books and wiring panels. A stereo played soft sitar music.

He glanced up and flashed a smile at Pickett. "Yo, Kel," he said. "I been waitin' on you, luv."

He uncoiled himself from the laser. He was tall and excessively thin, with pale skin. His blond hair, shoulder length, was done in dreadlocks. He wore a black T-shirt with a picture of Karma Moffett on it.

Kelli introduced Matt. Peter nodded perfunctorily and returned his attention to her. "Well, where is this mysterious thing you want scanned?"

Marquette took the sphere from his gym bag and unwrapped the toweling. He handed it to Dvikas. Peter studied it a moment, turning it over in his hand.

He tilted his head and gave Kelli a sly, under-the-brow grin. "Why's it got an EL unit on it? What the hell is this, sweetcheeks? Part of a dope drop?"

"Not dope," Matt said sharply. A tight little smile played

at the corner of his mouth. "It's actually stolen diamonds."

Dvikas's look was cool arrogance. His eyes flicked up, down. "Funky," he said.

Kelli gave Matt a warning glance.

Peter led them down a corridor and into a secondary room. Electrical conduits snaked all over the floor. There was a computer panel across one wall with a white CTX-5000 machine linked to it. It was a large machine and resembled a four-man winter tent.

As he set up, Dvikas explained the machine's workings to Kelli, completely ignoring Matt. "This is a boosted version of the standard FAA model. Uses hard X-rays in the nine-plus-nanometer range, which gives fantastic resolution layer clarity."

"How long will it take?" she asked.

"The feed's instantaneous and continuous. We've programmed the laser cycle to produce a constant chain of nanosecond bursts."

"Can you magnify?" Kelli asked.

Peter nodded. "Good enough for normal fieldwork."

Matt wandered around the room, peering at equipment. He came to a doorway that led to a larger room. A stenciled sign was taped over the lintel: CAPACITOR AREA—ONLY AUTHORIZED PERSONNEL ALLOWED. Inside were steel-framed banks of huge batteries connected by intricate wiring networks. The floor was highly polished, the color of raw copper.

Farther on was another door. Someone using a felt pen had written on it in precise block letters: BIG SALLY. He opened the door a few inches and peered in.

It was a large, ceilingless area lit by blue light. Long laser carriages and cable-connected computer workstations were scattered all around. In the center of the room was a huge target chamber looking like a Navy submersible. It was made of glistening stainless steel with bolted viewing ports showing a central matrix of beam cannons. The blue lights made it glow softly, as if in moonlight.

"Hey, buddy," Dvikas yelled sharply at him. "Don't go messing around in there."

Kelli threw Matt another frown. He strolled back.

The CTX hummed as Dvikas ran the scan, its X-ray drum whirling with a slapping sound as it took pictures of multiple series of thin cross sections. Instantly, the image of the interior of the sphere appeared on Peter's workstation monitor. The image was bright and clean.

Everyone leaned in.

Under the skeletal frame and innards of the locater unit, they could see three separate components within the sphere. On the left was a pencil-thin tube that protruded from the underside of one of the beveled surfaces. It was about two inches long, its tip nearly touching the second component, a core sphere about the size of a golf ball. The core was faceted with hundreds of plane surfaces. On the other side of it was a cone-shaped funnel that extended about an inch toward the center, ending in a tiny, flat plate.

Peter tapped his keyboard. Immediately, the monitor image began to revolve slowly, the closer locater lines passing around to the back side. As each image frame clicked rapidly past, the core facets reacted to the X-rays, glistening like a jewel under a beam of light.

Dvikas grunted and scratched at his jaw. "Where you say you got this thing?"

"I didn't say," Matt said.

Dvikas started to turn toward him. Kelli quickly asked, "So, what do you think it is, Peter? Could it actually be a bomb?"

Dvikas shook his head. "No, it ain't a bomb." He pointed at the core. "But that thing's plainly a crystal cluster. And I think that tube might just be a beam cannon."

He tapped at his keyboard again. The picture jumped in magnification, focusing on the tube. Now they could see a faint black shadow inside it.

Peter clicked his tongue a couple of times. "We're not getting complete ray penetration of the tube. Its molecules must be dense as hell. Probably something like carbon-carbon. But I'll bet that shadow image is a fiber-optic wire."

"Can you take pictures of it?"

"Sure." Within a minute, he had six snapshots. They were warm to the touch. The three studied them for a moment. Then Peter leaned over, shut down the CTX and extracted the sphere. He handed it to Kelli.

"So?" she said.

"Well, it's a crystal chamber of some kind, that's clear. But other components are needed to make it operate." He shrugged. "Could be part of a liquid-phase epitaxy beamer. Or maybe even a Molecular Curve Detection unit."

He leaned back in his chair and studied her appraisingly for a long moment. "This is precision-milled high-tech stuff, Kelli." His eyes looked directly into hers. "You realize it's obviously been ripped off by somebody, don't you?"

Outside once more, they crossed Steven's Way and walked back toward Guggenheim. The sun was warmer now, but there were still little patches of ocean chill hiding in the narrow shadows beside Kirsten Hall.

"At least we know part of what that thing is," Kelli said.

"But still not *why* it is."

She was thoughtful for a moment. Then: "I hate myself for thinking this, Matt. But could Rick have been mixed up in something? I mean, like smuggling expensive electronic gear? You heard what Peter said: this thing's worth a lot of money. And it *was* stolen."

Marquette shook his head. "Not a chance. The kid was straight."

"Then you better turn it over to the police. Right away. Obviously it's the reason they were killed, or at least part of it."

He gave her a wry, sad smile. "No, I don't think I better do that just yet."

"Why not?"

"The police think I did it."

"Did what?"

"Murdered Rick."

"Are you serious? That's insane."

"Not from their point of view. I'm the only one around with a possible motive."

"What motive?"

"I think they figure I was torching my boat for insurance. Accidentally or deliberately, I killed Rick and Julie in the process."

"How do you know they think that?"

"It's obvious from their questions."

Her face held a mixture of shock and tenderness. In all the months he had known her, Matt couldn't remember ever seeing that combination before. It gave an exploratory touch to the moment.

"You have to give the police the sphere," she said. "That'll prove that others were responsible."

"Smuggling stolen high-tech equipment could make an even better motive."

"I don't believe this," she said. She put her hands up as if in prayer, absently touched the fingertips against her lips. "Wait a minute. You were on the phone with me when the boat blew up. That's proof you couldn't have done it."

"Not necessarily. They'd claim I fired it and then called you for an alibi."

She shook her head to dispel the idiocy of it all. "Then what do we do?"

"Not we, Kelli. Just me."

"Don't talk stupid."

"No, I mean it. You're not part of this."

She started to say something, then stopped. She studied his eyes. "Something else has happened, hasn't it?"

He remained silent. Two girls walked past just then. They had book bags strapped to their backs, and both smiled at Kelli. She ignored them.

"I can see it in your face," she said.

"It doesn't matter."

"You're not going to tell me?"

"No."

She gave him a hot, flashing look, turned and strode off. After a few paces, she paused and turned back to him. "Apparently the obvious hasn't gotten through. If you're involved, I'm involved.''

"You don't understand."

"No, just shut up and listen. You're in serious trouble here, Matt. You're going to need help, *my* help. Don't hold me off.''

He studied her face, and a slow, warm smile gradually came into his eyes. "You're a real hard case, ain't you?''

"You got it.''

He finally told her about the helicopter and the attack on the ferry. They walked past Guggenheim Hall and sat on a cement bench near Drumheller Fountain. Its forty-foot geyser looked pure white in the crisp sunlight.

"Now do you see why I want you out of it?'' he said. "These people are after this thing. They've killed for it once; they'll do it again.''

"Then you have to go to the police.''

"I'd be arrested, or at least watched closely. If I'm to get to the bottom of this, I'll have to be on the outside.''

"All alone?''

"Yes.''

She put her head back, inhaled. She seemed to shiver.

A young man in a white smock had come out of Guggenhiem and was now walking toward them. Matt recognized him as a member of the CRYSTALBALL team.

He called to Pickett. "Hey, Kel, you just got an urgent call. Gal name of Bev Boudeen. She wanted to talk to you real bad.''

"Okay, thanks, Dan.''

He turned and walked off across the quad.

"Something's happening," she said.

"Is there a phone around here?''

"In the main lobby. Maybe I'd better call.''

"No, I'll do it.''

"Where in hell you at?'' Bev said the moment she heard Matt's voice. "No, wait, don't tell me. I don't know, I can't say.''

"What's up?"

"You gettin' some sticky manure on your boots, cousin. The police've been around here askin' all kinds of questions about you."

"When?"

"A coupla hours ago. They even talked to some of my customers. That big old lieutenant, Two Elks, and his deputies."

"What'd he say?"

"Didn't say nothin'. Jest wanted to know where you were when the kid and his girl got killed and what sort of fella you were. Stuff like that. But Lord, boy, you don't need no crystal ball to tell what he's thinkin'."

Marquette was silent.

"There's somethin' else," Bev said. "There's a pick-up warrant on you. One of the deputies told me on the sly. An' they're fixin' to search your house, too. He says they're lookin' for a murder knife." There was a long pause, then, "You better get yourself a lawyer, cousin."

He and Kelli talked over Bev's news. He wasn't surprised. But now that the police position was clear, Kelli wholeheartedly agreed with Boudeen about getting Marquette a lawyer.

Unfortunately, he didn't know any, nor did she. He also pointed out that he was too poor to hire a decent one, anyway. She dismissed that problem, said she'd pay for it. He refused. But she did finally convince him to at least talk to an attorney.

She suggested they ask Gilhammer about one. He knew a lot of people in the city. They found him talking to a student in the hall outside the CRYSTALBALL lab. They waited until the student walked off, then went over and asked him.

"A lawyer?" Troy said, grinning and arching an eyebrow. "For who? You?"

"No," Kelli said. "Look, you're familiar with people like that. Can you recommend somebody?"

"What kind of lawyer you looking for?"

"Criminal."

He gave them a silent study, his face sobering. "This sounds serious."

"It is."

"You in some kind of trouble?"

"Please, Troy, it's important."

Gilhammer frowned, thinking. Finally he shook his head. "All the lawyers I know work tax court or handle corporate suits."

"Then ask one of them. They'd know."

He agreed, and they followed him to his office inside the lab. It was cluttered with books, and there were skis and climbing gear stacked against the back wall. He rummaged around his desk until he uncovered a business card file, chose a number and rang it.

"Jo Ann? Hi, Troy Gilhammer," he said. "Say, is Vern in? Thanks." He waited. "Vern, I need some legal advice. Yeah. Could you recommend a good criminal attorney? No, not for me. A friend." He glanced at Kelli, then Matt. His eyes held for a moment before drifting off.

"Yeah, okay," he said. He lowered the phone. "How much money can you, or whoever, afford?" The question was directed at them both.

"That doesn't matter," Kelli said.

"Yes, it does," Marquette interrupted. "Make it as cheap as possible."

"Reasonable," Troy said into the phone. He listened again, thanked Vern and hung up. "Well, he says there're a bunch of attorneys around. Some good, some bad. One guy in particular he knows about does real well for his clients. A fella name of Grady."

"Grady?" Kelli said.

"Yeah, John Wayne, like the movie star. He's a civil liberties hotshot. Likes tilting lances at the establishment. But according to Vern, he's sharp as hell. In fact, he hasn't lost a single court case yet. And he does pro bono work."

Kelli nodded. "Thanks, Troy. Listen, can I take off for a couple of hours?"

He frowned. "We were just about ready to rerun the bridge sequence."

"I'll be back as soon as I can."

He sighed. "Okay," he said. "But make it fast?" He watched them thoughtfully as they walked out of the office.

"Je-zus H. Christ," Bobby Winterowd giggled. "Will you *look* at that asshole out there."

Seated at a table across the room, Samuel Catching's head shot up. "Hey!" he snapped. He was a big man with square, chiseled features and brooding dark eyes. He had been field-stripping a Cobray M-11 assault pistol. "I tole you about using the Lord's name like that around here."

"Sorry," Bobby said. "But, man, you gotta see this crazy Halberstadt."

"We know what he's doing."

A third man, Leroy James, chuckled. "Hell, he jest likes settin' in the snow."

"But the damn fool's nakeder than a blue jay's ass."

"He don't feel the cold."

"What?"

"Yeah." James said. He was sitting on an old Army cot beside several metal boxes of .45 caliber ammunition. Two sawed-off Winchester pump twelve-gauge shotguns lay on the boxes. "He's meditating. Some kind of Jap shit he calls Zen. Claims he don't feel nothin' when he's in a trance."

"Zen?" Bobby scoffed. "I figured it was the crank. The way he scoffs up that shit, it's a wonder he ain't bouncin' off the trees."

"He does that, too."

On the opposite side of James's bunk was a beat-up rolltop desk. On it was an IBM personal computer with a linked printer and a portable Sony ICF-2010 shortwave radio. James had been swinging radio stations, getting splurges of static-filled French programs out of Canada.

Winterowd continued to watch the German. He was sitting cross-legged about twenty yards from the cabin in a drift of snow. A quick March storm had passed in the night. Now the ground was blanketed with new snow over the older winter layers.

His head was down on his chest, eyes closed. His total nakedness gave the heavy, muscular lines of his body a look of Grecian repose. But that image was shattered by the stark black lines of several tattoos on his white skin. There were swastikas and a stiletto with a coiled snake, and a spiderweb on his elbow. That symbol proclaimed that he had killed another human at least once.

Sighing, Bobby finally left the window and dropped into a camp chair. He still had on his thick blanket coat and the yellow hard hat he'd worn driving up from Lowland with supplies for the cabin.

It was a single-room affair made of rough-hewn lodgepole pine logs and mill ends, situated in a small clearing in the mountains at the edge of the Sawtooth Wilderness sixty miles northeast of Boise. It belonged to Catching. A coal miner and part-time preacher, he'd used it for hunting. Now it was the secret headquarters of the Grassrooters' J-Cell.

"You know, I'm surprised a Nazi'd have anything to do with Jap bullshit," Bobby commented.

"Why?" James said. "They was allies in the war, wasn't they?"

"I guess."

Originally, the Grassrooters had merely been an amorphous collection of disgruntled, religion-based survivalists and antigovernment adherents scattered throughout the northern mountains of Idaho. Then the incidents at Ruby Ridge galvanized them, and the isolated groups began to coalesce. Their rallying point was the fiery call-to-arms raised at a convocation of Militia Movement leaders held in Estes Park, Colorado, in the fall of 1992.

Now the Grassers were tightly structured into pseudoindependent cells of five to seven men. Each cell had an "organic" commander, and Catching was J-Cell's leader. He oversaw training in guerrilla warfare, weaponry and small-unit tactics.

Close contact was kept with other militia and survivalist

groups around the country through the Internet and by short-wave. From these sources, they received further instructions on sabotage, battlefield first aid, logistics and methods to make or steal weapons. All for the inevitable day when the revolution started . . .

Bobby took off his hard hat and scraped fingers through his blond crew cut. He was twenty-seven, as athletically handsome as a Marine recruiting poster.

"You know what the kraut tole me?" he said. "He got in a fight one time over in East Berlin. With this Eeth-aye-o-pian? He sticks a knife in the guy, cuts him from just above his dick all the way up to his ribs. Slices the sucker open like a butchered hog.

"And then you know what he done? He stuck his finger inside the wound, sopped up the guy's blood and sucked it off his fingers like it was candy. *Damn!*"

"I don't like the man," Catching said solemnly. "He's got a viper's soul." He had reassembled the Cobray. Now he began to load its stick clip with Black Talon bullets capable of piercing class II body armor.

"Maybe so," James said. "But you gotta deal with the Devil's disciples to obtain the Devil's weapons, right?"

"The longer he's here," Catching said, "the stronger the chance he'll bring wrath down on us."

"Well, I don't know about his soul," Winterowd said, "but he's got the snake eye. You say something he don't like, he bores you with them black eyes. Make your balls shrivel."

"Aw, he's all right," James said. "Jest don't piss him off."

"Yeah, well, I'm glad he's goin' to Seattle with you, Dog-man, and not me."

"He'll be all right," James said. He was small and wiry, partially bald, with thick glasses and a perpetual two day's beard. He got his nickname from the fact that he raised fighting pit bulls. A onetime timber-mill worker, he'd been "gill-poked" when a log jumped the conveyor and crushed his hip. Now he owned a bleachered fighting pit in a barn in

Swan Falls, a twenty-foot fenced circle with red carpeting to hide the blood.

Catching glanced at his watch. "It's almost three o'clock. You best get Stackman's show on. And let's hope it comes today."

James punched in one of the radio's presets to shortwave station WWCR out of Colorado Springs. The men fell silent, listening. There was some bagpipe music and then a blue-grass song.

A few minutes later, John Stackman's talk show, *Freedom Hour*, began. Stackman started with a fiery, five-minute ha-rangue about the U.S. government's recruiting of Bloods and Crips gang members out of L.A. to be future troops for dis-arming the American populace. They and Sikh soldiers al-ready training in secret camps in Hong Kong, he continued, would soon be massing along the Canadian border.

At last, he started to take calls, first from a ranting Klans-man out of Duane, Arkansas; then a MOM Christian Patriot from Noxon, Montana. The third caller said, "Hello, John. This is Ka-Bar from Seattle."

All three men sat forward. Ka-Bar was the code name for Jack Stone's chopper pilot, Jay Basset, a Grasser from F-Cell in Boise.

"Good to hear from you, Ka-Bar," Stackman said. "What's on your mind?"

"I say it's time to cut out all the talk and get to kickin' some ass," Ka-Bar said. "You unnerstan what I'm sayin'?"

"I hear you loud and clear, brother."

"That's right. Those SOBs in Washington'll listen to only one sound, man. The crack and recoil of heavy weapons."

"Crack and recoil, I like that. Sings on the tongue."

"You bet your ass," Ka-Bar said. "An' here's another thing fits on the tongue. I read it once. Patrick Henry said it. 'If this be treason, then let's get to it.' "

"Hallelujah, brother."

"That's it," Catching said. He rammed the clip into the Cobray with a metallic snap and stood up. "Go get the German. It's time to go."

6

Kelli's houseboat was moored among hundreds of others on the west side of Lake Union, two miles from the campus. The dwellings were complete houses built on rafts of huge cedar logs. Many were ornate and very expensive.

Kelli parked her Chevy Blazer beside a stunted silver pine, and she and Matt walked down the narrow pontoon slip to her front patio. The house was shingle-sided, the shingles brown and rustically windblown. On the porch were boxes of cinnamon and water fern and tall *polystichum*. The brisk wind off the lake carried the smell of tar and wood smoke.

Inside, the single front room was spacious, filled with early afternoon sunshine from twin blocks of paned windows. On one side was a kitchen with a huge wood-burning stove. Opposite was the combined living and dining area, cherry-wood furniture accented with patterns of blue-and-white Wedgwood.

Kelli's workstation nearly filled the back wall. It consisted of a boomerang-shaped desk filled with folders and program binders and twin UNIX computers. One was code-linked to the CRYSTALBALL lab's Cray C-90 mainframe, code-named Orion, and also to the other workstations within the lab. The second UNIX carried a T-1 line to the Internet, capable of downloading a hundred times more data than a normal modem.

Beside the desk stood a combination stereo/bookcase filled with computer texts, journals and a few leather-bound classics. On top of the bookcase were four swimming trophies. Kelli had swum in high school and college. She'd even been considered a potential competitor for the 1988 Olympics. She swam the 200-and 400-meter medleys, loving the take-it-to-the-wall endurance required. That kind of staying power—along with a mulish tenacity in the face of a perplexing problem—she'd learned from her father, an aerospace engineer at Lockheed.

She got a Budweiser from the refrigerator and watched Matt pop the top and take a long draught. "You look beat," she said.

"I am, a little."

"Want some lunch? I've got ham."

"No, thanks."

He took another long pull of beer. When he lowered the bottle, he stared into her eyes. Then he put his hand in her hair and gently brought her against him. She locked her hands at the base of his spine. He could smell her skin, enjoying the solid contact of her body. And he felt a sudden, warm rush of desire come up through his groin, into his chest.

He kissed her.

The question of hiring Grady to represent him had been left undecided. They'd discussed it during the ride from the campus.

"I don't like the sound of this guy," Matt had said. "He's probably some ACLU-type only interested in political axes to grind."

"So he's political," Kelli said. "Who the hell isn't? At least he doesn't lose."

"Guys that don't lose come high."

"I've already told you that's not a problem."

Matt shook his head emphatically. "I'm not letting you tie yourself up to some shyster for me."

"But he does pro bono."

"So? Why would he give me freebies? I don't have any political ground to explore."

Exasperated, she guided the Blazer off Interstate 5, held it tight into the curve that came out on West Mercer Avenue. "Look, you can at least give the man a call," she had said. "Find out what he has to say."

"I don't know."

Now she broke their kiss, touched his cheek and moved across the living room to her workstation. The answering machine message light was blinking. She poked the play button. The machine clicked and scraped, and then a man's voice said, "Miss Pickett, this is Lieutenant John Two Elks of the Clallam County Sheriff's Department. I'd like to speak with you at your earliest convenience."

Kelli lifted her eyes to Matt with a silent, aching look.

"It's now nine A.M.," the tape continued. "My number is 360-555-8856. I'd appreciate a call. Thank you." The machine buzzed and clicked off.

She inhaled deeply. "Well? Do you call Grady or do I?"

He slowly took another drink of beer, watching her. He nodded. "Yeah, I guess I'd better."

Kelli turned back to one of her computers. Within seconds, she had the city telephone directory on her screen. She typed in Grady's name.

Matt went into the bathroom. It was done in solid white save for a magnificent copper bathtub in the center. Standing over the toilet bowl, listening to the foamy rush of his urine, he felt his heart beating. It seemed unnatural that he should.

His eyes drifted up to the mirror. He studied his face. Except for a slight weariness in the eyes, it looked strong, capable. A not-yet-aging athlete with a lot of stamina and reserves still going for him.

Yet, inside, encapsulated down there where he himself began, he felt the fear. And the knowledge of it humiliated him.

When he came out, Kelli handed him the cell phone. "His office is ringing now," she said.

A minute earlier, John Wayne Grady had leaned back in his Navaho-rug-draped chair and grinned at the ceiling of his office. It was braced with raw sugar-pine beams. Below, the walls were terra cotta, with the texture and rich beige color of desert sand. The whole room had the cool, sun-secluded scent and feel of a New Mexico mission chapel.

"I'd say that was a sticky question, hon," he said. He lowered his eyes. They were brown and held a merry, agile energy behind yellow-tinted glasses.

"I'm sorry," the female reporter from *Seattle Beat* said quickly. She was blond and bright in a chrome-blue business suit. "But don't you think most people would want to know? I mean, an attorney of your ... ah ... well, expertise, who's defended so many militia types, would he be sympathetic to their movement? Wouldn't you say they'd be interested?"

"Sweetheart, I try not to assume what other people want to know."

"Then you're *not* sympathetic."

"Quite the contrary. I'm always sympathetic to a client's need for a fair trial."

"Of course." Distractedly, the reporter uncrossed her legs, recrossed them.

Grady watched the maneuver, noting how smooth and tanned her legs were. Copper-colored pantyhose, he decided. He idly wondered if she also wore panties. He imagined himself peeking, pulling the edge of the hose between thumb and forefinger. Was she a real blond?

"Now, Mr. Grady, I—"

"Ah-ah," he corrected. "Johnny Wayne. You know, said all of a piece. With that little cracker accent on the 'Wayne.' "

"All right. Johnny Wayne. Is there a—"

The phone buzzed. He held up a finger. "You want to hold that thought, hon?" He punched the blinking light, picked up the receiver. He listened a moment. "I'll talk to him in two minutes." He hung up.

He looked at the reporter. Then he ran his hand along the side of his brown hair, the fingers finally nestling to fondle the thick, long curl below his collar. He had a lean face, narrow-mouthed and high-foreheaded, like a well-fed Dick Cavett.

"Hon," he said, "I feel downright regretful about this, but I'm afraid I'm gonna have to call a halt to our little chat."

"But I haven't even touched—"

"Duty first." He rose, moved around his desk and stood smiling down at her. She sighed resignedly, gathered up her purse and stood. Lightly touching her elbow, he accompanied her to the door and pulled it open.

"Well," the reporter said curtly, "I'm certainly sorry I couldn't get a little more of your time, Mr. Grady."

"Me, too," he said. "But tell me, you mind I ask *you* a question?"

"What is it?"

"You wear panties?"

Her face went slack for a moment. Then a hardness came into her eyes. "You like to shock, don't you, fella?"

"Yeah, yeah, I do," he said. "Like to fuck, too."

She stormed out.

He returned to his desk. Like his chair, it was adorned with delicately hand-carved Indian rosettes in nineteenth-century Spanish cedar. He lifted his phone and tapped the lighted button. "Tell me about it," he snapped.

"Is this Grady?" Marquette said.

"You got it."

"I need some advice."

"What's the charge?"

There was a slight pause. "No charge yet. But it concerns a double murder."

"Uh-huh." He scratched an eyelid. "What say we have some names here first." His speech pattern was quick, brusque, now. The slight Texas twang was still there, but gone was the slow, back-porch folksiness.

"We'll hold that till you've heard me out."

"Fair enough." Grady punched the speaker button. From a silver-and-turquoise humidor, he extracted a slender Andelusian Ducados cigarrito, lit up and began to stroll around the room. "Where'd these homicides occur?"

"In Dungeness."

"When?" Near the back wall, he adjusted the position of a foot-high bronze statue of an Hunkpapa Sioux chief in battle gear.

"Last night."

Grady hurried over to a side desk with a computer. As he talked, he brought up the PA filing section of the Washington State District Attorney's Office. All violent incidents occurring within the state were formally logged into these files within six hours after discovery.

He typed in: Dungeness, Clallam County—03/15.

"What's your connection to the crime?" he asked.

"One of the victims worked for me. I run a fishing boat out of Dungeness."

A tiny light on the computer flashed. On the screen he read:

```
CC/TAC//0045//PT:0703
FILE: 145-576-0023

BOAT FIRE
INITIAL REPORT CC: PT: 0112
TWO (2) FATALS
ID (VERIFIED BY MARQUETTE, MATTHEW—BOAT
    OWNER):
    HAMMIL, RICHARD: MALE, 24 YEARS
    POLK, JULIE: FEMALE, 19 YEARS
```

He scanned down:

```
CASE DISPERSAL: CC DET LT TWO ELKS, JOHN
ME REPORT (DR CD BYNER): PENDING
```

"Hey, you still there?" Marquette said.

"Why don't you fill in the holes," Grady said.

"Okay, but it's gonna sound a little weird."

"I thrive on weird."

Marquette began, slowly at first. He told about the taking

of the mako and the hovering helicopter, moved on to the explosion and fire.

Grady returned to his circuiting of the room, letting the man talk. He didn't interrupt until Matt told him about finding the sphere. "What sort of sphere?" he asked.

"It's made of some kind of plastic. About as big as a grapefruit."

"And it had a position locater attached?"

"Yeah."

Interesting, Grady thought. It opened a lot of possibilities. "You know what's in it?" he asked.

"Yes."

"How's that?"

"I got it X-rayed."

"Oh? Where?"

"I just got it X-rayed."

"And?"

"It's some sort of high-tech crystal chamber. Possibly off a computer chip layer machine."

More vistas . . .

Grady paused in front of his window. It looked out over the container docks of Salmon Bay to the lush green pine stands of Discovery Park and the Fort Lawton Military Reservation. Smuggling operation? he thought. A squabble among thieves? He sucked on his cigarrito, savoring the smooth brandy tang of the smoke.

"This chopper you saw," he said. "You get a good look at it?"

"Yes."

"Anything unusual about it?"

"Just an ordinary two-seater. White. I couldn't tell the make. But I saw what looked like a company logo on it."

"Mmm?"

"Yeah, three red *S*s, entwined."

Grady's cigarrito stopped in midair. Slowly he turned and stared at the telephone speaker. *What?*

"You sure about that?" he barked.

"Positive."

Grady walked to his chair and quietly sat down. *What the Christ is this? Three Ss? That's Jack Stone's company logo. Could it be possible somebody else had the same thing? No, logos were trademarks.*

"I find this fascinating as hell, Marquette," he said.

"How in hell you know my name?"

Shit!

"I've got it on my screen," he said. "The boat fire was logged into the DA's office."

Matt went silent. Grady had the stricken feeling he was about to hang up. Hurriedly, he said, "Look, I'll take you on." His mind raced. *He had to hold this guy, find out what in hell was going on.*

"Just like that?" Matt said.

Grady managed a casual laugh. "Hell, the thing intrigues me."

"What about the fee?"

"That can be worked out." *Hold him, hold him.* He got a thought. "Listen, Marquette, you're in a very dangerous position here."

"That ain't exactly news."

"No, it's worse than you think." He lied: "They've already filed an arrest warrant for you." He heard the man exhale slowly into the phone. "You gotta get out of Seattle. Damned quick. Give me a chance to feel out the parameters of this thing, see what the police actually have."

Silence.

"You hear what I'm sayin'?"

"Yeah."

"Have you got a place where you can hide out for a few days?"

"No."

His mind flew through options. "Okay, I know a place. My summer cabin in Moses Lake. You know where that is?"

"Wait a minute. Wouldn't that make you an accessory?"

"You haven't been formally charged with anything yet." He heard Marquette place his hand over the receiver. There were muted voices.

Marquette came back. "Okay, I'll go. Where is this cabin?"

He gave directions, adding, "Can you get use of someone else's car? They'll be watching for yours."

"I don't have a car. I don't drive."

"Then take a Greyhound. But do it fast, before the street cops start watching terminals."

Silence again.

"So what do you say?"

"All right."

"Have you a number I can call in case we miss connections?"

"I'll call *you*."

The line went dead.

Two Elks ate a banana and slowly flipped through photos of the *Big Blue* crime scene. Bananas were his favorite food. He usually snacked on eight or ten a day, big Bluefields from Hawaii that he bought at a small Korean market on Beverly Street.

The photos were eight-by-ten color prints, their images stark and raw. Such pictures of death and the particular places in which it occurred always struck him as containing a strange sense of collision, as if the victims and the places had somehow suddenly struck a time wall to be left scattered, sucked of all substance and dignity, like the windblown remnants of a carcass atop an ancient Sioux burial platform.

Before taking up the photos, he had finally completed his PSR-1, the Preliminary Summary Report of the Dungeness crime—a tiresome job of evidence logs, autopsy protocols, prelim forensic data and interviewee statements. Among the statement summaries were those of Rick Hammil's parents and Julie Polk's older sister.

Talking to the relatives of victims was always disturbing to Two Elks. Polk's sister had completely broken down with him, sobbed for several minutes in her three-room walk-up behind a Chinese restaurant in Dungeness. Hammil's father had sounded old and infirm on the telephone, yet his voice was slow and steady, void of hysteria.

He turned to the next photo in line. It showed the fishing boat's ice hold with its dead shark. Apparently the county photographer had been more than thorough. He studied the print. It seemed incorrect somehow.

After a moment, he realized it was the shark. In the picture, it was ungutted. Earlier that day, he had supervised two county divers attaching flotation tanks to the boat so it could be beached. While there, he'd noticed that the animal had been sliced open, its smelly entrails spewed onto the wet deck boards.

Why would Marquette do that?

"Hey, George," he called.

A young deputy poked his head around the door. "Yeah, John?"

"You used to work the salmon boats, right?"

"Yeah."

"When do you normally gut a fish?" he said.

"You don't. You just ice the suckers down and then off-load 'em ashore. Guts, assholes and all."

"Why would a guy cut open a shark in the harbor?"

The deputy shrugged. "Maybe he wanted chum for the next day?"

Two Elks grunted, turned back to his photos. Chum for the next day? Not likely. A puzzle.

His phone light blinked. He picked up the receiver. "Detective Division, Two Elks."

It was Sheriff Milt Lindsey. "Judge Cherry just okayed the Marquette search warrant," he barked. Lindsey had a booming voice and spoke in bursts like strobe flashes through the phone. "When you gonna execute?"

"Later this afternoon."

"Good."

"Did you get that BSU form off?" John asked.

Earlier, Two Elks had logged a request for a personality profile analysis of the unknown murderer through the FBI's Behavorial Science Unit at Quantico, Virginia. Around noon, the local FBI office had faxed him a twelve-page inquiry form, which he had duly filled out and sent upstairs for Lindsey's signature.

"Faxed it out a half hour ago," Lindsey said. "But we won't hear anything for at least ten days."

"I know."

"Talked to Parelli, too." Steve Parelli was the FBI station agent for the Seattle area. "Their files show Marquette was clean. They checked out his military records, too. Served as a SEAL, as an ordnance specialist. Two tours in Nam. With decorations."

Two Elks grunted. "So he knows how to kill if he wants to."

"Sure as hell looks that way." Lindsey hung up without saying good-bye.

Two Elks had worked ten homicides in his career. All but one had been routine: biker bar fights, domestic shootings. But the one that stood out was the murder of a Mexican illegal in Port Angeles two years before. It had taken diligent work to solve, along with coordination with the FBI and Customs. In the process, they'd uncovered the northern terminus of a drug network with connections all the way back to a major Columbian cartel.

The killer had been a hired shooter from San Francisco. Barely five feet tall, with the body of a miniature Hercules and the cold-blooded instincts of a Beirut terrorist. John had been allowed to be part of the strike team that took him in a hotel in Tacoma. Still, Clallam County had been denied prosecution because of FBI precedence.

He pulled off his Stetson and tiredly ran his hand over his thick, black hair. It was parted in the middle and pulled back into a small ponytail. His skin, marred only by a two-inch scar on his chin from the helmet of a San Francisco 49er, was the color of slowly tanned deer hide.

It was now almost thirty-six hours since he'd been to bed. He looked at his watch. Two-thirty. He decided to sleep for a couple hours, then go out and run the search of Marquette's house. He leaned back in his chair, laid the Stetson low on his brow and closed his eyes.

In the darkness behind his lids, he drew up the image of a white buffalo running in slow motion, the great head high, eyes ablaze, as the beast's powerful legs pounded the prairie dust in utter silence. It was a trance key, a mantra-picture to bring sleep quickly. It had been taught to him by his great-grandfather, who had fought with the warrior-shaman Smo-halla along the tule banks of the Blue Columbia.

Within a minute, he was asleep.

"I'm gonna ask you flat out," Grady said. "Is your company chopper out here?"

"What the hell you want to know that for?" Stone said.

"Just tell me."

"Yeah, it's here."

"Well, goddammit to hell."

Stone and Fettis had spent the morning frantically trying to get a trace on the owner of *Big Blue*. From the morning paper, they'd at least learned his name was Marquette and even gotten his address.

At 9:30, Jack had called Basset on the cell phone. He had to try three times before the pilot answered. Jack gave him Marquette's address and ordered him to watch the house, maybe even break in if he got a chance, see what he could find.

Basset called back an hour later. "There's a county cop parked down the hill from the place," he said.

"Dammit," Stone said. "That means he's a suspect."

Fettis said, "Who's a suspect? Marquette?"

"Yeah."

"That ain't good, Jack," Gus said. "He get picked up, the cops'll seize the unit."

"What you want me to do now?" Basset said.

Stone thought a moment. "Stick around the town, keep your eyes open. And don't forget you gotta make the Stack-man call."

"Yeah."

"And do it on time."

"I said yeah."

"All right, keep in touch. And stay the hell out of the bars."

Since that call, Jack had continued to make probes. He tried the state Marine Licensing Board on the chance that Marquette had listed a friend or relative on his boat license application. He hadn't. But Stone did manage to learn that the Pine State Bank actually held the paper on the boat.

He called the bank posing as an old Army buddy of Marquette's and asked for the names of credit references in the loan file so he could trace him. A brusque female bank officer told him such information could not be released without a written statement from Marquette.

By one o'clock, Stone had begun to sweat bullets. . . .

Now Grady said, "You all want to tell me just what the hell is going on here?"

"What're you talking about?"

"How is it your chopper was seen by the owner of a fishing boat just before the goddamn thing got torched and two people died?"

Stone was jolted. "How did you know about that?"

Fettis glanced over. In his jockey shorts, he'd been doing sit-ups and lifting furniture. He lowered a table to listen.

"Because I just got off the phone with the guy that saw you," Grady said. "In fact, he just hired me."

Stone looked wide-eyed at Fettis. "Who're you talking about? Marquette?"

"That's him."

"I don't believe this."

"Well, believe it," the lawyer said. "Now listen, Stone. You and me, we got important business going here. I don't want nothin' screwing it up."

"Where is he now?"

"You hear what I'm saying? Goddammit, now we're looking at two fatals here. For God sake, did you do this?"

"Where the hell is Marquette?" Jack yelled.

"I've got him sequestered," Grady said.

"What do you mean sequestered? He's there with you?"

"No, I sent him out to my cabin at Moses Lake."

"Where?"

"Moses Lake. It's in the Basin. Look, are you gonna tell me what this is all about or not?"

Agitatedly, Stone pulled at his jaw. "It's nothing, Grady," he said. "Look, don't worry about it. It's just a little side job, a skooch. He's got something of ours."

"Did you fire the boat?"

"Hell, no."

"Can I take that to the bank?" Grady said.

"You can shove it up your ass for all I care. Listen, did Marquette say anything about a sphere?"

"Yeah, he did."

"Does he have it with him?"

"Yeah. He says it's some kind of crystal chamber. That what you after?"

Stone made a fist, joyously punched at the air. "Is he at the cabin now?"

"No, he's on his way over. By Greyhound."

Stone said to Fettis, "Get out your road map." To Grady: "How do we get to this cabin?"

Grady gave directions, then said, "Get this real straight, Stone. I'm standing clear of this bullshit. You hear? You get this thing settled with Marquette, okay. But you damned well better do it away from my cabin. You understand? An' don't let nobody see you with him."

"Yeah, yeah." He hung up.

Gus said, "What's this shit about a cabin?"

Jack explained.

Fettis laughed. "You gotta be shitting me. Of all the attorneys in Seattle, the dude picks Two-Gun? What the fuck're the odds on that?"

"I guess we just been living right," Jack said.

They spread the Chevron road map out on the table. After a moment, Stone jammed his finger down onto it. "There she is, Moses Lake."

7

It sat cold in Marquette's mind, a thing totally contrary to his instincts: this running, hiding. He glumly stared out the Blazer's passenger window as Kelli eased the vehicle to the curb.

They were on Eighth Street, directly behind a bobtail freight truck. The driver whistled to himself as he hustled cartons off the truck bed and onto a small hand dolly.

Up the block on Stewart Avenue stood the main Greyhound terminal. It was an old brick building with turn-of-the-century cornices and cable-suspended metal porticos jutting out above the two main entrances.

Kelli turned off the engine. For a moment, she studied the distant mountains through the windshield. Banks of dark clouds, building up over the past two hours, seemed to foam along the high ridges.

"Looks like you might get some snow crossing the summit," she said.

He didn't answer. He continued to gaze out the window. A young man in a green smock stepped from the loading door of the building beside them. He lit a cigarette and stood watching the trucker. At his feet, little wisps of steam came up through a grill in the sidewalk and disappeared into the air.

One of the prime lessons Matt had learned in his life was that when dealing with an opponent, you first sized him up. It was the same in a school-yard fistfight or a tactical night mission in Nam. You learned parameters, your enemy's strengths and weaknesses. But how could you do that by fleeing him? he thought. Seeking refuge like a goddamned rat in a hole?

Kelli said, "I know you don't like doing this, Matt."

He turned to her.

"I can understand that," she said, "but you don't have much choice. You'll be safe out there in the Basin. And now with a warrant out for you, the cops'd pick you up for sure if you stay."

Someone tapped on her window. She turned, jumped. It was a policeman. She rolled down the window.

He gave her a smile, his light blue shirt looking fresh, the pleats knife-sharp. "Sorry, miss," he said. "You can't park here."

"Oh, I'm sorry, officer. I was just dropping off a bus passenger."

"Okay, but make it fast." He strolled back to his blue-and-white cruiser.

She watched him in the mirror. "God, he scared the hell out of me."

Matt reached over, squeezed her arm and opened the door. He got out, leaned down. "Take care of yourself," he said.

"*You* take care. And call me as soon as you get over. I'll be at the lab."

"Right." He closed the door and walked away. When the police cruiser passed him at the corner, the officer didn't even look over.

Inside the terminal, he found the ticket booth and bought a one-way to Moses Lake. At the far end of the building, a demo crew was dismantling a stairway, taking out the tarnished brass railings and pulling off marble facing. They made the air smoky with cement dust.

He walked out to the bus apron where several buses were parked in a line. The area was like a breezeway with huge doors at each end. A light, chilly wind funneled through the apron, smelling of diesel fumes and hot dogs and cold, rusty steel.

He waited beside a thick I-beam festooned with names and obscene graffiti, and felt, for the first time since that quick flashing explosion in the Dungeness night, the slow, icy coil of anger beginning in the pit of his stomach.

Stone didn't hit bad weather until he reached the foothills beyond North Bend, thirty miles east of Seattle. First came rain, which quickly turned to sleet as he climbed into the mountains. A muddy slush developed along the edges of Interstate 90.

After Grady's message, Jack had called Basset and ordered him to retrieve the helicopter at Port Angeles, then pick up Gus in the transient area of King County International. They were to fly directly to Ellensberg, the first Greyhound stop on the basin side of the mountains. There they would watch for Marquette's bus. Meanwhile, he took Fettis's Trans Am and headed directly to Moses Lake.

Near Snoqualmie Pass, it finally began to snow. The huge flakes flared upward before striking his windshield and then were whipped away by the wipers. Tiny ice breams formed on the blades. Beside the highway, the forest rose silent and dark, filled with gray snow mist.

So far, Stone had been gliding along on the high from Grady's news about Marquette. But as the storm thickened, his doubts began to assail him again. Time was slipping away with the irretrievability of words spoken into air. He glanced at his watch. It was ten minutes after four in the afternoon.

A sudden scattering of taillights shone ahead. He quickly braked, easing off speed. In a moment, he pulled to a stop behind a double line of cars. Far forward were clusters of flashing red and blue lights—an accident.

"Shit," he said aloud.

He waited. Several minutes passed with nothing moving. Then a Washington Highway Patrol four-by-four pickup went past him along the shoulder of the highway. Its flashers threw scarlet bursts through the falling snow.

Stone reached over the seat and brought up his briefcase. It lay beside Fettis's carry-on, which contained the subassembly units. He opened the case and set it on the passenger's seat. Inside were folders and note pads, a cell phone and a holstered Ingram P-11 assault pistol. He sat back.

"Come *on*, for Chris' sake," he growled and tapped his fingers agitatedly on the steering wheel. "Let's get this sucker going."

Six minutes later, his cell phone buzzed. It was Gus in Ellensberg. "We just come in," he said. "Where are you?"

"Stuck on the damn pass. It's snowing up here, and now there's a goddamned accident up ahead."

"We must be getting some of the storm overflow down here. The wind's stronger'n hell. And that stupid fuck, Basset, damned near killed us landing. The prick's half bagged."

"Goddammit, Gus, keep that son of a bitch away from the booze."

"Yeah."

"All right," he said. "You spot Marquette, see if you can get on the same bus with him. But don't let him see Basset. He could make him from the ferry."

"Right," Fettis said and hung up.

Stone sat glaring through the windshield. Finally, he rolled down his window. The cold air swept over his face with a clean, sharp bite. He began to honk his horn and shout out the door, "Come on, assholes. Let's get *moving*, here."

Gus and Basset had taken a taxi into town from the Ellensberg airport. It was a small Unicom field with a single runway, a cluster of hangars and a few dozen private planes cabled down in the wind. Surrounding it were alfalfa and wheat fields and long stretches of open grassland dotted with cattle.

The Greyhound depot was located in the lobby of the Columbia Hotel on Eighth and Okanogan. Across the street was the *1889 Cafe*, made of old sand brick with steel-shuttered windows. They went in and sat at the counter so they could watch the hotel through the wide front window.

The place was nearly empty. It had a large gold-rush-era mirror behind the counter, the corners covered with old snapshots and rodeo ribbons. There were mounted elk and deer heads and pieces of old cowboy paraphernalia—lariats and spurs—on the walls.

The waitress came up the counter. She was young and pretty, with short blond hair and dangling, gold leaf-shaped earrings. "Hi, guys," she said with a broad smile.

Basset gave her a slow, half-drunk grin. "Hi yourself, hon. My, but ain't you a sweet thang."

"So, what'll it be today?"

"How's about a little bite outta *you*?"

The smile stayed on the girl's face, but her eyes went wary. Across the room, two old men in dusty denim work clothes and baseball caps glanced up.

Fettis said, "A couple long-neck Buds."

The girl started away.

"Wait a minute here," Basset said. "I'm hungry. What kinda hamburgers you got, honey?"

"Hamburgers and cheeseburgers," the girl said. In the kitchen, a radio was playing country music.

"What else you got on them hamburgers besides cheese?" Basset, still grinning teasingly, put his elbows on the counter, his chin on his knuckles.

"A tomato slice, pickle, relish and a strip of bacon."

"A real uptown burger, huh?" he said.

"Bring him one," Gus said.

The girl gave the order to the cook, then pulled open an old cooler box. She took out two bottles of beer, opened them and put them on the counter. The bottles were wet. Basset ogled her, his gaze half-lidded. When she glanced at him, he pursed his lips and kissed the air.

She went back into the kitchen.

He took a long pull of beer and slammed the bottle noisily down onto the counter. He belched and lazily scanned the room. When he got to the two men in baseball caps, he stared hard at them until they looked away.

Gus watched sardonically. "You a real tough peckerwood, ain't you?" he said.

Basset glanced at him, then turned and looked at his face

in the mirror. "You bet your ass," he said. "I eat nails and shit glass."

"You talking about your stomach or your brain?"

Basset was silent for a moment, the little grin still playing on his lips. Then he said, "You like to fuck with the dog, don't you, Gus-oh?"

Fettis chuckled.

"Watch out he don't bite," Basset said.

Gus's expression didn't change. He was silent for a moment. Then he leaned forward and said softly, "Listen, shit-face. You figure you got enough to bust my nuts, let's get it on right now."

Basset stiffened—a minute tightening of the neck and mouth, the grin unslacking and then opening again—and he sniggered. He picked up the bottle between his thumb and forefinger, drank and put the bottle down lightly, almost delicately. He sniggered again, his head bobbing slowly.

When the waitress brought the hamburger, Fettis asked, "What time's the Seattle bus get in?"

She turned and glanced at a Coors clock near the mirror. "It's already ten minutes late," she said. "Must have hit snow up in the pass."

"She's comin' up the street now," one of the baseball caps called over.

Gus and Basset went to the window and watched as the bus pulled up in front of the hotel. Several people got out and went into the building.

Basset nodded. "That's him," he said. "The big sucker in the college jacket."

Fettis went back to the counter. He paid the bill, leaving a two-dollar tip. "What's the next stop for that bus?" he asked the waitress.

"Wanapum, I think," she said.

"Yeah, it's Wanapum," the baseball hat said. "Thirty miles east, beyond the river."

Gus looked around at Basset, then walked out, crossed the street and went up into the hotel to buy a ticket.

*   *   *

Once clear of Seattle, the Greyhound driver had lead-footed it all the way to the Cascade foothills, the bus whipping past slower traffic, wheels humming on the pavement. Matt had taken a window seat in the rear—and felt the immediate cold panic of speed envelope him, that tight grip of stomach and the perspiration beading his forehead.

Then the mountains came and finally the snow, and the driver slowed. They went through the long tunnels of pine and sequoia, misty and silent in the snowfall, and then downward again beyond the pass. The thick forests followed them, and there was Roslyn and Teanaway, and finally the forest was gone. They sped through Thorp and finally reached Ellensberg.

The lobby of the Columbia Hotel looked like a 1910 drummer's stop: faded carpet, dry walls of Phillipsboard, two potted palms beside the entrance to a cool, dim bar. Matt bought a beer and watched a girl in tight Levi's and high heels playing a pinball machine in the corner.

When the driver called for everyone to reboard, he noticed a new passenger: a short but powerfully shouldered man with a burr haircut and a yellow windbreaker. The man smiled at him as they queued beside the bus door.

"Damn wind blows cold around here, don't it?" he said easily.

"Yeah, it does," Matt said.

He took his seat and looked out the window. The shadows were long beside the buildings, washed in soft blue through the tinted glass. The engine started, tappets clacking for a moment, and then they pulled slowly along Eighth, swung onto Main and headed back to Interstate 90.

The panic returned. He closed his eyes. Synchronizing himself to the growling hum of the tires, he let it pull images through his mind—particular moments and places in his life that had left indelible imprints like shiny stones from a sand castle washed away by the surf.

He focused. Sounds, smells, touches. The scent of grass at spring practice in college; the icy-cold cloy of shoulder pads and jerseys still wet from the morning workout, and then the jolting, sweet ache of first contact . . . a little boy this time, his father big and grinning, home after a month on the rigs and smelling of crude oil and man-sweat . . . and his first dive into tropical waters, floating over a teeming reef fundament and then suddenly a pool of white sand, like an oasis in the reef, glowing in crystalline green sunlight . . .

He felt the warm drowsiness of the beer in his head and slowly, drifting, he fell asleep.

There was movement. He opened his eyes. People were filing off the bus. It was dark outside. They were parked beside a small store built of weathered boards. To the left of the store, set back off the service road, were a white farm-house and a water tank on struts. On the other side was a small pole corral. Three horses came to the fence and watched the passengers walk around the bus to the front of the building.

Inside, it was warm from a potbelly stove in the center. Along the walls were shelves of canned goods and fabrics and a small butcher's case holding sausages and thick cuts of steak. The floors sagged under his weight.

A young, bald man in coveralls and a Central Washington University sweatshirt greeted them. "Rest rooms are back that way, folks," he said cheerily. "Cold drinks and snacks up here. An' beer, if you want it."

Matt bought a pack of cigarettes and waited until the line to the restrooms dwindled. The men's toilet had a blue door with a rudely scrawled sign that said "hombres." Between it and the front of the store was a small storage room stacked with bags of rice and chicken feed, with bright harness on the walls. It had a doorway to the outside.

He went into the rest room. It was small, with a cracked tile basin and a single toilet, and it smelled strongly of disinfectant and fresh paint. A window above the basin looked out onto the corral, covered by thick wire and a burlap-wrapped desert cooler on a swingout frame.

Matt urinated, flushed, then washed his hands and face. The towel dispenser was empty. He took out his handkerchief and stood wiping off, gazing out the window. The darkness outside was not quite night yet, but he could see stars to the east and a solid expanse of rolling hills rising gently toward the Wenatchee plateau, all silhouetted against a ribbon of fading indigo.

He froze.

Parked about a hundred yards out in the cobbled traprock, its blades and white body glowing softly in the distant lights from the store and farmhouse, was a small helicopter.

Adrenaline hit his veins like a splay of ice crystals, hurled his heart up into a jolting pound. He swung around. The man in the yellow windbreaker was standing just inside the toilet door. He held his right arm down at his side. In his hand was a stainless steel Glock automatic.

The man lifted his left hand, forefinger extended for silence. There was a smile in his eyes. He nodded toward Matt's gym bag on the floor, pronated his hand and waggled his fingers.

Matt stared at him, motionless. Three or four seconds passed. The man tilted his head, a tiny frown between his eyes but the smile still there. Give it over, man.

Matt eased down, never taking his eyes from the other. He picked up the bag. It felt suddenly heavy, the weight of the Browning. For a flashing moment, he considered swinging it, heavy and fast, swinging and ducking, and the faint whisper of combat was in his teeth and with it the coppery taste of fear.

The man's eyes seemed to sense the thought. He shook his head.

Suddenly, the door was flung open. It knocked the man in the windbreaker off balance. A second man started in. "Gus, you in—*hey!*"

Matt's eyes flicked left, instantly recognized the man in the doorway. He was one of them from the ferry.

The man named Gus turned his head and yelled, "Goddammit, Basset!" He tried to recover, twisting, the Glock coming up.

Thought became action. All the adrenaline energy in Marquette's legs gathered, released. He sprang forward, his right arm swinging the gym bag up and across, the weight of the

Browning shifting against the canvas. It struck Gus high on the cheek, and he jerked away from it, his head down.

Still moving forward, Matt rammed the door against the other man, felt him stumble backward. For a moment, he saw his face, his right arm clawing behind him as if he were grabbing wildly for his spine. Matt's left arm shot out, fingers extended like a spider's legs, going for the man's eyes. He felt face flesh, the hard rim of eye socket. The man grunted as he struck the corridor wall and went down, shoulder first.

Matt's momentum took him through the door. He almost tripped over the man's extended leg, got past it, rolled his weight to the right, took two steps, turned and dove through the doorway to the storage room.

It smelled of feed dust and burlap. He reached the back door. Its handle was a worn strip of wood with a dowel. He flipped it up and shoved through, hearing the sound of boots slamming behind him in the corridor.

He paused on the small, hard-dirt driveway that circled the store. There were wooden skids of baled hay covered with canvas tarps stacked against the outer wall, a greasy Ford V-8 engine block. The wind chilled the sweat on his face as he frantically searched for a place to hide.

Across the road, the horses in the corral, spooked by the slam of the door, lunged away from the fence, turning in unison, their heads thrown back, their eyes catching the lights. In a clot, they circled the corral.

Matt raced across the road and went over the fence. Again, the horses flared away from him. As they did, he saw that one was trailing a hackamore rope. He glanced back. The two men had emerged from the storage room and were coming across the driveway, walking slowly, silently, separated, the wind flapping their jacket collars.

He ran to the opposite side of the corral. Here the pole fence gave way to a four-foot stone wall. The horses had now gathered on the left, dancing and stamping nervously. He moved toward them. Instantly, they charged away, skirting the fence again, creating a dust cloud that drifted up against the lights.

"Give it up, you son of a bitch," one of the men yelled.

As the horses came back past him, bodies huge in the shadows, he grabbed for the trailing hackamore but missed. The animals continued on around the fence, then stopped abruptly, wheeling as they saw one of the men ducking into the corral.

As the animals came abreast of him this time, Marquette caught the rope. Instantly, it jerked taut and started to slip out of his hand, the rope greasy-dusty. Before it went, he snapped his hand over, forming a loop, and was immediately pulled off his feet, the rope biting against his fingers.

As he was dragged, he flung his other arm with the gym bag over the horse's neck and desperately clawed for a hold in the animal's mane. Got it. Hanging, he let the animal's massive momentum pull his own weight up. He shoved off with one foot and then was airborne, and up and over onto its back.

The horse skidded to a stop, nearly hurling him off. It shot out a hind leg, jerked itself backward. He rammed his feet into its haunches. Instantly, the animal leaped forward, seemed to stumble, then recovered and headed straight for the stone wall.

Matt felt it gather itself, the muscles quivering under him, and then the forelegs snapped up. His buttocks came off the back for a fleeting instant; then the horse's head came up, and they sailed over the stone wall.

Then they were running full out as he leaned deeply forward over the animal's neck, feeling the pound of legs coming up through his thighs and the animal's breath blowing, the warm, expelled air sweeping back and his own heart's blood ringing as they fled into the darkness.

8

His name was Alex Stolowski. He had a broad Polish face under thinning hair and a body thick with the muscle bulk of his antecedents, shift men from the Pittsburg steel foundries.

When he was twenty-four, the steel industry took a nose-dive because of foreign competition, so Alex joined the Army and served two tours with the 82nd Airborne. That was where he met Jo-Jo Azevedo. Both earned hard-stripe E5 ratings on the same day.

Now Stolowski owned a small saloon, The Antlers, in the Pioneer Square section of Seattle near the King Dome. It was an eclectic, historically restored area of boutiques and art galleries that stood alongside cheap dives, mission houses and massage parlors.

Alex was bucking beer kegs in the back room of the saloon when Azevedo peered around the door jamb. "Hey, you goddamn Polack," he said.

Alex swung around, scowling. Then his face opened into a grin. "Well, look what the wind blew out of the gutter."

They shook hands warmly, then knocked their closed fists together, street style. "Lock and load, baby," Alex said.

"Right on," Jo-Jo answered.

"So, what the hell're you doing out here again?" Stolowski asked.

"Working a trace."

"You back with the task force?" When Azevedo was with

Drug Enforcement, he had often picked up tips from Alex. At the time, Stolowski had allowed some of the better-class street ladies to work his saloon for a percentage. In return, Jo-Jo always warned him whenever a police street sweep was going down.

Azevedo shook his head. "I'm with ATF now."

"Ow," Alex said. "You the guys got your cocks caught in your zippers at Waco, huh?"

"Yeah, that was a bad scene."

They walked out into the main saloon. Jo-Jo sat at the bar. There were pictures of boxers along the back wall between a row of aluminum kegs. While Stolowski drew him a draft beer, he looked around. The place was nearly empty—just a few old men looking like out-of-work seamen and two bikers in rivet-head leathers playing shuffleboard.

"So, how're things going?" he asked.

Alex slid the glass over to him. "Well, I'm hangin' in. That's about all I can say."

"The Pioneer's changed."

Alex snorted. "Yeah, now it's upscale snobs on one side and panhandle slug junkies on the other. A real paradise."

"What kind of weight are they dealing around here now?"

"Same old shit, same old routine. Except I hear heavy crank and PCP loads are coming in from the Indian reservations."

"Yeah?"

Alex nodded and drew himself a beer. "That's what I hear."

A little girl of six came running along behind the bar. She had yellow hair clipped in a pageboy and rosy cheeks. "Daddy, Momma wants last night's 'ceipts."

Alex lifted her. "Anna, honey, you remember Jo-Jo?" he asked.

She studied Azevedo solemnly.

"Hi, sweetheart," Jo-Jo said. "You were just a baby last time I saw you. But, wow, look at you now."

"How come you got two same names?" Anna asked.

"Because my momma loved me so much, she named me twice."

Anna continued to stare at him with her grave brown eyes. Then she twisted her head away. "Momma wants the 'ceipts." Her father squeezed her, lowered her to the floor and handed over the receipts. She scooted off.

Alex leaned his thick elbows on the bar. "So, who're you tracing?"

Jo-Jo pulled a snapshot from his coat pocket, handed it over.

Stolowski studied it a moment. "Looks like a goddamned skinhead," he said.

"He's one of the top-dog skins. Name's Hans Halberstadt, a real badass from Germany."

"And you figure he's here?"

"That's what we think."

"Well, there's a lot of these swastika lowlifes around here," Alex said. "They even got their own bars. Play that goddamned screwdriver music and beat the crap out of each other on the dance floor." He shook his head. "Dumb fucks."

"Like what bars?"

"Oh, the Spiderweb over on Jackson and the Celtic Cross up near Lander." He dipped his head, looked askance at Azevedo. "Watch out, Jo-Jo, they'll smell your badge a mile away."

A young woman came up behind the bar. She was strikingly pretty with long, straight blond hair and heavily made-up eyes. She wore a red tank top under a sleeveless denim jacket.

"Alex," she said, "you're missing the Olympia tags here." She threw Jo-Jo a cold stare. "Well, if it ain't the L train. What do you want around here, Azevedo?"

"Hi, Janet," he said. "You're looking as beautiful as ever."

"Honey, you ever seen this guy before?" Stolowski asked her, holding out the photo. She glanced at it.

"Nope," she said. "Where're the tags?"

"On my desk."

Janet left.

Jo-Jo watched her go. "Still in love with me, huh?" he asked.

"Don't pay her no mind," Alex said. "She just ain't never gonna like cops."

Janet Stolowski was an ex-hooker. With her good looks and class, she'd always worked the Uptown Track: the fancy hotels and conventions. Her pimp was a sleek, Robert Redford–lookalike hotel manager named Archie Bentencort. Stolowski had met her during a convention of Airborne vets. They quickly fell in love.

Soon afterward, Alex had taken Archie out behind his hotel and beaten the hell out of him. Then he pulled a banana from his pocket, ate it and left the peel neatly laid over Bentencort's bloody face: the traditional symbol signifying that he had just stolen Archie's whore.

Jo-Jo downed his beer and took out his wallet. He put a ten-dollar bill on the bar. "Let's have another one, Polack. I always said you had the best beer in town."

"Yeah, well, go tell that to the world," Stolowski said, shoved the money away, and turned to draw another draft.

"What the hell are you telling me?" Stone roared into the cell phone. "The son of a bitch got away from you? On a fucking horse, for God sake?"

"Yeah, yeah," Fettis said. "It was that asshole, Basset. I had him, I had the bastard. Then shit-for-brains comes slamming into the toilet and *wham!* Marquette bolts."

"Didn't you go after him?"

"We made a few passes out over the boonies, but it was too dark to see anything. We'll pick it up again at first light."

Jack glared through the windshield, trying to untangle the fury in his thoughts. He gradually became aware that he was approaching a hundred miles per hour, his rage having communicated itself to his foot. He quickly eased off, felt the car heavy up. Jesus, that was all he needed now, to have a goddamned cop pull him over, and him with weapons in the vehicle.

"Where are you now?" he asked.

"The chopper needed gas, so we rousted a guy at a duster strip. He sold us a fill-up. I'm using his outside phone."

"Where's Basset?"

"Out in the chopper nursing his eye." Gus laughed. "That's the only upside thing in this. Marquette damned near gouged out his right eyeball."

Another glitch, Stone thought. Another stupid fuckup. So what now? He tried to focus on Marquette, get into his brain, anticipate what the man would do now.

The first assumption that hit him was bad. Marquette would undoubtedly steer clear of the cabin. Worse, he might start putting things together and realize Grady was a part of it. After all, who else had known he was headed east for Moses Lake aboard a goddamned bus?

Wait a minute, he thought, maybe not. He *could* figure we'd simply picked him up in Seattle and then followed him over the mountains.

Fettis said, "Jack, you still there?"

"Yeah, I'm looking at options." An eighteen-wheeler rumbled past him, tires roaring. Its turbulence rocked his car. "There's still a chance he'll dump the horse somewhere and hook a ride to the cabin."

"Yeah, but he might also tumble to Grady's part in this," Gus said. "If he does, Christ only knows where he'll head." He grunted. "I got a feeling this cat's sharper than we know. He's either been in or trained for combat."

"Why do you say that?"

"From the way he moved in that toilet. Fast and decisive. And he went straight for Basset's eyes."

A goddamned combat vet, Jack thought disgustedly. A man with survival instincts and skills. "Well, shit," he said.

"But I think you're right; he might still try for Moses Lake. You'd best cover the back door if he does."

"Okay."

"Like I said, we're going out at first light. If he's still out there, and he's gotta be, we'll spot him for sure. There ain't nothing for miles around except flat outback and that pissant spit-in-the-road store where we jumped him.''

"All right," Jack said. He had a thought. "You know, maybe this might work out after all. You take him out way the hell and gone, his body ain't likely to be found."

"That's exactly what I was thinking," Fettis said.

Lieutenant Two Elks eased his car to a stop beside the county police cruiser parked a quarter mile down the hill from Marquette's house. In the cruiser, the deputy had his head back on the seat. The lieutenant tapped his horn and the deputy jerked forward, then hurriedly rolled down the window.

"Hi, Lieutenant," he said.

Two Elks took a half-smoked cigar from between his lips. "See any sign of him?" he asked. Seated beside him was Sheriff Sergeant Bob Satterfield.

"Nothing, sir," the deputy said.

Two Elks nodded. "Okay, go log back on patrol. You figure you can stay awake long enough to do that?"

"Yes, sir," the deputy said sheepishly.

Two Elks continued on up the hill. In his rearview mirror, he watched the deputy's lights come on. Then they swung in a U-turn and headed back toward Dungeness.

In front of Marquette's house, Two Elks switched off the engine, and he and Satterfield got out. They surveyed the building for a moment. It was a three-story Victorian with a porch partially crossing the front and ending at a three-pane bay window on the right. It was painted some sort of light color, beige or cream, with dark trim on the windows and eaves.

Earlier, he had traced its owner, a Theodor Lyons living in Pasadena, California. He called Lyons to notify him that an investigation was being conducted on Marquette and that a search warrant might be executed on his building.

"My God," Lyons said. "Marquette? But he was such a nice young fella."

"Did you know him well?"

"No, just saw him a couple of times when me and the missus went north."

"Do you use a rental agent up here?"

"Oh, yes, the White Water Realty in Bellevue."

"Would they have an extra set of keys we can use?"

"Oh, yes." Then, away from the phone, "Mother, come quick. There's a policeman from Seattle says Marquette killed somebody."

"We're merely investigating that possibility, Mr. Lyons."

"My God," Lyons said.

Two Elks and Satterfield went through the wrought-iron gate and circled the house, playing their flashlights on the windows. On one side was a small kitchen porch. Around the back was another door at the head of a narrow stairway. The yard slanted down to a low bluff above a dirt road and the edge of a wheat field. Fertilizer on the wheat made the air smell like popcorn.

Two Elks posted Satterfield at the rear door and walked back around to the front. He flicked his cigar over the fence and mounted the steps. The main door had a large, egg-shaped window made of leaded glass. He checked his watch. Eight fourteen. He knocked.

"This is the Clallam County Sheriff's Department," he called out, going through the formality. "We have a warrant to execute a search of the premises."

He waited. Nothing moved. Finally, he took out the keys the realty company had delivered that afternoon. There were three on a binder ring. The second one opened the door.

He walked in, feeling along the wall for a switch. He found it, flicked it on. He was in a small hallway. Several doors led into other rooms, and a stairway was at the end. The house held the warm scent of mustiness and wool, like a quilt that had been put away for a long time.

A moment later, Satterfield came in. Both men took out surgical rubber gloves and slipped them on.

"You take the upper floors, Bobby," Two Elks said. The sergeant nodded and went up the stairs.

Two Elks walked into the room with the bay window. It was a bedroom with heavy oak furniture and a canopied bed. The bed was casually made, the coverlet merely thrown over the pillow.

He caught sight of a pair of small, gold hoop earrings on the bed stand. He picked up one, rolled it between his thumb and forefinger. Was it Kelli Pickett's? Or did Marquette have other women?

He had tried to contact Pickett three times that day, using the number Marquette had given him. Each time, he had gotten her answering machine. Pretty voice, low and full. He had explained his reason for calling on the first message but simply hung up on the others. He intended to try again in the morning. If he still couldn't raise her, he would obtain an address on the number from Northwest Pac.

The rest of the room held normal male clutter: clothes and heavy-weather gear flung on chairs, rubber work boots and dirty running shoes on the floor, two ashtrays filled with cigarette butts. He looked in the closet. There were several button-down shirts, two pairs of slacks, a leather jacket, no suit.

He went through the dresser drawers, starting at the bottom. Marquette was not adept at folding things, he noticed. His underwear, sweatshirts and Levi's were merely stuffed in. In the top drawer, he found a half-empty box of 9 mm Winchester bullets. Beside it was a folded cleaning rag smelling of gun oil. It held an indentation where a weapon had lain.

Two Elks took a plastic evidence bag from his jacket. It had a snap seal and a small card attached. He placed the ammo box in it, sealed it and scribbled a notation on the tag. He placed the bag in his pocket.

In the bathroom, he checked the medicine cabinet, the wastebasket. He examined for any stains on a pair of towels on racks and a third draped over the shower curtain rod. There was nothing.

He went across the hall and into the parlor. More dark oak furniture of the twenties: an upholstered couch with a worn plaid covering, twin wingbacks, a twenty-one-inch television. He flicked the set on. It was tuned to the Discovery Channel. He turned it off and peered into the fireplace. A small mound of ash, gray as moondust. He scanned the room, then went into what had been the dining area.

Marquette had turned it into a workout room. There was a weight rack with bar- and dumbbells, a workout bench holding a bar for bench presses, and a metal frame, bolted to the floor, suspending a speed punching bag on one side and a heavy-impact bag on chains on the other.

Two Elks walked slowly around the room, studying the equipment. He inhaled the familiar gym odor of the place: dirty socks, the musk of male crotch. And he suddenly sensed the presence of the man, even more than he had in the bedroom: the sweat of him, the exhilarated determination of him as shown by the heaviness of his free weights. He had been power lifting, actually bench-pressing over three hundred pounds with still more weights lying beside the bench.

The lieutenant moved to the metal frame, studied the leather of the speed bag, then ran his finger over the underside of the bounce-back board and along the ball joint of the bag mount. Everything was worn smooth. He glanced at the heavy bag, noted the deep indentations where Marquette's fists, carrying solid body weight, had pounded.

The man had a great deal of strength and power, he could see. But he detected something else. There was a deliberate pushing of limits here, the going-beyond-normal workouts. A frustration, an anger. Apparently, something deep had been eating at Marquette for a long time.

He wandered across the hall again and into the kitchen. It was neat, clean, white. He peered into the refrigerator. Cans of Budweiser beer, a bottle of moderately expensive Chablis—another woman's touch?—milk, eggs, a half-eaten T-bone, no vegetables or fruit. Dishes, hand-cleaned, were still in their drying rack.

He examined the note pad beside the wall telephone. There was a sketch, surprisingly well done, of a woman's head turned slightly to the side: dark hair, a pert nose and lowered eyes, the shading giving depth. Her neck was smooth and narrow. But then the pencil lines swirled and went downward to doodles of circles and three-dimensional blocks.

The sergeant came into the kitchen. Two Elks turned, gave him a questioning look. Satterfield shook his head. ''Nothing upstairs, John. Doesn't look like he even goes up there much.''

They entered the room connected to the kitchen. It had a door leading out to the small porch. There were a washer and dryer and some housecleaning items. Marquette had also used it to store some of his gear. Two pairs of large scuba tanks with regulators attached leaned against the back wall, along with swim fins, a lead weight belt, assorted fishing equipment and heavy rolls of nylon netting yarn.

Nearby, hung on a wall peg, was another yellow rubber raincoat. Satterfield felt over it. His eyebrows suddenly lifted, and he said, ''Oh, yeah.'' He pulled the coat away. Under it was a wide leather belt carrying a knife in a military-green canvas scabbard. The canvas was darkly stained.

Carefully, he pulled open the snap and extracted the knife, holding the butt delicately between his fingers. He and Two Elks examined it closely under the light. The haft was wrapped with compressed leather rings from pommel to hilt. The leather was scored from use and had turned dark brown. The blade itself was black, epoxy-coated and about seven inches long, with a deep blood groove. Stamped on the hilt were the letters *USMC*.

It was a Marine Ka-Bar.

On the forward side of the crossguard and along the groove were streaks of dark, dried material. Satterfield sniffed at them, glanced at Two Elks.

He nodded. ''It's blood, all right.''

9

Under the oval glass viewer of the magnifier, the photos of the sphere's insides were blurry, their light-and-shadow interfaces attenuated by ray defraction. Kelli paused a moment, then continued to scan slowly, watching for something that would catch the eye—a mark, a glitch in the milling, any clue that might suggest the sphere's ultimate purpose.

She was alone in the Data Aquisition Machine room of the CRYSTALBALL lab. It contained several SunSPARC workstations carrying high-speed digital and ATM links for instantaneous access to databases around the world.

It was now 10:45 P.M.

After dropping Matt at the bus terminal, she had returned to the lab and found the crew already rerunning the previous day's aborted wind-vector simulations. For the rest of the afternoon, she tried to concentrate. It was no use. She was edgy, distracted. She continually missed Gilhammer's sequence cues.

Troy frowned but said nothing. The other crew members gave her studied looks. Apparently, they had found out about Matt's boat fire and the twin deaths aboard.

At six o'clock, Troy had called for a complete shutdown. He had decided to give everyone the evening off. He walked over to Kelli's console and sat on the edge of her desk.

"You weren't with us today, Kel," he said quietly.

"I know. I'm sorry."

He rolled his candy drop around his mouth. "I guess it was Marquette you wanted the attorney for. You want to talk about it?"

"No. But thanks."

"They don't honestly suspect him of anything like this, do they?"

"I guess they're investigating everything. He's just a part of it."

He nodded, inhaled and slipped off the desk. "Look, why don't you go on home. Take a long bath, have a few hits of wine. Things'll look better in the morning."

"Thanks, Troy."

She tried to follow his advice; sat in her copper tub, sipped Chablis and waited for Matt's call. He should have long since reached Grady's cabin, she knew. Why didn't he call? Her thoughts kept gathering a dark momentum that eventually forced her from the tub. Draped in a towel, she prowled the houseboat.

Anxiety was a confusing emotion for Kelli. It always carried with it a sense of helplessness, of vulnerability. Throughout most of her life, a natural optimism and innate awareness of capability had firewalled her against such disabling submersions. Of course, there had been moments of frustration, the acceptable jolts of normalcy.

But what to do in total impotence, when the firewalls were breached? Like when her mother died, two years before. Kelli had been in Sarasota, Florida, attending a conference on artificial intelligence. Just before lunch, a call had come in from her dad.

"I think you'd better come home right away." His voice was soft. Did it tremble? "Your mother had a stroke this morning."

"Oh, my God!"

"The doctors say—I—God—they don't think she has much of a chance." He began to sob.

Kelli had never heard her father cry. It frightened her. His voice was so soft and fragile and vulnerable. She had caught the first plane out, and all the somber way back to California she had felt an overwhelming sense of powerlessness against what was happening, inwardly knowing that it had already happened.

Now that same unnerving sense of disintegration and collapse was rushing at her, coiling itself around her heart. Had those men found Matt? Was he already dead? A stone terror was building.

By nine o'clock, she could no longer bear doing nothing. She hurriedly dressed and drove back to the campus. Before going upstairs, she checked one of the Physics research stations on the first floor of Guggenheim. She found two grad students working and talked them into letting her borrow a portable magnifying viewer.

Now she flipped another photo under the glass. So far, she'd been using 50x magnification. To go higher would have caused total blur. Still, she decided something might show in a higher amalgam. She clicked the viewer to 100x.

Now the pixel arrays were clearly visible. She scanned. At first, it was merely a meaningless skim over rectangular dot cells. But she noticed something she had missed before: a brightness throughout the entire inner surface of the globe. It resembled the facet refraction of the central core.

She leaned back. Could the inner surface of the sphere be coated with some sort of microscopic layer of crystals?

She continued her scan. On the third photo, something else appeared. It was a tiny squiggle in the barrel of the needle assembly. She had almost slid right past it. She delicately eased the photo back. There it was. She squinted at it. A scratch?

She clicked the magnifier to its maximum level of 150x. Instantly, the thing leaped at her. Only the bottom of it was visible, but it was clearly a deliberate mark. A two-turn helix. She elevated the photo, bringing the top of the mark into view. The helix was connected to the letter Z. A company trademark stamped into the barrel.

"Yes!" she cried.

She slid her chair over to one of the SunSPARC workstations. Checking the URL directory for the site address of the

U.S. Patent Office, she quickly accessed its main database. She scrolled through the file menu and chose the Registry of Trademarks and Symbol Assignments. She typed in a short description of the Z-helix and requested a search of the files.

Two minutes later, the computer buzzed. The search had revealed two helix-Zs. Neither matched the one in the sphere.

"Dammit!"

She got up, wandered around the room. And like a tiger leaping from brush, the anxiety lashed at her again. She glanced at the clock. 11:23. Nine hours since Matt had left.

She phoned the houseboat on the chance he had called there. It rang three times and clicked, and her voice came on. She punched in her code and listened to the message playback. There was Two Elks's message, then another. A man. Her heart leaped.

"Hi, Kel." It was Gilhammer. She heard music behind his voice. "Thought I'd give a ring, see if you're okay. Hope you're not picking up because you're asleep. See you in the morning."

She paced some more and felt a sudden, overwhelming hunger for a cigarette. She'd quit cold turkey six months before. For a brief moment, she fought it but finally said, "Oh, what the hell," and went hunting through desks. She found a crumpled pack of Kools and a Bic lighter, went out into the hall and lit up.

The menthol-laced smoke made her dizzy.

Gradually, she calmed down, started thinking. A thought emerged. Maybe she'd been searching in the wrong place. Matt had recovered the sphere in the sea, where the mysterious helicopter had been expecting to pick it up. So that could only mean the thing had come in from somewhere overseas. Across the Pacific.

She stamped out the cigarette and scurried back to the DAM room.

For the next hour, Kelli probed the national government databases of high-tech industrial countries along the rim of the western Pacific, accessing trademark registry files. Japan, South Korea, Hong Kong, Australia. When she found nothing there, she moved farther west, to Singapore, Thailand and India.

It was a complex balancing act, but still she came up with nothing.

She went out for another smoke. Afterward, she started to access European databases. The Common Market, the UN International Trade Classification Committee, UNIDO's *Continental Industry and Development Reports* out of Vienna. On and on, one database giving references to others.

At twelve forty-one, she hit pay dirt. From Germany's *Direktorat für Korperschaftlich Patentiers*, she obtained a perfect Z-helix match. It turned out to be the registered logo of a pharmaceutical and surgical instrument fabrication company in Frankfurt, named Tierkreis-Wickeln.

The file also gave her the company's Internet address.

The two prostitutes looked young, upper teenaged. Both were classy in sheath dresses with little jeweled evening bags and well-applied makeup. One was small, with golden hair and dimples; the other, heavier, about five-foot-four and a hundred and sixty pounds, heavy-breasted and buttocked but still shapely.

The heavier one smiled, showing perfectly straight teeth. "Good evening," she said. Dog caught her giving him a fleeting up-and-down. "You were expecting us?"

Dog James laughed nervously, glanced back at Halberstadt, came around again. "Yeah, yeah, we were. Come on in." He stepped aside and caught the faint, sweet trail of their perfume as they passed.

Over the past nine hours, James had learned caution. During the ride west out of Idaho, Halberstadt had been goof-crazy: one minute silent, sullen, glaring out through the windshield of Dog's 1989 Chevy four-wheel-drive pickup as its snow tires growled, the next minute going off into screaming German tirades.

Once he had suddenly slapped Dog across the right cheek. "*Verdammt, Scheisskerl!*" Spoken in a growling tone, an angry Arnold Schwarzenegger.

"Jesus," Dog yelped. "What in hell you do that for?"

"Loog at me when I speeg at you."

"Jesus."

And then Hans had giggled and hugged him, planted a wet kiss on his face. He smelled of chemical sweat and gross power.

Around eight that night, they had stopped for gas at a small roadside mom-and-pop outside Tyler, Washington. The proprietor was an old man with a phlegmy cough and a beautiful white Persian cat that purred beside the cash register.

Hans cooed to it, tickled it under the chin. Then, while the old man was out filling another customer's tank, he had, with a quick snap, broken the animal's neck and draped its carcass over the Hostess pastry rack.

Sweet Mother of Jesus, James thought, jolted. Even during the fiercest, bloodiest three-hour battles in his Swan Falls pit, he had never been so repulsed. This kind of killing was for nothing. Sick.

As they climbed the Cascades and hit snow, Halberstadt had stripped off his clothes and opened all the windows, the snowflakes whipping in like icy little puffs of cotton. Dog froze his ass off but hunkered down and kept his silence.

Once across the mountains, they had stopped at North Bend, thirty miles from the outskirts of Seattle. He followed his instructions and called the number he'd been given for their Seattle contact.

A woman answered immediately, even though it was nearly midnight. "Yes?" she said in a rich, throaty voice.

"Yeah, hey, we're here," Dog said.

"Who is this, please?"

"Leroy James and friend."

"Ah, yes." A smile came into the voice. "I've been expecting you, Mr. James. Where are you calling from?"

"A bar in North Bend."

"All right, would you care to proceed directly to your hotel in the city? Or perhaps stop there for the night? I imagine you must be exhausted."

"Yeah, I'm that, all right."

"Then I'll arrange accomodations for you at the Blue Pine Lodge." She gave him directions to it from the freeway. "Everything's taken care of, Mr. James. Now, do you intend to retire immediately, or would you care for some company?"

"Yeah, okay, we'll go for that."

"Do you have any preferences?"

"Just one," Dog said and sniggered. "My friend says he likes his a little *fettig*. You know *fettig*?"

"Indeed. He prefers a companion with a fuller figure."

"Hey, how come you know German?" James asked, surprised. He thought he would stump her.

The woman laughed. "In my business, knowing several languages always proves profitable."

"How about that."

"After tonight, a suite has already been arranged for you at the Seneca House Hotel in Seattle. You won't have any trouble finding it; it's just off Madison and East Union Street. Now, when you're settled there, call me and I'll dispatch your limo service."

Limo service? Dog thought.

"The driver already has your entire itinerary, and everything's taken care of. One thing, though. If you decide to deviate from the schedule, please notify the driver ahead of time so we can adjust."

"Sure thing."

"Well, thank you, Mr. James. We'll certainly try to make your stay here as pleasant as possible."

Now the girls strolled into the room, smiling, laying their bags on the bed stand. They looked at Halberstadt. He was sitting naked on the floor in the corner, grinning crank-eyed at them, his dark pubic hair and thick, flaccid penis flagrant.

The girls exchanged a quick glance. Then the petite one said, "Well, you certainly believe in being ready, don't you, honey?" She put her hand behind her back and began to unzip her dress.

The other did the same. "So, how's it going to be, boys?" she asked. "Who gets what?"

Dog felt himself oddly embarrassed, flushing. It wasn't that he was against occassional adultery. He had cheated on his wife in the past—a hot-pants waitress here, a faded lady with too much alcohol in her brain at the local honky-tonk there. But these girls were goddamn *beautiful*. He had a fleeting moment of terror that he might not be able to get it up.

Halberstadt watched the stout one. When she got down to nothing but stockings and a black garter belt, he hissed appreciatively. *"Ah, Du bist ein Schatz,"* he murmured. *"Dien Titten machst mich ganz heiss."*

She said, "What's that you're talking there, honey? Is that German?"

"Yeah, it's German," James said.

"What'd he just say?"

"Beats me."

"Can't he speak English?"

"Sure he can."

"Is he a skin?" the smaller girl asked, a tiny frown on the perfect skin between her eyes.

"Hell, he ain't no skin," Dog said.

"Well, I got a feeling he's mine," the stout girl said. She crossed the room and squatted in front of Halberstadt. "Am I right, honey?" She ran her fingers over his shaved head. Hans nuzzled her breasts and put his hand against her vagina. He roughly shoved two fingers in.

"Oh, easy, honey," the girl said. "Mama likes gentle. Come on, let's go utilize that nice big bed."

Halberstadt came to his feet with a clean, lunging litheness. He kissed the prostitute, then bent and picked her up. She squealed, delighted. He carried her to the bed and dropped her. She bounced, laughing, her huge breasts with their dark, thumb-sized nipples jiggling.

The other girl led James to a green satin loveseat. She gently eased him down into it, rubbed his crotch and nuzzled his ear. "Mmm," she said and ran her tongue around his earlobe. She began to unbutton his fly.

Dog inhaled the incense of the girl, the light lemoniness of perfume, the warm bouquet of her skin. He glanced over at Hans and his whore. The woman was blowing him, her head bobbing up and down while Halberstadt's own head swiveled slowly back and forth. He grimaced at the ceiling and uttered soft Teutonic invective through his teeth.

Oh, Lord, Dog thought and heard his girl chuckle, felt her fingers on his penis. It was shriveled.

"Come on, honey," she whispered, all hot-breathed. "Relax and let Connie make nice."

Across the room, Halberstadt growled suddenly, a guttural sound like the kind a man would make in a fight. Dog glanced around again. The German was dragging his whore by the hair, bringing her up to him. Her face was contorted as she tried to push him off. He manhandled her, swung her body around and lifted her buttocks.

"Goddammit," the girl yelled. "No!"

Dog's girl turned around. "Hey, what the hell you think you're doing?" she cried. She started to get off Dog's lap.

Halberstadt had positioned himself behind the whore's buttocks, holding her up and open by the hips. She squirmed and wriggled frantically, her head down, croaking and half-squealing, "No, I can't that way. Please, I can't."

"You bastard!" Dog's girl yelled, then snapped around and looked at him. "Stop the son of a bitch, for God sake. Adele can't ass-fuck. She just had a hemorrhoid operation."

Adele gave a tight scream as Halberstadt forced himself into her rectum, probing and ramming, going in slowly at first and then all the way. The whore groaned and dropped her head to the bed.

The next minute for Dog James was an eternity. He sat immobilized. Connie had finally flung herself to her feet, raced across the room and started shrieking and beating Halberstadt's shoulders with her tiny clenched fists as he thrust with rapid, powerful lunges and Adele writhed and whimpered below him.

Suddenly, he arched, and all the molded tendons of his body rose into flex state as if he were straining to lift a great stone. He quivered. Again. And still again. Then he relaxed and withdrew, flopped onto his back on the bed and looked at the ceiling, eyes half-lidded, momentarily sated.

Connie got Adele off the bed, holding her up, Adele walking stiffly. Her face was pale, makeup-smeared and tear-moistened. Connie quickly gathered up their clothes and purses.

"You fucking bastards," she yelled. "Oh, you goddamn shits. You wait, we'll fix you." They left, still partially undressed. Dog listened to them going off down the hall.

He finally breathed. On the bed, the German stretched sensuously, one hand toying idly with his still partially engorged organ. It glistened with drying semen that bore flecks of blood.

He finally turned his head and stared at Dog. Slowly, the stone hardness came into his eyes, the snake's glare. "*Willst du was, Hund?*" he said.

What? Dog quickly looked away. He felt his heart pounding. He sat very still and listened for someone to come up the hall to take them away. No one ever did.

Kelli's screen said:

```
SYN: 04:03:25
TIERKREIS-WICKELN KORPERSCHAFT (NET-TWK)
PHARMAZEUTISH/WERKSEUGEN MEDIZINISCH
SILBERSTRASSE 137
CH-11781 FRANKFURT
BUNDESREPUBLIK DEUTSCHLAND

NETNAME: TWK
NETNUMBER: 130.87.0.0

ABTEILUNGALEITER:
MESSINGER, FRITZ (FM88) BBKF@ID.TKK.CA
#22 58 88 3967
```

She scrolled the screen, scanning what she assumed were the names and IDs of other corporate officers along with company departments and managerial heads. Then the screen went blank for a moment, returning with a brilliant montage of whirling, intercoiling color variations of the Z-helix theme. Over it was an electronic female voice speaking in German.

She logged off, got up and walked around, arms folded over her breast, goose-fleshy in the chill air. From the SYN notation, she knew it was now 4:03 P.M. in Germany. That meant company personnel were still at their workstations, making it dicey to go prowling through files.

She considered waiting until the official workday ended. No, that would burn an hour or more. There could even be a night force on. And systems could be shut down for the evening or have security firewalls up.

She rubbed her face, ran fingers through her hair. ''You gotta do it now, girl,'' she said aloud.

But first she needed something else. Returning to her computer, she quickly accessed the university's library database. Within seconds, she'd downloaded the complete *Langenscheidt Standard German Dictionary*.

Next, she exited and then re-entered the Internet, only this time logging in from a remote, masked location so as not to compromise the CRYSTALBALL lab machine. She chose Denver. Lots of hackers and ankle-biters were there, she knew. Her new code name: SPHERE.

Through the remote, she quickly accessed Tierkreis-Wickeln again. She paused and mentally ran through basic hacker techniques. Rdist. Sendmail-e. Phoenix-t. She discarded these as too obvious. She chose instead to use the IP spoofing attack.

This attack was predicated on a weakness in the technical communications instructions for Internet traffic known as the TCP/IP system. By first overwhelming the Synchronize-Acknowledge sequence of TWK's data system with a flurry of Remote Procedure Calls, she could filter out the system's main sequence code. With this, she would then locate a "trust" computer within the system, gain its acceptance as root, and be able to roam the entire company system freely.

Kelli began her attack, her fingers keystroking with rapid sureness. Within four minutes, she'd gained root status. Next, she typed in a "sniffer" search command, a scan order to hunt out certain specific words within the company's files: *Kristal* (crystal), *Kristalkammer* (crystal-chamber), *Kugel* (sphere).

Almost instantly, a deluge of data began to scroll across her screen: inventory reports, fabrication schematics, e-mail files, sales statistics, on and on, nearly all of it in German.

She shoved herself to her feet and went out for another cigarette. The anxieties over Matt started again, an iciness down the spine. But she forced them from her mind, focused instead on the hacking problem. Before her cigarette was completely smoked, she had figured a new approach.

Once more at her computer, she said, "Okay, assholes, let's try it this way."

Now she focused solely on the corporation's chief executive officer's personal e-mail file, tightening down her scan focus to pick out only data that contained all three of her key words. Instantly, it was displayed. Two letters, a string of intercompany memos.

She studied the letters. The ID heading of one indicated it had come from a *Shausyau (Hauptfach)* Cheu Xinin, Beijing, CJK (China). The second was also from Cheu Xinin, but this one had originated from Hu nyau-Ge *Lujyunyiywan (Krankanhaus-Militarisch)*, Kunming, CJK (China).

The letters were from someone in Beijing and Kunming, China.

She copied the German references in the headings, then scanned through the memos, quickly noting that the same letter-number set headed each memo: HGL-0147N. A work order?

She returned to the company's main database and typed in the letter-number set. Data began to scroll. It looked like technical design and fabrication instructions. Then came

10

To the west, snow clouds were still clinging to the high ridges of the Cascades, their dark, puffy edges faintly etched with starlight. Marquette headed toward them in the face of a downslope wind that, freighted with the bite of the high snows, numbed his face and hands.

Far to the east and south, the sky was open. In the clean, wind-buffed air, the stars appeared sharp, as if a billion shotgun pellets had punctured holes in the sky's mantle to disclose a shimmering, white-hot field beyond.

He had been slowly walking his horse for the past thirty minutes. The animal picked its way gingerly through nopal and creosote brush. Now and then, they crossed the sandy sponginess of a gravel wash. He glanced at his watch. The luminous dials showed that it was nearly one in the morning.

He reached a stand of willow trees. The bare branches went straight up and looked like skeletal sentinels in the night. Nearby was a small stream, no more than a few inches deep. He dismounted and led the horse to the edge of the water. It blew noisily and then dipped its head and drank.

The stream water looked black as it murmured over the bottom stones. On its surface, the stars' reflections danced and whirled. He squatted and let his fingers drag in the water. Its cold stung his flesh.

He stood and leaned against the horse's side. At first, the animal shied, sidestepping. Then it settled, turned and looked at him and finally drank again. He could feel its massive warmth, smell its earthy, prairie scent. He closed his eyes, and the anger in him was like a bright light. . . .

After the first, wild flight from the store, Matt had driven the horse hard out into darkness. From behind him had suddenly come the sound of the helicopter engine turning over and then the solid whomping rap of its blades.

He had twisted to look in time to see the aircraft pull pitch and shoot up into the air, its lights spinning threads up into the whirling blades. It dipped hard and came sweeping after him. The spotlight popped on and cut a tunnel through the darkness.

Frantically, he had searched the shadowed landscape for a place to hide. A willow stand rose to his right. He made for it, went down into a shallow wadi, the horse dropping sharply, its front legs braced. Then they were level again. Matt hauled back on the hackamore and the horse stopped, snorting and throwing its head.

The wadi was suddenly filled with the cracking roar of the chopper. Its lights skimmed overhead, disappeared for a moment beyond the opposite limestone wall. Then it was back, farther down the wadi, its spotlight illuminating the rocky sides. It turned again, and Matt saw the spotlight beam touch for a moment the tops of the nearby willow trees. It made them shine like white sketch lines against the farther dark.

He moved up the wadi and watched as the helo continued its sweeps, back and forth and around in wide, sharply rolling circles, the spot probing the ground. He moved still farther up the incline and then came up out of the wadi and headed due west, away from the probing light. After a few minutes, the helo gave it up, turned southwest and was soon swallowed by the night.

The country Matt found himself in was high plateau desert—rolling, grassy hills and low caprock mesas. Then he crossed close to the edge of a winter wheat field and, afterward, a long stretch of alfalfa, the air heady with green sweetness. Now and then, he encountered small herds of cattle. Once he was startled by the sudden, rushing pound of hoofbeats as antelope fled his approach.

Farther and farther he had drawn away from the interstate. The land grew even darker, punctuated occasionally by the lights of a farmhouse that looked deceptively close in the clear air. To the southwest lay a town, its lights casting a fused glow upward as if it were a mound of radium.

As he had ridden, the anger he had first experienced at the bus depot grew in heat and power. He felt it in his shoulders, in the pressure on his temples, a flaming in the blood. It drew up old instincts, long dormant, hidden things rising through layers of darkness into shadow and finally sunlight.

In its glare loomed the single name of John Wayne Grady. . . .

He now remounted and rode on. His legs and buttocks were beginning to ache. Steadily, the night deepened with cold. His breath and that of his horse fumed and were whipped away by the wind. But in it now, he caught the spicy fragrance of river willows like fresh-baked berry bread, and the moister, rawer smell of masses of cold, moving water. He figured it must be the Columbia River somewhere up ahead.

He came to a cross fence, turned and followed it southwest until he reached a dirt road with a cattle guard. The horse balked at the guard, backing and jostling. He urged it forward, digging his heels into its flanks. It refused for a moment, then gathered itself and jumped across. They went on.

He heard the sound under the wind: a sharp squealing, like chalk being drawn across a blackboard, in it a sharp metallic clank. It came from his left. Curious, he turned toward it, moving over ground that was suddenly, oddly rutted.

It turned out to be a small windmill with a huge stock tank at its base. Beside the windmill stood a flat-roofed, one-room line shack built of boulders. Connected to it on the leeward side was a lean-to. The area smelled of cattle and wet manure.

He dismounted and, leading the horse, poked around the shack and finally knocked on the door. It was made of wood with a sheet of corrugated iron nailed across its face. The shack was silent save for the soft wail of the wind around its eaves.

He let the horse drink, then tied it in the lean-to and went into the shack. It was frigid and musty and carried the stench of tallow and slaughtered meat. He moved slowly around, his hands out in front of him. His knee struck something. A metal bunk. Another. Then the edge of a stove. On the stove shelf, he found a box of kitchen matches and lit one.

The room was like a cave. Spare harness hung from metal pegs drilled into the stone. The two bunks had thin, rolled mattresses and faded Indian blankets. A kerosene hurricane lantern hung from one of the cross beams. He shook it, then lifted the glass and lit the wick.

Using kindling from a sawed-in-half fifty-gallon drum, he got the stove going. While it warmed the room, he rummaged around, found some canned goods and a small bag of oatmeal. He took the oatmeal and one of the blankets outside. The horse nuzzled at the bag. He opened it and put it on the ground. He covered the horse with the blanket, retrieved his gym bag and went back inside.

He added wood to the stove and extinguished the lantern. He lay in the darkness, smelling the fetid, crotchy odor of the blanket. Nearby, the stove ticked with heat. Outside, the wind soughed against the eaves and made the door tremble.

Slowly, the wildness in him banked, and fatigue crept through his body, coming up through his legs, into his chest, like a narcotic. Drowsily, he focused on Kelli's face, suspended it in his mind.

Then a stiletto-sharp thought suddenly struck through. His eyes snapped open. What if his pursuers had gotten to Kelli? Forced her to tell them where he was? Had killed her!

He quickly discarded that possibility and calmed once more. There was no way these men could have picked him up that quickly in Seattle. No, he was certain it had been Grady. A Judas goat. Against all the odds, the attorney was somehow involved in this thing.

His eyes closed again. I'll find you, you son of a bitch, he thought. At first light, I'll move again, get across the river and hitch a ride back to the city. Squeeze your fucking neck between my fingers until you lay it all out. Yes.

He fell asleep.

Through the Starlight scope, the terrain was washed in dim, greenish light. Marquette scanned the field. Nothing moved in the swamp grass. He lowered the scope, listening, listening. Mosquitoes droned near his head. A spider the size of a saucer crawled softly across his hand. He brushed it away.

Suddenly, the metallic chunk of a weapon bolt sounded through the darkness. Throat going suddenly dry, Matt jammed the scope to his eyes. Less than sixty yards away, dozens of VC had lifted out of the grass, coming forward, their bodies dark silhouettes in the scope's green moonlight.

His heart leapt in his chest like a small animal exploding from its hole. Then he was firing. Tracers sliced the darkness like bolts of lightning. From his right and left came the throaty thunder of M60 machine guns, Stoners, the cannon-like slams of Mark 1 twelve-gauges.

The return fire swept over them in a fierce wind . . . again . . . a tumultuous screaming, rising, weaving through the gunfire. Himself bellowing. A thump, and then an M203 parachute flare arched into the night and burst, flooding the scene with hot, white sunlight.

He braced his legs, the fever in his blood now, coming up out of the mud and waist-high water, the others rising and plunging forward to collide head-on with the scattering VC, and the moments devolving down into separate black-and-white, stop-motion images of men and shadow and sound. While above the battle, the incandescent ball of phosphorus light hung in a close heaven . . .

He lunged up, still in the dream, feeling the sultry night heat, the wild pounding of his heart and there, the flare, holding motionless at eye level.

He put his hand up to shade his face from its light. The dream suddenly dissolved, and he was in a stone room. Silhouetted against the door-rectangle of pale-gray dawn light

was a man with a cowboy hat and long horse coat, and a
rifle in his hand, the muzzle resting against his boot. In his
other hand was a flashlight.

"What in hell you doin' here, mister?" the man said.

"Who are you?"

"I'm askin' the questions. What are you doin' here?"

Matt released his breath, wiped his hand across his forehead. He was sweating. "I was out riding last night and got
lost. I figured I'd get out of the cold until first light."

"Where you from?"

"East."

"Where east?"

"From one of those farmhouses back about ten miles. A
relative of mine lives there."

"What's his name?"

"Marquette."

"Never heard of him." The man was silent for a moment.
Then he waved the beam of the flashlight. "Light the lantern," he said. "They's matches on the stove there."

The kerosene light disclosed a tall man of about fifty, nar-
row-featured with a stubble of beard. He wore a sweat-
stained robber Stetson and a dirty neckerchief, and his horse
coat was made of yellow rubber with a black corduroy collar.
His rifle was an old Winchester 94 carbine, the metal buffed
gray from use.

The cowboy surveyed him silently, his eyes lingering on
the gym bag. He said, "You know you on private land?"

Matt nodded. "I figured that when I crossed the fence. But
I was hoping to strike a house, ask directions."

"Well, mister, you damned lucky it wasn't the old man
found you out here." He squinted. "Chris', you got this
place hotter'n a steam bath."

He crossed the room, took a battered pot from the wall
and went outside. Matt followed. The dawn was coming in
strongly now, the air sharp-cold and crystalline as if it were
made of molecules of glass. The land stretched off, hills
grassier than those around the store, with scattered patches

of wild blue chicory looking pale, almost white, in the gray light.

The cowboy's horse, a big buckskin, was cropping grass near the stock tank. Its saddle and rifle scabbard were black from sweat and wear. There was a lariat coiled across the pommel and a soogan tied behind.

The cowboy took a small cloth sack from his roll, walked over to the stock tank and dipped the pot in. He nodded toward Matt's horse. "Untie him an' let him browse."

"He'll run off."

"Why? He's your horse, ain't he? 'Sides, he'll chummy with mine."

They returned to the cabin, and the cowboy made coffee— grounds straight in the pot along with a thumbnail of salt. They drank it from chipped enameled cups. It was steamy and bitter as wormwood, but it went down hot into Marquette's chest, infusing outward.

The cowboy sat silently watching him, the Winchester resting against his right thigh. Outside the open door, the light steadily brightened, the grayness slipping out of the land, and strong colors coming.

Finally, the cowboy put down his empty cup. He took off his hat, scratched his forehead where the skin was stark white, put it on again. He stood, bringing the muzzle of the carbine up, pointed at Marquette.

"Okay, mister," he said. "They's enough light now. Let's you and me get started."

"What?"

"You got some explainin' to do." He nodded his head toward the outside. "I happen to know who owns that horse out there. An' his name ain't Marquette."

The helicopter came at them down low, skimming the hills, the sound of its blades muffled, absorbed by the open space. Then, seconds before it reached them, Marquette heard it, the distant popping slap of the blades. His horse's ears pricked forward as he caught it, too. The adrenaline hit Matt's heart like a sledgehammer.

He and the cowboy had been moving slowly along a shallow draw, Matt ahead a few yards, the horses walking over bunch grass still prickly with frost. The cowboy rode with the carbine across his thighs, whistling softly to himself.

Marquette twisted around and screamed, "Get down! Take cover!" In a single motion, he came off his horse, his eyes searching the earth. Behind him, the cowboy reined in, his mouth open, the carbine coming up.

The chopper hurled into sight, so close that Matt saw the bottom carriage clearly, the pontoons streaked with take-off oil. The bubble looked as polished as a crystal ball, the sun glistening on it and the two men, one leaning far out with a yellow windbreaker and dark glasses and a black machine pistol at the end of his extended arm. The aircraft swept past, its downdraft hurling a wind that smelled of hot engine and flattened the grass.

Matt dove for a small castle of rock, hit and rolled, pressing as tightly as he could against the stone. It still held the night's cold. Behind him, the cowboy was fighting hard to settle his horse, but the animal, spooked by the sudden roar of the helicopter, reared and skittered wildly. Matt's mount had taken off, panicked, up the draw.

The first volley of rounds came, blowing silently out of the aircraft's overriding noise. The bullets slammed into the ground in two distinct groupings, tearing divits of grass. Another burst, this one across open dirt. It threw dust puffs that were instantly dissipated by the downdraft.

The last of the burst struck the cowboy and his horse. With the impact, the man twisted sharply in the saddle, grabbing at his chest. His horse seemed to lift suddenly off its forelegs. It rolled in the air, screaming, and came down on its side, the rider still under it. There was blood all over its neck, bright in the sunlight. It thrashed its legs and tried to regain its feet, but couldn't.

The chopper had dipped into a hard turn, pitching as its momentum slew it out of sight beyond the grass ridge. Instantly, Marquette was up, running full out toward the downed horse and rider.

` He caught sight of the Winchester lying in the grass, bent to scoop it up, then launched himself into the air. He landed on the buckskin's flank, twisted over and fell onto the cowboy's boot. The man appeared dead, gray-pale, his wide eyes blankly staring at the sky. The horse had stopped screaming. It kept trying to lift its head, and a great, heaving moan came from deep in its chest.

The helicopter appeared again, sweeping over the grass ridge as if shot from a hydraulic chute. Matt saw the gun flashes and burrowed down deep against the horse's struggling body. He could feel the terrible heat of terror coming off it. Its flesh quivered as the rounds struck it with dull, heavy, absorbing impacts, as if someone were beating the animal with a baseball bat.

The chopper passed. Matt rose slightly, jacked a round into the rifle's chamber. Seventy yards away, the aircraft tilted sharply to come back. For a brief moment it seemed to hang motionless in the air as the pilot countered its forward momentum.

Marquette fired, the Winchester bucking sharply against his shoulder. He saw the round go through the bubble. It blew a spidery pattern of cracks in the Plexiglas. Below it, the pilot jerked backward.

Keeping the rifle butt against his shoulder, he continued to jack in rounds, firing immediately. On the third shot, he caught the faint, tinny slam as a bullet struck the blades. The next bullet made a spark of hot metal fly off the rotor's swash plate.

Then the craft was sweeping back toward him, still tilted over sharply. He hugged the buckskin, felt the craft go directly over him, felt the blades cutting through the air only a few feet away, their tips sundering it with the sizzling, cracking reverberations of artillery rounds.

A second later, the blade tips struck the grass ridge. Huge chunks of grass and sod and rock were hurled outward as the helicopter, engine screaming, plowed a raw, dark-earth swath across the top of the ridge, then slammed over, upside down, disappearing from Matt's vision.

He heard it crash, a metallic, iron collision like empty freight cars coming together. There was a wild hissing, then a deep, ground-jarring explosion. A concussion wave riffled over him, and he saw a huge ball of fire laced with white smoke hurtle upward, felt a sudden in-sucking of air.

Marquette lay still for a long moment, feeling his body pounding violently, his nerves and flesh and blood riding electricity. At last, he came to his knees. He could hear the chopper's wreckage and grass burning fiercely just beyond the draw's ridge. He bent to the cowboy, touched his throat.

The man's eyes moved, stared at him in a kind of forlorn, glassy bewilderment. His breath came in wet gasps. In the sunlight, his gray-black beard stubble looked as if his lower face had been sprayed with sugar and pepper. His tongue flicked between his lips.

"Kill my . . . horse," he croaked. "Jesus God . . . I can't stand . . . kill him."

Marquette did.

11

"Damn your black soul," Annabelle Frost said with cool, bitter rage.

"Duchess," Grady said, a morning smile in his voice. He thought: Oh, oh, trouble. "You sound a mite peeved this morning, darlin'."

"How dare you expose my girls to that Germanic cretin."

Germanic cretin? Halberstadt. Shit. "Ah?" Grady said. Although it was only 6:58 A.M., he was already at his office. One of the man's attributes was a tendency for early toil. "We have a problem?"

"No, *you* have a problem," she said.

Annabelle "Duchess" Frost was the progeny of one of the oldest lumber-baron families in the Northwest. She was forty-two, a product of the elitism of Sarah Lawrence and Princeton. She could speak seven languanges fluently and exuded chic elegance like a Tiffany vase.

Seven years earlier, strictly from ennui, she had created a "companion service" business, a crème-de-la-crème prostitution operation that catered only to the internationally well-heeled. Her telephone exchange and fax number could be found in little black books all over the world.

"That degenerate anal-raped one of my girls," she said.

Anal-raped, he thought. Sounded like a damned DA. "You're telling me he butt-fucked a hooker."

"Don't refer to them as hookers."

"I still ain't seeing the problem."

"Adele wasn't catalogued for that activity," Duchess said. "Besides, she'd had a recent operation. The whole thing was extremely traumatic for her."

"Okay, I see now," he said. "Well, the next time, just send out a hook—a girl who specializes in that kind of action. Problem solved."

"There won't be a next time," she said. "I'm canceling our contract."

"Whoa, hold on a minute here," he said. "Look, this operation's important to me, Duchess. You pull out now, you're gonna be dead-centering me."

Duchess remained silent.

"Okay, what say I add a little earnest money here," Grady said.

More silence.

"Come on, hon, negotiate with me."

She said, "All right. Let's just triple your fee."

"Double it."

A considering pause, then: "Double only if you cover my girl's medical expenses."

"Done."

"All right."

"And you keep the original itinerary?"

"Yes."

Grady relaxed. "Look, Duchess, it's only gonna be another twenty-four hours. Soon's them boys are on that ferry tomorrow morning, you all are home free."

"I'm looking forward to that moment," she said. "But be forewarned, Grady. If any of my girls is seriously injured, I'll make you sorry."

"Oh, that hurts," he said.

Annabelle Frost sniffed with contempt. "Well, as your German friend might say, *Das ist mir scheissegal*."

"What's that mean?"

"Look it up," she said and was gone.

Grady laughed as he put down the receiver. He eased back into his chair. But his smile faded quickly. That animal Halberstadt, he thought. He knew the bastard was going to cause rain on the corn. A fucking loose cannon with crank for brain tissue. But he also knew he had no choice. Without Halberstadt, Keck wouldn't deal.

He pulled his drawer open, extracted the fax that had come in twenty minutes earlier. It was from Keck. He studied it. Pure Teutonic terseness: *Arrived Victoria . . . Verify meeting time . . . D. Keck.*

Grady had immediately shot back his acknowledgment, along with the precise time for their meeting: ten o'clock the following morning in Victoria.

He lit a Ducado and drew up a picture of Dieder Keck. Round-faced, slope-shouldered with stony eyes. He had the secretive rat-look of a man who masturbated over kiddie porn. But he was still a power in the European neo-Nazi underground, with heavy contacts in the Middle East from which he could obtain weapon caches of astounding variety.

Through intermediaries in Berlin, Grady had met him six months before in a nudie *Nachtklub* in Heidelberg. He made his pitch fast: monies up front, possible delivery arrangements. He stressed the philosophical linkages between the American militia movement and the new *Hitlerzeit.*

Keck had listened without comment. As he rose to leave, he had said simply, ''I will zend my emizzary and zen I come myzelf.''

Grady blew a cloud of spicy smoke toward the beamed ceiling, watched it twine gently toward the air vent. Finally, he sighed and punched the turquoise button on his intercom. ''Get some coffee in here,'' he snapped. He returned to work.

Two minutes later, another Seattle phone rang. In the bathroom of room 14B of the Travelodge Motel on Dakota Street, Azevedo was shaving. He wiped off the last bit of shaving cream, rinsed the razor and went to answer the call.

''Yeah?''

''Hey, Jo-Jo,'' a man said. ''It's Alex.''

''Yeah, what's up, man?''

''I think maybe I got a line on that skin you're looking

for." Azevedo could hear music playing in the background. Garth Brooks.

"All *right*," he said.

This was the first hint of Halberstadt he'd picked since arriving in Seattle. The previous night, he'd spent most of the evening mousing the town, looking up old sources who might offer a thread indicating that the German actually was in the city. Mostly, he talked to blank faces.

Around eleven, he'd driven out to the Spiderweb, sat down the avenue in his car and watched the skinhead punks come and go in their *Sieg heil* leathers and Doc Marten boots, with their foul-mouthed, bleached-blond chicks in tow. But no Halberstadt. It was the same at the Celtic Cross. Around two o'clock, he'd said the hell with it and gone back to his motel.

"At least this sounds like the bastard," Alex said.

"Where'd you pick this up?"

"Well, the wife still knows some high-town hookers around here, you know what I'm saying? She likes to keep in touch. Anyway, this one, Adele, works for a madam that runs a high muckety-muck trick service. She tells Janet about some German punkass who bung-holed her last night. Rough as hell the son of a bitch was, hurt her pretty bad."

"A skin?"

"Yeah, judging from this gal's description—shaved head, spiderweb tattoos, all that shit. And he talked German. Was a strong motherfucker, too. She said there was this other guy with him, name of Leroy James."

"That's them," Jo-Jo growled happily. "Where are they now?"

"They were at the Blue Pine Lodge in North Bend last night. But I understand they've got reservations at the Seneca House Hotel."

"Seneca House? Where's that, in Seattle?"

"Yeah, just go east on Madison and you'll find it. You know, these pricks must be loaded, or somebody else's putting out a lot of scratch for 'em. I mean, the Seneca, limo service? And this madam, she don't come cheap. Sounds heavy, Jo-Jo."

"We think yeah, maybe."

Alex grunted.

"Listen, babe, you're my man," Jo-Jo said. "I appreciate this. You thank Janet for me. I mean, helping the fuzz and all?"

"She hates johns who get rough more'n she hates cops."

Jo-Jo laughed. "A fair comparison. But tell her I still love her anyway."

"Will do."

"Thanks, Alex."

"See you."

Jo-Jo didn't put down the phone. Instead, he dialed Kizzier's home in Boise. It rang five times before Kizzier picked up. "What?" he said gruffly.

"Al, Jo-Jo. I get you up?"

"No, I was on the crapper. How's it going?"

"The bastard's here, all right."

"Bingo."

"Dog James's with him." He explained about Alex and the hookers. "Now they're supposed to be staying at some expensive place name of the Seneca House. They're getting limo service, the whole ball of wax."

"High-priced hookers, limousines?" Kizzier said. "That shit sounds a little out of the 'Rooters' league."

"Somebody else wants something, that's for sure," Jo-Jo said. "But I don't think it's gonna be a whack. The kraut would have come alone if he was intending to take somebody out."

"Yeah, I agree. I smell a meet. What d'you think, dope or weapons?"

"Weapons, easy. Probably through someone in Europe with Halberstadt the go-between."

"Sure as hell looks that way. Okay, I'm coming out."

"You flying?"

"No, I'll be bringing heat and I don't want to have to fuck with them air marshalls. I'll be there late this afternoon. Where you staying?"

"The Dakota Avenue Travelodge."

Kizzier laughed. "The Travelodge? Jesus, man, you're on the Fed tab, you shoulda gone more upscale."

"This ain't bad," Jo-Jo said. " 'Cept the goddamned heater'll roast your nuts off."

"Okay. Look, we just got full clearance on the IAW. But we're still gonna play this thing low-key. I want Hans and whoever's coming from overseas."

"Right."

"Could that asshole James make you?"

"I don't think he's ever seen me."

"Good. Stay cool."

"Right," Jo-Jo said and hung up.

The cowboy had been hit twice. Marquette stripped off his horse coat, denim jacket, shirt and the top half of his soiled longjohns. The man's skin was very white where it had been covered save for a sunburnt *V* below his throat.

The smaller wound was on his right shoulder. The bullet had skidded through the deltoid muscle. It was creased open, and Matt could see the edge of bone down under the muscle and fat, white as a gleaming tooth.

The other wound was worse. The bullet had entered the cowboy's chest on the right side, under the nipple; had apparently curved left and was now lying just under the skin on the man's back, near his upper spine.

When he breathed, it made a soft sucking sound, and there was bloody froth around the pucker of the entry wound. A large area had already turned black and blue. Matt suspected the lungs had been nicked, and there was probably broken rib, too.

He checked the cowboy's pulse, the man still looking up at him with that distant, quivering, sorrowful stare. His pulse was weak, his skin pallid and clammy. Shock was coming on.

"Why'd they—shoot me?" the cowboy gasped.

"Don't worry about that," Matt said. "You gonna be all right, buddy. Just relax."

He pulled the soogan from the horse's body. Inside the

rolled blanket was a small packet containing a tobacco pouch, a snakebite suction cup, flashlight batteries and a small first-aid kit. Several cows, attracted by the burning wreckage, came and stood on the grassy ridge, looking down at them with round, dumb eyes. Grass was burning around the wreckage, crackling.

Using the cowboy's belt knife, Matt cut pieces from the blanket, then placed the small square compress from the kit against the chest wound and pressed down. At the same time, he used his other hand to put pressure on the man's throat just above the collarbone. After a few minutes, he bound the upper torso with blanket strips, making it as airtight as he could.

He worked quickly, efficiently, as training and old memories came up, drawn forth by the icy tingle of adrenaline, the smell of cordite and torn-open flesh. Beside them, the horse's blood steamed softly in the chilly air.

He bandaged the shoulder wound and then wrapped the cowboy's torso in the remnants of the blanket. He stood and looked north, the direction they had been traveling before the attack. The hills rolled away. Here and there, the wind made shifting patterns in the grass. His horse was nowhere in sight.

He spotted a house and barn, about two or three miles away, nestled in twin hillocks like a brooch sitting between a woman's breasts. He quickly retrieved his gym bag, tied it to a belt loop with his handkerchief and returned to the cowboy.

He knelt down. "Listen, buddy," he said. "I'm gonna carry you out. You understand?"

"Water," the cowboy croaked.

Matt shook his head. "No, not with a chest wound."

"Lord," the cowboy said.

"Okay, I'm gonna lift you onto my back now," Matt said. "It'll hurt." He took hold of the man's left wrist, shoved his other arm under his thigh. "You ready?"

The cowboy murmured something.

With a quick lifting and dipping motion, Marquette brought him up off the ground, his weight pure-dead, coming quickly, Matt's back muscles gripping up. The cowboy let out a stifled moan that trailed off into thick gasps. Matt settled him across his shoulders and started off.

The ground under the grass was irregular. It was like walking through a newly plowed field turned hard by night frost. Matt kept turning his ankles, the cowboy's weight pressing down. Several of the cows trailed him for a few minutes, then fell back.

By the time he'd covered two hundred yards, he was panting. His leg muscles burned. A barn swallow suddenly swept over a grass ridge, riding the wind. When it spotted him, it chittered and darted straight up, forked tail and wings flaring. He kept doggedly on.

After a while, he became aware that an animal was following him again. He heard a snort, the soft tread of its feet. He turned around. It was his horse, about twenty yards behind him. It stopped and began to crop grass. He called softly to it. It lifted its head and looked at him.

He lowered the cowboy. This time the man made no sound. He seemed to be unconscious, and there was a large spot of blood on the blanket-wrap. Matt leaned on his knees a moment to catch his breath, felt his legs trembling. Then, holding out his hands as if they contained feed, he walked slowly toward the horse, cooing at it.

It bobbed its head, blew through its nostrils. When he got a few feet from it, the animal sidestepped, then stood still, pushing out its neck to sniff at his hands. It shied a little when it smelled the blood on his clothes but allowed him to take hold of the hackamore.

But the horse wouldn't let him load the cowboy onto its back. It kept sidestepping and going out to the end of the hackamore. After two tries, Marquette cursed and stood glaring at it.

The cowboy said, "Blindfold the sum'bitch." Clear as a bell.

Marquette looked down at him. The man's eyes were open, the sorrowful look gone now, in its place an irritated anger.

Matt gently placed his jacket over the horse's head, hiding its eyes. It stood stock-still the moment the jacket was in place. Matt then wrestled the cowboy up onto its back, jack-knifed him over the animal's shoulder. The man made only one sound, a long, in-sucking hiss, and then he was silent again. Matt slipped up behind him, and they moved ahead in an even, rocking-chair lope.

They reached a dirt road and then a metal gate. Marquette dismounted, opened the gate, led the horse through and closed it again. He remounted, and they went on.

Twenty minutes later, they crossed a railroad embankment, the horse slipping slightly on the gravel ballast and then stepping high over the ties and quickly down the other side. A half mile beyond was the farmhouse.

The house was covered with weathered shingles, and its tall stone chimney rose above both of its stories. It was surrounded by a wire fence that enclosed a wide swath of brown grass, two smaller buildings and a barn that was the color of rust. Beyond the enclosure was a small, unkempt apple orchard, the trees leafless.

An old man was standing at the fence gate. He wore faded bib overalls without a shirt, and his arms were thin and wrinkled. As Matt drew closer, he saw that the old man's right eye was milky white.

"God a'mighty," the old man said, spotting the cowboy. "That's Jimmy Lennart." He opened the gate to allow Marquette to pass through, then closed it.

Matt dismounted. He caught sight of a woman in a cream-colored dress standing behind the screened front door. He said to the old man, "Call nine-one-one. Tell them to get a medevac team out here right away."

"Martha," the old man yelled. "Call the police, tell 'em send out some medical people right quick."

Martha disappeared.

The old man helped Matt get Lennart off the horse. They carried him into the house and laid him down on a moth-eaten couch. The rest of the furniture was in the same condition. There was a tall, 1930s console radio in the corner.

"Hey, Jimmy," the old man said. He smelled of sour clothes and pipe tobacco. "You all right?"

Lennart didn't answer.

"What in hell happened?" the old man asked Matt. "I seed that smoke out yonder an' I figured there was something a-goin' on. Ain't nothin' out there to make smoke 'cept prairie grass."

Martha came into the room. She looked like Mother Hubbard. "The police is comin,' " she said. "They gonna bring a heel-i-o-copter, the girl said."

Matt checked Lennart's pulse. Surprisingly, it had strengthened. Lennart's eyes watched him, slid to the old man, came back.

"You got a car?" Marquette asked.

"No," the old man said angrily. "Ain't got no need now. Dam' state took my license away. Whenever me or Martha want to go to town, we gotta call my son. Helluva note."

Matt returned to Lennart. "They'll be here real soon, partner," he said. "I'm sorry about this."

Lennart looked at him silently. Then he said, "Thanks."

Marquette went back outside, the old man following. He retrieved the horse and mounted. The old man held the gate open. "You want to tell me something, young fella?" he asked. "Ole Jimmy was shot, wan't he?"

"Yes."

"Damn! You do it?"

"No."

"No, I suppose not. He surer'n hell wouldn't be thankin' you if'n you had."

"Take care of him."

"Oh, me 'n Martha'll handle it till the doctors get here. Where you headed now?"

"I don't know."

"Damn," the old man said. "Helluva note."

Marquette rode off.

He'd covered about a mile at an easy canter by the time the blue-and-white medevac helicopter arrived at the farmhouse. He watched over his shoulder, now far enough away that he couldn't distinguish people. After a few minutes, the aircraft rose and headed southeast.

He was following the rail track now. It curved gradually until it pointed due west. To the south, the grass was still burning from the wreckage, sending thin, dirty-brown smoke into the sky. Far to the west, the mountains rose, their high peaks clear of clouds now and coated with snow between the trees.

The wind dropped, and it grew hot. Once, a truck filled with Mexican orchard workers passed on the other side of the rail embankment. The men in their sweat-stained clothes and straw hats watched him silently as the dust fumed off the truck's wheels and hung in the air.

Two hours later, he reached a wheat station. He'd been watching it for a long time, the thing huge and protruding above the low hills. It shimmered like a mirage with what looked like smoke rising gently from it.

There were six cement silos, all a hundred feet high and connected like batteries in a cell. The sides were roughened by the wind to the color of old bread. Long metal conduits protruded from the lower ends of each silo and were suspended on cable lines. Spread out below the silos was a compound of warehouses and smaller tin buildings.

A train made up of two locomotives in tandem hooked to about fifty ore and closed-hopper cars stood in the siding beside the silos. It was taking on bulk wheat, four cars at a time. The loading tubes hissed as the wheat came down and chaff dust boiled out of the hatches, coating the cars and tin buildings like a fine volcanic ash.

Now and then, the lead engine would put on a burst of diesel power, a short, whirring whine, as the engineer repeatedly positioned the loading cars under the conduits.

Matt circled the station. On the other side of it stretched more open pasture and a wheat field. A harvester was parked on the side of a paved road. A thin black man was sitting on a drainage culvert near the tracks eating a strip of beef jerky and drinking from a wine bottle.

Matt headed over. "How you doin'?" he said.

The man squinted up at him. He wore a faded Army fatigue coat and a filthy sailor hat turned inside out. "Right enough," he said. "How *you* doin'?"

"You know where that train's headed?" Matt asked.

The black man took another bite of jerky before answering. "Sure," he said. "Seattle."

"When?"

"Soon's them boys gets her loaded. Maybe in a hour or two."

Marquette nodded. He dismounted. The horse ambled over to the edge of the culvert and began cropping tufts of grass. He sat down.

The black man studied him, particularly the dried bloodstains on his sweater. "You look like you been in a fight, man," he said.

Matt didn't answer. He turned and looked over at one of the hopper cars. "They have bulls on these things?" he asked.

The man laughed. "Bulls? Man, I ain't heard that for years. No, they ain't got bulls. Sometimes the comp'ny hogs gets fat nuts and the train boys tells you to get off. But mos' time, they don't pay you no mind."

"You riding?"

The black man nodded. "Yeah, I jes' be dozin' here till she goes. Headed for the Dinosaur, see my chil'run."

"The Dinosaur? Where's that?"

"South Central L.A."

They sat in the sun and talked. The man's name was Rothelle. He'd been riding freights off and on for twenty years, he told Matt. He shared his wine, gave a few pointers on jumping a hopper car. "Jes' remember, don' *never* fall in a full one," he said. "You know what I'm sayin'? You be sinkin' to the bottom, *wham!* That wheat jes' suck you in like quicksand."

After about an hour, Rothelle turned and squinted at the line of cars for a moment. "Better be gettin' ready, man," he said. "She be goin' pretty soon." He turned around. "What you gon' do with your horse?"

"Leave it with somebody in the station. They'll take care of him."

"I suppose."

The locomotives were starting to throw off heavier sound now, in combination, the cars' couplings slamming as the line moved slowly forward.

"You better make it fast," Rothelle said.

Matt walked the horse along the fence, talking softly to it and rubbing the hard bone of its jaw. There was a small guard shack at the main entrance to the station compound. No one was inside.

He tied the hackamore to the doorknob. The horse looked at him, nuzzled his arm. "So long, pal," he said. Then he turned and sprinted back along the fence.

Two men came out of a building and looked at him and then over at the horse. One of the men yelled, "Hey, what the fuck you doing?"

The train was beginning to move faster now, the locomotives coming up into a solid churring roar. Rothelle had already jumped aboard the third car from the end and was nestled under a metal strut, grinning and waving for him to hurry.

Matt cut over the culvert and ran along the tracks, his gym bag and jacket bouncing against his thigh, the cars jostling and clanking iron-loud beside him and the chaff dust powdering off. He caught up to the third-from-last hopper, grabbed hold of the step brace and deftly pulled himself aboard.

Within a few minutes, they were racing west.

Chapter 12

Lieutenant Two Elks had been going over the FBI's preliminary BSU psychological/personality report just faxed through from Quantico. The full report was still ten days off. He'd noted immediately that there were inconsistencies.

His phone light blinked. He picked up. "Detective Division, Two Elks."

"Big John, Byner."

"Mornin', Doc."

"I just got your analysis on the knife," the ME said. "A mixed bag."

"Oh?"

"The blood analysis on the primary shows very low readings on the Lundsteiner/Wiener Rh scale, and oxygen levels indicate a single circulation pattern. There's also traces of the blue pigment hemocyanin."

"What does all that say?"

"It's nonhuman. The primary's undoubtedly fish blood, probably from a shark. And the hemocyanin's from a crustacean—a crab, something like that."

Two Elk grunted, took a pull on his cigar. "What's the other side of the bag?"

"The blade and hilt configurations fit the wound pattern perfectly. I'd give it ninety-nine percent it *was* a Ka-Bar did the dirty deed."

"Could he have cleaned it?"

"Possible. But I didn't pick up any traces of cleaning solvent. If he'd just wiped the blade or washed it, there'd have been fragments under the FS scan. Besides, the hemocyanin was badly decayed, quite old.''

''Okay, Doc. Thanks.''

''No problem.''

He replaced the receiver. So, Marquette's knife wasn't the murder weapon. Did he have another? After all, he apparently liked Ka-Bars. But if there had been a second knife, it could be anywhere—starting at the bottom of the estuary.

He returned to the BSU prelim fax, began at the top again. It was a list of initial comparisons made between the traits of the unknown killer, suppositionally deduced from Two Elks's PSR-1, and the available data on Matthew Marquette.

It said:

UNKNOWN	MARQUETTE
blitz attack (disorganized)	organized personality
spontaneous aggression	controlled aggression
crime scene, random/ sloppy	organized personality
low intelligence	above av. intelligence
unskilled	skilled
did not know victim	knew victim
age: 35—45	age: 44
carry weapon (knife)	carry weapon (knife)

He saw that the only true matches were the age factor and the fact that both profiles contained a carried knife. That constituted a twenty-five-percent match-up. Statistically, an affirmative should have contained at least a sixty-percent match.

He knew, of course, that these P/P profiles were based on parameter assumptions drawn from data available in the FBI's files of past homicides. The whole thing was always a guess. Still, the Bureau had an astounding record of correct suppositions.

There was a short summary of further analysis approaches

at the bottom of the list, the whole thing signed off by the Agent Assigned, a Robert Choney. One sentence struck Two Elks's eye: *Investigative suggestion: Be alert to possibility Marquette is not perpetrator.*

He frowned at that one.

His phone light blinked again. This time it was Lieutenant Stu Walters of Seattle PD's West Precinct. After identifying himself, he said, "I just came across something on the Highway Patrol CA line I thought you might want to check out, John. Might have to do with that pickup notice you put out on a—shit, where the hell is that thing? Here—on a Matthew Marquette."

Two Elks sat forward. "What about it?"

"Well, apparently there was a helicopter crash this morning out in the basin, near Wanapum. Damned thing exploded on impact, burned all to hell. Possible two fatals, but nobody's sure yet.

"Anyway, sometime after the crash, these two men showed up at a farmhouse a couple miles way. One had been shot twice, a cowboy working for a ranch out there. But from the descriptions he and the farmer gave, the other guy just might be your man."

Wanapum?

"Is the WHP holding him?" Two Elks said.

"No, but they've already issued their own APB on the guy," Walters said. "Apparently he just left the cowboy and took off. Listen, John, that's all I've got on it. You should give the WHP a jingle. Go through the Westlake Division; they're handling it. Check with a Sergeant Muldauer."

"Thanks, Stu."

"Good luck."

Sergeant Muldauer was very military. "Yes, sir," he said. "A helicopter crash did occur at approximately oh-five-hundred hours this date. Pursuant to that, our command is now coordinating with the FAA, and a National Transportation Safety Board team has already been dispatched from Portland, Oregon."

Two Elks tapped cigar ash into the tuna can he used as an

ashtray and said, "You want to give me details?"

Muldauer quickly went through it. When he got to the eyewitness account of the helicopter attack, the lieutenant's hand pulled the cigar from his mouth very slowly and his dark eyes went dead.

Muldauer ended with the wheat station sightings. "Employees out there said the unknown tied the stolen horse to the station gatehouse and then boarded a train that had just completed loading. He was accompanied by a black man. Apparently the black had ridden in on the same train earlier in the day."

"Let's go back a minute," Two Elks said. "This cowboy claims the unknown suspect brought down the chopper himself?"

"Yes, sir. He fired on it with Lennart's rifle and either wounded the pilot or struck something vital on the rotor."

"About this train—where was it headed?"

"To a mill in Seattle."

"When did all this take place?"

"Let's see. The initial medevac request was logged at—"

"No, when did the unknown jump the train?"

"The call from the employee of Colucktum Company was logged at eleven-thirty-one hours, sir," Muldauer said.

"Does the train go right through to Seattle?"

"No, sir. It's scheduled to stop at Roslyn to take on another engine for the pull through the pass."

"When?"

"I believe its TOA is fifteen-thirty hours, sir."

Three-thirty P.M. He glanced at his watch. It was now 12:01.

"Are you people going to run a search of it in Easton?" he asked.

"Yes, sir. Two units in coordination with Kittitas County officers."

"Okay, thanks."

"Sir?"

"What?"

"Your name's Two Elks?"

"Yes."

"Did you by any chance play for the Seahawks?"

"Yes."

"Oh, wow," Muldauer said, unstiffening. "I saw you twice. Jeez, this is an honor."

"Thanks," he said. "And thanks for the information."

"Man, oh, man," Muldauer said.

Two Elks sat and stared thoughtfully at the tiny glow of his cigar and thought: What the hell is this? Marquette—and he had the solid sense inside that it *was* Marquette out there—in a battle against a helicopter assault? Stealing horses, jumping trains?

He mused out loud, "This boy's running from something besides me."

Then he was out of his chair, pulling on his Stetson and heading for the door. He had just over three hours to get to Easton.

The station attendant in George was tall as an NBA forward. He whistled while he put gas into Stone's car. It was 2:30 in the afternoon. The station was just off the highway, beside a pancake house shaped like a beehive.

Stone walked around the pumps, restlessly studying the rolling hills that went south. He was hungover, with a sour stomach and a headache, needles piercing his eardrums. Most of the night he'd cruised on Jack Daniel's.

He'd arrived at Grady's "cabin" about nine o'clock. It was situated in an exclusive Moses Lake area called Laguna Estates. A two-story structure made of hand-peeled cedar logs, running about four thousand square feet, it sat on a two-acre lot full of short silver pines. It faced the lake, and its porch extended out over the water. To the right were a boathouse and a small pier.

He had parked his car a block away from the entrance gate. He wore the Ingram assault pistol, with a six-inch silencer attached, in a holster under his jacket. He also carried a flashlight and his cell phone.

Once inside Grady's gate, he crept toward the house, darting from tree to tree. Finally satisfied that it was empty, he went around to the porch and listened at the lakeside door. The breeze off the water was cold, and the lights of houses ranged around the other side of the lake looked like ships anchored in a roadstead.

He broke the lock and went inside. It smelled of cedar and metal polish. He flicked on the flash. The front room was huge and sunken, adorned with sunburst bancos and cabinets and Nambe brasswork. There was a boulder kiva in one corner, woolen Navajo rugs on the floors and walls, and a big, silver-laced sombrero near the kiva. In the kitchen were bunches of red chili and Zuni corn. The place looked and smelled like a Mexican bordello.

He found a bottle of Jack Daniel's in the wet bar and sat on a white leather sofa that gave him a view of the driveway and gate, the Ingram and phone beside him. Drinking steadily, he waited for Marquette.

The night went by in sluggish clicks. His inebriation gradually reached that point of soddenness in which there was only a petulant anger in him. Now and then, he'd wander through the darkened house, peering out windows, running into furniture. Once, he went out to the porch and listened to music drifting past from a house up the beach.

Around two in the morning, he finally fell asleep, going to a black place without time. It was as if he had simply closed his eyes and then opened them again to find the room flooded with light.

He bolted upright. The headache instantly struck like a skewer of lightning. He checked his watch: 7:31 A.M. Frantically, he tried to raise Gus on the cell phone. All he got back was a taped intercept saying the unit he was trying to reach was turned off.

For the next three hours, he ranged through the house like a caged animal, cursing and sweaty with frustration. Each time he tried to get Fettis, the same taped message came on. It was obvious that something was terribly wrong.

By ten o'clock, he couldn't stand the inactivity. He walked

back to his car and returned to the interstate. But where to look? He drove west, all the way to the Columbia River, watching buses, checking the sky for the chopper. At Wanapum, he turned off the highway and took dirt roads out into the hills—tore all over hell, whirling up dust and spooking cattle among the bunch grass.

He found nothing. . . .

Now the attendant checked his oil, and he and Stone went into the station. A pretty teenaged girl was painting her nails at the counter, a small portable radio playing beside her arm.

As the attendant rang up the sale, she said, "Hey, the news just said they think that guy's on a train headed for Seattle."

"Is that right?" the tall attendant said.

"Yeah, he left the horse at the Colucktum wheat station."

The attendant shook his head and handed over Stone's change. He said, "Man, that sure is something."

"What's that?" Stone asked.

"There was a big shoot-out hereabouts this morning."

"Yeah? I didn't hear."

"Oh, man," the attendant said. He leaned on the counter. "These two fellas got into it with a helicopter out on the Damapage Ranch. Gunfire, the whole shebang. This one guy shoots down the chopper, carries his wounded pal in, then runs off."

Stone stared at him, his face suddenly pale and hard. "What kind of chopper was it?"

"I dunno—some little two-man thing, from what I hear."

"Any survivors?"

"Nope. Friend of mine at the Sheriff's office said they think there was two people aboard, but nobody can tell yet. Everything was burned up too bad."

Stone went out and sat in his car for a long time. Finally, the attendant tapped on his hood and asked him to move. He started the engine and drove across to the pancake house parking lot and sat again.

There was no doubt in his mind that the crash involved Gus and Basset. He thought about Fettis. He'd known him for nearly thirty years, and the impact of the news gripped at his heart like a squeezing hand.

Then, slowly, the rage came through. He looked at his watch, calculating. He had twenty hours to finish this thing off. Well, he didn't know how he was going to do it, but he *was* going to do it. He'd find Marquette somehow, the bastard returning to Seattle. And he'd blow his goddamned head off, then carry out the rest of the mission.

For Gus.

For himself.

He rammed the car into gear, leaving tire marks on the asphalt as he returned to the interstate and headed west.

Gilhammer said, "Okay, what the hell's going on here, Kelli?"

"I can't tell you yet," she said. "Not just yet."

He shook his head, sucked a cherry gumdrop while he studied her. "Look, I know how personal this is for you," he said. "I understand and I sympathize. But, dammit, your involvement's beginning to disrupt the team. We're eating up too much unnecessary track time waiting on you."

"I'm sorry, Troy." She put her head down, rubbed her temples, then looked up again. "Just give me one more day. Okay?"

"To do what?"

"I think I'm on to something." Before he could speak, she said, "Don't ask. It's all still too—complicated to explain."

Gilhammer sighed and slid off the desk. "All right, one more day." He started for the door of the DAM room, stopped. "Do you want any help? Maybe if we work together on whatever the hell it is you're doing, it might speed things up."

"No, I have to do it myself. But thanks."

He went out.

Kelli had worked till nearly five that morning. After downloading the sphere data from Tierkreis-Wickeln, she had attempted probes of the Chinese computer network, trying to locate and access the Hu nyau-Ge military hospital system. After several attempts, she found it nearly impossible. There were simply too many layers of security within the Chinese system.

Although their network was quite antiquated, its databases were all protected by multi-escrow encryption systems in which the digital code keys were kept at independent computer sites. All of these sites were part of the Military Intelligence System of the Chinese Central Communist Party.

Although access was easily achieved through Internet and WWW sites in China, these databases were ciphered, cleared of any data the CCCP felt was State-sensitive.

She thought about using some advanced hacker techniques—possibly breaking into the MIS network and running "dictionary" sniffers or e-mail loops. But she quickly realized that to do so would leave incriminating footprints in too many places. She simply couldn't risk compromising the university.

With dawn light beginning to filter through the window, fatigue had finally overwhelmed her. She checked her home message machine. Still nothing from Matt. After a last cigarette, she'd gone downstairs to the building's small infirmary, found a bed and climbed in with all her clothes on.

She had lain there listening to the silence in the building and feeling the cold ache of anxiety. Eventually, with the sounds of slamming doors and voices beginning out in the halls, she fell asleep.

The day nurse woke her when she came on duty at 10:30. For a moment, Kelli couldn't remember where she was. Then it all came back, the stunning reality of what had happened. She felt her blood heave and bolted upright, checking the time. Where was Matt? She immediately called the houseboat. There was still no message from him.

Desperately, she tried to convince herself he was all right. He's still alive, she thought. He can handle this. And slowly, forcing the anxiety away, she managed to calm herself.

She washed up in the infirmary's small bathroom, staring at herself in the mirror. She looked haggard, her eyes dull, lifeless. Afterward, the nurse insisted she eat something. So she forced down a cup of coffee and one of the woman's blueberry muffins.

When she returned to the CRYSTALBALL lab, she went straight for the DAM room, saying nothing to anyone. Everybody watched her transit the room in silence. . . .

She renewed her attack on the Chinese network. This time, instead of approaching the Chinese system directly, she attempted to backtrack the fax messages from Hu nyau-Ge to Tierkreis-Wickeln in the hopes of isolating password signals or finding a niche through which she could enter the CCCP's multi-escrow system.

She got as far as the satellite telephone switching network in Singapore before hitting a snag. Once the main circuit trunks entered China, they were all filtered through the MIS network and encryption-guarded.

Frustrated, she tried tracking Internet and WWW transmission logs out of Beijing to Kunming, using a logic-watch on all e-mail loops to find those directed specifically to the Hu nyau-Ge site. But without key ID codes in Chinese, her logic-watch program miscued, isolating data on a military garrison in Kuangnan and an agricultural *xiang* commune in Lichian.

Kelli paced around for awhile, studying the ceiling in the chill air. Another idea came to her. What if the work on bacterial transmutation at Hu nyau-Ge had been published somewhere? In journals or governmental reports, through regular medical research channels? If so, she might obtain some insight as to the sphere's part in it.

She quickly accessed the listings of governmentally cleared data sources pertaining to medical and scientific research within China. It turned out to be a complex montage of both ancient and modern Oriental medical practices. Most of the texts were untranslated. Those that were contained endless esoteric terminology.

·Okay, she thought, what about American or European journals? She started in the U.S., pulled up clearinghouse data on articles published in bacteriology, epidemiology, pharmacology, and every other -*ology* she could think of that might pertain to bacterial research.

Her query scan turned up numerous articles. Fine-tuning, she focused on specific reports that dealt with metamorphosis and the transmutation of bacteria cells for the years 1990–96. Again a mind-boggling conglomeration of medical terminology turned up, most of which seemed to center on bacteriophagesal DNA manipulation and transduction for the purpose of interdiction of infection sequence.

No mention of any Chinese research.

She turned to international journal sources. The World Health Organization, the Pan-American Health Organization, UNICEF. More: European medical libraries, the data bank of the prestigious London Dispensary, *poliklinika* reports of Russian clinical research.

At 2:30 P.M., she found a single mention of the research being done at the Hu Nyau-Ge hospital.

It was in the January 1993 issue of the journal *Bakteriologisch*, published at the University of Zurich—only a single line saying that the Chinese were conducting transmutational research on bacterium T-cell suppression.

But in the notation references, she saw that the data had come from a Russian source, the in-house journal of the Russian State Research Center of Virology and Biotechnology in Koltsovo.

She made a surprisingly rapid login to the RSRC's data bank. Her query scan quickly located the specific article containing the references to the Chinese military hospital in Kunming. It was in phonetic Russian.

She had suspected that it might be and already had the solution. While at Stanford, she had once roomed with a girl named Helen Kleinsmith, a postgrad in Slavic languages. The last she'd heard, Kleinsmith was an assistant professor at Willamette College in Oregon.

Within three minutes, she had Kleinsmith on the phone. "Helen, Kelli Pickett," she said. "I need your help."

"Kelli?" Helen laughed. "My God, how long's it been?"

"Too long. Listen, girl, I don't have much time."

"Hey, this sounds serious."

"It is, believe me. I need a translation of part of a journal article. It's in phonetic Russian."

"No problem. What's your RDL?"

Kelli gave it. "I want the portion covering research at a Chinese hospital in Kunming. The name's Hu nyau-Ge." She spelled it. "Hurry, Helen. And thanks."

"Will we talk about this sometime?"

"Yes."

It took eleven minutes for Kleinsmith to link with Kelli's computer, download and then send back the translated portion: a single paragraph, clothed in scientific jargon. Still, she managed to grasp its essentials.

The article said that Chinese virologists had been experimenting with the transmutational effects on bacterial gradient proton plasma from laser bombardment. Following Lamarchian nonrandom, survival mutational theories, their primary focus was to track the precise, speeded-up sequence of metamorphic synthesis within bacteriorhodopsin molecules in the so-called "purple mass" state.

But it was the last sentence that jarred her. She stared at it blankly and felt something cold and obscene slip into the air. She rose to quarter the room. But her screen repeatedly drew her back, like a suspended steel ball to a magnet.

Lord God, she thought.

She knew there could be no turning back now. She must follow this out, all the way. And something that had been working in her through the afternoon rose into the clear: a possible way to determine precisely what the sphere was, what its purpose was.

She went to the door and called to Gilhammer. It took several minutes before he could break away. He came into the room scowling.

"I need the lab," Kelli said. "Alone."

"What?"

"Send everybody home," she said. "I want to run an AI Platform."

Gilhammer shook his head. ''That's crazy. I can't authorize something like that, and you know it.''

''Listen to me, Troy,'' she said, staring right into his eyes. ''I've uncovered something that could be potentially catastrophic.''

His eyes narrowed. ''What catastrophic?''

''I can't tell you now; I'm not sure of it yet.''

He shook his head. ''Sorry, no can do.''

She flared. ''Goddammit, didn't you hear what I just said?''

''I heard what you said. But this is personal business, Marquette's problem. I can't let you—''

She cut him off. ''It's much more than that. Oh, God, much, much more. This could be *all* of us.'' Again her eyes locked with his. ''Please, Troy, trust me on this.''

He studied her for a long moment, then cursed. ''I ought to have my goddamned head examined,'' he said. ''All right, you got the lab. For tonight. But that's it, Kelli. You don't come back to us tomorrow, you're off the protocol roster. Understood?''

''Yes.''

He slammed the door going out.

She returned to her workstation, once again looked at the translated paragraph, at the final sentence. It said:

''For the tracking of the accelerated electron transfer of enzymatic and acid cycles, Chinese scientists have been using the active bacilli agents of *Halobacterium halobium* and *Bacillus anthracis . . .*''

Anthrax . . .

13

The train bored through the afternoon heat across an endless expanse of open land. Soon after leaving the wheat station, it had crossed the Columbia River, rumbling over a rail bridge with the strut shadows flashing past and the sound echoing down and up again. Twin jet skiers swept under the bridge, their wakes ribboning out and then fading back into the swirls and dimples of the brown-green water.

Marquette sat on the right side of the hopper car, in the shade of a brace. Rothelle sat on the other side. It was too difficult to speak over the rush of the wind, the jerking clang of couplings and the rhythmic slam as the car's wheels crossed the rail joints.

After the river, the land flattened out completely, the earth covered with short brown grass and rock castles, and then there were green expanses of wheat and corn and alfalfa. Now and then, they passed through tiny towns, and the locomotive's horn riffled back to them as if from a ship at sea.

They thundered past little boys on bikes who threw rocks at the cars, and once, at an intersection, there were teenagers parked with their three pickups, sitting atop their hoods, drinking beer. The girls waved and shook their breasts at them.

It all seemed so acutely alive to Matt. A profound vibrancy seemed to suddenly inhabit him, a rising of sensual appraisal that came with a clarity he had not known for a long time. Within it was an awareness, the feel of wholeness and capability coming like youth's own blood warming through the veins after a slumber.

With his back absorbing the drowsing tremble of the hopper car, eyes half-lidded, Marquette's mind was easy, expansive. In that state of half-repose, he set things out, one by one, and looked at them.

There was no doubt, if there ever had been, that his primary target was Grady. From him he'd obtain all the rest, the faces of those others involved in this deadly charade. And he'd find them, too, and bring them all down. How? Simply by utilizing the one advantage he had: the possession of the sphere.

They passed through Ellensberg, then Thorp and Teanaway. A wide sheet of blue water glistened in the sunlight far to the northeast. The land changed, rising off the basin bottoms into foothills covered with scrub oak and then meadows fringed with Douglas fir that thickened into the Snoqualmie National Forest. Close by, the true mountains rose.

The train slowed. Rothelle waved at him, pointed ahead. "We comin' into Roslyn," he shouted. "Get us some mo' power."

They passed a cemetery. Another. Then still another. They sat in glades of overgrown grass with ornate eighteenth-century wrought-iron gates, the gravestones gray in the sun. Beyond the cemeteries, up in forested hollows, were the tops of several abandoned coal mine cage derricks.

The train moved ever slower, skirting the edge of the town. They caught a glimpse of the main street, cafes and false-front buildings. A moment later, they passed another train parked on a siding. It was made up of empty ore gondolas. Up ahead were two locomotives sitting beside a long, open platform constructed of old wood. It resembled a fruit packing shed.

Rothelle suddenly jerked his head farther around the edge of the hopper car. He stared a moment, then skittered over to Matt. "Hey, man, are you on the run?" he said.

"What?"

"They's poo-lice up there," Rothelle said. "An' they look

like they fixin' to run a search of this train. They sure as hell ain't lookin' for me.''

Matt's heart jumped. He quickly crossed to the opposite side and peered around the slant of the bin. Two Washington Highway Patrol cruisers were parked beside the engines. Farther back were two Kittitas Sheriff's cars and a gray sedan. The officers were standing near the tracks, watching the train ease in. One was Lieutenant Two Elks.

''Dammit!'' Matt growled. ''Not now.''

He went back to the other side of the car. Rothelle was studying him narrowly. ''Go awn, man, you better disappear fast,'' he said. ''They gon' be here in a couple minutes.''

Matt looked off to the left. At this point, the tracks paralleled a dirt road. On the other side of the road was a strip of grass and then heavy brush, the branches and leaves coated with clay dust and road oil. The brush quickly merged into a thick stand of fir.

He glanced back at Rothelle.

''Don't worry, man,'' Rothelle said. ''I tell 'em I ain't seen shit.'' He grinned. '' 'Cept some white dude who jumped off way back yonder.''

They shook hands, then Matt scurried to the step. He hung there for a moment, trailing a leg, and at last went off, his foot hitting the gravel and his body coming with it, already running. He sideslipped down the embankment and crossed the road, hearing the train's brakes squealing and the locomotives' diesels whining a moment and then dropping into a low throb.

He crashed through the underbrush and broke out onto a thick carpet of pine needles. Branches slashed at him as he bore deeper into the forest, the sunlight slanting sharply down through the trees and making the air look smoky.

A hundred yards in, he rose on a slight incline. He could see the train through the trees. Two police officers were talking to Rothelle beside the hopper car, the black man pointing back down the tracks.

One of the officers talked on his handheld radio. A moment later, a county cruiser crossed the tracks, bouncing hard over the rails and down the embankment. A moment later, it sped past Rothelle and the officers, going south, the tires whirling up a cloud of dust.

Marquette turned and moved off through the trees.

Stone reached Seattle just before five o'clock that afternoon. Earlier, coming off the west slope of the mountains, he'd called Grady's office, was told the attorney was in court. Grady's secretary gave him directions to the Civic Center.

The downtown streets were crowded with home-going traffic, made him crazy as he sat in stop-and-go lines while the traffic lights sluggishly went through their colored sequences.

He finally got to the Municipal Courthouse, located between James and Cherry Streets, just off Interstate 5. It was made of red brick and sat among bare sweetgum trees. He found an underground parking lot near Pioneer Square and walked the two blocks back to the courthouse.

The woman at the information desk told him Grady's case was being heard upstairs in Courtroom 2B. When Stone pushed open the mahogany door of the courtroom, a husky bailiff stopped him.

"Sorry, mac," he said. "Court's in session."

"This where Grady is?"

The bailiff nodded toward the defense table. The attorney was seated beside a hulking Indian with jet-black hair trailing down his back. "That's him," the bailiff said.

"I gotta speak to him," Stone said. "It's extremely urgent."

The man gave him a slow up-and-down. "This got anything to do with the case in hearing?"

"Yes," Stone lied.

"What's your name?"

"Jack Stone."

"Wait here."

Stone paced. The corridor was tiled with marble that had turned yellow with age. A Vietnamese janitor was polishing it with a rotary buffer, and the air smelled like all courthouses: a combination of old cement and chicory.

Grady didn't come out for ten minutes. When he did, he was frowning, stepping through the door, looking around and then coming down to Stone. Today he was wearing a brown cowboy-cut suit with a red bolo tie.

"What the hell is this?" he snapped.

"We got a problem," Jack said.

A red-headed girl in a navy-blue business suit went past, gave Grady a flirtatious smile. "Hi, John," she said.

He flashed on her. "Hey, sweetheart." He made his fingers into a pistol, pointed it at her, clicked his tongue. "Lookin' killer."

When he turned back, the smile was gone. He took Stone's arm, guided him to a secluded pillar. "What problem?" he said. "An' make this fast. I only got a five-minute recess."

"Marquette's still on the loose," Stone said. "And the motherfucker killed Fettis and Basset."

Grady's face went still. He stared hard at Stone through his tinted glasses, and then his upper lip tightened subtly as if it would come up into a grin which was not a grin.

"Jesus Christ," he said softly. "This is bullshit. What in hell happened?"

"I ain't got time to explain," Stone said.

For the first time, Grady's downhome cool seemed penetrated. He kept turning to look behind him as if someone were creeping up. "Goddammit," he said. "You were supposed to settle this thing. God*dammit.*"

"Look, I'm gonna nail that bastard," Stone said. "You can make book on that. All I need from you is an address."

"Address? What address?"

"You said he called you on the phone, right?"

Grady nodded.

"I want the address he called from."

Grady looked away, then back. "A telephone trap trace takes days. And you can't get one without a judge's order."

Stone glared at him, his eyes sparking with energy. "Horseshit," he said. "You're a big-time operator, Grady. I figure you got ways around that kind of legal crap."

"Yeah," Grady said. "I got ways."

"Then put 'em to work."

Grady checked his watch. "I can't do anything until court adjourns."

"Call for a postponement."

"I can't." He studied Stone's face again, his eyes narrowing. "Man, are you on somethin'? Your goddamned eyes could light up a TV set."

"Don't worry about what I'm on," Stone said. "Just get me that goddamn address."

"We jest keep gettin' deeper here, don't we," Grady said.

"The address."

Reluctantly, the lawyer nodded. "All right." He thought a moment. "There's a lounge over in the square, Telesco's. I'll meet you there soon's I get outta here."

"How long?"

"Depends on when Judge Kennedy stops blowin' wind." Grady put his hands together, cracked his knuckles. "This shit's gonna blow the deal with Keck."

"No, it won't. Not after I take Marquette out."

"We play stall games with that bastard, he's gone."

The bailiff opened the door down the hall. "Mister Grady," he called, waving him back.

"Telesco's," Stone said. He looked balefully at the attorney for a moment, then turned and walked away.

The Roslyn Sheriff's station looked like Marshall Dillon's office. It held a scarred rolltop desk, captain's chairs and a gun rack with pump shotguns and a deer rifle. The only things modern in it were a field radio, a computer on the desk and a small air conditioner in the window. In back were two cells, in one of which an inmate was drunkenly singing "Blue Moon" and talking to himself.

Deputy Hatter poked his head around the door. "Hey, shut the fuck up back there," he snarled. The man stopped singing.

Near the window, Lieutenant Two Elks looked down toward the train station. Directly across the street was a bar with a delicately painted moose head on the door and antlers nailed along the eaves. Several dusty pickups were parked out front.

"So what d'ya want to do, Lieutenant?" Hatter asked. "You request a hard search, we can have dogs up here by dawn." It was now 5:43 P.M. "Ain't much sense in working the woods now with dark coming on."

Two Elks nodded to the woods beyond the rail platform. "What's up through there, anyway?"

"Houses, cabins. Farther back, some timber operations."

"That's where he's at," Two Elks said.

"This far in?" the deputy said. "Then you figure the black was lyin' about where he bailed out?"

Rothelle had been taken back to the Westlake Station by the WHP officers for questioning. Two Elks considered that a waste of time. The black wasn't a part of this. He'd just been there when Marquette had tried to get back to Seattle.

And the man would do it, too—he knew, was certain of it. Long before dawn, Marquette would hitch a ride out, steal a car, maybe even jump another train. But he'd get back to Seattle.

Hatter lit a cigarette, scratched his nose. "This whole thing's startin' to sound like a goddamned movie, you know what I mean?" he said. "Four fatals, a goddamn firefight that turns a chopper into a pile of cinders. Jeez, James Bond shit. And you say this Marquette was a Navy SEAL?"

"Yes."

"Then he'd know how to survive up in them mountains, wouldn't he? Hell, I bet he heads straight northwest and holes up in the wilderness."

No, Two Elks thought. Things were playing themselves out now. He could feel the tension in the atmosphere, sense the approaching climax. Whatever it was Marquette had to do, it was obvious he was going to carry it out back in the city. And that's when he'd become vulnerable, the moment he resurfaced. Vulnerable to everybody that was chasing him.

He turned and walked to the door. "Thanks," he said and went out to his car.

"Hey, Lieutenant, what about the search team?" Hatter called after him.

Two Elks simply shook his head and kept walking.

Marquette ran steadily, an Indian trot, running high, smoothly, eyes scoping the ground ahead and the balls of his feet touching lightly and lifting away. He had tied the gym bag to his back with a strip of shirt around his neck and now it bounced lightly with each footfall and merged into the rhythm of his body.

Evening had filtered into the forest, molding sounds out of the air. It was as if something were draped above the trees, absorbing the soft rustlings, the light pound of his shoes on the needled forest floor, and drawing silence out of the earth. Gradually, ever deepening, night began to come on.

He knew he had to make distance. They would be coming after him soon. Maybe at night, maybe in the first light of dawn. And they'd probably have dogs and four-ups, and his journey would end right there.

Already he was mentally tabulating the components of survival. He listed his assets, the little things he carried: shoestrings, matches, a weapon, weather clothing. Sometime in the night, he would stop and shelter. But for now there was only the clean thrust of himself through the lowering gloom and the steady pumping of his heart.

Gradually, he was forced to slow. In the darkness, he began to misstep, and there was danger of his twisting an ankle. A few minutes later, he reached a break in the forest. Downslope was a highway, cars moving with their lights on, casting scurrying shadows into the trees as they passed.

He waited until the road was empty and then fled across, feeling the faint warmth of the asphalt come through the soles of his shoes. Then he was into the opposite side and down a small ravine clogged with thick brush that swept scathingly across his face and arms. On flat ground again, he moved forward, squinting in the last, dim light.

The sound of the dog seemed as if it came from a well, hollow and distant. But soon he saw the lights of a house through the trees, and in a moment he came upon a dirt road that led to it. A second dog began to bark.

The cabin was flat-roofed, and there was a pickup parked beside the front door. The windows flooded light onto the hard ground and over a stack of firewood piled beside the door. The two dogs crossed the light, their back hairs erect, and came up through the darkness, barking.

A man opened the cabin door and stepped out, whistling. He wore a pair of walking shorts and combat boots, the straps unbuckled. "Goddammit, Billy," he yelled. "You and Suzy get your asses back here."

Matt melted off into the forest again. He heard the dogs barking up the road. The man whistled again, and they went back. He heard the man curse and the cabin door slam. He went on, very slowly now, into dimness.

It was surprising how much his eyes could distinguish in the night. Some substance of light seemed to come from the air, defining dark-on-dark silhouettes. But near the ground there was utter blackness, and he continually stumbled, falling into tangles of brush and across timber slash.

Then his ears picked up a sound. It was like a sudden, short burst of thunder, muffled through the trees. There was the tinkling jangle of chains. Soon afterward, light appeared from somewhere ahead, and Matt heard clearly the human-made sounds of engines growling, whining up and fading, and the movement of mechanical metal.

It turned out to be a timbering concentration yard, two acres of cleared, scarred ground with lights strung around on poles. There was a small company office shack and stacks of huge, bucked logs that had been hauled in by skid tractors from the cutting zone. Two crab loaders scooted about, lifting logs onto trucks strung out in a line, long flatbeds and timber dollies. The thunder he'd heard was from the logs dropping into their bunks.

He squatted in the shadows and studied the line of trucks. Two were from the Iron Horse Mill in Easton. The remaining four belonged to the Cascade/Pacific Lumber Company, Richmond Beach, Edmonds, a suburb of Seattle. Some of the drivers stood around, smoking and waiting their turn to load.

He focused his attention on the third truck in line. It was a flatbed, white-cabbed with the red lettering of the C/P company. He edged his way around the yard, crossed the entry road and went into the brush near where the loaded trucks parked so the drivers could cable their cargo before pulling up onto the road.

The night was cooling rapidly, drying his sweat and making him shiver. Two drivers came walking up to the road. They stood twenty feet away and urinated, arguing about someone named Trask.

One laughed. "Yeah, you tell him that, he'll kick your ass up around your ears."

"Yeah?" the other said. "I like to see him try it, the fat bastard. I like to see him try."

They zippered up their pants and walked back down into the yard.

Matt lay watching the loaders scurry, their engines straining and the trucks moving slowly up the line, the flutter plates on their stacks popping. The air turned crisp and smelled of wood chips and diesel fumes and the babbitt odor of hot bearings.

The first truck had left, then the second. Finally the third came up and parked. The driver began to cable up, cranking the cables down tight with a bar winch. He wore a padded vest and a cowboy hat and hummed softly to himself. When he was finished, he made a final check, circuiting the truck and whanging the cables with the winch bar to listen to the sound of their tension.

Then the truck was moving, the cab jerking momentarily as it broke its inertia and, groaning, took on the tremendous weight of the logs. Matt waited until the flatbed was abreast of him, quickly glanced toward the yard and rose, moving with the truck. He gripped a cable and swung himself aboard.

He had earlier chosen a hiding spot within the load. It was between the cap log and the one below it and to the right, a curve in the upper log that formed a narrow slit. He pulled himself back to it, shoved his gym bag in and then squeezed in himself. He just fit.

The bark of the logs was rough with deep, sharp indentations like fractures in the wood. They were dripping wet, which formed mushy patches of soaked sawdust and mud. He lay tightly wedged in, feeling the tremble of the truck's engine and its movement come back through the logs. There was a slight pause and then a jerk each time the driver shifted, working up through his lower gears.

At last, they were moving steadily, smoothly through the dust of the road. He listened to the logs, squeaking like ship's hawsers under terrible strain, and the cables, twanging and humming, a foot from his head as they headed for the highway and Edmonds.

14

At precisely 6:23 P.M., Albert Kizzier pulled into the parking lot of the Dakota Street Travelodge. The place had a Western motif, half-log facings on the outer walls and the office with twelve-over-twelve windows and frilly curtains.

He flicked his cigarette away and went in. A teenaged girl with acne scars was reading a book in a chair behind the counter. She rose and smiled at him. Her T-shirt was very tight, and he could see her nipples through the material like dark jelly beans.

"Good evening," she said and slid the register pad around to face him.

"Which room is Azevedo in?" he asked. "Joe Azevedo?"

"Let's see," the girl said. She consulted her card file. "That would be number fourteen B."

From a back room, a man called out, "Hey, he askin' about fourteen B, babe?" Kizzier could hear an NBA game on television, the Sonics and Lakers.

"Yeah," the girl said.

"Wait a minute." A young man came out. He wore a plaid shirt under which his belly formed a dome. When he leaned down to glance at the file, Kizzier caught the yeasty smell of beer.

The man glanced up at him. "You mister Kaizer?"

"Kizzier, yeah."

"Mister Azevedo left a message for you. Said for you to go to the Antlers saloon. He said he'd call you there."

Kizzier nodded. "How do I get there?"

The man gave him directions, adding, "You gonna want a room?"

"Can't I bunk with Azevedo?"

"No, he's in a single."

"Okay, I'll take one." He signed the register, flicked it around.

The man checked it, then handed him a key fitted to a red plastic disk carrying the number 12A. "That one's down the end of the first line. That be okay?"

"Whatever," Kizzier said.

Twenty-five minutes later, he walked into the Antlers. It was crowded, mostly working men in construction clothes and a group of six noisy young men, obviously students, drinking pitchers of beer. Behind the bar, Stolowski hustled, sweating down into his blue golf shirt.

"Hi," Alex said. "What'll it be tonight, pal?"

"Bud dark."

"Comin' up."

Kizzier put a five on the bar. Stolowski brought his beer. It had a thin head of creamy yellow foam, and the mug was frosted with ice.

"You Alex?" Kizzier asked.

Stolowski's eyes flicked up. "I know you?"

"I'm Jo-Jo's partner."

"Oh, yeah. Kizzier?"

"Right." They shook hands. "He been in tonight?"

"No, but he's called a couple times. He figured you'd be in earlier."

"So did I."

All in all, it had been a shitty day for Kizzier. He'd been held up in Boise and then had to listen to another lecture from Williams on exercising caution in Seattle. Finally, coming in, he'd pulled off the interstate at Ritzville for gas and was stopped for speeding by a cocky city cop with no chin who hadn't been impressed with his BATF identification.

For the next half hour, he sat and sipped beer, talking with Alex during the pauses. He met Janet Stolowski, who gave

him the hard eye and then made it a point to ignore him.
After awhile, the students began to get rowdy and almost got
into it with two construction men.

"Well, I guess it's time," Alex said finally, looking narrow-eyed over the bar at the young men.

"Need any help?" Kizzier asked.

"No, but thanks, anyway." He winked. "I kinda enjoy
kickin' smart-mouth, college-boy ass."

Stolowski got the six out without physical confrontation.
They cursed and grumbled and, once outside, threw threats
and went on up the block hooting.

At 7:25, the phone rang. Janet answered it, then turned,
pointed at Kizzier and walked away. He went around the bar
and picked up the receiver.

"How come you so late?" Jo-Jo said.

"It's a long story. How's it going?"

"I'm in front of the Celtic Cross watchin' the freak
show."

"They inside?"

"Yeah, been there since six."

"I'll be right out."

"Okay."

Jo-Jo's car was parked down the block from the skinhead
club, beside a pawnshop with bars in the windows and a
thick, wire-mesh gate across the doorway. The Celtic Cross
was at the other corner. There were colored lights out front
and entwined swastikas on its red, padded door.

Several Harley-Davidson motorcycles with high antelope
handlebars and Nazi symbols on the tanks were cranked
against the curb. Three skinhead punks in black leather jackets and chains sat on them, passing around a bottle of whiskey. Back up the block was a long, gray limo with
black-tinted windows and CB and television antennas.

Kizzier opened the passenger door and slid in. Jo-Jo was
eating a burrito. He nodded silently at him and went on
chewing.

"They alone?" Kizzier asked.

"Nope." Jo-Jo swallowed, wiped the back of his hand

over his mouth. "Got a coupla hookers with 'em. High-class stuff." He laughed. "Apparently, one of the boys likes his pussy stout."

Kizzier studied the limo. As he watched, the uniformed driver got out and stood, smoking. "That thing private-owned?" he asked.

"Nope. She's got a B-class license."

"Damn, I'd like to get in there, see who the hell the Hun's with."

Azevedo snorted. "We go in there, we might as well wear a fucking sign."

"Well, I don't figure this is the meet site, anyway," he said. "He wouldn't have the hookers along if it was."

Jo-Jo nodded.

Kizzier sighed and watched as his partner stuffed the last of the burrito into his mouth. "That thing smells pretty good. Where'd you get it?"

"A Taco Bell back that way. You hungry?"

"I ain't ate shit since I left Boise."

"Might as well go get something," Jo-Jo said. "I got a feelin' this is gonna be a long night."

On the way back from the Taco Bell, Kizzier retrieved his weapons bag from his car. He tossed it onto the back seat of Jo-Jo's sedan and settled in.

Telesco's was an upscale cocktail lounge—smoothly diffused light from crystal candles and red leather booths with two beautiful waitresses dressed like jockeys. A tall, sleek Italian sat at a piano on a dais, surrounded by stools, and softly played show tunes.

Stone had been there for nearly an hour, downing straight-ups and surveying the other patrons sullenly. The crowd was made up of business types and lawyers, all winding down after their routines of legal confrontation. Now everybody was chummy, the day's battles momentarily quiescent. Here and there were a few women, still chic in faintly rumpled business suits.

It was 7:30 before Grady showed up, weaving his way

through the orange glow of the crystal candles, slapping shoulders and giving out with his affected barn-dance affability. Some of the men returned him stony faces.

Jack waved at him and the attorney hurried over, put his briefcase on the table and slid into the booth.

"What the fuck took so long?" Jack asked, glaring from under his eyebrows.

"A little problem at court," he said. His face broke into a wide smile as one of the waitresses came over.

"Good evening, Mr. Grady," she said. She had a beautifully shaped mouth and light blond hair tucked under the rakish jockey's cap.

"Hi, Monica."

"The usual?"

"Of course. And another for him."

The waitress went away. Stone started to speak, but Grady held up his hand. The girl returned with the drinks. Grady had a margarita. As soon as she left again, he leaned forward.

"Okay, Stone," he said, keeping his voice low and tight. "Now whyn't you tell me just what in hell happened out there."

Jack did so, giving everything he'd picked up from the radio—the firefight, the crash, particularly the report that an unknown man suspected of being implicated had jumped a train bound for the coast.

The attorney listened, sipping his drink. The light from one of the crystal candles flickered in his tinted glasses, made it look as if a tiny fire were burning in his right eye.

When Stone finished, Grady said, "You figure he's headed for Seattle."

"Where else?"

Grady hissed. "This little side job of yours has got us on the downwind side of a shittin' duck."

"I told you I'd take care of it."

"But what if the police pick up Marquette? An' he starts draggin' me into it?"

"He won't get picked up."

"Oh, you're sure about that?"

"I'm sure. He's too smart to get busted now."

Grady studied him. They had been talking close together, but now the attorney pulled back slightly. Stone's breath was thick with sour-stomach smell.

"It ever occur to you," Grady said, "this old boy's put things together and is fixin' to come lookin' for *me*?"

"I'm hoping the bastard does. That'd make it a helluva lot easier."

"I don't like the sound of that."

"If he shows up, you just get hold of me."

"That's before he decides to blow my fucking belly open, of course."

Stone snorted. "Hey, you're the big-shot mouthpiece— talk him out of it."

Again Grady stared at him. "You know, Stone," he said finally, "I'm beginning to suspect that you-all're a rather stupid and dangerous man."

That went into Stone's eyes and came back out hot. He thrust himself forward. "Listen, you pile of corral shit," he said, his voice hoarse with threat. "You give me any more smart lip, I'll put your fucking head through that wall."

Grady was taken aback at Stone's vehemence. He felt the man's lethality wash over him and turned away from it. The waitress, noting his looking her way, started over. Grady waved her off with an angry flick of his hand.

"I want that telephone trace," Stone said. "Now. And you tell whoever the hell does it to make it damned fast."

Grady exhaled and pulled his briefcase to him. He snapped it open. Inside were brief folders, a laptop computer and modem, and a worn cell phone. He quickly hooked the phone to the modem and dialed his office. A moment later, he was scanning through his telephone logs.

He made a notation on a blue pad and logged off. Then he disconnected the cell phone and tapped in a number. After a few seconds, he said, "Grady. Cell number." He hung up.

They waited. Stone ordered another round. The piano player finished one song and started into "The Way We Were," giving it lots of wistful flourishes and runs.

Grady said stiffly, "I been thinking. Maybe we better put Keck on hold for now. Settle this Marquette thing first."

"No way," Jack said. "Like you said, he'd bolt."

Grady shrugged. "If he does, he does. We could set it up again with somebody else down the line." He scowled thoughtfully out at the crowd, came back. "What if Marquette used a public phone to make that call? Then we got nothin'."

"My gut tells me he used a friend's phone."

"And *my* gut's tellin' me this whole thing could unravel on us. Goddammit, we've only got till ten tomorrow morning. That's cuttin' it close to the halter."

"Don't worry about it."

The phone gave a tiny, hushed chime. The attorney picked it up. "Grady," he said. "Right, a hurry-up TT." He read the time and date of Marquette's call from his log. "Someone'll be at my office." He hung up.

"How long?" Stone said.

"Two, maybe three hours."

"Dammit."

"That's as fast as he can work it." Grady reached into a pocket in his briefcase, took out a key. He flipped it onto the table. "That's to my office. I've got a dinner date I can't afford to miss."

Jack downed his drink, slid out of the booth.

Grady said, "Wait a minute. How do I get you?"

"Gimme a piece of paper."

Grady gave him the blue pad. Jack wrote down his cell phone number, handed it back. The attorney looked at it, tossed it into his briefcase and shut it.

He glanced up, held Stone's eye this time. "You-all get one thing straight here, Stone. Nothin', and I mean *nothin'*, goes down in my presence. Understood?"

"Don't like your hands getting dirty, huh?"

"You got it."

Jack snorted with contempt. "Don't worry about it, Two-Gun." He smiled contemptuously, "Enjoy your dinner date." He turned and walked out just as the piano player finished "The Way We Were" and segued smoothly into "One for My Baby."

Marquette felt good, cruising on an unheralded sense of optimism. Everything was going to be all right. He knew it, felt it—the kind of sureness he'd known in the past, like fresh blood infusing into muscle.

He lay snugly in his wooden cave and watched the night rush past, the truck continually climbing but occasionally coasting down momentary slopes with its exhausts back-popping, the sound echoing off into the dark trees.

Around 9:30, it began to rain. That quickly turned to sleet. Water dripped down through the logs, chilling him. Outside, the cables hummed like the backstays of a small yacht, and then ice formed on the steel, tightening it, and he could hear it biting into the bark of the cap log. Now and then, slivers of ice, whirled by the air currents, snapped in over his face and left hand, stinging like tiny jolts of electricity.

Despite the cold, he was getting drowsy, the fatigue like a thickening of tissue. He closed his eyes and let his mind drift.

Kelli's face came softly. He kissed it, felt her lips touch his cheek, light as a butterfly. He ran his hands over her, let her come quickly from her clothes. But he did not make love to her. He merely lay and held her, the warm contours of her body scented with the faint essence of jasmine. He fell asleep.

Kelli disappeared.

He was in deep water, black as pitch. It pressed down on him, in it a current filled with silt that lightly buffeted his face mask. He reached bottom, and his hand went into soft sand. He paused to check the tiny glow of his compass. Ten more feet.

The communications conduit had metal collars that kept it off the bottom. There were streamers of seaweed that coiled around his fingers like awakened snakes. He quickly attached his C-4 UDE charge and pressed the timer key, the tiny metal box suddenly clicking through the darkness, the clicks coming faster, humming, as he hurtled away....

He opened his eyes. The truck was stopped. He stiffened, listening. The humming came again, one of the load cables being struck. He looked out. A flashlight was playing on the logs from the opposite side of the truck.

A car suddenly sped past, its tires hissing on the wet pavement, the lights flooding for an instant and then snapping back into darkness in a whirl of wind.

The driver came around to Matt's side, boots crunching on the unmelted ice. He tested the cables and skimmed his light over the load. It crossed Marquette's slot, passed on, then suddenly swept back again and finally went on past. A minute later, the driver went back around the truck.

Matt heard him slam the cab door. He relaxed.

The driver sat for a moment absorbing the warm cocoon of his cab. His radio was playing Reba McEntire, singing about starting over again. He lit a cigarette, turned Reba down and picked up the mike of his Motorola Nextel.

He keyed. "Six-oh-three to truck boss."

There was a splay of static, then: "Truck boss, go ahead."

"I got me a stowaway, Steve. He's up in the logs."

"Dammit, roust the bastard."

"I dunno. I been thinkin' this dude could be the guy the Smokeys are looking for. If it is, he's carrying firepower. I ain't messin' with him."

"Then flag down a patrol."

"No, they're liable to hold me up on the summit for a coupla hours. I'm gonna bring him in. Don't notify the cops yet, but you be sure some Edmonds PD are at the yard when I get there."

"What's your ETA?"

"Twelve thirty, quarter to one."

"I copy. Hey, be careful, John. Truck boss clear."

"Six-oh-three clear."

John sat smoking, wondering. The guy had to have come up on him at the concentration yard, he thought. Yeah. He'd been scanning WHP transmissions earlier in the afternoon and heard them mention something about a train search at Roslyn. Sure, this was the sucker, all right. He'd simply slipped away from them.

He put out his cigarette and brought Reba back. A moment later, he geared and pulled back onto the highway, his boot extra-heavy on the accelerator, prickly-shouldered with the realization that he had a killer less than twenty feet from his back.

The trap trace call came at 11:03.

By that time, Stone had circuited Grady's Navajo office a couple dozen times, sipping on one of the attorney's pinch bottles of scotch. It was like he was on speed, nerve endings jamming, everything wired and adrenaline-hyped. It seemed to absorb the whiskey like a flame, wouldn't even form a low-grade buzz.

When the phone rang, he leaped for it, punched the panel light and scooped up the receiver. "Yeah?" he said.

A man's voice said simply, "Pickett, Kelli . . . 3524 West-lake Drive."

3524 Westlake Drive. He scribbled it onto a memo pad.

"Where's that exactly?" he said.

The man hung up.

"Dammit." Stone glanced around the room for a city map. Nothing. He tried Grady's drawers. They were locked. Then he got an idea. He dialed Information.

The operator came on. "What city, please?"

"Seattle. Say, would you happen to know where Westlake Drive is?"

"Westlake Drive?" the operator said. "Sure, it skirts the west side of Lake Union."

"Thanks." He started to hang up.

"Would you like a number?" the operator said.

"No, that'll do it."

He lowered the receiver. 3524 Westlake Drive. A house-boat? Sure, a good place for Marquette to have hidden.

He took one last pull of scotch, flipped Grady's key onto the desk and headed for the door.

15

Kelli had entered, slowly and methodically, a dark, bizarre landscape that made her stomach grip down. For some odd reason, it drew up the icy impression of falling buildings, dust rising from ruins. The impression was almost palpable in the chill lab air. . . .

Earlier, she had been annoyed at Gilhammer. He'd deliberately dawdled in releasing the team from the CRYSTAL-BALL lab until well after eight o'clock—like a teenage boy pouting, showing that he still ran the show. It wasn't like Troy, and she knew she had angered him more than she realized and was sorry for it.

Throughout the early evening, bone-tired and stiff from tension, she'd repeatedly checked her home answering machine. Still nothing from Matt. Out of a deliberate twist of her mind, this fact actually buoyed her. If anything desperate had happened, she was sure she would have gotten some word by now. She clung to that thought.

Finally, alone at last, she set up the construct for her AI Platform search. The most time-consuming part of it was writing the software toolkit and inputting as much as possible of the sphere's data—schematics, measurements, known components—into the code language of Fuzzy Logic systems called PRUF. It took nearly three hours to complete.

Essentially, Fuzzy Logic dealt with the gray areas between absolutes. It located a thing's precise, fundamental "self." In practice, it was like analyzing an echo. According to FL set theory, the subject echo was never considered in "crisp" state. It existed neither in absolute silence nor in absolute sound. Instead, it lay somewhere along the line of gradation continuity, referred to as the C-line.

Once its exact position on that line was established, the second phase of a Platform search was initiated. This theoretical transform was referred to as a Bayesian Probability Inference Engine. By considering every conceivable way in which the echo could have been created, fitted within its C-line parameters, a precise fix might be obtained as to the conditions of its creation.

In essence, the BPIE run read backwards from the echo to its original sound—from effect to cause, shadow to object.

Once Kelli was able to isolate and precisely pinpoint the sphere's real "self," her Bayesian Probability construct could deduce its "target function" or true purpose.

Hopefully.

It was nearly midnight when everything was set. Hesitant to actually begin, she stalled, went to the bathroom, made coffee. While it perked, she went out for the last cigarette in her pack and stood around listening to the silence of the huge building. It seemed suddenly ominous, foreboding, like the still-emotion-charged hush of an empty church after a funeral.

Once more at her workstation, she clicked on and started the run.

Although the lab computers were equipped with the latest Tera-FLOPS processing speed and multilinked, integrated circuitry, it still took nearly twenty-two minutes to complete the data scan, working through literally trillions of IF-THEN and TRUE-FALSE domains of reference.

The machines clicked and hummed as Kelli scooted her chair from workstation to workstation, watching the splay of numbers and code scatter like white and green insects on the screens.

At last, the buzzer on the master computer sounded. She leaned in, studying the lines of code on the MC display. It contained the final DCID, the Deduced Conclusion of Ingested Data. Quickly she translated the code language back into normal speech.

She scanned the screen and felt her bones chill. Once again, that dark, unseen presence seemed to cross through the air. Her fears had been manifest. The sphere *was* a bomb—or at least part of one. Unfortunately, the Inference Engine had failed to define it completely. Instead, it presented three possible scenarios:

SCCON: BPIE-1-XXXKL: A BIOLOGICAL BOMB
                      DESIGNED TO CON-
                      TAMINATE A WATER
                      SUPPLY OR FOOD
                      SOURCE . . .
SCCON: BPIE-2-XXXKK: A   ZONE-SPECIFIC
                      DEMOLITION CHARGE
                      USING AN UNKNOWN
                      GAS . . .
SCCON: BPIE-3-XXXKJ: A COMPLEX TRIGGER
                      ASSEMBLY   FOR   A
                      LARGER,   NONSPE-
                      CIFIC DEMOLITION . . .

She rose to pace, head down. A single word kept jolting her mind. *Anthrax.* It reverberated like the menacing footfall in the dead of night. It was the key, she was certain of it. Her data had simply proven insufficient. A fundamental element was missing.

But what?

She ran back through the construct, focusing particularly on the anthrax input. Hurriedly accessing the campus's Magnusun Medical Center library, she downloaded text material pertaining to the disease and entered it into a reformed construct. Then she ran another BPIE search.

The results were the same.

*   *   *

It had been biting cold up on the summit; the logging truck moved through small snow flurries that whipped flakes into Marquette's crevice. But soon they were through the pass and headed on the long downslope to sea level, passing through patches of fog sometimes thick enough to obscure the gallery of trees rising on each side of the road.

They passed North Bend and then Issaquah and finally came into the outskirts of Bellevue. The driver crossed the southern end of Lake Washington and turned north on I-5. There it was overcast and the air off the sound felt comparatively warm, but there was a mist of fog over the city.

A few minutes later, the driver swung onto a cloverleaf, the truck gearing down to a near crawl in order to make the tight curve. It crossed under the freeway on 185th Street and headed west. Before it could gather speed again, Matt slipped from his hiding place and squatted for a moment on the edge of the flatbed, then jumped to the road.

He walked two blocks to First Avenue and then down Corliss. A huge shopping mall was on the corner. It was closed, but there were lights everywhere, which made the place look like an abandoned gas works. The fog gave the lights faint, colored halos.

Several teenagers were skateboarding in the parking lot. They wore dark baggies and turned-around baseball caps, and the wheels of their boards *shooshed* on the pavement. They belittled each other's skills and surveyed Matt with cocky looks as he crossed the lot to a phone booth near the mall entrance.

The booth smelled of marijuana smoke. He dialed Kelli's houseboat. The phone rang four times, clicked, and her voice came on: "Hi, this is Kelli. I'm not here at the moment. Please leave a message at the sound of the tone and I'll get back. 'Bye."

Beep.

He said, "I'm back. It's one-oh-four A.M. I'll be there in twenty minutes." He hung up.

Where was she? For a moment, he experienced a sharp

anxiety. Had they somehow gotten—? No, she was probably at the lab. He started to call there but suddenly realized he couldn't remember the number. Feeling stupid, he paged through the phone directory and called the main campus number. The sleepy-sounding girl who answered told him she wasn't allowed to give out the numbers of research facilities.

He walked back across the parking lot to 185th. His earlier sense of euphoria had dissipated. In its place was a nervous restlessness.

A Yellow Cab was parked in front of a bar called The Fat Lady up near Second Avenue. Matt pulled the front passenger door open and slid onto the worn seat.

The driver was listening to mariachi music, his eyes closed, his tongue clicking in time with the beat. He glanced over, a rotund Mexican with a thick brush mustache and horn-rimmed glasses that gave him a look of incongruous scholarliness.

He studied Matt's clothes, nose twitching. The cowboy's blood had long since dried and was now chemically breaking down. It had the foul smell of a tallow barrel.

"Goddam, meng," the Mexican said with repugnance. "Chu smell like sheet."

Matt silently rested his head back on the seat, closed his eyes.

"So, where chu wanna go?"

Earlier, Marquette had decided to stop at the CRYSTAL-BALL lab before going on to Kelli's houseboat. Now he hesitated. Would the police be checking cabs in the city? He shook his head. He was getting paranoid. *The Fugitive.* Well, maybe, but it was safer not taking chances.

Instead, he chose a point six blocks from the campus: "Forty-fifth and Latona in the city," he said.

The driver flipped down his meter flag and started the engine. He gave Marquette another disgusted look. "Chu gonna steenk up my focking cab, meng."

*   *   *

Marquette's voice sounded mechanical and hollow in the darkness of Kelli's front room: "I'm back. It's one-oh-four A.M. I'll be there in twenty minutes."

Click.

A hand reached out of the darkness and punched the replay button. There was another click, the sough of tape, and the message played again.

Jack Stone grinned, whispered triumphantly, "Oh, yeah."

He stood, moved about the room. He could hardly contain his whiskey-laced glee. The dumb prick was coming right to him. And in twenty fucking minutes.

He'd had little trouble finding Pickett's houseboat, just drove slowly along Westlake Avenue, flashing his light on mailbox numbers. Her houseboat was moored in a small bight of the shoreline.

He parked beside a tiny beach-park a block away and walked back to the houseboat, stood in the shadows for awhile to be certain no one was about. Then he quickly darted down her walkway. Using his jacket to muffle the sound, he broke one of the door panes, pulled back the bolt and went in.

Now he wondered just who this Kelli Pickett was. From the looks of her place, she was obviously single. Marquette's chief poke. But how much did she know? Since the call to Grady had come from here, she must know all Marquette knew. That meant he might have to kill her, too.

When he had first come in, poking around with his flashlight, he'd immediately noted the high-tech computer gear, the T-1 line and the twin UNIX machines. No amateur, this one, he decided. Pickett was probably a software designer, maybe even a computer researcher.

He came across snapshots of her on the shelf among the swimming trophies. He studied her image. Good-looking broad. At least Marquette had taste in women. Then he came across one of Marquette himself, leaning against the cabin doorway of his boat, smiling at the camera.

Stone stared at the snapshot, particularly at Marquette's eyes. It was always difficult to kill a man when you looked into his eyes. That was where his life hid. Yet Jack felt no remorse now. There was only a sense of anticipated pleasure—and the old feeling, the tingle, coming up through his blood.

This one would be for Gus. As for the repossession of the sphere, that had long since passed far beyond rage or revenge. It lay deep within him now, down where he himself began, a thing withheld and fermented into maniacal desire. At all and any cost, like a nearly forgotten buckskin stallion in a long-ago Red Elm corral . . .

He went out to the porch of the houseboat and crept up the walkway, checking for entrances on the dock side. There were none. Marquette would have to come to the front door. And that's where he'd take him, before the bastard saw the broken window and ran.

Stone studied the huge houseboat next door, listened for movement. It was silent and dark, save for a single green light on the dock.

He returned to Kelli's porch, stood inhaling the breeze off the lake. It was cold and invigorated his lungs. A few yards away, a small yacht with canvas coverings on its sails creaked gently at its buoy moorings, and a thin mist lifted off the dark water as if the lake were steaming.

Once more inside, he investigated the rest of the houseboat. The bedroom carried woman's scent: skin like warm milk, perfumed silk. In the bathroom, his flashlight cast a shattered sun on the copper tub.

For a tiny moment, he pictured the girl in the snapshot climbing from it, wet and naked, graceful as a deer rising from meadow grass. Then the picture changed, and he watched a bullet strike her in the belly, and then another, making tiny holes like puckered lips, red as the flesh of a pomegranate. He found that particular image oddly distasteful.

He went back into the bedroom and sat on the bed. With his flash off, the only light in the room was from Kelli's clock; tiny glowing numbers in the darkness. Sitting motionless, he became aware of the subtle shift of the floor as the houseboat rocked.

He checked the Ingram P-11, sat there toying with the breech bolt, slipping it back and forth a fraction of an inch and listening to the soft metallic clicks it made. Then he stopped, closed his eyes and turned his ears to catch the slightest sound of someone coming.

The phone rang in Two Elks's bedroom at 1:15 A.M. His wife, Tusi, answered it. "Hello?" she said gruffly. "Who?" She ticked her tongue and handed the phone to him. "Seattle PD."

Tusi was Samoan. Two Elks had met her in Honolulu when he played in the 1986 Pro Bowl. She had been a dancer with a Samoan hula troupe, a lovely, mischievous girl. After four children, her dancer's body had expanded into butter-chocolate broadness. Two Elks loved her dearly.

"Yeah?" he said, sitting up in his undershorts.

"John, Stu Walters. Hate to get you up, but I got something that could be Marquette."

Two Elks stopped rubbing his face and frowned. "Go."

"Edmonds PD got a call around one o'clock this morning from a lumber company, Cascade/Pacific. One of their drivers had a stowaway as he came in. The guy bailed before the truck got to the mill yard. But get this: the driver's pretty sure he got aboard at a loading yard outside Roslyn."

"Roslyn," Two Elks said. "That's gotta be him."

"That's what I figured. The driver said he was on the interstate all the way in until he got to one-eighty-fifth up there. So Marquette musta got off somewhere along there."

"He get a full description?"

"No, just got a glimpse, said the guy was wearin' what looked like a letterman's jacket. Edmonds's alerted their street cruisers, and they're checking with cabbies in the area now."

"You better red-line your APB," Two Elks said. "I got the feeling this thing is about to bust open."

"Already done. Along with an A and D tag-on."

"I'm coming in."

"Right. See you, John."

He hung up.

Tusi said, "What, you going out a-*gain*?"

"Yeah."

He dressed quietly. Tusi twisted and turned, murmuring to herself. When he finished, he leaned down and kissed her cheek. "I might be gone for a couple days, mama."

"Shoot!" Tusi said.

After the cabbie dropped him off, Matt hurried down Roosevelt and turned left at Forty-second Street. He knew there would be campus security guards posted at Gates One and Five on this side, so he stayed on Forty-second. It would take him to the campus's small Kitsip Lane turnstile, just south of the university's Memorial Museum.

The fog was thickening. It coated the streets with a sheet of moisture that glistened under the lights, and the sound of Interstate 5 came like hushed surf in the distance. From somewhere beyond it drifted the single mournful echo of a ship's horn. He entered the campus and walked through the huge, empty Central Plaza Garage; crossed Grant Lane and finally the Drumheller Quad to Guggenheim Hall. The huge doors were closed but unlocked. He went in and up the stairs, his shoes squeaking on the polished cement floor. The CRYSTALBALL lab lights were all lit.

Kelli didn't move for twenty whole seconds when he stepped quietly through the door. She had glanced up, startled for a moment that someone was there. Then her mouth slowly opened, and she stared at him.

At last, she rose, quickly, a lunging upward, went to him and threw her arms around him fiercely. They stood wordlessly holding each other.

He finally broke the embrace. "Hi," he said, grinning down at her.

There were tears in her eyes, and she kept squeezing his shoulders. "God, I thought you were dead," she whispered.

"Almost."

"What happened out there? Why didn't—" Then she noticed his clothing, and a new anxiety leapt into her eyes. "Is that blood? You're hurt!'

"No, it's not mine."

"What happened, Matt?"

"It's a long story." He caught sight of the coffee percolator. "I could sure use a little of that."

She hurried to it, poured him a cup and brought it over. Holding it, he walked to a workstation and laid his gym bag on it. He leaned tiredly against the desk and drank.

Kelli watched him for a moment, then looked down at the bag. Her eyes narrowed. "Do you still have it?"

He nodded.

"I've been running an analysis on that thing," she said, still staring at the bag. "It's horrible."

He slowly lowered the cup. "Tell me."

She did, going back through the entire run. He listened, the coffee suddenly forgotten, his eyes growing colder and colder. When she finished, he quietly put the cup down and stared at his hands.

"We've got to destroy it," Kelli said, "or give it to someone who can. Even though I don't have all the data, I know enough. It's filthy and evil and godawful dangerous."

He lifted his eyes to her. He didn't say anything.

A shocked look crept into her face. "You don't agree?"

"We can't do that yet."

"For God sake, why not? We're talking the possibility of mass murder here."

"Not as long as we have it."

"But those . . . people out there aren't going to give up. We don't know who they are or what they are. What if they find you and take it back?"

"That's just it, Kelli. As long as I've got it, they'll have to come to me."

"And kill you."

"It's the only way I can expose them."

"Then go to the police. With what I have, they'll listen to you now. They'll have to."

He shook his head. "No. Once these bastards found out the police were into it, they'd go to ground, disappear. We'd never find them."

"Let the filth disappear. We'll at least have stopped them."

"How can we be sure? What if there are other spheres like this one, Kelli? Already planted in the city? Or in some other city?"

The chilling reality of that stunned her into silence.

"No," Matt said. "There's only one way to get at them. And that's through me."

He pushed away from the table and walked slowly among the workstations, thinking. Finally, he stopped. "Which one of these computers has that DCID run?"

"That one."

He went to it, stood reading the suppositional scenarios. He shook his head. "This thing's not a demo charge trigger. A gas bomb? Maybe. But I think it's more likely some sort of anthrax chamber. Have you rerun the construct?"

"Yes. I even downloaded everything the university medical library's got on anthrax. But there's still something missing, some key element preventing specificity in target function."

Matt began to pace, head thrown back, eyes closed. He tried to bring up the memories of lectures on biological warfare he'd attended when he was in the SEALs. The content came back scattered and spotty across the years:

Bacillus anthracis . . . common form: cutaneous with malignant pustule and anthracitic meningitis . . . vector system: animal meat by contact . . . German troops contaminating Romanian cavalry horses: 1917 . . . Iraqi experiments, Russian . . . the treaty ban of 1970 . . . at present technology, impractical for ordnance dispersal due to slow vector contagion . . .

Impractical for ordnance dispersal.

Something hovered on the periphery of his mind. It hung out there, elusive.

Kelli said, "Should I try another run?"

"Wait a minute."

Then it started coming. There: a name, a place. *Sverdlovsk*. He swung around, eyes snapping open. "Access the medical library again."

She hurried to her station. In a moment, she was logged in.

"Run a search for anything on the Russian town of Sverdlovsk. Nineteen seventy-six—no, nineteen seventy-nine."

She did. Nothing came up.

"What other medical sources can you access?"

"Anything. Journals, associations, hospital records—"

"Try the American Medical Association."

She brought it up. Listed publications. Marquette studied the list, and Kelli ran a search for the Russian town. Still nothing.

Matt cursed, walked around a bit, came back. "How deep can you penetrate military security?"

"Probably pretty deeply, but it'd take some fancy technique and a lot of time."

"What about Freedom of Information stuff?"

"Easy. We can start with the Library of Congress."

Within six minutes, she had isolated an item on Sverdlovsk/anthrax within the LOC archives. It was from a Department of Defense white paper on Russian biological experimentation during the years 1978–79. In a historical footnote, it said:

Intelligence reports (DOD-2546DIA and DOD-3647DIA) indicated a Soviet team headed by Dr. Nikolai Karolov of the military-run Institute for State Medical Logistics performed experiments during 1968–9 at the Nathpockti Shakh facilities in the coal town of Sverdlovsk on Bacillus anthracis *organisms for the purpose of creating biological ordnance.*

Mission goal was the creation of an inhalative genome-state of the anthracis through the use of pico-second bursts of heat, which hurled the bacterium's DNA spirals into rapid, survival-threshold mutative

*meiosis. Experiments were discontinued, however,
when an accidental release of the spores into the atmosphere surrounding the facility took place. It is believed that over eight thousand civilian deaths resulted
from this accident. The rate of fatality after infection
was said to have been 100%.*

"That's it," Matt snapped. "Your key element. Airborne
anthrax."

Kelli was still looking at the last line of the entry: *. . . rate
of fatality . . . 100%.* At last, she turned and looked up at
Matt. Her eyes held sharp, dark lights and seemed to quiver
with a strange meloncholy. "Oh, Matt," she said softly, as
if her voice might shatter the terrible silence.

He put his hand on her shoulder. "Download the entry
into your construct and run it again," he said.

Thirty-one minutes later, a new DCID had been formed.
It was all there.

16

Stone toiled within a kind of soul pain. Frustration and anxiety drew nausea into him, a sourness like a wound. It was now 2:31 A.M. Obviously, something had gone wrong with Marquette's coming.

Restlessly, he paced Kelli's bedroom, glared at her clock. Then he went out to the front room and finally the porch. The breeze had picked up, turned very cold. He stood there hurling maledictions across the lake.

Where in Chris' Almighty was Marquette? Could he have sensed ambush? Was he even at this moment lurking somewhere close by? No, he couldn't have suspected anything. Perhaps he'd gone after Grady. Stone also discarded that possibility. He wouldn't have called to the boathouse and specified such a short arrival time.

Then an icy thought struck him. Had Marquette been picked up by the police? For a moment, Stone experienced a wild urge to flee, eveything suddenly coming apart, exposed like a nakedness. He went back into the houseboat, huddled near the door, peering out.

Slowly, he quieted himself. Marquette hadn't been arrested. If he had, and had talked, Grady would certainly have known about it and would have called on the cell phone.

No, Marquette was still loose. But where? With Pickett? Could they have another safe house? He slumped. If that were the case, everything was lost. There was too little time left for him to again pick up Marquette's trail.

Then again, maybe . . .

He hurried to Kelli's workstation, brazenly turned on the overhead light and began to rifle through drawers and data folders. Somewhere there must be a clue to where Marquette's bitch could be. If he wasn't actually with her, she'd know where to look for him.

The accumulated material on the CRYSTALBALL lab quickly disclosed Pickett's identity as a staff researcher at the university. He paused. Were they at the campus? Not likely at this time of night. Then again, it *was* possible. Pickett might actually be the one in possession of the sphere. He had noted that she was an expert in AI and computer technology. Could she have been running computer analyses on the sphere? A wild thought.

He went back through the folders, slower, searching for ID and access codes. He was sure her machines were linked to a secure net at the university. He scanned downloaded material, checked headings and finally found it: 2X18813.cs/ kp:orion.comm.

Again he paused. Should he make deliberate contact with her? That would expose his position. But it would also show Pickett, and thereby Marquette, that they could never escape; give the illusion that their pursuers were everywhere, even here. And that might force them into exposure—or a deal.

Outside, the wind rustled Kelli's ferns, made the neighbor's green walkway light bob slightly in the chop. Beyond was utter silence.

He reached out and clicked on one of the computers. . . .

Kelli's screen said:

SCCON: BPIE-4-XXXKL: TARGET DEVICE IS
                       ANTHRAX - CHAMBER
                       BOMB. CAPABLE OF
                       DNA ALTERATION OF
                       BACILLUS ANTHRA-

CIS GENOME INTO SPIRAL FORM WITH AIRBORNE CHARACTERISTICS. ATTACHED LOW-YIELD EXPLOSIVE DEVICE CAPABLE OF SCATTER PATTERN IN RANGE OF 30-60 METERS.

Cold, precise.

Matt and Kelli read it. Again. Then looked at each other. Although partially expected, the reality stunned. Earlier, their humanity had balked at the full premise.

It was unspeakable, so they did not speak. The night paused, a tiny lapse. The lab's air conditioner seemed to cease its soft breath. Everything stopped. And then started again, and Matt said, "Jesus!"

His eyes turned to the gym bag. It exuded its dark, ineffable presence. He tried to think ahead. Now there was a completely new landscape. One false step, one wrong choice . . .

Kelli said, "We can't deal with this alone anymore. We need help."

He didn't answer.

"Matt, listen to me." She moved to him, stared into his eyes. "This is airborne anthrax, the same thing that was loose in that Russian town. One-hundred-percent fatality rate! How can we play games with this thing any longer?"

"We don't have a choice."

"Are you willing to risk this kind of—of chaos? With monsters like that?"

"*Dammit*, Kelli," he said sharply. "You think I want it this way?"

She put her head down for a moment, looked up again.

"Then let's at least contact the Centers for Disease Control in Atlanta. They'd tell us what to do."

"No. Once they knew, the whole thing'd blow open."

"Not if we explained, not if they realized the situation. They could handle it discreetly."

"How can you handle something like this discreetly? There'd be a red alert in every emergency agency in the city. Maybe even mass evacuations, total panic."

She put her fingertips to her temples as if to stifle a scream. "Then what in God's name can we do?"

"I'm going after them."

"How?"

"Through Grady."

"You won't stand a chance. They'll kill you."

"No, they won't."

"But what—"

Suddenly, all the lab's computers that Kelli had not been using for the DCID run clicked on, their screens lighting. For a moment, they stood blank.

Matt said, "What's happening?"

Kelli frowned, puzzled. "Someone's accessing the entire lab net." She walked to the closest machine, stood watching.

Then letters began snapping up onto the screens:

KELLI PICKETT

Her name repeating, scrolling down:

KELLI PICKETT
KELLI PICKETT
KELLI PICKETT

She punched a key. Instantly, an identification code for the accessing machine appeared in the corner of the screen: PROCESS (2×18813.cs/kp:orion.comm).

"Oh, my God," she gasped. "It's one of my machines."

She twisted around, stared at Matt, her face open with shock. ''They're at my houseboat.''

The computers continued printing out her name, like a soft, obscene whisper from the darkness.

A Yellow Cab was parked just inside the gate of the cruiser yard of Seattle's West Precinct station on Third and James when Two Elks pulled in. The driver was talking Spanish with one of the department mechanics, joshing, senorita-rapping.

The yard was quiet. It was now nearly three o'clock, an hour before the normal shift change. Two Elks got out. He glanced at the two men and then walked over to them.

''You the one picked up the fare on a hundred eighty-fifth?'' he asked the cabbie.

The man looked him up and down. ''You a cop?''

''Lieutenant Two Elks, Clallam County Sheriff's Office.'' The mechanic turned and walked away.

''Oh, yeah,'' the cabbie said. ''Wow, chu a beeg dood.''

''Tell me about the man.''

''Like I say before, he jump inside my cab on hunnart-eighty-fifth. Meng, he steenk bad, chu know?''

''What do you mean bad?''

''Jus' bad. Hees clothes are all dirty, covered with stains, chu know? He smell like *un matadero*.''

''What's that?''

''*Matadero*, where they kill the cattle.'' The cabbie's eyes narrowed behind his glasses. ''Hey, chu play futbol, no? Sure, I joos to see you on telebision in Tia-*hua*-na.''

''He say anything during the ride?''

''No, he jus' sit there with hees head back.''

''Where'd he get out?''

''Forty-fifth an' Latona.''

''You notice where he went?''

''No, I jus' get my money and take off, meng.''

''Thanks.''

"*De nada*," said the cabbie.

Upstairs in the main squad room, Two Elks found Lieutenant Walters in his office. He was a tall, slender man with curly gray hair and a lean face long since immune to expression. "Hi, John," Walters said. "You just missed the cabbie who picked up Marquette."

"I talked to him in the yard."

"Spot anything?"

"No."

"Well, so far we haven't gotten a sighting. North Precinct's put a couple extra cruisers into that area along Roosevelt. It's a nonresidential."

"I know." Two Elks had spent his college years at the University of Washington and was familiar with the Wallingford district, bisected by Latona and Roosevelt Avenues. Back then, a pizza and beer saloon had sat off Forty-third. It was called the Second-and-Ten. He and many of the Huskies football players had hung out there between seasons.

He studied the wall map behind Walters's desk. On it, the campus formed a large area marked in light purple a few blocks east of the Roosevelt section, right along the edge of Union Bay.

"Coffee?" Walters asked.

"Thanks. Black."

Walters went over to the black coffeemaker near the door and began to pour.

Two Elks asked, "Did North Precinct alert campus security?"

Walters turned around. "You think he's headed over there?"

"Possible."

"Why?"

"Just a hunch."

Walters shrugged. "I'll tell 'em," he said.

"Answer him," Matt said.

Kelli's head snapped around. "What?"

"Answer him. Tell him you're here."

"Why?"

"Just do it, Kelli."

She sat down at the workstation, quickly keystroked: *i'm here.*

The answer was immediate, the letters popping rapidly up on the screen: *where's marquette?*

"Tell him I'm here, too," Matt said.

"No."

"Kelli, we've got—here, I'll do it." She gave up the chair. Using only his forefingers, Matt typed: *hello asshole.*

Stone: *so we finally meet. where's my property?*

Matt: *i have it.*

Stone: *i want it. now.*

Matt: *what's in it for me?*

Stone: *your lives.*

Matt: *unacceptable answer.*

There was a pause. Then Stone came back: *what do you want?*

Matt: *a million dollars.*

Kelli stood around watching, her mind saying, "Oh, God!" She couldn't believe what was happening. These two men were interfacing, horse-trading, their words as casual as two sales reps discussing the price of fish—yet the content was death. It was too weird, pure freakery.

She turned and strode way across the room; stood there staring at the wall. Over the past two days, her mind had absorbed a mountain of stun, heavy input. She could feel the exhaustion in her like a lead glove. She caught the faint odor of her own body, her clothes: gamy, woman-soiled.

Then a chill seeped out of the air and into her skin with the realization that this man, this faceless entity who at this moment hurled electronic letters onto her screen like darts to a board, was a killer who actually *intended* to kill them ... to kill thousands!

She turned. The screen said: *don't be stupid. where do i get that kind of money?*

She walked back, stood behind Marquette again. She
touched his shoulder. It was steel-hard, the same shoulder
she had held, had bitten during those delirious moments of
passion that seemed, here, so distant in time. Now she sensed
a strange ironness beyond muscle. An elation? She looked
at his fingers. They were rock-steady.

Matt: *get it from grady.*

A pause.

Without turning around, Matt asked, "Does the campus
have an ROTC armory?"

"What?"

"An armory, an armory."

For a moment, she was confused. "Yeah, I think so. Sure
it's in Clark Hall."

"Does it have an ordnance inventory?"

"You mean weapons? I don't know. There's a firing range
down near the sport fields."

Stone: *all right, a million.*

Matt: *i want grady to make the exchange.*

Stone: *why?*

Matt: *i owe the prick.*

Stone: *yeah, i'd say you do. where and when?*

"I need an isolated place," Matt said. "Lots of cover,
woods."

Kelli squinted, trying to think. "How about the Washington Park Arboretum? It's full of woods."

Matt frowned, thinking. He'd been to the park twice. What
was there? Sure.

He typed: *washington park arboretum. near the japanese
garden. dawn.*

Stone: *too early. we'll have to get money from bank.*

Matt: *then nine a.m. sharp.*

Stone: *accepted.* A pause, then: *i hope you choke on the
goddamn money.*

Matt: *fuck you, too.*

Grady's beeper sounded like a tiny bubble of sound drifting around the bedroom. The attorney was asleep, lying on

his side. Beside him, curled against his back, was a girl whose lush, red hair lay in disarray on the pillow. Her name was Jean. She was an assistant producer at the Channel KTNT studio in downtown Seattle.

Slowly he came up into consciousness, blinking. The room smelled of sex and hair spray. He fumbled around on the bedside table and squinted at the tiny screen of his beeper unit.

It said *STONE: 206-555-8836.*

Oh, Lord, he thought, what the hell now? He turned on the light and elbowed the girl. "Hey, honeybunch, get up."

"What?" Jean lifted her head. She had violet eyes. "What's the matter?"

"Go make some coffee."

"Now? My God, it's three in the morning."

"Go awn, I gotta do some business."

"Well, shit," Jean said. She got out of bed. She was naked, and there were red hand-marks still on her buttocks where Grady had gripped her as he plunged.

He dialed the Stone number, not recognizing it. It rang once, and Stone said, "Grady?"

"Yeah."

"I've made contact with Marquette."

"You got the trace address, then."

"Yeah. He's agreed to sell us the sphere."

"Sell it? Us?"

"Us. He wants a million."

"Wait a minute—"

"And you're gonna deliver it. He wants it that way."

"Are you outta your mind?"

"Shut up and listen. We ain't gonna give him nothing. You just show up with a lot of cash. I'll do the rest."

"No," Grady said. "You're the one wants the damned thing; *you* pay him."

"Grady."

"I ain't gonna do it."

"Yes, you are."

"I told you before, I ain't part of *this*."

"Listen, crackerass, you *are* a part of it," Stone said. "And you're gonna stay a part of it until I tell you you're finished."

"No, goddammit."

There was a string of silence. When Stone came back, his voice hissed with threat. "Don't fuck with me, man. You bail out now, I'll blow your goddamned head off."

The attorney fell into anguished silence.

"You hear what I'm saying?" Stone said.

"There's gotta be another way. Don't you realize I'll be exposing myself?"

"We do it this way."

Grady inhaled, let the air out slowly, figuring. Maybe it might be all right. He could jive Marquette long enough to make the exchange and then get the hell out fast. "All right, Stone," he said. "Where does this meeting take place?"

"Near the arboretum in some place called Washington Park. You know where it is?"

"Yeah. When?"

"Nine this morning."

At least that part was in his favor, Grady thought. The Park was a secluded enough place to cut down on eyewitnesses. He inhaled again, squinted at his hand. "Are you gonna kill him?"

"What the fuck do you think?"

"Not around me," Grady said quickly. "You get him the hell away from me when you do it. Either you guarantee me that, or I'm out. And y'all can threaten all you want."

"You got it. I do it after you've cleared the area."

"All right," Grady said, relieved. "Okay."

"Remember, make it look good," Stone said. "Briefcase full of cash, the whole bit. Nine o'clock." He hung up.

Grady sat staring at the floor. It was carpeted in a thick, white wool. After a while, Jean came back, still naked, carrying a ceramic mug with an elf forming the handle.

"Here's your damned coffee," she said disgustedly.

*   *   *

While Matt washed up in the men's room, Kelli sequestered her findings in her workstation machine and was pacing
near the front door of the lab when he came out. She looked
at him, nervously brushed her hair back. Her face looked
drawn, pale.

"You can't do this," she said flatly.

"I have to."

"Oh, Matt, they'll kill you."

"They'll try."

She studied his eyes. "You're turned on, aren't you? In
some crazy way, this is putting a high in you."

For a moment, he turned his head slightly, his expression
wistful. He turned back. "I've been dead a long time, Kel.
Can you understand that?"

She stared at him, then hugged him fiercely, turned and
went out the door.

Clark Hall was a half mile northeast of Guggenheim, an
old red-brick building with four slender Doric columns at the
head of the front steps and twin barbicans framing the entrance. To the east of it spread the vast open spaces of the
university's playing field complex.

Kelli eased her Blazer off Steven's Way onto Skagit Lane
and slowly circled the building. Matt studied it through the
open window. No one was around. The night had turned
crisp, cold. A wind blew off the lake across the playing
fields, carrying the smell of spring grass and newly turned
earth and sawdust from the jump pits.

They circled it again, and Matt told her to stop on a short
gravel path near the vehicle yard at the side of the building.
He checked his watch. It was 4:16 A.M. He put the tools and
flashlight he'd brought from the lab into his pocket and got
out. For a moment, he glanced up at the eastern sky. It was
partially overcast and still night-dark.

He leaned down. "Park somewhere away from here. Give
me twenty minutes."

"God, be careful."

"Don't worry. It's a piece of cake." He turned and

sprinted to the wire fence surrounding the vehicle yard, his
shoes crunching on the gravel, the tools clinking softly. With
easy grace, he went up and over the fence and dropped down
into the yard. Behind him, the Blazer moved onto Steven's
Way and turned right.

There were several vehicles parked in a line: jeeps, a Hum-
vee, two three-quarter ammo carriers. On the other side were
a field-kitchen truck and a communications van. They were
all painted field green.

Marquette moved along the back of the building, staying
in the shadows as best he could. He reached a large steel
door that slid on wheels. It was securely padlocked. He
checked windows. Everything was covered with heavy mesh
and hard-wired, foil strips running through glass. Several
pieces of field equipment covered with canvas were stored
under an overhang.

He crossed and recrossed the entire yard, looking for access. Nothing was open or loosely locked. He cursed and
studied the yard, the trucks. He spotted an outside grease pit
close to the back wall. He darted to it and slipped down the
steps.

The yard lights cut sharply over the upper edge, illuminating the bottom. There were two hydraulic lift cylinders
with hand control boxes. He moved along the wall until he
found the inspection hatch for the pressure tanks. Quickly,
he unscrewed the wing nuts and pulled it open.

Inside was a narrow tunnel beside a single tank. Above it
was a pressure gauge and valve panel with relay piping feeding down to the lift cylinder sleeves, which went through the
wall. Beyond the tank was another access door.

This door opened onto a low tunnel that passed through a
maintenance room containing a small boiler. Beyond were
cement steps and a door at the top that broached the main
lobby of the building.

An old 75 mm howitzer stood in the lobby. It was black
and glistened like glass. Across the room was a tall trophy
case holding awards for marksmanship and loading drill
competition. Beside it were crossed purple-and-gold battalion

flags, pictures of ROTC units of the past and two World War I campaign hats, sugar-stiffened, their robin's-egg-blue cords and acorns faded with age.

Matt scurried through a small sally port into a huge assembly room. The floor was worn brown tile, but it was waxed to a high gloss. The space was cold and smelled of saddle soap and gun oil.

Kelli had driven out to the university's golf driving range to wait. She sat on Walla Walla Road and listened to the range flags snapping in the wind.

Desperate for a cigarette, she felt her nerves send continual little riffles of energy through her skin, like waves on a beach. She thought: What the hell am I doing? Knew and agonized. The night hung a dark danger in the wind, so she closed all the windows and sat hugging herself.

The car lights came across the vast, empty E1 parking lot swiftly, lunging over the dips, straight at her. She watched them come, and her heart started beating wildly. Then they were close enough that she could make out the white cruiser, see the university logo on the passenger door. A campus security patrol.

The cruiser pulled up beside her window, and the driver got out. He wore a blue jacket with a fur collar. He directed his flashlight onto her face.

"Is there some problem here, miss?" he asked. He bent and played the light inside the Blazer.

"No problem." She laughed, aware of the nervous lift in her voice. "I just came out for a smoke and a breath of fresh air. I've been working late."

"Where?"

"Guggenheim Hall."

"And you came all the way out here for a cigarette? You got any identification?"

She took her lab ID tag from the glove compartment, handed it over. He put the light on it and glanced up, comparing the photo. He handed it back.

"I wouldn't sit out here alone, ma'am," he said. "We just

got a priority alert from Seattle PD. They think a fugitive might be on campus.''

''Really?''

The guard nodded. ''Big man, filthy clothes, university letterman's jacket. You see anybody like that, give the main guard station a call.''

''All right.''

''Well, be careful.'' He touched the brim of his hat, got back into the cruiser and left.

Kelli started the engine. Her hands were shaking. She returned to Montlake Boulevard and drove slowly back toward Clark Hall. She looked at her watch. There were still ten minutes left before she was to pick up Marquette.

He located the small armory in the basement. The outer door easily broke open with his weight. Just inside was a thick, floor-to-ceiling wire mesh. It had a clerk's port in the center with a sliding metal panel. Beyond were a desk and a door to a second room. He could see the edge of rifle racks back there.

It took him several minutes to loosen the screws of the panel with a screwdriver from the lab. He finally slid it open, squeezed through and slipped into the second room. The racks contained at least a hundred M-16 assault rifles. In another, smaller rack were a dozen Winchester Marine twelve-gauges. There was also a large metal safe that probably contained handguns.

He studied the M-16 racks. They were all triple-barred with an entire series of carbon-hardened, heavy-duty locks. It was the same with the shotgun rack. Again, he cursed. There was no way he'd get weapons from here.

He wandered around, peering into cubbyholes. He came to a closet. Inside were a half dozen Kevlar bulletproof vests. They were dark blue and bore the stenciled word RANGE. The material was scuffed and stained and had obviously been used by cadets working the targets on the firing range.

Matt grabbed one. He took off his jacket, slipped into the vest and then put his jacket back on. It felt heavy, yet suddenly familiar. He checked his watch. Kelly would be returning in six minutes.

He went back into the front room. The desk was military-neat, regular Army. There were two locked filing cabinets beside it, a shortwave radio, a coffeemaker. His eye caught the glint of something against the wall between the cabinets.

There were two World War II M1-A1 carbines there—competition weapons, the barrels and breeches chromed, stocks sporterized with hand-molded grips. Nearby was a small military ammo box. It contained cleaning gear, spare clips, score pads and six boxes of Ball M1 copperpoint carbine rounds. Obviously, their owner had carelessly left them unlocked.

Matt quickly filled two clips. He put one in his jacket pocket, the other into one of the carbines. It made a solid metallic rap in the stillness, an ordnance sound, a soldier's sound. The weapon felt good and clean in his hands.

Four minutes later, he scaled the yard fence just as the Blazer pulled up. He hauled open the passenger door and slid in. Kelli looked at the carbine, squinting.

"I was stopped," she said. "Campus security. He said the Seattle police are checking for a fugitive on the campus."

Matt's head snapped around. "Dammit, they must have traced the cab. They're getting close. That means they'll likely be checking gates."

"We can go off campus out near the range," Kelli said. "Montlake goes right onto Forty-fifth with no gate."

She geared and went slowly up onto Steven's Way just as one of the campus jitneys came past. It was empty save for a young couple necking in the back. Behind the little bus was another campus patrol cruiser.

"Oh, God," Kelli said.

"Smile and wave at him," Matt snapped.

She did. The patrolman waved back. A moment later, he and the jitney disappeared beyond Clark Hall.

Matt relaxed and glanced toward the east. Far away and high beyond the city lights, the line of the mountains and the clouds held the first, faint glow of dawn, indigo on black.

17

"They're moving," Jo-Jo said. Kizzier's eyes opened instantly. He sat forward, coughing phlegm in his throat. He glanced across the wide stretch of Madison Boulevard to the front of the Seneca House Hotel.

The Seneca resembled a French château: two stories of rich cream-colored walls, a bright blue roof with four-corner pinnacles at each end and a brass widow's walk. A doorman stood in red livery under a portico. Spread around the building was a complex, perfectly manicured garden.

Kizzier immediately spotted Dog James. He stood under the portico, hunched up in his lumberman's jacket. In the plush surroundings, he looked like a beggar stopped for a handout. Idly, he looked up and down the boulevard, then spat onto the almost-polished cobblestones of the driveway and went back into the hotel.

"I got a feeling it's gonna be today," Jo-Jo said. "They're up too early." It was now barely 5:30, dawn light coming in all gray and somber.

"Yeah," Kizzier said.

It had been a long night. They'd followed their targets to several bars after the Celtic Cross and finally ended up at the top of the Space Needle. Halberstadt and James were in the intimate Emerald Suite, boisterous as hell, while their whores looked uncomfortable. One was husky-fat as a Russian peasant but pretty, the other slender as a New York model.

Afterward, the group went upstairs to the Top of the Needle Lounge. Jo-Jo and Kizzier hung outside rather than risk a make in the confines of the small bar. They wandered around, looking at Kodak displays and peering through the high-powered telescopes at the hulking, conic shadow of Mount Rainier, then down at the waterfront. After awhile, bored, they started checking out lighted windows to see if they could catch somebody screwing.

There had been a close moment with their quarry. With all the messed-up eating, Kizzier had developed a touch of diarrhea. Desperate, he'd had to sneak into the lounge's men's room, squatted disgustedly there amid the antiseptic-smelling gray-black and mauve tiles.

Someone came in, slamming back the door. Kizzier listened to him urinate, groaning sillily to himself. Silence. Then a hard impact against the door of the stall next to his. Then on his.

What the hell?

He pulled the door open a few inches. Halberstadt was standing in front of the mirror, grinning crazy-eyed at himself, his bald head shining in the overhead fluorescent lights. He caught the stall door opening and whirled around.

"'*Ey Arschlock*," he growled menacingly. "*Du kannst mich mal am Arsch lecken!*"

"Sorry," Kizzier said and quickly closed the stall door. Shit! He'd been seen. Halberstadt once more threw a fist against the door and went out.

On the platform again, Kizzier said, "Hans saw me."

"Aw, no."

"Yeah." He sucked air through his teeth. "Man, that sucker's cranked up to his eyeballs. He ain't gonna come easy."

After the Needle, they'd followed the group back to the Seneca. Jo-Jo parked down the boulevard beside a laundry building, and they settled in to wait for dawn or whatever. Around four, the two prostitutes left, going off in the limo, looking decidedly relieved.

Now James's shabby pickup came swinging around the corner of the hotel and pulled up under the portico. The attendant got out and slipped the tag off the wiper. He walked off, shaking his head.

Hitler-Hans and the Dog came out a moment later. The doorman smilingly led them down to their vehicle and got stiffed for his troubles. They tossed their suitcases into the bed, James's a leather affair faded to a chaparral color with a cord holding it together.

Jo-Jo started the car. "Yeah, I got the feeling, baby," he said. "That meet's right down the road."

Kizzier reached back for his weapon bag. He unzipped it, took out two Uzis. After checking the clips and making sure there were rounds in the chamber, he laid them on the seat. Then he took out two lightweight armored vests and laid them down, too.

The pickup moved down the drive and swung right on Madison. Jo-Jo waited a moment, then pulled a U and merged neatly into the traffic several car lengths behind.

Kizzier checked his watch. 5:41. He logged it.

Kelli had been correct; Matt *was* riding a sort of high—not the full adrenaline rush just yet, but more a mental psyching up for what lay ahead. It was familiar ground, rockin' and rollin', like being aboard the Hueys of Light Helo Fire Team Three just before the first M60Cs opened up with covering fire.

A preparing.

He knew there was a good chance he'd have to kill again. He thought about the two men in the chopper back out in the Basin; beyond them, to all the others. And he realized, with a sudden pleasurable shock, that the deep guilts that had haunted him since Barcelona were now, somehow, almost evaporated—not completely gone, but almost.

Still, there were moral injunctions, yet even these seemed caught in the web of Battle Immunity now. Self-survival exempted certain moralities. Nam had been pointless; but here, the real survival of literally thousands of people disarmed his prohibitions. Kill or be killed: the soldier's prerogative.

Kelli turned the Blazer off Washington Boulevard into the

north entrance of Washington Park, easing past the small stone caretaker's cottage at the gate. Beyond lay the lush, golf-link meadows of the park. The scattered groves of Douglas fir and cedar held faint wisps of fog like hairnets.

She continued along Arboretum Drive toward the shore of Lake Washington and finally pulled up beside a small basin constructed of granite stones with a water pipe for drinking. Across the drive was the marshy edge of the lake, tall water grass and mud flats and rocks covered with sweet algae.

Beyond were the rolling fairways of Broadmoor Golf Course and, farther still, the Evergreen Point floating bridge with thickening morning traffic, some of the cars running with their headlights on.

Neither had spoken much after the armory run, each partitioned off with thoughts. They'd exited the campus without incident and then spent time in a McDonald's parking lot, waiting for daylight. Marquette ate ravenously, wolfing down Egg McMuffins.

Kelli's coiled fear had also engendered a kind of hunger, and she'd managed a hamburger, too, then discreetly got out and vomited behind the Blazer. Two counter girls watched from the door of the restaurant.

Now they sat in the car and watched joggers pass and Steller's jay birds go gliding through the trees. Earlier, Kelli had stopped for cigarettes. She opened the pack, methodically pulling away the cellophane wrap. Her hands were still shaking.

They both lit up, inhaling deeply.

Kelli put her hands on the steering wheel, her head down. "Lord, I'm scared," she said. "I don't ever remember being this scared before."

"I know."

She looked at him, her eyes sorrowful. "Can you really do this?"

"Yes."

"But why take the sphere with you? If they—"

"They have to see it."

She took a drag, blew the smoke at the header. "You don't

even know how many you'll have to deal with."

"Two are already dead. Besides Grady, there can't be many more."

She grunted. "Somehow that doesn't comfort me."

He checked his watch. 6:15. He bent down and unzipped the gym bag, took out the Browning Hi-Power. He checked it as he talked, extracting the clip and putting it back, jacking a round into the chamber and easing the hammer down to half-cock. He shoved it under the band of his Levi's, near his left hip.

Kelli watched silently.

"Here's how we work it," he said. "At exactly nine-fifteen, call Lieutenant Two Elks at the Clallam County Sheriff's Office. Tell him the whole story, convince the bastard it's true. He'll take it from there."

She nodded.

"Then you call the Centers for Disease Control in Atlanta. Let them download everything you've got."

"All right." Her eyes flitted over his face. As he rezippered the bag and straightened, she lunged across the seat, drew him in. The carbine was in the way. She roughly shoved it aside, held him, her face against his jacket.

"I can't bear this," she murmured.

He kissed her hair, felt the line of her neck gently with his fingers, looking out through the windshield to see if anyone was coming. And then he disengaged, opened the door and stepped out, the gym bag and rifle in the same hand. He lightly tapped the top of the window, turned and sprinted toward the woods.

Right at the edge, he paused, turned and looked back over his shoulder. He smiled at her, then disappeared among the trees.

Eight minutes later, Jack Stone pulled his car up near a grove of Douglas fir a hundred yards from the park's Graham Visitor's Center. Having come in the south entrance, he'd had to traverse the entire park.

After talking with Grady, he'd immediately returned to his

hotel for the bomb's secondary components. Then he'd traced a meticulous back-trail from the bomb target to Washington Park, memorizing the exact route in reverse. The actual time it was going to take him from park to target would be close.

Now he studied the area. At the center was a squat building of dirty brown aggregate stone with a trellised walk across the front. Behind it sat a low glass greenhouse. There were two vehicles parked out front: a Volkswagen van and a Park Service jeep.

To the right of the visitor's center was the entrance to a Japanese garden, a small sign saying it was a replica of the Kameishi-Bo garden in Fukuoka, Japan. It was situated at the border of heavy woods that seemed to creep thickly over its edges.

Stone fixed his gaze on it. He thought: Marquette was stupid to set up the meet so close to such thick cover: perfect for an ambush. Or maybe he was being slick as a goddamn fox. Cover worked two ways. He went meticulously over the entire garden, noting particularly the best areas of cover, fixing imaginary lines of fire.

Satisfied, he got out, removed the car's license plates and tossed them into the backseat. He climbed back in, slipped the Ingram up under his jacket and drove slowly toward the center. He swung around and backed into the slot beside the jeep.

He heard the sound of someone sawing wood. After a moment, he got out of the car and quickly walked around the corner of the building. The windows of the greenhouse were frosted with moisture. No one seemed to be moving around inside. Tools and a small riding mower were near the wall, and a pathway led off into a stand of red cedar and dogwood that came right up to the greenhouse.

He plunged into the thick underbrush of salmonberry and hardhack that stretched beneath the trees. Everything was wet and immediately soaked his jacket and pants. Soaring above him, the tree trunks were coated with moss and spongy gray

knots of bracket fungus. A hummingbird darted past his face
with the delicate sound of a dentist's drill.

This was going to be a contingency operation, Stone realized. He'd have to go with the flow as Marquette laid it
out, adjust to it. Still, the advantage would always be his: an
ambush scenario. He'd let Grady make the swap, and then
he'd take out Marquette once and for all, him sitting right
out there off the tip of the Holbey silencer.

For a moment, Stone relished that image as he moved
stealthily through the underbrush, pausing to listen and scan
every few seconds as he gradually worked his way around
to the rear of the Japanese garden.

Suddenly, he stopped. He heard music—jazz, the wailing
alto sax of John Coltrane. It was coming from somewhere
close. He instantly dropped to the ground, then wriggled forward until he could see the edge of a small pond inside the
garden. The water was clear, strewn with lily pads and tiny
stone-tortoise islands. Now and then, the black, white and
red heads of koi jerked through the surface as they darted
for gnats.

To his left, a stream fed into the pond, coming off a rock
waterfall. Near the pond, a stone dragon-bridge arched over
the stream. A young man and woman in sweat clothes, towels around their necks, were standing at one end of the
bridge, nuzzling. The girl wore a radio on her waist. The
young man playfully bit her neck, hands toying with her
buttocks. Then came a little subtle bump and grind. She giggled.

Dammit, Stone thought viciously. He glared at the pair,
then hurriedly scanned the rest of the garden. Directly across
from him was a small Japanese teahouse. It had a porch and
shoji doors and upswept roof tips. The porch stood out over
the water on log pilings.

A pathway led from the house around to the entrance of
the garden, secluded under plum trees and crimson maples.
There were stone lanterns beside the path and a *tsukubai*
fountain with a bamboo dipper on a long handle. Just inside
the entrance was a six-foot guardian stone.

Jack estimated the distance to the entrance: about forty or forty-five yards. A bit long for accuracy, but it gave him a clear line to anyone moving on the pathway to the teahouse.

He swung his gaze back to the pair on the bridge. The young man was getting serious, pawing, kissing his girl all over her face and neck. Go ahead, jerkoff, Stone thought, take the little bitch back in the woods and fuck the shit out of her. Just get the hell out of here.

He flipped up the edge of his sleeve to check his watch. It was 6:43, a long wait until nine. Cursing silently, he rested his chin on the bend of his elbow and continued to watch the pair at the bridge.

The Dog didn't seem to know where in hell he was going. He just drove around and around, getting in the wrong lanes and pissing everybody off in the morning traffic, a country bumpkin in the big city.

Jo-Jo had stayed right on the pickup, four car lengths back, in order to keep them in sight. The targets didn't seem to notice anyway, Hitler-Hans giving James an occasional cuff on the back of the head like Moe smacking Larry in the Three Stooges.

Earlier, they'd stopped at a small cafe for breakfast. Halberstadt got into a scuffle with two big blacks in suede jackets and *chulo* turtlenecks. James was scared shitless trying to hustle the husky German out and back to the pickup.

"Oh, looka here," Kizzier had said, watching from a half block away. "There goes our fucking bust."

But now the pair were wandering aimlessly around the Wallingford district, stopping now and then for Dog to look anxiously at street signs. He finally pulled into a Shell station and talked to one of the attendants, who rattled off directions, pointing here and there. James nodded and pulled back onto Forty-fifth Avenue, headed west.

Azevedo swung his car into the station a moment later. He leaned out the window and whistled to the attendant. "Hey, pal, you wanna come over here?"

"Sir?"

"That pickup that was just in here. Where'd the guy want to go?"

"What?"

"That pickup that just left."

"You guys cops or something?"

"Yeah."

The attendant shrugged. "He was looking for the place where the Victoria ferry docks."

Jo-Jo swung around and gave Kizzier a look. Kizzier said, "Oh, oh."

"Which one?" Azevedo said to the attendant. "Elliott Bay or Kingston?"

"Elliott Bay," the man said.

They pulled back into traffic, the pickup far up the avenue now. Kizzier said, "Looks like the meet's gonna be in Victoria, don't it?"

"That puts us shit out of luck."

Kizzier thought. "Maybe not. Could be it's supposed to happen on the ferry."

"Could be," Jo-Jo said. "But don't bet on it."

"Then we take 'em down before they cross the B.C. line."

Azevedo hissed disgustedly.

The huge white-and-blue Seattle-Victoria ferry *Spokane* was already at Pier 48 when Jo-Jo and Kizzier followed Dog's pickup under the Alaskan Way overpass and turned onto the long Elliott Bay waterfront promenade. The place was crowded, full of small tourist shops and galleries and al fresco eateries.

They watched James park near the Victoria Line office and go inside. Halberstadt spat out the window of the pickup and said something to two young girls passing nearby. They looked over their shoulders at him and then walked off, their heads together, laughing.

"I don't like this," Kizzier said. They were parked near the corner of the VL building. "It's too goddamned crowded."

"We better take 'em in their vehicle."

"No, I want to give the pricks a chance to go topside. Just in case the guy they're meeting's aboard." He watched a group of Japanese tourists pass, flashbulbs popping, their guides herding them along with small Nippon signal flags. He stuck up his middle finger just as one of the group pointed a camera his way.

"Well, you better go get our tickets before that ferry pulls out," he said. "What time does it usually take off?"

"Eight o'clock, I think."

Jo-Jo got out and walked to the office entrance just as James came back out. He went right past him.

When they drove onto the ferry, the pickup was two rows ahead in the wide parking zone. Azevedo cut the engine and took his baseball cap out of the glove compartment. He put it on bill forward, cocked back on the black curls. Both men adjusted the vests under their jackets, checking the Velcro belts.

A few moments later, the ferry blew its horn, and they felt the huge diesels rumble up. Slowly, the vessel eased away from the pier. Once out into open water, it turned slightly to starboard, moving between Bainbridge Island and the ship derricks off West Point. Once past, it settled into a steady power speed.

"There they go," Kizzier said. As they watched, James and Halberstadt got out of the pickup and headed up the stairway to the upper deck. "How long have we got?"

"You mean when do we cross the British Columbia line?"

"Yeah."

"It's about three-quarters of the way over. Maybe two hours."

"Okay, follow 'em and hang close. I'll come up in a minute. But I'll stay in the cabin area so the shitheads don't see me."

Jo-Jo got out and darted between the parked cars to the stairs. He located the pair out on the passenger deck, sitting on one of the big, striped boxes near the railing. The boxes looked like huge tool chests.

He crossed right behind them, overheard James say,

". . . I tell you, man, I'm gon' be sick. Goddamn puke my guts out right here." And Halberstadt snorted with disgust, now in a leather jacket with the collar pulled up, his bald head making him look like a Gestapo *Obergruppenfuehrer*.

Azevedo went on by and stood beside one of the viewing windows. He looked through the tinted glass. A moment later, Kizzier came into the cabin area and took up a position just inside the same window.

Twenty minutes went by. No one approached James and the German. After awhile, they went up to the top deck. There were tables up there, and a small, open-air coffee vendor with trays of pastries. The waiters wore red aprons, and everything was behind a high wire barrier.

Jo-Jo went up, too, and stood near the stairs for a moment, watching. Then he went down and got Kizzier. "There ain't gonna be no-meet," he said. "I think we better do it now."

Kizzier looked out over the sound. At the moment, they were passing Port Gamble, its cranes near the waterfront and its small piers surrounded by day-sailors and motor launches, with two freighters off-loading.

He came back. "How many people're up there?"

"Maybe fifteen, twenty."

"Where are Dog and Hans located, precisely?"

"At a table just about right overhead, near the wire fence."

"Anybody close by?"

"Not when I was there."

"Are they facing the stairs?"

"Hans is."

"Shit," Kizzier said. "All right, take a spot to the right. Get a clear field of fire. I'll give you a couple minutes, then we'll go in fast."

"Okay."

"Watch it, Jo-Jo. That crazy German's probably still cranked. There's a good chance he'll go for it."

"Right."

He went back up the stairs.

Kizzier gave Azevedo two minutes precisely, checking his

watch. 8:24. Then he pulled the Uzi from beneath his jacket and went up the stairs, two steps at a time, the weapon down at his side.

It was windy on the top deck. Women held their hands against their hair, their dresses curving snugly against breasts and legs. A waiter with two coffees crossed in front of Kizzier as he cleared the top of the stairs, scanning, taking in the total layout of the deck in one sweep. Most of the passengers were down at this end, save for two old people now at a table about fifteen feet from James and Halberstadt. The German was saying something, and Dog nodded. The flag on the stackhouse snapped in the wind, and the smell of diesel fumes and salt was in the chilly air.

He saw Jo-Jo check him and reach under his coat. Kizzier headed straight for Halberstadt, the Uzi coming up.

The German's eyes caught him on the second step. Even from thirty feet away, Kizzier could see them go solid: hard, black agates in the fleshy mass of Halberstadt's face.

And then he and Azevedo were bellowing in unison, "FEDERAL AGENTS—DON'T MOVE!"

James's head snapped up, and a look of utter shock swept over him. Then Halberstadt's body was rising, hurling back the chair, and his hand fumbled for a moment inside the leather jacket.

"DON'T DO IT!" Kizzier yelled.

But the German's hand came out lifting the biggest-bored revolver he'd ever seen. Kizzier fired a burst, the Uzi jerking almost softly in his hand. Then Jo-Jo fired, too, and the bullets went into Halberstadt with the sound of someone striking a hung rug with a paddle. The strikes twisted him up against the wire barrier, his hand still coming up. In reflex, his finger pulled off a round, the crack of it like a shotgun going off. Kizzier actually heard the round go past him and impact.

James was down on the deck, cowering. Jo-Jo jammed a foot into the middle of his back, pointing his Uzi at Halberstadt, who was now on his hands and knees, retching. Then his mouth opened wide, and he vomited a red ball of blood and fell facedown onto it.

Kizzier, his own blood thundering, rushed over, his weapon in both hands. Gingerly he reached down and felt Halberstadt's neck. The man was dead.

From behind him, someone screamed. He whirled. The old lady who had been sitting near Halberstadt's table was lying on the deck. Her face was ashen, her lips moving.

''Oh, Christ!'' Kizzier cried, leaping up and going toward her.

18

Marquette lay very still, letting his eyes scan slowly from point to point: the brush on the other side of the pond, the edge of the woods, the dragon bridge and shadows under it. He caught no movement. The leaves were as still as a painting.

He was lying under the garden teahouse, in a narrow space, with his head and back touching the cedar floor beams. The ground was cold, slightly damp. Beside him rested the gym bag and the carbine, its chrome surfaces stained dark brown.

Earlier, he had come through the woods, the canopy trees cutting off light, casting the understory and ground brush into a still twilight. He passed slowly, easing gentle footfalls into pine needles and carpets of kinnikinnik and salal, skirting open meadows, holding to the shadows. All the old instincts bristled to catch the slightest sound or movement, a flutter of wings, the snap of a twig. Now and then, distant voices drifted in from the Broadmoor greens.

Out of habit, he even sniffed at the air, enemy searching. But this wasn't Nam. There were no VCs with their sweat odor of pickled beets and peppered fish, the dung stench of the dog grease they used to waterproof their weapons. Instead, there was the clean odor of pine bark and spruce, the watermelon scent of huckleberries.

Once into deep cover, he'd paused long enough to camouflage himself and his weapon. He took off his jacket, discarded it, and rubbed dark earth over his face and hands. Using the licorice-smelling juice of skunk cabbage, he stained the barrel and breech of the carbine to keep it from reflecting light.

Upon first entering the woods, he'd estimated the Japanese garden to be about a half mile east-northeast. As he moved, he periodically took bearings, using the position of the hour hand on his watch to locate south. Now and then, he'd cross a path. Once, a jogger came past along a path under the trees, panting in the silence. Matt quickly darted into undergrowth and waited until he was gone.

He neared the garden, heard music—tinny sounding, coming in surges. He slowed, crept forward. A few minutes later, he came upon a young man and woman lying on spread towels at the base of a cedar tree. The girl's sweatpants were off, tossed aside. She wore only black bikini panties, her sweatshirt pulled up, her bra down, the young man suckling her breasts.

Matt moved around them, silent as a ghost.

He reached the back of the garden, coming at it from the rear of the teahouse. For nearly fifteen minutes, he lay near a stand of bamboo and carefully surveyed the area. The garden seemed caught in a vacuum of silence, only the faint radio music in the air and the soft soughing of the wind in the high trees—all of it external, beyond the still sanctity of the garden.

At last, he moved quickly from the bamboo, going to his belly and slipping under the building. . . .

In Nam, a line soldier usually killed by firing at brush, returning bursts at muzzle flashes—unlike the SEALs, where it was down-and-dirty and very personal. The kind of killing that resonated in the soul for a long time afterward.

Here, Matt realized, it would probably be line fighting, skirmishing. Locate and destroy at a distance, from cover. Somewhere out there would be the enemy. One man, maybe two.

Were they already in place? If so, they were in good concealment. Once Grady arrived, he knew he'd probably have to expose his position in order to pinpoint them by drawing fire.

He set about preparing the field for that moment. He shoved the bag out, right to the edge of the porch's shadow, so that Grady would have to bend to retrieve it. At that precise moment, he'd go right at him, and past, the lawyer probably falling back out of shock, giving cover as they opened on him.

That's when he'd have them, their positions isolated out there in the brush by their gun flashes. He'd hit and roll and come up firing right at the bursts that would still be pulsing on his retinas. It was a big risk, total exposure. But if he did it fast enough, the element of surprise would balance out the odds.

He eased his way back to where he'd first gone under the house, then stopped. Directly above him, he noted, a panel was cut into the building's floor. He'd missed seeing it as he came in. Vaguely, he recalled something he'd learned when he spent R and Rs at the geisha houses in Japan. There were always trapdoors in a Japanese house. They were called *age-buta*, throwbacks from the ancient days when household women could flee while their samurai fought off attackers.

He listened for a moment, then gently eased the panel up. It fitted neatly into the tatami mat. He slid his rifle onto the floor and pulled himself through.

The room was small, built of open cedar beams with ricepaper walls and sliding shoji doors. Scrolls hung from the walls, showing bold-stroke calligraphy and misty mountain scenes. The tatami mats were made of tightly woven straw. In the center of the room was the only piece of furniture, a low gold-and-black lacquer table. On it were tea ceremony utensils and the stones and squares of a *Go* game.

He crossed to the door, which faced the pond, hunkered down and slid it open a fraction of an inch. Something suddenly darted across the pavilion. He felt his heart heave, then settle. A squirrel. It went off down the path, chittering.

He glanced at his watch. It was 8:39.

*   *   *

Stone's mouth was sawdust-dry, felt like acid on the tissue. His stomach and crotch were soaked, too, cold and clammy, and the goddamned music drove him crazy. In the stillness, it was just quiet enough to seem to filter out of the underbrush from no particular direction.

Occasionally, a car drove past the entrance to the garden. Each time, Stone tightened inside until it continued on along Arboretum Drive. Once, a man in work clothes had passed aboard a huge riding mower, the blade barrels cranked up like the wings of parked carrier aircraft.

He checked his watch constantly. Time seemed nearly stopped in the serenity of the garden. Stealthy things moved in the underbrush; birds flashed past. A beautiful gray squirrel startled him as it darted across the porch of the teahouse, bringing an icy breath to his skin.

His eyes watered from peering so steadily at motionless things, and he was sick of looking at faked Jap artifacts, listening to the tiny swirls of the goddamned fish. "Come on, motherfucker," he murmured deep in his throat.

Sometimes, his mind drifted off and was caught momentarily in the snare of his fatigue. Once he actually dozed, for just a few seconds, and then, rousing, came up with a start. And always, there was the faint music, like a memory of sound. Dizzy Gillespie, Wynton Marsalis . . .

But suddenly, there was an abrupt cessation of it, as if a switch had been thrown. The pause lingered for several seconds. Then the announcer was saying, "We interrupt this program for an important news bulletin."

Curious, Stone tilted his head to listen.

"One man was killed and a woman wounded during an exchange of gunfire aboard the Victoria Line ferry *Spokane*. The incident occurred this morning at approximately eight-twenty-five. The ship immediately returned to Seattle.

"Reports are still sketchy as police officials and VL spokesmen remain discreet on specific details. However, unofficial sources claim that the man was killed by federal agents and was a known German terrorist wanted by the police throughout Europe."

Stone stiffened. *Halberstadt!* Oh God, oh God. He felt his insides like heated rocks in the belly, in his chest. One killed. What about James? Oh *God*, this wasn't supposed to happen.

For a long moment, he lay stunned, no longer hearing the announcer, the returning music. He looked unseeing at the brush close to his face.

In one single snap of a second, all of it had just gone down the toilet. All the beautiful intricacies of his plan, the complex mergings of its scattered parts, were wasted now.

He'd been so close. Within a few minutes, he would have had the sphere—and the time to place it, to totally destroy, in one quick strike, the things that stood between him and victory, riches: *William Ballard and his PrimeData Corporation.*

The sphere would have taken Ballard out, killed him with incurable anthrax, along with every senior official of his company. And in the vacuum created by the catastrophe, Stone's own BODYGUARD-t security platform would have instantly dominated the world of electronics.

The sharp image of Ballard came to him. Arrogant, nerdy-brilliant. He felt the hot, groin-aching urge to reach out, to slice that image-face into bloody tissue. And take it—

Wait. No, goddammit. It could still work.

But what if James talked? Undoubtedly, he'd do that— openly admit to the police what he and Halberstadt had been doing here, their meeting with Keck in Victoria to set up shipments of arms from Germany for the Militia Movement.

Would the police believe him? Or, more importantly, would they instead believe he and Halberstadt had been sent to kill Ballard in an act of urban terrorism against American technology and government?

That had been their single function in Stone's plan, the only reason he'd meticulously set up their visit to Seattle— right down to their itinerary, which had been designed to have them actually seen by ATF agents, whom he'd enticed to Seattle through the arrest and killing of Goodell, at the target zone last night.

Even the bombings by the Horseman in Denver and Silicon Valley had been Stone's doing, all of it to create the image of blame toward the American Militia Movement. In today's atmosphere, no one would have doubted their culpability.

For a moment, Jack weighed his options. But there was little conflict now. His mind, caught up in the fanatic dream, allowed no space for surrender. Yes, he could still carry out the mission.

He came out of his thoughts just as Grady's sleek red Jaguar pulled up in front of the Japanese garden.

The lawyer switched off the soft purr of his engine. He sat there looking around, trying to absorb the landscape. It was a cool morning, gray overcast across the sky. The neatly trimmed lawns and meadows of the park looked like those of an English estate. No one was around save for a maintenance man on a mower a quarter mile off.

He put both hands on the wheel and inhaled slowly. His hands felt clammy. Goddamn, he didn't like this. He felt utterly exposed, a man in a downpour. Some of the spray was bound to soak him. That fucking Stone.

Grady was used to dealing with social misfits, paranoia, even true psychosis. And he was certain Stone had long since entered that particular territory. He had all the symptoms—that look of imbalance, the absorption by some self-seen intent that could trigger ferocity if frustrated—only he was worse. A goddamned robot homing to a target, going at it until everything was spent.

A flat-out dangerous man.

He pivoted his head this way and that, slowly, taking it all in. He thought, where the hell are you, Marquette? He glanced at his watch. Three minutes after nine.

Beside him on the seat were two briefcases. He opened the smaller one. It contained a hundred and fifty thousand in one-hundred-dollar and single-dollar bills, the hundreds facing the packets with singles down under. It looked very good at a glance.

It wasn't his. All his funds were in banks. If this thing

blew up, he certainly didn't want bank records to show such a huge withdrawal. Instead, he had gone to a bookie he knew, had had to talk some fancy jive to get the man to front that much on his word.

He closed the briefcase and waited another two minutes. Then he slowly opened the door and got out. He walked around the Jag, pausing to study the landscape, leaning with a casualness he didn't feel against the rear fender.

He glanced into the Japanese garden. It was empty. Where the hell is Stone? Had he made a mistake in the place? Was he too early? Or too late? No, Stone had said the Jap garden at nine sharp.

Maybe he was suppoosed to go *inside* the garden, he thought, circuit the place, let all the players see that he was there and straight. He reached into the car and brought out the smaller case. Bracing himself, he crossed the sidewalk and entered the garden, passed the guardian stone.

It was very still inside, a kind of vacuum. The pond was placid now, its rocks covered with moss and the willows and red maples hanging limp in the motionless air. He caught the smell of the pond water, a faintly fetid odor, like dirty feet.

Slowly, he moved along the pathway toward the teahouse, alert, tense. Each step was a gentle touching, as if he were treading gingerly over booby-trapped ground. The crunch his soles made on the gravel sounded like the crush of glass shards. He felt his heart tapping hurriedly against his chest wall.

He reached the edge of the teahouse, paused. Was that music? It sounded muffled. Blues in a Nip-pawn garden? Something rustled in a nearby bamboo thicket and he thought, Here we go!, stiffening.

"Grady," a voice said flatly.

He froze, waiting. Only his gaze darted about.

"Put the briefcase on the porch."

The timber of the voice seemed oddly hollow. Enclosed. It wasn't coming from the bamboo thicket. He focused on the teahouse. Yes, the man must be there.

"Do it," the voice hissed. "Keep your eyes down, or you're dead where you stand."

God Aw'mighty. Grady dropped his focus, studied the herringbone patterns of his glistening cowboy boots. Head down, he stepped forward, leaned way out and placed the briefcase, upright, on the cedar planking of the porch. He straightened and stood stock-still.

Thirty seconds dragged past.

"Where is it, Marquette?" he finally asked.

Silence.

Grady got the sudden, frigid feeling of impending explosion, a sudden crawling up the back of his neck. He physically shrank from it, shoulders drawing back as if to shield his face. He had an overwhelming urge to turn, hurtle himself back along the path and out of this dangerous place. But he didn't.

"Godammit," he said shakily. "You got your money. Just give over the damn thing an' I'll get out."

More silence.

Stone had not heard the first word spoken, but he saw Grady jerk up slightly. His hand instantly closed tighter on the Ingram's grip. Then he heard Marquette's voice, coming softly, furtively, across the pond.

Put the briefcase on the porch.

Where is he? Where is he?

Frantically he searched the brush and bamboo beyond the lawyer. No movement. Marquette was close, had to be. Again he scanned the entire area around the lawyer.

Do it. Keep your eyes down, or you're dead where you stand.

Then Grady leaning out, placing the briefcase.

Stone still saw nothing—no movement, no telltale spot of cloth or tuft of dark hair.

Wait. Of course. There was only one place Marquette could be. In the teahouse. Or under it. He brought the weapon up, cupping his left hand under the stock. He moved the muzzle to the left, fixed the tip of the silencer on the first piling below the house. He squinted hard into the shadows down there, trying to make out dark on dark.

Nothing.

He wondered: Would Marquette trap himself like that, unable to move freely? No, he wasn't that stupid. Then he must be inside. He lifted the weapon slightly, passing the tip across the porch, stopping on a shoji door sash. The rice paper looked as white as a sheet of light, the sash intersections like dark crosses.

Was a shoji door slightly open? Yes. He felt his body go hard, felt the killing sensation come up into his mouth: copper pennies on the tongue. So concentrated was he, even the music had faded from his consciousness.

He lay poised, motionless, waiting for Marquette to give up the sphere and for Grady to check it and make the exchange and then turn and walk away. It was then that he'd open up, throw bursts through the goddamned rice paper and cedar sashes and cut Marquette to pieces.

His finger tightened on the trigger.

Marquette's body also hummed with nerve impulses. Synapses and neurons glowed with electricity. He heard, felt, smelled everything—the cedar and straw redolence of the teahouse, the deeper pine of the forest. He felt the near-motionless shift of air and the faint musical notes like molecules fluttering. A daddy longlegs spider went trembling along the paper wall, and it was as if he could hear its dainty tread.

Grady was still standing stock-still out there, a slick cowboy dude with a black Stetson and Levi's jacket, yellow-tinted glasses. His face was slick with perspiration.

"I ain't gon' do this, Marquette," Grady said desperately. "You-all want to make the switch, then let's flat do it and get it over with."

"Under the porch," Matt said.

Grady straightened slightly, then quickly knelt and peered under the edge of the porch. He reached in and brought out the gym bag, straightened.

"Check it," Matt said.

Grady obeyed. He unwrapped the toweling and lifted the sphere out—and gave it away, lifting it higher, like a trophy, showing it off.

Matt thought: Oh, yeah, they're out there, all right.

Grady put the sphere back into the bag and zippered it. He seemed undecided now, looking around. Matt watched his eyes intently, following their direction. They seemed aimless.

"Put the bag on the porch and open the briefcase."

Hurriedly, the lawyer complied, wanting to play out the rest of it rapidly now. The briefcase hasps clicked. He pulled it open. The money was neatly packed in, bundles side by side.

Marquette was coming to it. In his mind, he saw it proceeding, each move, each piece of each second. Almost unconsciously, his body braced itself, legs tightening, muscles flushing with blood. His thumb flicked off the carbine's trigger-guard safety. Blood thundered in his temples.

Now!

He sprang forward, bursting through the shoji door. His feet hit the porch running, he himself bending over, the shards of cedar sash and paper falling away, his head turned, eyes hotly scanning brush and rock and tree limb.

In his peripheral vision, he saw Grady's eyes and mouth fly open with shock and sudden terror. Then the lawyer's body seemed to unweave itself, his arms and legs going in all directions as he scrambled to get away.

Matt went right past him, knocking the briefcase aside, packets of money flying out. He leaped off the porch, stretching out, the carbine in both hands.

There!

He caught a small burst of muzzle flashes in the brush beyond the pond, caught the sibilant spit of a silenced weapon. The sound was like pebbles being flung in rapid sequence into still water. Bullets tore into a porch beam, two impacting something soft. One went zinging off with the sound of a high-speed drill taking the first bite into plate steel.

Matt struck the ground, the carbine butt hitting first. He rolled, his eyes riveted to the spot from which the burst had come, as it turned upside down and upright again. Then he was on one knee, bringing the rifle up to hip level and pulling off seven rounds as fast as flesh and muscle could move. The gun bucked gently, its reports making a rip of sound in the stillness.

On the edge of his vision, he saw Grady thrashing on the ground beside the teahouse porch. His hat was off; there was blood all over his face. Then he went still, and one leg slid almost softly down into the pond.

The sharp odor of cordite lifted around him as Marquette shoved with his legs, starting another roll to his left. He never completed it. There were three muzzle flashes across the pond, six feet to the right of the original bursts. They were so rapid, they almost merged into one bright back-blown flame.

At the same precise moment, he felt a violent double impact in his chest, hurling him backward into the bamboo. The carbine, stock shattered, fell to the side.

He couldn't find his breath. It was as if all the air in his body had been instantly sucked out through his mouth. He fought to draw it back, heard his own agonized choking, heard something crash into water.

Time became his gasping. Seconds. Then a shadow loomed into his vision. The horse-faced man from the ferry. He stood over him, his features twisted into a wild, devilish grin. In one hand he held Matt's bag; in the other, a small assault pistol. He lifted the pistol. It was dark, and its muzzle was absurdly long. He pointed it right at Marquette's forehead.

"Get ready for hell, motherfucker," the man growled.

A woman screamed. It was so shrill, so high, it seemed to come from everywhere, bouncing off wood and rock and soft moss, rebounding. Another scream.

The horse-faced man jerked his head up, looked frantically

around him like a thief caught in sudden light. Then he turned and leapt away.

Marquette closed his eyes. In the darkness he sought air, but it hung out there just beyond his mouth like a mockery.

19

Fifteen minutes earlier, Kelli had overridden Marquette's instructions. . . .

Since she'd returned to the CRYSTALBALL lab, the anxiety of waiting had become unbearable, like bugs in the brain, a deep-tissue chill that kept her constantly on the move, around and around the big, cold room with the entire team staring, nobody doing any work.

"Goddammit," Gilhammer said for the third time. "You're driving me nuts, Kelli. What the hell is the matter?"

Kelli checked the wall clock. 9:02.

"I can't tell you yet."

Troy grabbed her arm. "Stop right there, girl. Now you're *gonna* tell me. Right now."

"I can't."

"Jesus, look at you."

She jerked her arm free and started off again. Then she stopped, turned and looked back at him. She shook her head as if in reprimand of herself. "I can't do it," she said. "This is wrong. I can't wait any longer." She twisted, grabbed up the phone.

To Troy she called out, "Get the CDC headquarters in Atlanta."

Gilhammer said, "The what?"

"The Centers for Disease Control."

Everyone looked at each other. *What?*

"I don't understand," Troy said.

"Just do it," Kelli shouted.

She dialed information, got the Clallam County Sheriff's number. Three rings, and a woman officer answered. "Clallam County Sheriff's Department, Deputy Lopez."

"I want to speak to Lieutenant Two Elks," she said. "It's an emergency."

"Your name?"

"Kelli Pickett. He'll know it."

"What sort of emergency?"

"Please, there isn't much time. I must speak with him."

"Hold on a minute."

She turned. Gilhammer was on another phone, speaking with the Atlanta information operator. "Yes, just the main number," he said and scribbled it down. "Thanks."

Kelli, waiting, snapped her fingers at one of the team members. Her name was Laurie. Kelli ordered her to boot up the machines she had been using to track the sphere, gave her the code references. The girl looked quizzically at her.

"Move it!" Kelli barked. Laurie looked at the others, shrugged and went over to the workstations.

Gilhammer said into the phone: "Yes, I'd like to speak with someone there about—" He looked at Pickett. "About what?"

"Biological contamination by rapid mutational anthrax," Kelli said.

Everybody's expression said, "Anthrax?"

"Tell them to prepare for data transference. Give them our IA codes."

The deputy came back. "Lieutenant Two Elks is not here at the moment."

"Where is he?"

"I can't give out that information. What does this concern specifically?"

"The Matthew Marquette case."

"I'm going to let you talk with the sheriff."

"I don't want the sheriff," Kelli said. "Look, contact Two Elks and have him call me back. Right away."

"What's your number?"

She gave it. The deputy hung up.

Kelli hurried to Gilhammer, took the phone, cutting him off in midsentence. She said, "Who's this?"

A man with a low, resonant voice said, "This is Deputy Administrator Russell Sullins. Who's *this*?"

She identified herself, her affiliation with the University of Washington. Then she said very slowly, "I have data relating to a biological device containing anthrax. It creates a mutated, airborne form of the bacteria."

Sullins was silent a moment. Then he said, "Are you serious?"

"Dead serious."

"Well, my God," Sullins said. "Where is this—device?"

"Here in the city."

The other phone rang. One of the team members answered it, said, "Yes," and held it out to Kelli.

She handed Gilhammer's phone back to him. "Tell this man to access our machines immediately. All the data's there." She flew back to the other phone. "Two Elks?"

"Yes."

She went over it, everything, speaking rapidly but distinctly. She could feel the words forming, coming, tumbling out as if they had all been waiting just inside her mouth. The team members stared, their faces open with puzzled shock. The lieutenant did not interrupt—not a sound, not a grunt. At last, she finished.

Calmly, Two Elks asked, "Where's Marquette now?"

"At Washington Park." She glanced at the clock on the wall. It said 9:17. Across the room, her machines were clicking softly as Atlanta accessed data.

There was a short pause, then the lieutenant said, "I'm handing you over to Dispatch. Remain on this line." He was gone.

After a short pause, a woman came on. "This is dispatcher fourteen. Would you repeat your name and number, please."

"Where's Two Elks? What's he going to do?"

"Your name and number, please."

Behind her, Gilhammer said, "Yes, of course." He lowered the receiver, cupped it in his other hand. Kelli swung around. "They're evaluating," he said.

The air came back to Matt in a rush as his solar plexus muscles came out of spasm. His lungs sucked it in, the taint of cordite still in it. He twisted his head.

The horse-faced man, running low with the assault pistol and gym bag swinging, fled through the garden entrance and disappeared beyond the guardian stone and the sculpted hedges.

Marquette sat up. There was gunsmoke in the air, layered like the last wisps from a dying campfire. He came to his feet. A shock of dizziness struck him, and his chest burned where the rounds had gone into the armored vest. A single, flattened round fell from the hole it had made.

He glanced back at Grady's body. The water had soaked into his pant leg, and his face was turned to the sky. The left side of it was a raw mass of bone and flesh. It dripped blood gently down into the mossy stones beneath him.

Matt picked up the carbine. The stock was splintered, and there was a ragged, thumb-sized hole in the breech. He hurled it away, shoved himself to his feet and broke into a run along the pathway toward the entrance, his head pounding.

As he cleared the huge guardian stone, he spotted his assailant. He was in a blue Trans Am parked near the visitor's building. As he watched, the man slammed the car into gear and hurled away, the tires screaming on the pavement.

Marquette pulled the Browning Hi-Power from his belt, clicking it off safety and bringing it up, two-handed, the thumb snapping the hammer out of half-cock. He held for a tiny second on the rear window of the rapidly receding automobile and then fired, twice. The weapon jerked upward, and the casings flipped out and tinkled to the sidewalk.

One of the rounds smacked into the car's trunk with a sound like a clapper striking a cracked bell. The other bullet shattered the rear window. But the vehicle continued on, taking the slight curve that led to the Washington Boulevard entrance at high speed.

Matt saw the stark faces of two women peering around the corner of the visitor's building. Far down the other way, the park maintenance man had stopped his mower and was standing on the seat, staring Matt's way.

Oh, Jesus, Marquette kept frantically repeating in his head. Oh, sweet Jesus! He's got the sphere.

He swung around, stared at Grady's Jaguar for a moment. Then he leaped for it and flung open the door, tossing the Browning onto the floor between the seats.

He slid behind the wheel. The car smelled of plush leather and wood polish and the faint tang of cigar smoke. The key on a silver-and-turquoise medallion was still in the ignition. He snapped it on, heard the muffled whine of the starter motor and then the almost imperceptible purr of the engine. His right hand reached for the gear shift. . . .

It all came back. A wind hurled through tunnels, the feel of the steering wheel in his hands, the metal odor of mechanical power, harnessed and waiting for the touch of his foot, the terror-laced memory of speed. It all merged into the jolting image of a fireball climbing into the blue Barcelona sky and tiny silhouetted bodies whirling in their midair dance.

Sweat instantly coated his forehead. He trembled, caught for a panicked moment within the coils of the vision, and heard himself groan as if in sorrow or regret.

But then, by sheer will, he focused his mind, drove the vision back and away. There was a moment of desperate struggle. Gradually, he felt himself untighten. He breathed.

Instantly, his fingers bore down on the gear shift, shoved it home. Then, with blood pounding through his veins, he rammed the accelerator to the floor, felt the Jag lift and leap out of inertia into life, the tires screaming like stallions in combat.

At precisely 9:21, an aide to Seattle mayor Norman Kerberry approached him at the guest table in the Banners restaurant's banquet room in the Sheraton Seattle. Kerberry was a handsome black man with a dazzling smile and soft, brown eyes.

He'd been guest speaker at an awards breakfast for executive officers of the Seattle Aquarium. Scheduled to leave soon to attend the press conference for PrimeData at the Space Needle, he assumed his aide was coming to remind him.

Instead, the aide said, "May I speak with you a moment, sir?"

Kerberry excused himself. He and the aide walked out into the lobby, crossed it and went into a small conference room. The aide closed the door.

"The police commissioner's on the phone, sir."

Kerberry frowned. He walked to the table and picked up the phone. "Gary, what's up?" The commissioner's name was Gary Tiener.

"Is your phone secure?" Tiener said tensely.

"What's that?"

"I don't want anybody but you hearing this."

"Well, yeah, I assume it is. I'm in the conference room."

"We just might have one catastrophic problem on our hands," Tiener said.

"What?"

"I just got a call from North Precinct. A woman from the university is claiming there's a biological bomb somewhere in the city. She says it's a goddamned anthrax bomb."

Shocked into silence, the mayor lowered himself to the tabletop. *Terrorists!* "An anthrax bomb?" he said dumbly. "What—is this a hoax?"

"We don't know. The woman's an associate professor over there, apparently legitimate. The thing seems to have some connection with recent killings in Dungeness and out in the Basin. I don't have particulars yet. But whatever it is, we've got to assume this thing is for real."

Kerberry tried to push through the rush of desperate thoughts flooding his mind. He rose off the table and walked around in a tight circle at the end of the phone line.

"What have you done so far?" he said.

"I'm in the process of activating our segment of the Status: Emergency Plan. I'm tagging it Category four."

Category four, Kerberry thought wildly. *Catastrophic Emergency.*

He tried to recall the precise sequence of protocols that had been laid out during past in-city and federal conferences. It was all a jumble. Nobody ever thought it would happen in their city.

Oh, Mother Mary.

He finally managed to say, "I'm going to notify the governor right now. I think all decisions must be made in coordination with him. Have any federal agencies been brought in yet?"

"No, I'm waiting on you to decide that." Someone said something to Tiener. He said, "I didn't get that. Yes." To the mayor again: "The Centers for Disease Control in Atlanta's on the line. They're actually analyzing data from the university right now."

Oh, God, Kerberry thought. CDC, solid data. This is no hoax.

He snapped his fingers at the aide who was standing by the door, open-mouthed. "Get the governor on the phone," he roared. To Tiener, he said, "Is Atlanta on a conference line?"

"No, but I can patch you through. Hang on." There was a short silence, then twin clicks. A woman said, "Operator three on line seven."

Then a man said, "Is this the mayor of Seattle?"

"Yes. Who am I speaking to?"

"I'm Deputy Administrator Russell Sullins of the Special Pathogens Branch of CDC. Have you been briefed on this situation?"

"Partially. Is there actually a bomb here?"

"Initial analysis of the data from your university out there indicates there is a very real possibility of that."

Kerberry's whole body went cold. "You mean it's true, then?"

"It could be. There's a high probability it is. Because of that, we've passed on the data to USAMRIID for their take on it. They're the in-depth experts on hot strains of anthrax."

"The what?"

"USAMRIID, the Army medical research facility at Fort Detrick, Maryland," Sullins said. "We're also putting our field teams on full-up alert—those on the West Coast, San Francisco and Portland. I assume USAMRIID will be doing the same."

Kerberry had the helpless sensation that things were flying away from him, going uncontrollably off in all directions. Federal field teams? The military? The politician in him wondered obliquely: Isn't there supposed to be a specific chain of command here? Then realized what a stupid thought that was. It didn't make any difference *who* the hell came in, as long as they did.

"Yes," he said. "We'll need as much help as we can get."

"I'll keep in tight coordination with you. Has your governor been notified?"

"I'm doing that right now."

"Good. I'd recommend that he go directly to the President with this matter, cut away some of the red tape. Our office's already sent a pre-situation report to FEMA. But, as you must know, any official request for FEMA participation must come from your governor."

"Yes, of course." Kerberry thought a moment. "What about the public, Sullins? Do we tell the public at this stage?"

There was a long moment of silence, then, "You and your governor will have to make that choice. If this turns out to be a hoax, you'll be risking mass panic. On the other hand . . ." Sullins let the words trail off.

On the other hand, Kerberry thought, and felt his heart twist.

The Jag XJS shot past the caretaker's cabin and blew out onto North Twenty-sixth, Matt getting the sense of the car, the responsive touch of the wheel, feeling the muffled roar of the twelve-cylinder powerplant hurtling it into smooth velocity. His mind was in that crystalline place, as in the teahouse: energy, sureness, instincts returning, tingling in his fingertips, his entire body moving as a single unit.

A half mile to his right, he saw the Trans Am go into a sharp left turn, combing off dust along the edge of the road. He followed, cars flashing past, the drivers' faces looking angrily across at him for a tiny second before they were gone.

He held the Jag hard down, watched the curve coming, and then he was into it, swinging the wheel over, left foot popping the brakes but keeping the accelerator down full to maintain maximum RPMs. The car heeled, its suspension damping the centrifugal pull.

As he powered out of the turn, he caught sight of the Trans Am just before it disappeared under the overpass of Highway 520. A few seconds later, it reappeared, shooting up the farside on-ramp, bullying its way into the freeway traffic.

Marquette continued along Roanoke Avenue until he reached the overpass, barrelled through and then jammed the XJS into a hard left onto the on-ramp, sideslipping past a slower-moving car, the chassis jolting for an instant as it bounced over curbing. He pulled onto the freeway.

For a moment, he flicked his eyes around the dashboard. Hand-laid walnut, butter-soft Connelly leather padding—but no phone. A briefcase was sitting on the passenger seat. His attention once again on the road, he felt for the hasps, pulled it open. It contained a small computer modem and cell phone.

As in his racing days, his senses were far ahead of the car, anticipating, flicking the wheel into the tiniest adjustments that instantly hurled him past other automobiles, weaving, darting, slicing lanes. He was gaining on his quarry.

He scooped up the cell phone, automatically tapped in the lab number, surprised that he had suddenly remembered it. He cocked it against his shoulder, pressing it hard to his ear.

It rang once.

An eighteen-wheeler suddenly cut in front of him, and he had to quickly veer away from it, skimming past the tarped boxes and huge whining wheels. Then he was out front, cutting back and across to the speed lane. In the movement, the phone had dropped into his lap.

He shoved it against his ear again. A woman's voice said, "Hello? Hello?"

"Kelli," he yelled.

Up ahead, he saw the Trans Am cut suddenly to the right and go bounding down an off-ramp. "Oh, shit!" he bellowed. He flashed a quick look over his shoulder and swung back across lanes, cars honking and swerving to avoid him. He made the lane and a few seconds later tore down the off-ramp, a sign zipping past—Mercer Avenue—the Jag lifting and settling as it crossed a dip in the pavement.

Kelli was yelling, "Matt? Is that you?"

Once more he jammed the phone to his ear as he followed the ramp into a long right turn. "Kelli . . . Kelli."

"Yes, I'm here."

"He's got it. The bastard's got it."

"Oh, dear God! Where are you?"

"In Grady's car on Mercer Avenue. Did you get Two Elks?"

"Yes."

He had to break hard suddenly as traffic ahead slowed for an intersection light. He swung to the outside, zoomed past three automobiles and crossed through the intersection. To his right, a car skidded, making a half pirouette before stopping.

"Get him out here," he shouted. "Mercer Avenue, westbound. The guy's in a blue Trans Am."

"All right, all right."

From beyond the sealed cocoon of the Jag, he heard a siren, a a short, faint wail; then it was gone. He accelerated, feeling the weight of the XJS pulling itself up into speed again.

He couldn't actually see the Trans Am, but he was aware of distant traffic dodging away from it, creating a wave movement that translated itself back to him. He bore on.

"The CDC," he yelled. "Did you get the CDC?"

"Yes," Kelli came back, her own voice shrill with excitement. "They're still evaluating."

"Goddammit," he shouted. "I don't need evaluations. Tell them I want instructions for defusing this thing. The bastard triggers it, I want to know how to stop it."

"Yes," Kelli said. "Yes."

The girl jogger was crying, hugging her partner. One of the North Precinct detectives had the pair beside the garden entrance, taking their statements. Her face was flushed; her neck, red, showing a dark hickey. Four patrol cars were pulled up beside the garden entrance, and several joggers had stopped to gawk.

Next to the teahouse, Two Elks rose from his squat beside Grady's body. He was with Lieutenant Walters.

"Yeah, this is John Wayne Grady, all right," Walters said.

Two Elks grunted and walked slowly around the area, squinting at the ground. He paused, staring at the packets of money, the open briefcase. He took out his pencil and righted it. There were several envelopes in the pocket, all addressed to Grady.

He moved on, stopped beside the shattered carbine. He bent over to examine it without touching the weapon. He noticed a slug on the pathway. He picked it up. The front of it was flanged outward like the head of a hammer. He rolled it in his palm. A nine millimeter.

After awhile, he and Walters walked back to talk to the joggers.

"Oh, shit," the girl said. "I've never seen anything like this." She shook her head with revulsion.

"Who did the actual shooting?" Two Elks asked her. "Which man?"

The girl shook her head, looked as if she were holding back vomit. The young man answered instead. "We don't know for sure. We were back there, you know, like, fooling around? And all of a sudden *wham! wham!* there's these five, six shots.

"When we get to the edge of the garden, right there, we see this man, looks dead, blood and all. And a second guy down on the ground, thrashing around. Then a third guy comes out of the bushes, right there, and goes wading across the pond. He stands over this thrashing guy with a gun to his head, like he's gonna blow it off, you know?"

"What did he look like?"

"Tall, kinda long-faced, mean-looking."

"What kind of weapon did he have?" Walters asked.

"Jeez, I don't know," the young man said. "One of them compact Israeli things, shoots about eighty billion rounds. Anyway, the guy's ready to shoot this other guy, and then Carol screams and the guy looks up and takes off. After a few seconds, the other guy gets up and takes off, too. Then *wham! wham!* we hear firing, and I'm saying fuck this, you know? Me and Carol just hit the ground and stayed there."

"You didn't see either man actually leave the area?" Two Elks asked.

"No way. We just, like, hid, man."

A patrolman approached. "Lieutenant," he said, "we got descriptions on the two cars. One's a blue or gray Trans Am; the other, a red Jag. And a gal back there says the guy in the Jag was wearing some kind of armored vest."

Walters's patrol car radio sputtered into life. "Two-one-eight, fourteen, four-one, Walters."

The lieutenant walked over and slid onto the seat. He keyed his mike. "Two-one-eight, Walters. Go."

"Suspect ID'd Matthew Marquette has been reported in a ten-fifty-three pursuit of unID'd second suspect. Westbound Mercer Avenue. Second suspect is reported to be in a blue Trans Am."

"All right, code-eight that whole sector," Walters snapped.

The dispatcher rogered and cleared off.

Walters started the engine. "Let's go, John," he barked,

waiting till Two Elks had climbed aboard before spinning the patrol car in a tight 180 and roaring off.

Thirty seconds earlier, Sullins of the CDC had spoken with Kelli. His voice was grim. "USAMRIID's running a probability model," he said. "So far, all your data are accurate."

Kelli put her head down, felt her whole skull throbbing. "The person with the device has been spotted. We're waiting—"

Sullins cut her short: "You mean you don't know *precisely* where this thing is?"

"No."

"Dear God."

"If it's triggered, is there any way to defuse it?" she asked. And the asking, the actual forming of the words, sent ice through her veins.

But Sullins wasn't listening; he was shouting to someone else. When he came back, he said, "I've just ordered our field teams to Seattle."

Kelli repeated her question. Sullins was silent for a moment, then said, "Until USAMRIID's model indicates the precise triggering sequence, we can't know that."

"But *is* a defusion possible at all?"

"We can't know that," Sullins said again.

20

There were thirty or forty journalists milling about in the plush, gray-black intimacy of the Space Needle's Emerald Suite restaurant. Most were in scruffy sweaters, with beards, ponytails; a few were in suits. They were schmoozing with several PrimeData senior executives, everybody waiting for the official start of the PD news conference.

Most of the journalists were business and science writers from national newspapers and magazines. But scattered around were several local television and newspaper people, a few wire-service stringers. Whenever PD founder Bill Ballard did anything, it was big news.

He was already seated at the main table, framed by the wide, slowly changing expanse of the city behind him as the restaurant turned in its ponderous 360-degree rotation. A tall, slender man in a navy-blue sweater, tousled red hair and puffy eyes behind thick, horn-rimmed glasses, he looked like some second-year philosophy student who'd wandered in by mistake.

He was definitely more. Starting in the basement workshop of his frat house at Oregon State, he'd literally created a computer software dynasty. He was a millionaire by graduation, a billionaire by thirty.

Now he sat quietly, smiling his bland, almost quizzical smile, while the more sycophantic of the journalists chattered enthusiastically around him. Everybody's expression said, "Wow, he's really *here.*"

Out in the room, the other PD execs drifted from cluster to cluster, wearing their unified corporate face of faint condescension. After the announcement, Ballard would personally host a tour of his recently completed mansion on a hill in Redmond.

Everyone already knew all the details of the company's new security system, the STAMINA-2000. But they wanted The Man's take on it, to listen to him play with the numbers. PD's stock was expected to go through the ceiling once the official announcement hit the market. Billions on billions. And the newsies were well aware that the general public always ate up the inside tidbits when money at that level was concerned.

The dining room tables, crystal and magician-wand lamps had all been removed so folding chairs could be lined up. At the back of the room, there was a long buffet adorned with beautifully coordinated floral arrangements and a huge ice sculpture of the PD logo. Delicate pastries and Northwestern finger food filled out the rest of the table.

Near the entrance, a Seattle morning news anchor was talking with a pretty computer columnist from L.A., sipping mineral water and making moves. He was scheduled to conduct a short on-camera interview with Ballard after the conference.

Now he was saying, "I tell you what, Suzy, you drop by the station tomorrow morning, I'll put you on. We'll rap about computers. And, hey, you're a skier, right?"

"Yeah, I love it."

"There you go. We'll swap slope stories, too."

"But I'm supposed to be back in Portland this afternoon after the house tour."

"What Portland?" he said. "You're in Mellowtown now, babe. Kick back, enjoy it."

"Maybe."

"Come on. Look, we'll have dinner tonight, talk about it."

She thought a moment, then flashed him a big grin. "Okay, sounds like it might be fun at that."

"Sure," he said.

His beeper sounded. He took it out, glanced at the screen. It was his station boss's number. He touched the girl's shoulder. "Don't go 'way."

He found a phone. "What is it, Al?"

"You and Bobby get your asses over to the mayor's office," Al said sharply. "Stat!"

"What? You forgetting I got a one-on-one with Ballard?"

"Scratch it."

"What the hell is this?"

"Something's up. Word has it, Kerberry's calling in all his top people for an emergency meeting."

"Whoa," he said. "I'm outta here."

He hung up and searched the suite, spotted his cameraman and gave him an emphatic jerk of the head. A moment later, both of them slipped through the entrance and ran for the elevators.

Mayor Kerberry didn't get ahold of the governor, Frank DeJohn, until he was in his limo on the way back to City Hall. The governor was on a business trip to Yakima and spoke from a golf cart on the eighth tee of the city's Hillrun Country Club.

"What the hell's the big to-do, Kerberry?" DeJohn demanded.

"We have a potentially devastating situation developing here, sir," the mayor said, sitting back there and sweating in the air conditioning. "We have word that a biological device could be loose in the city."

"What did you say?" Someone with the governor laughed loudly. DeJohn reprimanded him sharply, "Knock it off, George." Then, to Kerberry, "Now what the hell is this about a device?"

Kerberry explained the situation as his driver swung the limo off Pike and onto Fourth Avenue. When he finished, he paused, aware of the phlegmy sound his voice had made and he realized how frightened he was.

After a long silence, the governor exploded. "God *damn*

them," he said. "Fucking, *stinking* terrorists. I want—wait a minute, how do we know this isn't a hoax?"

"Nobody's certain about it yet. But the CDC thinks there's a very good chance it isn't a hoax."

"CDC? In Atlanta? You've pulled them in already?"

"They were already in, sir."

"Who the hell's responsible? Have there been any calls making claims? A warning?"

"Nothing."

"Jesus, Jesus, Jesus," the governor said.

"I think we'd better contact the President, sir."

"What?"

"The President. We need all the federal assistance we can get—and guidelines. As you know, FEMA won't come in until you make an official request."

"Yes." There was a pause as the governor attempted to draw back his control. "Yes, of course. I'll call him immediately."

"We'll also need your authorization for a WDP activation."

"Yes, I'll authorize that, too."

In a catastrophic emergency, the Washington Disaster Protocol instantly placed all state, disaster and civil defense agencies under the overall control of one authority: the governor himself. It gave him expansive constitutional contingency powers to assist in mobilization of the state's resources and in the coordination with FEMA and other federal emergency agencies.

"Are you returning to Olympia, sir?" Kerberry asked.

The governor thought a moment. "No, I'm coming to Seattle. I want to be on this thing myself. In the meantime, you work through Preston." Tray Preston was lieutenant governor.

"Yes, sir."

There was another pause. The mayor heard the soft soughing rustle of fairway wind passing over the mouthpiece of the governor's phone. He put his head down, fingered sweat off his forehead.

Finally, he said, "There's one other thing, sir. What about the public. Do we inform them now? Or do we wait?"

There was more silence. Then DeJohn said, "WDP policy is flexible on that issue. It depends on the particular situation and its ramifications."

"What about this one?"

"Lord, I don't know." The governor's voice held agony. "You realize that if we let this get out too quickly, there'll be goddamned panic in the streets. We still don't know if it's a phony threat yet."

"But if it isn't, we could be compounding an already horrendous situation."

"No, we need time. We must know exactly what we're up against. And I want the federals in on the decision-making before we start shooting off our mouths. No, I want a lid kept on this thing for now."

"The news people'll be all over it, sir. Undoubtedly, they already are."

"Then deal with them."

"All right, Governor, I'll try."

"Don't *try*, goddammit. *Do* it, Kerberry. Stonewall the hell out of this thing."

"Yes, sir."

"Look, I'm heading for the airport right now. I'll try for the President on the way. And I'll contact you again once we're in the air. Until then, you keep Preston apprised of everything. Is that understood?"

"Yes, sir."

"All right." The governor gave a deep groan, as if wounded. "And we all better start praying goddamned hard that this turns out to be nothing more than some big mistake."

"I've already done that, sir," Kerberry said as the facade of City Hall rose into view through the windshield.

It happened with lightning speed.

Marquette was on an open stretch of Mercer, the traffi

banked to the right, a line of cars and then a city bus. He started past the bus, flying.

Up ahead, little more than a block away, he caught sight of the Trans Am, swerving to the inside lane as it crossed an intersection and made a sharp left onto Broad Street.

Suddenly, a motorcyclist shot into Matt's lane from in front of the bus, a red-white-and-blue crotch rocket, with the rider hunched forward over his handlebars. His rear wheel was less than fifteen feet off Matt's right fender.

In pure reflex, Marquette rammed the brakes on, hurling the wheel hard over to the left. He felt the Jag hesitate for a fraction of a second. Then it snapped across, heeling over, rear tires still powering as it went into a wild skid.

He threw the wheel back over into the skid. The Jag momentarily began to recover, then went into a counter-skid, the car drifting almost leisurely into a near 180. Out there, the motorcyclist's head was turned, looking back through the black mask of his helmet, oncoming traffic dodging out of the way. The huge bulk of the bus loomed to Matt's right.

There was a sudden violent, metallic impact as the Jag slammed into the rear of the bus. The bus was stopped now, and the Jag's trunk slid under the high bumper, lifting it. The back window shattered, and Matt was hurled against the driver's door.

There followed a moment of near silence filled only with the heated ticking of metal, the junkyard odor of crushed steel, tire smoke. Outside the window, people stared with faces gone slack.

Instantly recovering, Marquette shoved the accelerator to the floor. The engine whined up, but the vehicle wouldn't move. It was jammed too tightly under the bus. He tried to open his door but couldn't.

Frantically, he shoved across the seat and got out on the other side. People were approaching now, stepping off the curb. Out on the boulevard, the traffic had slowed to a stop, bunching, the drivers gawking.

Matt glanced desperately down toward Broad Street, scanned far to the left. He couldn't see the Trans Am, just

the tops of automobiles. He twisted, climbed onto the bus
bumper and leaned far out, searching again. People glared at
him through the rear window. Where is it? There? No. He
looked still farther to the left. Nothing. Back again, slower.

He stopped.

Pinioned in his view was the soaring, spindly shaft of the
Space Needle, four blocks away. The glass mushroom at the
top reflected the gray, thickening sky, the red strobe light at
its apex flashing.

And he knew.

Ice came to his teeth. He felt his lungs constrict as if he
had just sucked in a violent contaminated breath of air.

He leapt off the bus bumper, raced back to the car. He
leaned in, searching for the cell phone. It had been slammed
against the steering column in the crash. It lay on the floor
beside the Browning Hi-Power. He scooped them both up,
straightened as people came up, stopped when they saw the
gun and then swung around to scurry out of the way.

He broke into a run across the boulevard, dodging between
the stopped cars, shoving the pistol under his belt. Then he
was on the opposite sidewalk, turning, going full-out toward
Broad Street.

A few reporters met the mayor's limo as it pulled into the
underground parking area of City Hall. Two state marshals
and one of Kerberry's aides met him as soon as the car
stopped rolling, the sound of the tires echoing in the vaulted
cement space.

The reporters rushed up, shouting questions. Kerberry
quickly slipped out of the backseat and, shielded by the marshals, scurried to the elevator, head down, saying nothing.

After the elevator doors closed, the newsies stood around
cursing for a moment, then headed for the stairs—all except
one, a young reporter from news radio station KERA. His
name was Marvin Port. He had spotted a small, yellow T-
bird that had just swung down the ramp into the garage.

He hurried over to it, arriving as the driver, a tall, frizzy-
haired girl, got out. Her face was pale, strained. She spotted

him and held up her hand. "I can't talk to you, Marv," she cried.

He took her arm and hurried her to the back of the car. Her name was Claire Voorhees, an assistant on Kerberry's staff. Port had often garnered bits of news from her since they'd shared a couple of nights of good Peruvian Red marijuana and several hours of raunchy sex.

"What the hell's going down here?" Port demanded.

"Dammit, Marv, I don't know anything."

He tilted his head, gave her a sly grin. "Oh, yes, you do. I can see it in your face."

"No."

"Claire, come on." She tried to pull away. "Claire . . . my God, you're trembling."

"Oh, Marvin," she cried. Her eyes began to tear up.

"Jesus, girl, what the hell is it?"

She closed her eyes, shook her head. "It's bad."

"What bad?"

She opened her eyes, moved very close to him. "If I tell you, you can't tell *any*body. Not this time. You promise?"

"Of course."

"Promise me," Claire said fiercely.

"Sure, you know me."

"They're saying a terrorist has planted a biological bomb somewhere in the city."

Port jerked back as if someone had spat in his face. "Hooooly shit," he said slowly. Then his grip tightened on her arm. "What kind of a bomb? Where? Who?"

"I think they said it was an anthrax bomb. And some agency called the CDC said it's really for real."

"You mean the Centers for Disease Control?"

"I think so, yeah. And the Army's in it, too."

"So they've got federal agencies involved already?"

"Yes."

"Who did it? What terrorists?"

"I don't know."

"Do they know where it is?"

"No."

Port stood for a moment, glaring at her with hot excitement in his eyes. Then he let go of her arm, turned and sprinted off.

"Marvin!" Claire shouted frantically after him. "God damn you. You promised."

At precisely 9:35 A.M., USAMRIID began to feed in the first results of their suppositional model on the sphere data. All of it was being sent through the mainframes of the Army's Medical Research and Development Command in Maryland, with everything going simultaneously to the White House, the Pentagon, the FBI, the National Security Council, the CDC. The computers at CRYSTALBALL were included in the network since they were the only highline link the Army and CDC had with Seattle.

Kelli stared at the scrolling screen, her mind riding on frenzied anxiety. She'd still been on the phone when Matt had had his accident; she'd heard the screech of tires and then a sudden cutoff of the phone's signal. Oh, God, was he dead? Hurt badly? Her mind listened desperately for the phone to ring.

Meanwhile, the entire lab team had finally understood the import of what was happening. Faces were haunted; nobody spoke except in hushed whispers. Now they huddled behind Kelli, reading the incoming data:

1735 UCT

USAMRIID: close-hold// code AP 183
Path/Dis HYPO Model//Run:1:
Bacterial Mutation Track: phasing AB-NB

Model device appears to be a bacteria meta-phasing/dispersing chamber. Active strain: *Bacillus anthracis*.
Mutational DNA with rapid bacteria evolution resulting in basic amino acid/enzymatic

ALTERATION SUFFICIENT FOR CREATION OF
SPEEDED-UP FUME OF HIGHLY VIRULENT SPORAL,
AIRBORNE FORM OF THE BACTERIUM.

METAPHASING SEQUENCE IS INITIATED
THROUGH RAPID-CYCLE LASER (SECONDARY COM-
PONENT) EXPOSURE OF INFRARED IN DISCRETE
SPECTRUM ESTIMATED IN RANGE OF 275 TO 285
MICROMETERS.

DISPERSION WILL BE ACHIEVED THROUGH SMALL-
YIELD EXPLOSIVE (TERTIARY COMPONENT) CRE-
ATING 50-75-YARD OUT-THROW.

The phone rang. Everybody's head snapped around. One
of the team leaped to it, scooped up the receiver. She listened
for a moment, then said, "Stay off this line." She hung up,
shook her head.

Everybody turned back. The screen scrolled on:

VICTIMS WILL BREAK OUT WITH SYMPTOMS 3-4
HOURS AFTER EXPOSURE. FULL PULMONARY CRASH
AND CASCADE OF DECAY WITHIN 18-30 HOURS.
INITIAL CHILL FOLLOWED BY GENERAL, TETANUS-
LIKE MUSCULAR SPASMS, DELIRIUM AND POSSIBLE
HEMORRHAGIC MENINGITIS. MORTALITY RATE ES-
TIMATE: 91-98%

AGENT NONFILTERABLE THROUGH CHAMBERLAND.
APPEARS TO BE TOTALLY RESISTANT TO PASTEUR
AND DEV VACCINES. ALSO TO ALL CURRENT AN-
TIBACTERIAL DRUG THERAPY.

POSITIVE CONTROL OF ANTIPATHOGEN ACHIEVED
ONLY THROUGH EXPOSURE TO OPEN SUNLIGHT OR
ELECTROMAGNETIC SPECTRUM WAVES IN RANGE
BETWEEN 10(9) TO 10(12) CYCLES PER SECOND
(MW).

EXPLOSIVE CHAIN OF TRANSMISSION WILL BE IN-
STANTANEOUS. DEPENDING ON CLIMATIC CONDI-
TIONS, DOWNWIND CONTAMINATION WILL CREATE
EXTREME HOT ZONE OF AMPLIFICATION. ESTIMATED
TIME TO CHAIN OF INFECTION PEAK WITHIN HOT
ZONE IS 8–10 HOURS, WITH SUBSEQUENT BREAK-
OUT INTO ENTIRE WEST COAST POPULATION
WITHIN 1 WEEK. FATALITY ESTIMATE IN SEATTLE
AREA PROPER WILL BE IN THE RANGE OF
200,000 TO 250,000.

RECOMMENDATIONS:
IMMEDIATE SATURATION OF HOT ZONE WITH BIO-
HAZARD SWAT TEAMS TO ACHIEVE BIOCONTAIN-
MENT OF LEVEL-4.
POLICE-ENFORCED EVACUATION ALONG PATHWAYS
BASED ON WIND DIRECTION AND FORCE.
MASSIVE (AFEP) AIRLIFT OF ISOLATION AND BIO-
CONTAINMENT EQUIPMENT INTO ACTIVE HZ, AND
CONSTRUCTION OF BIOCONTAINMENT PAVILIONS AT
CENTRAL SITES.
TAKEOVER OF LOCAL HOSPITALS AND ALL AVAIL-
ABLE MEDICAL FACILITIES, INCLUDING VETERINARY
CLINICS AND . . .

Kelli couldn't read any more. She turned, and walked
away, stood near a window. Outside, the fountain quad was
sunk in an overcast gray light. The trees swayed gently in a
rising wind.

Gilhammer came up behind her, put his arm around her
waist, hugged her. "He's all right, Kel," he said softly.
"We're all going to be all right."

She turned her head to look into his eyes. "After reading
that thing, can you really believe that?"

"I have to," he said.

Together they started back toward the workstations, but Kelli paused beside the high-speed printer softly humming off hard copies of the USAMRIID data. She lifted the top copy, read from the beginning—and stopped on the entry she had missed when the phone rang.

She stared at it, felt her heart stop for a tiny moment and then start again. The entry gave the suppositional time span between the triggering of the unit and the moment of maximum bacterial fume and explosive out-throw.

The phone rang. Startled, she blinked, then leapt to it. "Matt?" she cried.

Through the receiver came Marquette's faint, breathless voice shouting, "It's the Space Needle."

Three minutes earlier, Jack Stone had reached the number-four gate of the Seattle Center, swinging up to it from Broad Street. He hauled to a stop at the barrier arm, plucked the ticket from the meter and sped through. Across the way, a young attendant leaned around the corner of his booth and looked at the broken back window of the car. He shrugged and went back to his *Playboy* magazine.

Stone had now crossed into a complete state of manic focus, like an athlete staring down the ramp at the high-jump bar, a single, brilliant goal with everything else closed out.

He was unaware that Marquette was chasing him, but it wouldn't have mattered if he had known. Matt's bullets back in the park had merely locked in the focus, the shattering glass and slam of the slug into the car's header giving a tighter click to his brain's concentration.

No longer were the mules involved, he thought with a kind of fierce exhilaration, all the stupid, secondary characters he'd been forced to inject into his broad scheme. Only Fettis had been one with him; the rest, pawns who had fucked up and created glitches.

Now it was all in his own hands. And nothing, nobody, would prevent the possession of its completion.

The parking lot was sparsely filled. He waved off a valet parker who started toward him and pulled into a space about a hundred yards from the Space Needle, where its great, soaring sweep rose out of the southeastern corner of Seattle Center.

From the lot, he noted several dozen tourists wandering among the shops in the base plaza. Others stood out on the ramp, gazing upward at the graceful, six-hundred-foot-high structure. Two stories above the plaza, the broad, oblique windows of the Skyline restaurant reflected the gray tone of the sky, resembling sheets of thin pewter.

Quickly, Stone retrieved the secondary components of the bomb from his suitcase. He unsheathed the needle on the laser/computer unit and snapped it into the sphere. It made a soft hiss as the negative pressure within the globe formed an instant, airtight connection. He then mounted the explosive charge in the same way.

Next, he checked the trigger switch on the computer. Beneath it were two pinpoint-sized lights, one white, the other green. The white light was now lit, indicating that the unit's minuscule computer was functioning. The green light would go on when he pressed the triggering switch.

He leaned forward and whipped off his belt. He looped it around the sphere and tightened it until it was snug. Then he placed the assembled unit back into Marquette's gym bag and got out of the car.

There was a small line at the ticket kiosk: two flush-faced Chinese men and an old woman with a small boy. The old woman had blue-white hair and a Band-Aid on her nose. She checked out his damp, splattered trousers, then smiled brightly at him. "Playing in the mud again?" she asked.

He stared at her in stony silence. Her smile faded, and she turned away.

She and the boy, along with a dozen other people, rode up with him in the elevator. At this time of the morning, only one of the three elevators was working. There were yellow velvet ropes across the open doors of the others. Some of the passengers gave his filthy clothes quick, furtive glances, as if they could sense the dangerous energy field surrounding him.

The elevator gave an almost imperceptible jerk and began to rise on soundless cables. Through the window, they watched the monorail track pass, and then they were rising more swiftly, able to see down into the Fun Forest and, beyond that, the walls of Memorial Stadium as the perspective from the window changed.

Finally they were high enough to actually see down into the stadium, beyond it to the complex gardens around Center House, and at last the broad expanse of roof that covered Key Arena, where the Sonics played.

The old woman cried with mock fright, "Oh, my God, we're flying!" The little boy grimaced and murmured with embarrassment, "Aw, come on, gran'ma." Everyone chortled—all except Stone, who stared straight ahead, holding the gym bag in both hands against his stomach and feeling the solid, reassuring weight of the bomb under the canvas.

In the Emerald Suite high above the elevator, Ballard leaned close to Cornell and whispered, "What the hell's going on? You notice those guys leaving?"

Cornell nodded. "And they're all local reporters. Something big must have come up over the last half hour."

"Go check it out."

"Right." Cornell rose. "Dammit, wouldn't you know it would happen today." He moved off.

A scholarly looking writer from *Scientific American* approached Ballard, smiling. "Mr. Ballard, might I ask you something?"

"Shoot."

"What are your feelings concerning the latest government efforts to censor the Net?"

At that moment, twenty feet above the restaurant, a young man lifted his three-year-old daughter to the eyepiece of the number-eight telescope on the outdoor observation platform. For a moment, the child fumbled with the rubber buffer, then peered grimly through the right lens.

"See the big city, baby?" the father said. "See way down there, the big boats?"

The little girl giggled.

Marquette's shoes hit the pavement lightly, bouncing off, his wild momentum lifting weight off the soles. He reached Broad Street, turned left. Here, the traffic was moving smoothly, cars whipping past. Pedestrians, catching sight of his running figure, his wild, mud-smeared face, darted aside. Someone yelled, "Hey, watch it, man," as he passed.

Across the wide street and slightly to the south was the spire of the Needle, silhouetted against the gray overcast. The cloud cover was dark now, filled with rain. Beyond the structure lay the cluster of downtown Seattle buidlings, some actually challenging its height.

He hadn't taken his eyes from the structure since starting his run, his breathing climbing as he fumbled with the cell phone buttons to re-raise Kelli. The car crash had disconnected his line with her. And then, suddenly, he had her again, and he shouted into the phone, the thing bouncing with the rhythm of his strides.

She came right back to him, "Repeat, repeat. I can hardly hear you."

"It's the Space Needle," he panted, screaming. "The bastard's target . . . the Needle."

He heard her shout to someone, then to him again, "Where . . . I . . . you?" The phone was cutting in and out. Apparently, it had been damaged in the crash.

"Broad Street . . . get cops."

"Yes, we're doing that. . . ."

"What did . . . from the CDC?"

"Oh, Matt, it's horrible. Hundreds of thousand . . . going to die."

Through the heat of his body, he felt a wave of pure cold tremble in his skin. *Hundreds of thousands!* From there, the Needle, high in the sky, the infection riding the wind.

"How do I . . . defuse?" he managed to shout before having to leap over a section of pavement under repair, coming down hard, the phone lifting away from his face for a moment.

He had now covered two blocks of Broad Street and was directly opposite the southeastern side of Seattle Center. He shot a quick glance to the right and then dashed into the street.

"What?" Kelli cried. "I can't hear."

"Give me . . . options."

"Yes, yes. Open sunlight kills the bacterium. Do . . . understand? Bright sunlight. And electromagnetic wa—"

From the corner of his eye, Matt caught a flash of green and silver, the startled, grimacing face of a driver through a windshield. Tires screeched. Without thinking, he twisted to the left, his feet shoving his body into the air in an effort to get out of the way.

The car struck him in the right thigh. He felt the impact, a quick, sharp blow of pain, and then he was going over the curve of the fender and falling onto his side on the hood. His moving weight continued to pull him all the way across, and he fell off onto the road, down on his hands and knees.

Around him, cars were screeching to a stop. There was a sharp slam of metal. Another. A man suddenly appeared from around the front of the car that had hit him. His face was ashen.

"Oh, Jesus Christ," he kept repeating in anguish. He frantically tried to help Marquette up.

Matt brushed him aside and leapt to his feet. His right leg felt numb. He picked up the telephone and started across the street again, limping, partially dragging his foot.

The muscles, already flushed with blood, quickly began to regain feeling. His whole leg throbbed. Around him, all the cars had stopped, people sitting immobilized with amazement.

He could hear the tinny sound of Kelli's voice screaming through the phone. He brought it to his mouth. "Say again," he bellowed. "Goddammit . . . say again."

"Are you all right?" Kelli cried. "God, are you all right?"

He reached the other side of Broad Street, turned directly toward the number-four Center gate. The attendant stared out at him as he went hurtling past the toll booth.

"Tell me," Matt yelled.

There was a spurt of static as he crossed under the iron overhang of the booth. Then Kelli again: ". . . bomb to complete its fume cycle . . ."

"Say again." He started across the parking lot, slipping between cars, sprinting, his chest beginning to ache badly now, and his leg still partially numb.

Her voice, clear and precise, came back, "Once activated, the bomb will take precisely six minutes to complete its fume cycle and explode."

Six minutes!

"How do I stop it?"

"Once started, the sequen . . . can't be stop—" The phone was crackling with static again, cutting out, as the great mass of steel in the Needle increased the interference of its tiny signal. "You must . . ."

"Shit!" Marquette bellowed. "Say again."

". . . enclosed space, strong en— . . . no other . . ." And then she was gone.

The elevator doors slid open on the observation level. Stone was the first out. For a moment, he paused to get his bearings. Then he darted to the steps that led to the outside platform.

It was windy out there, a cutting wind that made the cables of the platform barrier hum softly. The barrier curved up and back like a prison fence, the cables stretching a foot apart. Just below the rim of the platform spread the wide beams of the structure's sun louvers, which formed an umbrella-like fan around the entire span of the observation platform.

There was only a smattering of people outside, the wind whipping their hair, their coats pulled up. The wind carried sea smell and rain in it, overlaid with the sharp, woodsy odor of pine resin.

Stone moved to the first telescope. It was number five. He

continued around the platform, checking off numbers until he reached number eight. A man and tiny girl in a snowsuit were using the telescope, the man peering through and the child squealing, "Boats. Boats."

Stone looked at his watch. It was 9:43.

He moved up beside the telescope and looked over the edge of the barrier. Long ago, in Boise, he'd studied the architectural drawings of the Needle's observation area, particularly the schematics that showed the air-conditioning system for the upper level. Now he spotted the three-foot-square opening of the main induction vent precisely where the drawings said it would be.

This particular vent, he knew, linked into the enclosed conditioning system's main air reservoir, which automatically kept the system fed with outside air through pressure seals. When the bomb exploded, its high pressure traveling back through the conduit would instantly break these seals. Then the highly imbalanced pressure gradient would suck the anthrax-laden outside air into the system and eventually out through the inside vents.

The man and his child finally left the telescope and moved off around the curve of the platform. Now Stone was alone on this side.

He unzipped the gym bag, reached in, touched the bomb, gripped it.

For one crystalline moment, he hesitated, something in his mind balking, something deep. Conscience. A sudden, nearly overwhelming sorrow.

He stood there caught in its web, the wind singing through the cables, the air rife with the smell of ocean distance, and the vast, open sky stretching away like layers of molten lead. . . .

Long ago, when he and Fettis had first evolved the thought of using the anthrax device, they'd hesitated, too—a simple human reaction. The immense potential for uncontrolled lethality was too devastating. If it got loose in the city?

Instead, they'd turned back to the use of conventional ordnance, a compact bomb of high, intense charge. But there was a big loophole there. No matter how strong and well-placed a normal bomb was, it could leave survivors. Only the anthrax would kill with totality, with a single breath.

No, they'd have to use the anthrax, they decided. Once done, they sought rational parameters, convinced themselves the contagion *couldn't* break out. Sucked into the completely enclosed area of the Needle restaurant and its slightly negative atmosphere, it would remain isolated. Perhaps a germ or two might escape on the wind, create a handful of deaths. But those would be battle casualities. Acceptable . . .

Now, again assailed by doubt, Stone remained immobilized. But his mind, plunging at speed, drove against it, and gradually the old rage came back, the laser focus.

Kill them!

His hand tightened on the bomb, lifted it out. He grasped the end of the belt with his other hand and deftly shoved the bomb between the cables, holding it high with his thumb and forefinger on the belt.

He punched the trigger button.

The tiny green light popped on.

He let the bomb fall to the end of the belt, swung it once, guiding the arc, and then let it go. It hit the bottom of the vent, rolled nearly out of sight until it stopped against the filter screen several inches inside. The end of the belt hung down over the vent lip.

He took one last look. Then he whirled, his heart pounding wildly in his head, and sprinted back toward the elevator.

21

Time to detonation: five minutes, fifty-six seconds

One microsecond after Stone pressed the trigger switch, the bomb's laser unit, powered by a high-density chlorine-arsenic battery, had hurled tetra-phased bursts of ultraviolet light through its needle assembly to the central crystal matrix. Instantly the matrix, composed of iodine crystals, began to glow like a burning ruby as the crystals deased the UV light into specific infrared wave frequencies. Heat radiated throughout the partial vacuum within the sphere.

The thin coating that covered the inner surface now began to seethe, forming blisters and bubbles. Within this coating, which was a nutrient-rich broth, were billions of inert anthrax organisms. Immediately, these were roused into life by the intense heat.

Although the heat had awakened the bacteria from dormancy, continued exposure to it would bring the organisms to death threshold. To escape it, the bacteria's recombinant enzymes quickly began to create a corrective genetic mutational form of spiral *anthracis* capable of lifting away from the heat source.

Clumping into groups called "random walkers," these altered bacteria then drifted through the nutrient broth, replicating in a tremendous surge of DNA exchange.

Meanwhile, the initial burst of heat had also activated a

detonation timer on the explosive unit. Calibrated for 360 seconds, it would reach detonation point at the precise moment the mutational fume reached maximum phase. . . .

At precisely 9:45, station KERA interrupted its regular news format with a special bulletin: ''A reliable government source has just revealed that there is a possibility a terrorist's biological bomb is at this moment somewhere within the city of Seattle.

''Efforts to contact Mayor Kerberry and other city officials for confirmation or denial have proven fruitless. It is known, however, that emergency meetings are being conducted at City Hall and at other official locations within the city.

''Governor DeJohn was also unavailable for comment. One member of his staff emphatically disavowed the rumor. He did admit that some sort of emergency reaction is in effect but said it was merely a scheduled Washington Disaster Protocol drill. Subsequent telephone calls to the offices of the WDP were not answered.

''Our reliable source further states that officials believe the bomb to be composed of *Bacillus anthracis* organisms, which cause the highly infectious disease commonly known as anthrax. Medical consultants say that . . .''

Throughout the entire Puget Sound area, people instantly stopped what they were doing and turned toward their radios. A terrorist bomb here? Could it be true? If so, where was it? In the wave of paranoia that had recently swept across the nation, following the bombings in Oklahoma City and New York, the unbelievable easily became the possible.

Sixty seconds after the broadcast, telephone switching stations immediately experienced a record surge of traffic. As word of the broadcast spread through the populace like a storm wind off the sea, the first stages of mass panic began to appear, not only in Seattle, but also in the suburbs of Bellevue, Renton and Kirkland. People drew together in agitated, whispering groups, confused, seeking reassurance of what to do. . . .

*   *   *

Jack Stone had never felt such a rush of euphoric triumph. It glowed in his mind like a sun, rendered to his heart's beat a fine glory.

It was short-lived.

When he reached the only operative elevator, a single man was waiting in front of the door. Stone stopped, frantically glanced at his watch.

The man turned and looked at him. "We just missed her," he said pleasantly. "But she'll be back in three, four minutes."

Three or four minutes!

No, he had to be off this level when the bomb went. He glanced to his right. There was a steel door with CENTRAL STAIRS stenciled across it. He ran to it, jerked the door open and started down.

The stairwell shaft was unpainted, and it smelled of cold and bare cement. There were large windows at each landing. The glass panes had slight waves in them, which gave the panoramic view of the city a gentle magnification and also cast the gray outside light into geometric patterns onto the landings, like storm light on the bottom of a swimming pool.

Down he went, taking four steps at a time, hurling around the landings to the next set of stairs, his heart now racing with a rising desperation. The holstered Ingram under his coat slapped heavily against his shoulder and deltoid muscles at each jolting step.

The phone was nearly useless, riding blows of static like the crackle of firewood exposed to sudden gusts of wind. Now and then, Kelli's anguished voice rose into clarity and then quickly faded again as if she were screaming from a distant room.

From somewhere came the sudden wail of sirens, as if the sounds had just sprung from the trees and building corners, drifting on the wind.

Marquette's breath rasped, and his leg throbbed in powerful spasms. Each impact of his shoe felt peculiar, as if his leg were partially asleep and his foot was something disconnected from the rest of his body. As he ran through the parking area, his eyes darted here and there, searching for the Trans Am. He didn't see it.

The girl in the ticket kiosk watched him pass, openmouthed. He reached the crowd idly moving about the base. People stared at him, shocked by this running, dirty-faced, wild-eyed man wearing an armored vest punctured by bullet holes.

He caught sight of the working elevator. Fifteen or twenty people were waiting for the doors to open. He skirted it, saw the second elevator with the yellow rope.

He turned back, headed for the stairwell. He slammed the door open and started up, lifting his right leg from the hip, slightly crookedly, feeling the throbbing in bone and muscle. He put the peculiar half-pain from his mind and continued, his right arm pulling on the railing.

He reached the first landing. He heard women's voices directly above him. The sound of their laughter was made hollow by the shaft of the stairwell. A moment later, two pretty, young girls rounded the corner of the stairs. They were both dressed in blue ski clothes. They stopped, gasping in sudden fright as he panted by them.

He passed the Skyline level, bore on. Landings came, went. Eight, nine. He had to pause on the tenth to ease the burning in his lungs. Sweat poured off his face, and his head rang from the exertion.

Six minutes! his mind cried.

It drove him on. He reached the fifteenth landing, stopped again. Air whistled through his nostrils, the cement walls ricocheting his wild breathing.

He heard a spaced thudding above him. Someone was coming down. Fast. He held his breath to listen, feeling the high pump of his heart in the sudden stillness of his body. The footfalls were heavy, widely spaced. Whoever it was was coming down jumping steps.

He slipped his hand to the grip of the Browning Hi-Power.

Keeping the gun under his belt, he pressed his back against the wall, listening as the footfalls get louder. Then a hand appeared on the railing ten feet above him, and, swinging into the turn of the stairwell, lunging down, was the horse-faced man.

The man stopped dead when he spotted Marquette, his downward momentum carrying him against the wall. For one tiny instant, they looked at each other, and then the man was clawing at his jacket, his face gone wooden, his hand exposing the long, black holster and the weapon coming out.

Marquette's Hi-Power was coming, too, lifting away from the warmth of his belly. Don't kill him, his mind cried. He's the only one who knows.

But as he watched, the man's weapon came sliding out of its holster, the long silencer clearing the edge, and the man's shoulder lifted awkwardly, his wooden face narrowing its eyes, the lips tightening as if he were already feeling the jerk of the gun.

"No!" Marquette bellowed, the butt of his own gun already seated in the palm of his other hand. But the man didn't stop. Up came the silencer, steady, steady. . . .

Marquette's finger tightened. He fired twice, the Hi-Power jarring against his hand. The reports were like cannons blowing upward in the confined space.

Both bullets struck the horse-faced man in the chest, twisted him around and backward as his weapon went off with a chain of soft, sibilant outbursts of high-pressure air. The rounds slammed into the cement walls, cutting the air over Marquette's head. One shattered the window. The patterns on the landing dissolved into pure gray light as the man crumpled to the stairs, falling straight down as if suddenly deflated.

Marquette leapt to him, grabbed his jacket and lifted his head. It hung down, limp, the man's eyes looking at him with a hot, steady light.

"Where is it?" Marquette screamed into his face. "You son of a bitch, where is it?"

The man said nothing. Only the heated sheen of those eyes showed life. Then their lids fluttered, and the life went away.

Cursing wildly, Marquette hauled the man up, lifted him bodily into the air. For a moment he stared into the dead face, growling at it like an animal. A thick drop of blood oozed onto his hand and ran downward, leaving a crimson trail through the hairs of his wrist.

He let the body drop, going down without structure. Then he dove over it and started up again.

Four minutes, forty-six seconds

In the ruby-red light inside the sphere, grotesquely beautiful fractal patterns now swirled within the nutrient broth, whorls and spirals and convoluted octagons and polyhedrons shimmering with a scarlet iridescence. And lifting off the surface was a smoke of mutated anthrax organisms. . . .

One of the senior execs of PrimeData was at the podium. It was now 9:51. He was to work the crowd for a minute or two, then pass the lectern to Cornell, who would introduce Ballard. Everyone dutifully took their seats as he started off with a lukewarm joke. There was a ripple of polite laughter.

Ballard lifted his glass of mineral water. Over the rim, he watched Cornell come back into the room, skirting the chairs. His face was clouded. Beyond, in the other part of the suite, waitresses were looking out the window.

Cornell bent close. "It's crazy," he whispered softly. "The maître d' told me that he heard on the radio something about a terrorist bomb in the city."

"Oh, oh," Ballard said.

"It's gotta be a hoax," Cornell said. "Somebody's out to screw up our announcement."

In the seats, the journalists were beginning to whisper.

Ballard had turned, was studying the waitresses near the far windows. "What the hell are they all looking at?" he asked. But before Cornell could answer, he rose and moved to the window behind their table.

The platform of the Needle had turned enough so that now it was facing Mount Rainier. Snow-covered, its jagged ridges formed bare up-thrusts through the white mantle. Down in the city, he noticed cars pulled over to the curb, people huddled in little groups, everything far beyond the cushioned silence of the restaurant.

Then, so faint it might have been no more than the gentle keening of the wind, he heard sirens. He glanced to his right. On Mercer Avenue, about three blocks away, the traffic was completely snarled. Here and there, he saw the red, flashing lights of police cars caught in the tangle like phosphorescent fish in a net.

Marquette barely made the final observation landing before he collapsed to the steel floor and knelt there, his chest heaving. Sweat stung his eyes; his leg hammered along his bones.

He had deliberately passed the restaurant level, knowing in some instinctive way that the horse-faced man had wanted the observation level—open space where he could sow the anthrax directly into the wind.

He finally pulled himself to his feet, slammed his hand against the bar of the door and lunged out into the enclosed visitor's section. It was empty. Information desk, display counters, nobody around.

He glanced outside. People were on the platform, some wearing the light gray smocks of Needle employees. Everybody was looking out over the city and pointing here, there. He ran to the stairs to the outside observation area, vaulted them and rushed out.

The wind enveloped him, icy cold on his wet skin. It smelled of rain and the acetylene scent of approaching storm. He started around the platform, moving to his left. His eyes frantically scanned to catch the tiniest glint from the polished sphere . . . the back wall and balustrade, the steel deck, along the overhead barrier cables. He paused to peer down onto the spokes of the louvers.

Nothing.

He moved on.

He passed a telescope. Another. A balding man and two women were standing just beyond. The man leaned against the cables, gripping them like a prisoner staring out. The women's blond hair whipped and feathered in the wind.

The man said, "Man, lookit that! There're cops all *over* the place."

"Oh, Norman, I'm getting scared," one of the women said. "Maybe we better go down."

The man laughed. "What, and lose a ringside seat?"

They didn't even notice Marquette dash by.

He passed another telescope. His mind was zinging, thoughts hurtling through like flashes of sharp light. Under them was the deadly expectation of an explosion at any moment—the out-blow from some niche, a muffled sound like the resonance of a kettle drum and then the engulfment of . . .

He forced the image away.

Suddenly he stopped, stared. A small, crumpled object lay beside the outer balustrade near a telescope. He started toward it, his eyes narrowed to make out what it was. Then he was running again.

It was his gym bag. . . .

Three minutes, thirty-nine seconds

The laser pulses ceased. For a few seconds, the crystal matrix continued to glow with heat and light energy. Then it faded, and the inside of the sphere sank into total darkness.

By now, the smoke of mutated anthrax had thickened until it was almost a plasma. But deep within the churning nutrient broth, other random walkers continued their DNA exchanges, all in black silence save for the soft pulse of the explosive timer. . . .

*   *   *

The belt-end flapped in the wind, now and then whipping against one of the I-beams that formed the frame of the lower part of the louver. Marquette stared down at it, followed it back to the vent lip.

He saw the edge of the bomb, the sphere rolling slightly, nudged by the wind. He felt the skin of his scalp move as if suddenly infested with insects.

Then he was climbing the cables of the barrier, upside down, going hand over hand to the top, the little cell phone in his mouth. The barrier didn't directly abut the inner wall of the platform. Instead, there was a three-foot space. He swung himself up and over the last cable, started back across the top.

A woman gave a muffled scream, "Look at that man! Oh, God, he's going to commit suicide."

A man's voice yelled, "Hey, don't do it."

Marquette reached the outside of the barrier, climbed down and stepped onto one of the main I-beams. He could feel the wind funneling up through the lower, canted frame. It formed pockets of twisting air that made the edge of the metal sheathing at the tip of the louvers hum. The beams themselves seemed to tremble slightly under his shoes.

He quickly lowered himself to the bottom frame. He didn't look down. With his legs wrapped around a beam, he leaned forward, reaching for the bomb. The air being sucked into the vent made a sound like water curving around a stone.

His fingers grasped the sphere. It felt warm. He lifted it off the vent ledge, drawing it in, staring mesmerized at its mute, shiny surface.

"Jesus, he's got a bomb!" a man cried out above him.

Startled, Matt glanced up. The bald man named Norman was staring down at him with a look of horror contorting his face. An instant later, he was gone.

"Bomb!"

The word was like the explosion itself. It swept from mouth to mouth around the platform, was turned into creams. People were momentarily stunned into motionlessness. Then they leapt into hysterical flight, running, knocking others down.

A wild scramble formed in front of the working elevator. The doors were closed. People began to yell and frantically pound on them.

Others turned away, dashed for the stairs. Another blockage was created as people tried to squeeze through. Fistfights broke out. A woman fainted, sinking right down to the floor. Someone stepped on her face.

A few seconds later, one of the first down the stairs stopped long enough to yell out into the restaurant level that a man with a bomb was on the top floor. Again there was the same stunned silence and then a wild exodus for the elevator and stairs.

In the Emerald Suite, the journalists began to stand up, looking confusedly about for the source of the distant shouting. Quickly the words became clear. Faces went stark.

Then, as if set off by a starting gun, everybody headed for the doors, knocking over chairs and drinks. Someone was shoved into the buffet table. The ice carving went over onto the rug amid plates, flowers and tableware.

Near the window, Ballard and Cornell looked at each other, shocked. Like all rich and powerful men, Ballard had long lived with the threat of kidnap or assassination. Now the look in his eyes said he believed that moment was here, now. Somebody was actually in the process of trying to kill him.

He quickly roused himself and burst across the room, dodging nimbly around fallen chairs. Halfway to the door, he turned and looked back. Cornell was still beside the window, paralyzed with fear.

Ballard turned and rushed back. He grabbed his CEO's shoulders and roughly shook him. "Move, Jerry," he screamed into his face. "Goddammit, move! We've got to get out of here." Half-dragging Cornell, he started across the room again.

In the melee, the doors had been flung wide with such force that they were now all locked open. . . .

*   *   *

His Stetson pulled down low over his eyes, Two Elks sat in seeming equanimity as Lieutenant Walters hurtled the patrol cruiser along Mercer Avenue with a grim, old-hand expertise.

Since leaving Washington Park, they'd kept a tight link to Dispatcher Fourteen, who constantly updated them on police bulletins and reports from Pickett at the university. When she told them about Marquette's message that the bomb target was the Space Needle, both men had exchanged silent, baleful glances.

Then came the stats from USAMRIID about the anthrax— its deadly, infectious nature; its rapid spread, the potential deaths. The dispatcher's voice choked up as she read the summary of statistics.

This time, Two Elks took off his hat, brushed his hand agitatedly over his hair and put the hat back on.

Through clenched teeth, Walters said, ''Big John, we're in some deep shit here.''

Mixed into the messages from CRYSTALBALL was a constant radio cross-chatter between dispatchers and patrol cruisers. Things seemed to be getting crazy out there, all over the city. Citizens flooded the switchboards, stopped patrolmen in the street with desperate questions. A sense of mass hysteria was openly beginning to spread like a wildfire.

''How the hell did word get out?'' Two Elks growled, swaying as Walters flashed around a car.

''I know how,'' Walters boomed. ''Some fucking pissant official shot his mouth off, that's how.''

Then they got word that the first announcement had come from station KEMA, which had quoted a reliable government source.

Enraged, Walters slammed his palms against the wheel. ''See? I told you. God*damn* that bastard.''

He had to slow suddenly as they approached a traffic snarl created by an accident. They saw a city bus near the curb, but any other vehicles were hidden. Several patrolmen were out in the street, surrounded by people, trying to get traffic moving again. On both sides of the road was a logjam of cars.

Walters cursed and whirled the cruiser into a 180. He bumped over the median strip and headed east again. A block away, he made a hard right onto Westlake Avenue. They roared past Harrison and then hung another wheel-screeching right on Thomas. Once more, they were facing the Needle.

Two Elks rolled with the swaying tilt of the patrol car, watching out the window. People waved frantically at them, their faces holding the strange mixture of confusion and shock that witnesses to sudden, rending accidents have. But Walters sped right past them.

Over the past three minutes, an ominous premonition had begun to build in Two Elks. They were all going to be too late, he felt. Inexorable things had already begun. Some deep, inner Indian consciousness seemed to tell him that the best and only thing they were going to be able to do was to merely, helplessly, witness this horror unfolding itself into chaos.

But what of Marquette? Where was he? Could *he* stop it? Would he know how? And, if so, would he have enough time? Enough courage?

The Space Needle was still three blocks away. It rose up out of the perspective of Thomas Street, towering above the buildings along each side. Looking beyond, Two Elks saw rain squalls over the sound, close beyond the dock area and coming in—willowy, gray-white curtains slanted by the wind. He watched for a moment; then his gaze was again drawn to the Space Needle.

Suddenly he thrust forward. "Jesus, look at that," he yelled.

"What? Where?"

"On the top of the Needle. Somebody's crawling around the apron."

Walters ducked his head, squinting. He caught sight of an object out on the louvers. "Oh, shit, it's him. He's planting the fucking bomb!"

Two Elks stared hard through the windshield, trying to

draw definition from the tiny figure clinging to the flaring span of the sun louvers. But it was too far away.

"We'll have to try and take him from the ground with handguns." Walters cried. "Can we reach with any power?"

Two Elks shook his head, almost sadly. Then he frowned. "Wait a minute—that might be Marquette up there."

Behind them, a second cruiser came skidding off Dexter Avenue, rocking for a moment before falling in behind, lights and sirens going full.

Two Elks stared at the little stick figure far above, his mind focusing, reaching out. Is that you, Marquette? he thought with a desperate hope. If it is, do it. Dear God, stop this thing. . . .

Marquette froze.

For a moment of pure agony, the fear overwhelmed him. He simply sat there on his beam and stared at this thing in his hand, his teeth biting hard into the plastic case of the cell phone. Seconds seemed to coalesce, cramming themselves together like steel filings drawn inward by a powerful magnet.

Into a single second.

This second.

He was as certain as he had ever been that the bomb was going to explode in his face. He heard himself groan aloud. His mind seemed to blot out everything except the overpowering impulse to hurl it away from himself.

It didn't explode.

In a desperate attempt to regain control, Matt looked down for the first time. Far below, little clusters of people stared upward. Farther out, beyond the Center complex, he saw the red, flashing lights of police cars converging; heard their sirens, coming up to him in surges.

He watched the first cruiser come barreling through one of the gates, disappear for a moment under the gate overhang, then reappear beyond, racing through the parking lot. Its siren rose powerfully for an instant, then dropped off abruptly.

They're here, he thought. He turned and looked at the bomb again—and ordered his fingers to open, to release it. Why not let the thing fall down the long slant of the Needle? he thought in sudden, childlike petulance.

I can't do this. I won't. Let *them* deal with it.

His fingers refused to obey.

From outside his concentration of fear, he felt the tiny, feather-soft tremble of the phone's static against his lip. Remembering it in a rush, he jerked the unit from his mouth, and screamed supplication into it. "Kelli! God, oh God, come back to me."

Only a wash of heavy static returned.

A sudden, strong gust of wind slammed into him from below, nearly knocking him off his beam. Frantically, he grabbed for a hold with his right hand. The phone was in the way. He tried to reach around it, fingers clawing. It slipped out of his grasp.

Helplessly, he watched it drop straight down, slowly turning over and over. The crowd below saw it coming and drew away from its point of impact like oil on water at the touch of a soap droplet.

Near the ticket kiosk, the police cuiser fishtailed to a stop. Two men leapt out and ran up the slight incline of the structure's ramp just as the phone struck the cement and blew apart. . . .

One minute, forty seconds

As the maximum fume state neared, the mass of already mutated organisms had become so compact that it began to generate its own heat. Ripples of energy swept through it, formed vacuum pockets that instantly closed on themselves. The gradual increase in temperature immediately speeded up the replication process of the remaining, unmutated anthrax within the broth. . . .

*   *   *

Twenty feet from where the cell phone had smashed to earth, Lieutenant Walters braced himself, bent sharply backward like an archer readying to send an arrow over a castle wall. Both his arms were extended upward; in his hand was a chrome-plated Glock .38 Special revolver.

To his right, Two Elks also had his weapon out. But he hadn't lifted it yet. Instead, he kept moving from side to side trying to see around the louver beams.

Then the man up there on the apron turned his head, looked down again, and Two Elks could see him plainly. Something was in his hand.

Instantly, Two Elks grabbed Walters's arm and jerked it aside. "Don't shoot," he cried. "It's Marquette. And he's got the bomb."

Both men stood there, gazing wildly, helplessly, upward. Marquette didn't move, just sat there. Six seconds clicked past, and finally Two Elks broke into a run toward the base plaza. Walters came right after him.

They headed straight for the elevators just as a clot of hysterical people came surging out at them, yelling. Then the stairwell door slammed open and another group came stumbling out, screaming about a dead man.

The elevator doors began to close.

"Hold those fucking doors!" Walters screamed. Nobody paid any attention to him, instead scattering past them, running hard. When the two policemen reached the elevator, it had automatically started up again. Walters gave the doors a vicious kick.

It would take forty-seven seconds to reach the top. There it would open, wait thirty seconds, move on to the observation level and again wait thirty seconds before starting down once more. A total of two minutes, thirty-four seconds.

Two Elks started for the stairs, paused, came back. It would be wiser to wait for the elevator, he realized. He felt his insides gripping down so tightly that it was as if he had to have a bowel movement.

He looked back outside. A squall had just crossed into the western side of Seattle Center, a thick gray front of rain sweeping in over the coliseum, the wind it created whirling fine, misty spray ahead.

He turned back to the elevator and waited, staring fixedly at the thin crack between the doors and listening to Walters's choked curses.

It was the rain.

The first droplet, hurtling in on the wind, struck Marquette on the cheek, stinging like a pellet of mercury. It left a tiny medallion of water on his flesh.

The impact riffled through his nerves, a pinprick of sensual feedback. It expanded through his head, down into his chest. He felt his heart respond with sudden life, and with it came a violent rush of fury, a quick, fiery blast that blew through the fear.

He glared down at the bomb in his hand. The heightened sensitivity of his fingertips felt its surfaces getting even hotter. The rage spiraled upward like a kind of lunacy. Bellowing curses, he began to wrench at the bomb, trying to dismember it.

He couldn't.

Then the rain came in a sudden, blowing, frigid deluge, hissing against the I-beams. He turned his face away from it, his eyes closed. In the darkness behind his lids, he drew the energy of his anger into a sharp focus.

Think, his mind roared, think.

Kelli had said it. When? Somewhere back along the fragile evolution of seconds that had brought him to this moment.

Open sunlight, she had said, her voice hiding in the static. But that was useless. The sun was gone. Why the sun? How?

Electromagnetic wa—Waves? Radiation. The sun's radiation. His thoughts reeled through the spectrum. Gamma, ultraviolet, infrared, X-rays, radio—

But how here?

Suddenly, something flashed across his mind. He lifted his face to the rain. Could it work? He didn't know, couldn't know. But now he grasped at it, clinging.

One last chance . . .

He rose quickly, hugging the bomb close against his body lest it fall. The I-beams were slick with water, and the rain hammered against the louver tip plates.

Using a single hand, he pulled himself to the top layer of beams, threw a leg over one and scooted to the wall. Going crookedly, spider-crawling, he scaled the cable barrier, made it across the top and dropped to the observation platform.

Sixty seconds . . .

The fume had become a boiling, churning mass of anthrax organisms that light could not have penetrated even if there had been light. Internal heat was still increasing as the last droplets of nutrient broth were used up.

Meanwhile, within the explosive unit, a tiny wheel clicked over, aligning a striking pin made of carbon-carbon fiber with its firing channel. The movement immediately compressed borax-based springs along the pin's shaft.

The moment the detonation timer reached 0000, a swing arm would release the springs. Instantly, the striking pin would plunge into a small friction-fired charge of PETN explosive, which would then ignite a capsule of fulminate of mercury. . . .

As the elevator doors opened on the observation platform level, the few people still remaining there lunged aboard. Two men paused long enough to drag the woman who had fallen into the car. Everybody huddled at the back like terrified cattle herded into a slaughterhouse holding pen, screaming for the thing to move.

Then one of the women caught sight of Marquette as he came leaping up the stairs from the outside platform.

"Oh, God, it's him!" she screamed. "He's got the bomb! He's got the bomb!" Like stalks of corn in a wind, the people shrank away from him.

The doors closed softly, gently.

Matt headed past the elevator to the main stairs and blew

through. In the furious exit, someone had dropped a purse
and a parasol. In an odd, flashing moment of astounding
visual acuity, Marquette saw, absorbed, the delicate, spidery
lines in the parasol's design.

Down he went, four steps at a time, all body pain now
gone.

He rushed through the restaurant-level door. He could feel
the heat of the sphere actually infusing through the vest material. A soft, terror-filled murmur escaped his lips. With it
came doubts, sudden, horrible images shafting into his mind.
He clamped down, forced them out again.

He sprinted by a reservation desk. A white computer on
it was running, endlessly scrolling through names and ad-
dresses. All the buttons on a small telephone panel were
flashing. He turned left, headed for the main entrance of the
Emerald Suite.

Twenty-five seconds . . .

He entered the hushed elegance of the restaurant. To his
right was a maître d's pulpit in front of a delicate mural of
converging, black-and-white triangles.

Across from it was the entrance to a conference area. Folding chairs were scattered all over the floor. Near the wall, a
buffet table was lying on its side. Directly ahead, an arch
separated the lobby from the main dining room. Spotless
linen-covered tables bore crystal candle-bowls and gold-
rimmed plates.

He headed through the dining area, wildly searching for
the kitchen doors. He spotted them: twin, swinging doors
faced in copper formed into the triangle motif.

He darted to them and plunged through.

Seventeen seconds . . .

The kitchen was a mass of white tile. Long, stainless-steel
tables ran the full length of the room; utensils and pans hung

from racks. There was a thick-doored, walk-in freezer toward the back, and wash basins and steam racks and cartons of produce. A New York–cut steak was still on a grill, charred black. The smoke from it was being sucked up into the stove vents.

Marquette stopped in the middle of the room, his eyes desperately scanning. In his chest, his heart pounded so violently he could feel its trembling devolving down into his groin like a strange, orgasmic ache.

His scan stopped. Against the wall near the freezer, he saw what he wanted: a small microwave oven for sauces. He leapt to it, flung open the door. He tried to cram the bomb into it, couldn't; it was too small.

He gave an agonized, helpless bellow.

Twelve seconds . . .

In moving to the small oven, he was now able to see around the corner of the room. There, up against a wall, were three larger microwave ovens. In one bound, he was in front of them, yanking open the door of the first. He shoved the bomb into it, slammed the door.

Nine seconds . . .

He squinted at the control facing, trying to find the timer and start buttons. The facing was in black with silver numbers. He punched his forefinger at the number five, missed. Cursing, he tried again. The number lit up.

Five seconds . . .

He rammed the side of his fist against the start button. It didn't take. Again. There was a soft whirr as the oven came on.

*   *   *

Three seconds . . .

Marquette turned, moving like a tiger leaping to quarry, yet, in his mind, he moved with sluggish slowness, his legs rising and going down and his heart pulsing out there into the air.

He crossed beside a deep basin, his arms coming up to cover his face like a fighter fending off blows, and the kitchen doors were there, just ahead, and then he gathered his feet and weight and propelled his body into and through them.

Detonation

The microwave oven blew apart. Glass and metal shards were hurled against the white-tile and stainless-steel surfaces. The entire room was instantly filled with a thick, yellowish-white smoke that whirled and twisted in the currents from the grill fans. . . .

aftermath

The four figures, dressed in bright orange Racal bio-hazard suits, moved slowly through the fog of bacteria like helmeted divers at the bottom of the sea.

Members of CDC's Portland biohazard SWAT team, they were working in the hot zone of the Emerald Suite kitchen. Everything from floor to ceiling was coated with bacteria, a fine, yellowish powder smelling of grape juice. It lifted off surfaces at the slightest movement of air.

The only sounds within the entire restaurant were the soft purr of the team's air motors and the BioCon suction collectors. The hoses from the collectors, connected to three-foot-high aluminum flasks, snaked across the floor.

The team had arrived at the Needle thirty-two minutes after the explosion of Stone's bomb, carried in by a Washington National Guard helicopter. They had immediately sealed off the entire Emerald Suite, taping exterior doors and windows with plastic sheeting and military duct tape.

In different, less-contaminated "gray zone" parts of the restaurant, other team members ran field tests on the bacteria. Several "hot boxes" of organisms had already been choppered over to the pathology department of the university's Magnuson Medical Center, where they were put under electron microscopes to establish biotic state.

So far, two hours after detonation, all tests were showing that the anthrax bacteria were dead.

Down in the city, the momentum of hysteria had steadily increased. The exodus from Seattle, begun slowly after the radio announcement, now worsened. Inner-city streets and highways were clogged. All the bus and airline terminals became swamped with frantic Seattlites trying to get away.

Police resources were quickly overwhelmed. In response, Governor DeJohn called out the National Guard, and the first units were just now beginning to stage. The moment his plane had landed at King County Airport, DeJohn went on television to reassure the populace. His words had little immediate effect.

Hospitals and doctors' offices all over the city also became mini battle zones. Already alerted and gearing up for the possibility of a catastrophic biohazard disaster, they were now deluged with terrified people begging and threatening violence in order to obtain anti-anthrax vaccine.

Small riots erupted in scattered sections of Seattle; widespread looting immediately followed. Fires broke out and shootings occurred as business- and homeowners tried vainly to protect their property.

It would be a long, tense afternoon and night. Not until the following day would some semblance of order return to Seattle and its suburbs.

For Kelli Pickett, it was a horror of waiting.

Within minutes of the bomb's explosion, FBI agents had entered Guggenheim Hall and the CRYSTALBALL lab. Everything within the lab, including all AI-F/B-3 team members, was immediately placed under a National Security hold. Then the agents, working in pairs, began to interrogate people.

But no one would tell Kelli what had happened to Matt Marquette.

At last, she'd had enough. Still being questioned in Gilhammer's office, she put up her hands. "Look, I don't answer another question until I know where Matt Marquette is."

"We're not at liberty to tell you that yet," one of the agents said.

"Then I shut the hell up."

"I wouldn't advise that."

Kelli gave him a steely eye. "Well, fuck your advice."

The agents gave each other a glance.

"Who's your boss?" Kelli demanded. "I want to see your boss."

"Sorry."

"All right, then I want to talk with Sullins at the CDC."

"Look, we have—"

"Now!"

One of the agents finally rose and went out. Four minutes later, Troy's telephone rang. The remaining agent pointed at it. Kelli picked it up.

"Yes? Who's this?" she snapped.

"Miss Pickett? This is Sullins."

"Where the hell is Matt Marquette? What's happened to him?"

"They haven't told you yet?"

Told you yet? Her heart shuddered. "No."

"He's in a biocontainment pavilion at the Needle."

"Is he . . . dead?"

"No," Sullins said.

She felt relief go through her like warm honey.

Sullins went on to explain. Immediately after the explosion, Marquette had frantically tried to seal off the restaurant. Two police officers, Two Elks and Walters, found him and assisted. By the time the SWAT team arrived, the three men were sitting out on the observation platform in the rain.

"They've been deconned and heavy-dosed with Pasteur vaccine," Sullins continued. "So far, all their tissue, blood and serum tests have come up negative. Apparently Marquette completely destroyed the anthrax hot agent."

"How?"

"He put the bomb in a microwave oven and turned it on. From what our analyses show, the radiation destroyed genetic material and broke down amino-acid shells. Intracel-

lular pressure then literally blew the organisms apart.'' He
chuckled. ''I still don't understand how your young man
knew exactly what to do, with what he had on hand. But
thank God in heaven he did it.''

''I want to see him.''

''I don't know. They're scheduled to remain in isolation
for another ten hours.''

''I want to see him now.''

Sullins sighed. ''Yes, I understand. All right, I'll see what
I can do.''

Twenty minutes later, the two FBI agents drove her to the
Needle. It was still raining. The entire Seattle Center and
several blocks adjacent to it were cordoned off by police and
fire units. The agents' car was stopped four times before they
reached the base.

The Skyline restaurant at the hundred-foot level had been
turned into a biocontainment pavilion. Like the upper levels,
all its external doors and windows were sealed.

Inside the largest of three dining areas, the Puget Sound
Room, all the furniture had been removed and replaced by
field trunks and battery units, surgery packs and collapsible
dissection tables. Twin portable decon shower stalls had been
erected in a corner along with two bubble pods. Two doctors
and a nurse worked inside, dressed in green scrubs and full-
face masks like scuba divers.

Kelli stood outside the sealed door and peered through.
She could see across the room to the facing windows. They
were slick with rain, which made the view of the sound look
misty and diffused.

In one corner, Marquette, Two Elks and Walters sat at a
table. They were dressed in white jumpsuits. Incongruously,
they were playing cards. She tapped on the pane. The three
men looked up. Then Matt down put his cards and walked
over, limping.

They stood and looked silently at each other for a long
moment. Kelli felt tears well in her eyes, and she wanted
suddenly, desperately, to reach through the glass, to take
Matt into her arms and hold him, listen to the beat of his

heart. She put her hand on the pane, fingers splayed.

Matt grinned at her. He lifted his own hand and placed it directly opposite hers, palm to palm, fingertip to fingertip. A fragile touch of non-touching. And it seemed that Kelli could feel his energy flow to her through the glass. Then he was saying something, his lips forming the words. She watched.

He said *I love you* . . .